Y0-AGT-915

JANE KIDDER
PASSION'S BARGAIN

ZEBRA BOOKS
KENSINGTON PUBLISHING CORP.

ZEBRA BOOKS are published by

Kensington Publishing Corp.
475 Park Avenue South
New York, NY 10016

First Printing: April, 1994

Printed in the United States of America

To my dear friends
Christine Flynn
and
Susie Van Orden.
Nobody plots them better!

Chapter 1

"I won't do it, Papa. I absolutely refuse."

Frederick Taylor frowned at the beautiful young woman sitting across the table from him. "You can't refuse, Megan. I have signed a contract."

Megan Taylor's dark eyes widened incredulously and the stubborn set of her mouth gave way to slack-jawed disbelief. "A contract? What kind of contract?"

"A contract promising that you will marry Peter Farnsworth."

"You can't do that!" Meg gasped, rising from her chair in agitation. "Fathers don't betroth their daughters anymore. Why, it's like something out of the Middle Ages!"

"I'm sorry," Frederick said quietly, "but I felt it was for the best."

A long moment passed as Meg considered her father, trying to determine what might have prompted him to sell her off like an unwanted parcel of land. "Why did you do this to me?"

"I just told you, I felt it was best."

"Best for whom?" she snapped, trying hard to hold on to her fast-rising temper.

"Best for everyone!" Frederick shot back, his own temper suddenly igniting. "Besides, you brought this on yourself, Meg. For five years I've asked you to find a husband, and for five years you've ignored me. Now, with my health the way it is, I felt I had to take the matter into my own hands. Someone has to take care of you after . . . after I'm gone."

"Calm down, Papa," Meg said, concerned by the angry red splotches that suddenly suffused Frederick's hollow cheeks. "You know the doctor said you're not supposed to get upset."

Frederick drew a deep breath, trying to still the erratic pounding of his heart. "Then stop upsetting me!" he wheezed.

"I'm sorry," she soothed, hurrying over and placing a light hand on her father's bony shoulder. "But Papa, I don't need anyone to take care of me. I'm not a child. I can take care of myself."

Frederick felt a familiar tightening in his chest and reflexively rubbed his fingers up and down his breastbone. "I know you're not a child," he rasped, his face becoming more and more pale as the clenching chest pains increased. "You're a grown woman of twenty-three who should have been married years ago. But since you've refused to heed my requests that you find a husband on your own, I have done it for you."

Meg's lips compressed into a tight line as she girded herself for yet another battle on the wearisome subject of her marrying. "Papa, we have discussed this more times than I can count. Why can't you accept the fact that I don't *want* to get married?"

"Because it isn't natural!" Frederick retorted, his voice stronger now that the stabbing pain was starting to subside. "Every young girl wants to get married. Just look at your sister. She's been married to Lawrence for ten years now."

8

"My sister is one of the biggest reasons I *don't* want to marry," Meg muttered.

"That's nonsense. Virginia is a very happy and contented wife and mother."

"That may be, but I'm sure I don't know why. All she does is cook and clean and . . . and have babies."

"But Megan, that's what women are supposed to do! Cook, clean, and have babies!"

"Oh, Papa," Meg sighed, seating herself next to him and picking up one of his thin, dry hands. "Please try to understand. I'm different from most women. I *like* my independence. I *like* running the mill. What I don't like is Peter Farnsworth, and I won't marry him."

"Liking Peter has nothing to do with it," Frederick snorted. "People get married every day who don't particularly like each other. That all comes later."

Meg closed her eyes for a moment, willing herself to remain calm. *Don't get angry,* she told herself sternly. *Getting angry will get you nowhere.* "Papa, I want you to listen to me," she said, her voice quietly beseeching. "I more than dislike Peter. I detest him, and I wouldn't marry him if he was the last man on earth."

For a long moment, Frederick gazed at his beloved daughter. She was so pretty—so slender and graceful with her lustrous dark hair and large, velvety brown eyes. Just like her mother—that vivacious, sparkling woman whom he'd loved so passionately that he'd beggared himself to make her happy.

Frederick hated himself for heaping the burden of his excesses on Meg. Hated the fact that he'd had no choice but to barter her off like a prize filly. Signing the agreement with George Farnsworth had been the hardest thing he'd ever faced, but it was done now and Meg had to accept it.

Besides, he silently assured himself, she *would* be better

9

off safely married to Peter Farnsworth, regardless of her protestations to the contrary. The doctors had told him he had no more than a few months to live; after he was gone, Meg would be left with no protector. Frederick couldn't bear the thought of his favorite daughter alone and destitute. Signing the agreement had alleviated that fear, and even though it was obvious that Meg was harboring some sort of maidenly aversion to young Farnsworth, Frederick was convinced that she would get over it quickly enough once they were married.

"Megan," he sighed wearily, "you must accept the fact that the contract has already been signed. Regardless of how you might feel, you are bound to marry Peter. I'm sorry if that distresses you, but there's no help for it."

Meg dropped her father's hand and rose, her bright yellow day dress hugging her slender hips as she paced the length of the dining room. "It can't be binding," she argued. "I'm over twenty-one. You can't betroth me to someone without my consent."

Frederick looked down at his untouched breakfast. "I didn't say it was a betrothal contract," he muttered.

Meg whirled around, casting him a wary look. "What are you talking about? If it's not a betrothal contract, what is it?"

"It's more of a business agreement."

"Business? What kind of business would you have with Peter Farnsworth?"

"I don't have any business with Peter," Frederick admitted. "The agreement is with his father."

Meg swept around the corner of the mahogany dining table and sat down again. "Enough of this evasion, Papa. I want you to tell me exactly what's going on."

Frederick swallowed hard, knowing that the moment he had dreaded for so long was upon him. He was going to have to confess his deepest secret to his daughter—a secret so humiliating that even his beloved wife had never known of it. "It was a long, long time ago, dear," he began. "I borrowed some money—a great deal of it, actually—from George Farnsworth."

"I know," Meg nodded. "He lent you the money to get the sawmill started. But surely you must have paid that back long ago!"

Frederick shook his head and looked at the floor, unable to meet Meg's eyes. "No, I didn't."

"What?" she gasped. "Why not? The mill has been very successful. Why, since I've been helping run it, I know that we've made an enormous amount of money."

"Yes, the last year has been good. But unfortunately there were many years that weren't nearly so profitable." Frederick glanced up, wincing at the startled look on Meg's face, and quickly amended, "Oh, I've always been able to make a living from it. At least, enough to build this house and give your mother and you and your sister a decent life, but there's never been enough left over to repay George. For a long time he let it go, but now that I'm sick . . ." Frederick paused, his voice trailing off as he was suddenly seized by a dry, wracking cough. "Now, George has come to me, demanding that I settle up."

"Settle up?" Meg questioned. "What does that mean?"

"It means that he gave me a choice: either come up with the money to pay him back for the original loan and all the interest he has added over the years, or . . ."

"Or agree to marry me off to Peter," Meg finished, the terrifying reality of her situation finally dawning.

"Yes."

"But why me, Papa? Surely Mr. Farnsworth must know how I feel about Peter."

"I think he does, but apparently Peter has told him that

he's taken with you, and you know how indulgent George has always been with the boy. Since Peter has been away in Texas, George has approached me several times about arranging a marriage between you two."

"Do you know why Peter went to Texas?" Meg asked, looking at her father speculatively.

"Not really. I just assumed he went away to try to forget that tragic incident with Jenny Thomas."

An angry flush of color crept up Meg's neck as she thought about the *real* reason Peter Farnsworth had fled Oregon. She was not surprised to hear that her father didn't know the truth. Regardless of how strained their financial circumstances might be, he would never have betrothed her to Peter if he had. But it was a secret Meg could not discuss with her father. She simply couldn't.

"So," she said slowly, "what you're telling me is that you have signed an agreement with George Farnsworth that states he will forgive the loan if I marry Peter."

Frederick nodded, the heavy mantle of guilt becoming more weighty by the moment. "Yes," he nodded. "It's that, or turn the mill over to him."

"Fine," Meg said curtly, "then that's what we'll do."

"What?"

"Turn the mill over to him. It's the only answer."

Frederick's mouth dropped open in horrified astonishment at Meg's unexpected selfishness. "Meg, please! We can't! The mill is all we have. If I turn it over to Farnsworth, there will be nothing for me to leave to you or Virginia."

"Virginia and I will be fine," Meg assured him. "As you just pointed out, she's married and settled, and even though I have no love for Lawrence, he does make a good living at the bank. And as for me, well, I'll find something to do to support myself."

Frederick's lips thinned with frustration at his daughter's

unyielding stubbornness. "You can't do that! How many times do I have to tell you that a young, unmarried, gently reared lady cannot live alone in Wellesley? This is a rough town, Meg, and you know it. Why, there's no telling what might happen to you living alone in this house. Besides, I don't understand what you have against Peter. He's young, handsome, and the richest man around, next to Geoffrey Wellesley himself."

"Young and handsome he might be," Meg spat, rising from her chair and clearing their still full plates off the table, "but he's the most odious creature I've ever met!"

Realizing that he was getting nowhere, Frederick changed his tactics. "Meg, please be reasonable. I am bound to honor this contract. I gave my word, signed my name. I can't believe you'd be so selfish as to dishonor me by forcing me to renege on an agreement. I don't think I could live with the shame."

Meg's fingers dug into the edge of the oak sideboard as she tried to keep herself from screaming. "I'm sorry if you think I'm selfish, Papa," she gritted, "but try to remember that I did not cause this situation. I did not borrow the money from George Farnsworth, nor did I make the decision to build a huge, lavish house instead of paying him back. I'm also sorry if you think my lack of cooperation is shameful, but I will not be used as the payment for this loan. I don't care if we have to sell the mill, sell the house, or sell our souls to the devil himself, but *I will not marry Peter Farnsworth!*"

And with a swirl of lemon-yellow silk, Meg pivoted on her heel and flew out of the dining room, leaving her exhausted, ailing father to stare after her in disbelief.

Chapter 2

When anyone asked Meg to describe her older sister Virginia, the first word that came to her mind was "practical." Practical, stable, and level-headed to the point of dullness, Virginia Lombard could not have been more different from her volatile younger sister. But it was this very difference that always prompted Meg, at every crisis of her life, to turn to Virginia for counsel and advice.

The untenable situation in which Meg now found herself was no different. After her heated confrontation with her father, she had gone upstairs, changed into a riding habit, and headed straight over to Virginia's.

Virginia and Lawrence Lombard lived in a plain clapboard house situated just off Main Street in Wellesley. Although Virginia would have preferred a home farther outside the rowdy logging town, Lawrence insisted that they live close to the bank where he was vice-president. Virginia had never been exactly sure why it was so important, but it never occurred to her to question her husband's preferences. Instead, she had happily set up housekeeping in the simple home he had purchased at the time of their marriage ten years before, and in the ensuing years, had presented him with five children. Lawrence wanted a big family, and with the unshakable determination of a woman born to be a wife, Virginia found her greatest happiness in giving her husband what he wanted.

Virginia's contentment with her marriage had always been a mystery to Meg, who thought Lawrence an arrogant, domineering, and totally humorless bore. She kept this opinion to herself, knowing how much it would hurt Virginia if she knew that Meg disliked her husband.

Riding into the Lombards' front yard, Meg dismounted, throwing the reins over the hitching rail while muttering a brief prayer in hopes that Lawrence had not come home for lunch today. She desperately needed to talk to Virginia about her situation, but she didn't care to listen to one of Lawrence's long-winded dissertations on the "inappropriate" way she lived her life. She walked up to the front door and pushed it open a crack, poking her head in and calling, "Ginny, are you home?"

"In the kitchen, Meg."

With a relieved smile, Meg closed the front door and walked through the sparsely furnished dining room into her sister's big, airy kitchen.

"Hello, dear," Virginia sang out cheerfully, rapping a wooden spoon sharply against the lip of a large pot she was stirring. "I didn't know you were coming into town today."

"I wasn't," Meg said shortly, trying to disentangle herself from the cluster of small children who were excitedly attaching themselves to her skirt. "But something has happened that I must talk to you about. I hope I'm not catching you at a bad time."

"Not at all," Virginia assured her. "Lawrence is having lunch with a prospective customer, and I've already fed these wild Indians and put the baby down for her nap. You couldn't have timed your visit better." Expertly detaching the children from Meg's skirt, she shooed them out the back door, closing it firmly after them. "Now, what seems to be the problem, assuming there is one?"

"Oh, there is," Meg nodded. "Probably the biggest I've ever faced."

Virginia's smile faded. Generally, her younger sister's "problems" were relatively minor and easily solved, but she could tell by Meg's tense expression and anxious stance that this time, something was seriously wrong. "Sit down," she offered, "and I'll fix us some tea."

Meg shook her head. "I'm too upset to sit, Ginny, and what I need is a shot of whiskey, not a cup of tea."

Virginia's eyebrows disappeared into her fringe of bangs. "My word, Meg, what could be so bad that you would consider spirits the answer?"

Despite her anxiety, Meg couldn't help but smile. Virginia's shock at her request was so . . . Virginia.

"I'm only joking," she responded, "but Papa has done something so awful that it might drive even you to imbibe."

"Papa?" Virginia asked, sitting down at the table and looking at Meg in confusion. "What could Papa have done to upset you so?"

"He sold me!" Meg blurted. "He signed a contract with George Farnsworth, selling me into marriage to Peter."

Virginia's mouth dropped open. "I don't believe you. Papa wouldn't do that."

"Well, he did!"

"But why?"

"It's a long story," Meg sighed, ceasing her agitated pacing and sitting down across from her sister. "Apparently, Papa borrowed a lot of money from Mr. Farnsworth years ago and never paid him back. Now that Papa is sick, Farnsworth wants payment, and since Papa doesn't have the cash, he agreed to forgive the loan if I marry Peter."

Virginia shook her head in disbelief. "I can hardly believe Papa would force you into a marriage you don't want just to pay a debt. He must have another reason."

"He does," Meg admitted. "George Farnsworth told him that Peter is 'taken with me,' so Papa thinks Peter will take good care of me after he's gone."

Virginia gazed out the window thoughtfully for a moment, chewing on her bottom lip. "You know, Meg," she murmured, "he has a point."

"What?" Meg gasped, leaping to her feet. "Ginny, how could you possibly agree with him about this?"

"I'm not saying that I agree with his tactics," Ginny hedged, "but he is right about one thing: you do need a husband."

"No, I don't."

"And you could do a lot worse than Peter Farnsworth," Ginny continued, as if Meg had not spoken. "He's wealthy, charming and handsome. Actually, the more I think about it, the more I think that he would be a good match for you."

"Well, you're wrong! If you only knew the truth . . ."

"What truth?"

Meg quickly turned away, cursing her runaway tongue. "There are . . . things about Peter that you don't know."

"Surely you can't mean that gossip about Jenny Thomas killing herself because he threw her over and went to Texas!" Virginia snorted.

It was Meg's turn to look surprised. "I didn't know you'd heard that."

"Oh, it was all over the place for a while," Virginia scoffed, "but I never paid it any heed. Jenny didn't jump off that cliff. She just fell, plain and simple."

Meg drew a long, shuddering breath, debating whether she should confess what she knew. If she was going to avoid marrying Peter Farnsworth, she definitely needed Virginia

17

as an ally. Looking at her sister's set, disbelieving face, she knew that the only way she could gain her support was to tell her the truth.

Wearily, she sank back into the chair she'd so recently vacated and gazed at Virginia earnestly. "Ginny," she murmured, "I'm going to tell you something I swore I'd never tell anyone, but I think you need to know." She paused a moment, then said quietly, "Jenny did jump off that cliff."

Virginia blanched, her eyes widening in horror. "How do you know?"

"Because she sent me a letter telling me she was going to do it."

"Oh, my God!" Virginia gasped, reaching out and clenching Meg's hand. "Didn't you try to stop her?"

Meg's eyes welled with tears as the whole terrible incident came flooding back. "I would have, but I didn't receive her letter until the day after she'd killed herself."

"Did she give you a reason?"

"Yes," Meg nodded. "She was . . . she was going to have Peter Farnsworth's baby."

"Oh Lord . . ." Virginia groaned, "why didn't they just get married?"

"Jenny wouldn't marry him."

Virginia lifted her head and stared at Meg in bewilderment. "Why not? Everyone knew Peter had been courting her. If they'd gotten married as soon as Jenny realized she was in the family way, they could have lied and said the baby came early. Even if the gossips in town didn't believe them, they'd have no way to disprove it, and the Farnsworths are certainly important enough in this community to squelch any rumors."

"Ginny," Meg whispered, "Jenny didn't get pregnant because she loved Peter Farnsworth. He . . . he raped her."

"What?" Virginia cried, clapping her hand to her mouth. "Oh, Meg, no. You must be wrong!"

"I'm not wrong," Meg assured her. "Jenny told me that at last year's Fourth of July picnic, Peter drank too much and afterward, he, well, forced his attentions on her. She tried to resist him, but he was too strong." Meg's voice trailed off as Virginia continued to stare at her in disbelief.

After a long, silent moment, she added, "Jenny wouldn't see Peter after that, and when she found herself in the family way, I guess she just couldn't stand the disgrace."

"Did you know any of this before you received her letter?" Virginia asked.

"Yes," Meg nodded miserably. "Jenny told me Peter had . . . attacked her, but I didn't know she was going to have a baby until I got the letter."

"Who else knows this?"

"No one, I don't think, except maybe Peter's father. It's my guess that Mr. Farnsworth knew about Jenny's pregnancy and sent Peter to Texas to get him out of the way, in case she started making a fuss."

Virginia shook her head, appalled by all she'd just heard. "Well, one thing is for sure. Peter should be punished."

"That will never happen," Meg said bitterly. "There's no proof except Jenny's suicide note, and I threw that away."

"You did?" Virginia asked, astonished that Meg would destroy the only piece of evidence that could link Peter to Jenny's death.

"Yes."

"Why would you do that? You could have taken it to the authorities."

Meg shook her head. "I couldn't disgrace Jenny's family that way. Besides, who'd have believed it? Everyone would

19

have just thought that Jenny made the whole thing up to get back at Peter for leaving her and going to Texas."

"You're probably right," Ginny agreed. She hesitated a moment, then looked at Meg thoughtfully. "Don't you suppose that is a possibility, Meg? I mean, Peter Farnsworth seems like such a nice, polite young man. Maybe Jenny really *couldn't* cope with him leaving her and decided to try to ruin his life at the same time as she took her own."

Meg shook her head. "No. I believe every word in Jenny's letter. First of all, she had no reason to lie to me, and second, I was around her and Peter enough to see how nasty he could be . . . especially when he'd been drinking."

"What a tragedy," Virginia moaned. Getting up, she walked over to a cupboard and pulled out a small bottle of sherry and two glasses. Splashing a little of the amber liquid into each glass, she returned to the table and offered one to Meg.

"Ginny!"

"Oh, be quiet and drink it." Seating herself, Ginny took a tiny sip, then set the glass down. "Meg, you have to tell Papa everything. It's the only way he'll accept your refusal to marry Peter."

Meg threw her head back and in one long swallow downed her sherry. "I can't do that. I just can't bring myself to discuss something so . . . so personal with him. Even if I did, he probably wouldn't believe me. Look at you—you're not even sure *you* believe it."

"But Meg, you have no choice."

"No," Meg repeated stubbornly. "When Jenny told me about what Peter had done to her, she made me give my word I wouldn't tell anyone. I feel like I've betrayed her already, just telling you. If I told Papa, he'd go straight to George Farnsworth and confront him, and even if Mr.

20

Farnsworth is aware of what Peter did, you know he'd deny it."

"Then what *are* you going to do?"

"I don't know," Meg said wearily. "I was hoping you might have an idea."

"You know," Virginia murmured, tapping her nail against her teeth, "I just might."

Meg's eyebrows rose hopefully.

"I think what you need is to marry someone else before Peter gets back from Texas. When is he returning?"

"I don't know, but that's not the answer. I don't want to marry anyone. I just want to go on running the mill."

"I don't think that's going to be possible, unless you can somehow come up with the money to pay back the loan."

"I've been thinking about that," Meg nodded. "Do you think Lawrence could help me get a loan at the bank?"

"They wouldn't lend you money," Virginia snorted. "You're a woman!"

"Well, then, maybe Papa could borrow it."

Virginia shook her head. "I don't think they'd give him a loan either—not with his health the way it is. He would be considered what Lawrence calls a 'high risk.' No, Meg, our only answer is to marry you off to someone else, and as quickly as possible."

Meg smiled fondly at her older sister, noticing that she had unconsciously started to think of her problem as "ours." It had always been that way between them. Despite the six-year gap in their ages and the very marked difference in their attitudes toward life, there was a bond between them that was unshakable.

Virginia rose and for several minutes thoughtfully paced the length of her large kitchen. Suddenly she halted in midstride, her eyes lighting with excitement. "Oh, I've got it! You can marry Geoffrey Wellesley."

Meg promptly burst out laughing. "Ginny, be serious!"

"I am!" Virginia exclaimed. "He's the perfect answer. He's the only man in town who's richer and more influential than our family or Peter's. George Farnsworth would have to tear up that contract if you were married to someone that powerful."

"You have lost your mind," Meg giggled. "I have about as much chance of marrying Geoffrey Wellesley as I do Cornelius Vanderbilt! You know he's a confirmed bachelor. Why, he doesn't even come into town, except to go to church once in a while. And besides, every girl in three counties has set her cap for him, and no one has received so much as an invitation to a dance, much less a wedding ring."

"I don't care," Virginia said stubbornly. "We can figure out some way to pique his interest."

"Ginny," Meg said slowly, as if speaking to a stubborn child, "Geoffrey Wellesley does not want to get married . . . and neither do I!"

"I know! That's what makes this so perfect. You two could come up with an agreement of some kind. You know, a marriage in name only."

"He wouldn't agree to that."

"Sure he would," Virginia insisted, her eyes shining with a vitality that Meg had not seen in years. "All we have to do is figure out a reason why it would be beneficial to Geoffrey Wellesley to marry you. Then you can go to him and lay out your proposition."

"Proposition is an interesting choice of words," Meg commented wryly.

Virginia planted her hands on her hips and glared at her sister. "Would you please stop making light of this? I'm trying to help you!"

"I know," Meg answered, sobering, "and I appreciate

your efforts. But Ginny, this idea is so ridiculous that I can't take it seriously."

"Well, you'd better, or you're going to find yourself walking down the aisle with Peter Farnsworth before you have time to blink an eye."

"Okay, okay," Meg relented, holding up a hand. "Let's say that I do talk the elusive Mr. Wellesley into a titular marriage. That still isn't going to solve the problem of paying George Farnsworth back. We would still lose the mill, so what's the point?"

Virginia hesitated a moment, then said, "I think after a woman gets married, her debts become her husband's responsibility, so Mr. Wellesley would probably be legally bound to pay Mr. Farnsworth."

"Virginia!" Meg gasped, truly shocked by her sister's outrageous idea. "That's so deceitful I can't believe you'd suggest it. I couldn't do that to Geoffrey Wellesley. I don't even know the man, except from doing business with him, and he's never been anything but honest and polite with me. I couldn't possibly deceive him like that."

Virginia waved a dismissive hand. "Nonsense. We'd figure out some way to pay him back."

"Like what?"

"I don't know. Let him mill his lumber for free for the rest of his life . . ."

Meg's eyes narrowed as she mulled over this possibility. "You know, you just may have something there. I could set up a credit at the mill for the amount of the loan, and whenever Mr. Wellesley brought in a load of lumber, I could deduct the charges against the balance I owe him. Why, with the amount of lumber he mills, I'd probably have the loan paid back in just a couple of years. Then, if I offered him another free year as interest, it would more than repay him for the use of his money."

23

"Right," Virginia nodded excitedly. "Everybody wins. We get to keep the mill, you're safe from Peter Farnsworth, and Geoffrey Wellesley saves a fortune."

"Then I don't really see any reason why I have to ask Mr. Wellesley to marry me," Meg noted. "Why don't I just go to him and ask him to lend me the money?"

"Because that won't save you from Peter Farnsworth," Virginia countered. "You know what he's like. He hounded Jenny unmercifully until she finally agreed to allow him to court her. If he's turned his eyes toward you now, I don't think simply paying off the debt will stop him. What you need is protection, and marrying Geoffrey Wellesley will give you that."

"But I still don't think Mr. Wellesley is going to agree to marry me. How would I approach him?"

"Play on his sympathies. You just said that you and he have a good business relationship, which must mean he likes you. Tell him about the deal you're willing to offer him, and if he argues, confess that you're being threatened by Peter. Wellesley hates him, so he'll probably take pity on you."

"Why does Mr. Wellesley hate Peter?"

"Don't you remember that incident a few years ago, when Mr. Wellesley's younger sister came to visit him?"

Meg nodded thoughtfully. "Now that you mention it, I do. Wasn't there some trouble between Mr. Wellesley and Peter over her?"

"Yes. Mr. Wellesley's sister Paula came to spend a few weeks with him, and Peter Farnsworth asked her to go buggy riding. Geoffrey allowed her to go, but something must have happened, because afterward, Mr. Wellesley went after Peter and beat him half to death."

"That's right!" Meg exclaimed. "I do remember now.

24

Did the Farnsworths ever press charges against Mr. Welles-ley?"

"No," Virginia said, "and everyone was really surprised that they didn't."

"And yet no one started to suspect that Peter's character might be different from what he tries to present?"

Virginia shrugged. "I think most people just believed that Geoffrey Wellesley had overreacted to something Peter might have said or done during the buggy ride. I've heard he has a temper and is terribly protective of his sister. Lawrence told me that he comes from a big family and that this Paula is the only girl."

"Knowing what I know now, I hate to think what Peter might have said or done during that buggy ride," Meg shuddered.

"There have certainly been hard feelings between Geof-frey Wellesley and the Farnsworths ever since," Virginia agreed. "Anyway, knowing how he feels about Peter, if you tell him you're being forced into marriage with him, he just might agree to help you."

"I don't know . . ." Meg said doubtfully.

"You have nothing to lose. The worst he can do is say no."

"I suppose you're right. I just hope he doesn't laugh in my face when he says it."

"He won't," Virginia said, pushing away from the counter and giving her sister an encouraging hug. "After all, he can't be all bad. He did beat up Peter Farnsworth, and that right there is enough to commend him!"

Chapter 3

"Boss, there's a lady out here says she needs ta see ya."

Geoffrey Wellesley threw down his pen and frowned at the scruffy-looking man standing in the doorway of his crude office. "Who is it?"

"That lady who works down to the sawmill," the lumberjack replied.

"Megan Taylor?" Geoffrey asked, his voice registering his surprise.

"I don't know her name, boss, but she's some looker."

Geoffrey smiled, amused by his workman's assessment of the pretty and sophisticated Miss Taylor. "All right, Ned, tell her I'll be right out."

With a nod, Ned turned and clumped down the shack's rough steps, calling, "He's comin', honey."

Meg's eyes flared with offense at the man's unthinking forwardness, but she held her tongue and nodded graciously. "Thank you, sir, I appreciate your assistance."

"Any time," he grinned, then picked up a huge ax and hefted it over his shoulder, sauntering off toward the dense forest which butted up nearly to the back wall of Geoffrey's office.

Turning her attention back to the shack, Meg drew in a

sharp breath as Geoff's huge bulk suddenly filled the narrow doorway. Although she'd met him many times, his sheer size and astonishing good looks never failed to awe her.

Tawny. That's the only word to describe him. Tawny hair, tawny skin, tawny eyes—and a body so big and muscular that even the most contented of wives secretly speculated about what he would look like with his shirt off. No man should look that good in faded denims and a flannel shirt, Meg thought, as her eyes covertly roved his muscular physique. And here she was, getting ready to ask this godlike creature to marry her!

She swallowed hard, suddenly not at all sure whether she could go through with this wild scheme. It had taken her more than a week to summon enough courage to make the trek up the side of the mountain to Geoffrey Wellesley's lair, and now that she was here, she feared she would not be able to actually put voice to her outrageous proposition.

"Good morning, Miss Taylor," he greeted her, squinting into the bright summer sunshine as he walked down the steps toward her. "You wanted to see me?"

"Y . . . yes," Meg stammered, mesmerized by the way the sun made his long, thick hair gleam. She paused, and he looked at her curiously.

"What can I do for you?"

His whiskey-colored eyes and deep, rich voice made her somehow feel as if she couldn't draw an even breath. "I . . . I need to talk to you about something," she managed.

Geoff nodded expectantly, but when Meg again lapsed into silence, his expression became even more quizzical. "Is something wrong at the mill?" he questioned.

"No," she answered quickly. "It's just that . . . Do you suppose we could go into your office for a moment?"

Geoff threw a dubious look at the shack behind him,

loath to take the beautiful woman into its squalid confines. "I suppose, if you want to."

"Please."

Turning, he headed back up the steps, pausing to hold the ill-fitting door open for her. "I'm afraid I'm not really set up for business meetings," he apologized, as he followed her into the cluttered, dusty room. Gathering up a pile of papers on the seat of a hard chair facing his desk, he gestured for her to sit down.

Meg perched on the edge of the chair and waited while he tossed the papers down and seated himself opposite her. "Okay," he smiled. *"Now,* what can I do for you?"

Marry me, she returned silently. *Don't ask me why, just marry me.*

Out loud she said, "I have a business proposition to present to you. One that I think could greatly benefit both of us."

Geoff's eyebrows rose. He didn't know what he'd expected her to say, but certainly not that. Noting her rigid posture and the tense lines around her mouth, he astutely guessed that she was greatly disturbed about something, but unable to fathom what it might be, he answered simply, "All right, I'm listening."

Meg drew a deep breath, praying that she wouldn't faint or throw up before she got out what she'd come to say. "I'm here to offer you free use of my mill's services for the next three years," she blurted.

A long silence ensued as Geoffrey tried to absorb what she'd just said. Three years' timber production, cut free? Who did this girl want him to kill? Careful not to betray his astonishment and give her the upper hand in whatever she was going to suggest next, he nonchalantly leaned back in his chair. "Go on."

"That's it, really," Meg shrugged, so relieved he hadn't

28

laughed at her that she didn't immediately realize she hadn't yet stated her terms.

Geoff gazed at his guest speculatively. "That's quite a generous offer, Miss Taylor. Care to tell me why you're willing to do this for me?"

"Oh, yes," Meg giggled nervously. "I suppose you are wondering that, aren't you?"

Geoff nodded, further bewildered by her obvious discomfiture.

"Well," she gulped, "it's because . . . because I need something from you in return."

"I thought you might," Geoff smiled wryly. "And just exactly what is it you need?"

Meg averted her eyes, suddenly unable to meet his golden gaze. "I need for you to marry me," she mumbled.

"What?"

She raised her head, forcing herself to look at him squarely. "I said, I need for you to marry me."

To her complete astonishment, Geoff burst out laughing. "Okay, Miss Taylor," he guffawed, "who put you up to this? Was it Tom Bosacki?"

"Mr. Wellesley, I assure you . . ."

"It's okay, you can drop the act now. I knew Tom was going to do something to get back at me for telling the Widow Anderson that he was sweet on her, but I never gave him credit for being so original."

"Mr. Wellesley!" Meg interrupted, appalled that he obviously was not taking her seriously.

"Tell me, Miss Taylor, how did Tom ever convince you to be part of this?"

"Mr. Wellesley! Please! I don't even know who Tom Bosacki is."

Geoff's broad grin gradually faded. "Are you telling me this isn't a joke?"

"Absolutely not!" Meg bristled. "I assure you, I'm very serious. In simple terms, I am offering you unlimited use of my sawmill for the next three years in return for you marrying me."

"You can't be serious!" Geoff snorted, rising from his chair and rounding his desk.

"Well, I am."

"This is the most ridiculous thing I've ever heard."

Meg's expression registered a combination of embarrassment and outrage at Geoff's blunt assessment of her offer. "I'm sorry you feel that way," she murmured, rising and turning for the door. "I'll not take up any more of your time."

Geoff frowned at her rigid back, chagrined that he had unwittingly offended her. "Just a minute."

Meg hesitated, but was too embarrassed to turn around.

"Why don't you . . . I don't know . . . sit down again . . . and we'll talk."

Meg wanted nothing more than to dash out the door of the rough little shack and never look back. But knowing how desperate her situation was, she slowly returned to her chair.

When she was seated again, Geoffrey leaned a hip on the corner of his desk and said, "Okay, now why don't you tell me what this is all about?"

"There's nothing to tell," Meg hedged, finding it impossible to confess the real reason she was trying to bargain with him.

"Oh, really?" Geoff countered. "You mean you suddenly just decided I'm the man you want to marry?"

"Something like that," Meg mumbled.

"Oh, come on, Miss Taylor! Do you really expect me to believe that? We don't even know each other! It hardly seems plausible that you just spontaneously developed an overwhelming longing for my affections."

This last eloquent statement made Meg look at him in surprise. *Plausible? Spontaneously?* Where had the rough-and-tumble Geoffrey Wellesley learned such words? Well, he was right about one thing—his unexpectedly urbane grammar was in itself a testament to how little they knew each other.

"Of course I didn't just 'develop a longing for you,' " she said quickly.

Geoff frowned at her a moment, trying to figure out her motivation. Then, it dawned on him. "You're in the family way, aren't you?" he asked softly.

"What?" Meg cried, her eyes widening in horror at his outrageous assumption.

"And you need a husband—quick," he added.

"That's not true! How could you even think that? Why, in order to be in that condition, a woman has to . . . and I never would . . . I never have . . . That's preposterous, Mr. Wellesley, just preposterous! How dare you insult me by even suggesting such a thing?"

The indignation in her voice, coupled with the bright spots of embarrassed color that had risen to her cheeks, were so genuine that Geoffrey knew without a doubt that pregnancy was not what had driven the beautiful woman to make this outlandish proposal.

"I'm sorry, Miss Taylor," he said contritely, "I didn't mean to offend you. Look, why don't we stop playing games? This, ah, proposition of yours might be easier for me to understand if you'd just tell me why you're here. You say you're not in love with me, you also say you're not in the family way, so what is it? Certainly *something* made you approach me."

Meg exhaled a long, shuddering sigh, stalling for time as

31

she tried to sort out how much she should confide. She couldn't tell him about the debt her father owed. She just couldn't. No, better to do as Virginia had suggested and appeal to Geoffrey's protective instincts by telling him she was being forced into marriage with Peter.

"All right, Mr. Wellesley," she said finally. "I'll tell you why I'm here."

"Good," Geoff nodded, settling his hip more comfortably on the corner of the desk and directing his full attention toward her.

"I'm . . . I'm in need of protection," Meg began. "For reasons which I am not at liberty to discuss, my father contracted with George Farnsworth to marry me to his son, Peter."

Hearing Geoff's sharply indrawn breath, Meg knew she'd hit a nerve and quickly plunged on. "I don't want to marry him," she said bluntly.

"I can well understand that," Geoff agreed. "But what do *I* have to do with all this?"

Meg cleared her throat, then forced her gaze upward until she was looking directly at him. "The contract my father signed is binding, and the only way I can think to escape it is to marry someone else before Peter Farnsworth returns from Texas."

"And you've decided I'm the one."

Meg nodded.

"Why?"

"Because I know you don't want to get married, and neither do I. I thought you and I could come to an agreement where we would be married in name only. I would be free of Peter, and you would turn a tremendous profit by being able to cut your timber at my mill free of charge. I can assure you there won't be any . . . entanglements."

32

"You're wrong, Miss Taylor. There are always entanglements."

"I promise you, there won't be," she said quickly. "Besides, think of the benefits! This plan could make you very rich."

"I'm already very rich, Miss Taylor," Geoff said carefully, hoping to let her down without further embarrassing her, "but, you're right about one thing. I don't want to get married. In name only, or any other way."

Meg's heart sank. "So you won't consider my offer?"

"I'm sorry, but it's out of the question. I'm flattered you thought of me, though."

"Well, don't be," she retorted, suddenly angry that he'd not even given her the courtesy of telling her he'd think about it. "The only reason I 'thought of you' is that you're the one man in town powerful enough to intimidate the Farnsworths. So if you're entertaining the delusion that I came to you because I found you attractive or . . . or desirable . . . well, you're dead wrong."

For some reason, her insulting words offended Geoffrey to the core. For a long moment, he just looked at her, then he rose and moved toward the door. "I think we've said all there is to say here. Good day, Miss Taylor."

Her eyes flaming with anger and humiliation, Meg bolted out of her chair and rushed by him, not even bothering to return his farewell.

Geoff watched her fly down the steps and race over to her tethered horse. He started to follow her, his innate good manners demanding that he at least offer to help her mount, but before he was halfway down the steps, Meg had hurtled herself into her sidesaddle and charged off down the rutted path.

"So what'd she want?" Ned asked, hurrying over from a nearby copse of trees.

"A husband," Geoff answered, shaking his head. "The lady asked me to marry her."

"She did?" Ned exclaimed. "What'd ya say?"

"What do you think I said? I said no."

"And she accepted that?"

"Of course she accepted it. What else could she do?"

"Nothin', I guess," Ned shrugged. "She don't seem like the kind who would make a scene."

"She's not. Anyway, it was no big thing. She asked, I answered, she left. That's all there was to it."

Ned looked at Geoff speculatively for a moment, then said, "Ya know, boss, women are funny, the way they always seem to go for the wrong man. Hell, if she'd asked me, I'd a said yes so fast it woulda made her head swim. Why, a woman that looks like she does could have any man in town—'cept you, of course. Everybody knows you're the one man hereabouts who ain't interested in a wife. Not even one who looks like that."

"Right," Geoff agreed absently, still looking down the trail where Meg had so recently disappeared, "not even one who looks like that."

"He turned you down flat?"

"Yes," Meg nodded miserably, taking a sip from the tea Virginia set in front of her, "and so fast that it was downright insulting. I'd hardly finished telling him my idea before he said no and showed me the door."

Virginia sighed, disappointment clouding her pretty face. "I'm sorry, Meggie," she murmured. "I feel guilty for even suggesting you talk to him. I really thought he might look more kindly on your proposition."

"Well, he didn't," Meg sighed. "In fact, he seemed hor-

34

rified by the very thought of marriage. I don't think he likes women. It's almost as if he's scared of them . . ."

"That's odd," Ginny mused. "After all, he was engaged once."

"He was? When?"

"Five or six years ago. I'm surprised you never heard about it, but maybe it was when you were away at school."

Meg nodded. "That would be about the time I was gone. Who was he engaged to?"

"Francine MacGregor. But something went wrong between them and they broke it off. Francine immediately left town and went to San Francisco to live with an aunt. I don't think she's been back since, even for a visit."

"Do you know why they broke the engagement?" Meg asked, curious despite her anger with Geoff.

"No. But it must have been something pretty serious, because it happened just two weeks before the wedding. Everything was all arranged, and then, suddenly, Francine just disappeared. Mr. Wellesley was even building that gorgeous house up in the high meadow for them to live in, and after Francine left, he just abandoned it."

"That half-built house near the waterfall belongs to him?"

"Yes, and he's never made any attempt to finish it. He lives in a little cabin up at his timber camp and the house just sits there. Lawrence says it's an eyesore and that Mr. Wellesley should either finish it or tear it down. The city council even met once to decide whether they should demand he do something with it, but they decided that since it's on his land, he has the right to leave it like it is. It's kind of sad, though, that big frame just sitting there so stark and lonely."

"Yes, it is," Meg agreed.

"Well, as I said, something terrible must have happened

between him and Francine, and after what you said about his reaction to your proposal, it looks as if he isn't over it yet."

Meg shook her head and nibbled disinterestedly at an oatmeal cookie. "So, now what do you think I should do?"

"I don't know," Virginia shrugged. "Maybe you should marry someone else, even if he isn't rich and powerful like Geoffrey Wellesley. At least that way you'd be safe from Peter."

"But I don't *want* to marry anybody!" Meg wailed. "I just want to be left alone to run the mill. Is that such an impossible request?"

"No," Ginny said, "except that you're a woman, and women usually aren't allowed to do what they want to do—unless what they want is to get married and raise families."

"Like you," Meg noted.

"Yes, like me," Virginia smiled. "I'm doing exactly what I want."

Meg wrinkled her nose, her distaste so obvious that Ginny couldn't help but chuckle. "Look at it this way, sweetie—as long as Papa is alive, you don't have much to worry about."

Meg looked at her in bewilderment. "What does that have to do with anything?"

"Simple. If Peter comes back from Texas and starts demanding that you marry him, you can simply tell him that it's impossible, since you have to care for Papa."

"Papa doesn't need caring for," Meg argued. "He's not an invalid. He just has a bad heart."

"I know that and you know that, but Peter probably doesn't. If nothing else, it will serve to put him off for a while. At least until we can come up with a better, more permanent plan."

"If only Geoffrey Wellesley had agreed," Meg said wistfully.

"You know, you almost sound as if you'd enjoy being married to him."

"Oh, Ginny, don't be ridiculous. He is just the most convenient choice."

"Yes," Virginia smiled, "convenient and handsome and rich."

"And definitely *not* interested," Meg finished.

"I don't know," Virginia mused, "maybe you're giving up too easily. Maybe all you need to do is think of another way to approach him."

"How?" Meg asked, throwing her hands out in exasperation. "What would you have me do? Trick him, threaten him, blackmail him?"

"I didn't say that, but there must be *some* way to convince him to agree. Every man has his weakness. We just have to figure out what Geoffrey's is."

"Well," Meg sighed, rising, "when you figure it out, let me know, because it's my opinion that nothing short of threatening his life or his livelihood is going to make Mr. Geoffrey Wellesley marry me. And even then, I'm still not sure he'd agree!"

Chapter 4

"I think what she did to me stinks!" Geoff slammed his beer glass down on the crude plank that served as a table at the Skid Road saloon and glared at his friend Greg.

"Oh, come on," Greg Stevens chuckled, "she didn't do anything to you. She just asked you to marry her. You refused. She left. What's so bad about that?"

"What's so bad about it is that it's put me in a hell of an embarrassing position. I have to do business with this woman and now I don't know if I can even look her in the eye."

"Forget it," Greg advised. "Just act like nothing happened."

"That's pretty hard to do," Geoff snorted, tossing back a shot of whiskey and chasing it with a swig of beer.

Greg looked at his friend for a long moment, surprised by his vehemence. "Why don't you just marry her?" he asked slyly.

"Are you nuts? I don't want to marry her. I don't even *know* her!"

"She's awful pretty . . ."

Geoff shrugged. "So what?"

"God, you're stubborn, Wellesley! Can't you even admit

38

that much? Megan Taylor is the prettiest, most desirable woman in Wellesley, and she asked *you* to marry her. Aren't you even the least bit flattered?"

Geoff hesitated a moment, then reluctantly nodded his head. "A little, I suppose, and you're right, she *is* pretty. But that doesn't mean I want to marry her."

"You've got to get over Francine sometime," Greg said quietly. "Not every woman is like her."

"Oh? And how do you know that?"

"How do I know that?" Greg chuckled. "Are you forgetting I'm married?"

"Well, Vickie's different. You got the best woman in the whole state of Oregon."

"That may be, but it doesn't mean there isn't another good one somewhere, and I think Miss Taylor is a hell of a fine lady."

"I've always liked her, too, what little I know of her," Geoff admitted. "I just don't want to marry her, and now that I've told her that, it's going to be damned uncomfortable the next time I have to face her."

"Well, I think you should reconsider. You need a wife, whether you realize it or not, and I hate to see Megan Taylor marry that slimy Peter Farnsworth. I still think he had something to do with Jenny Thomas's death last year."

"I don't want to see her forced into marrying Farnsworth, either, but I'm not willing to sacrifice myself on the altar of matrimony just to prevent it."

Greg threw his friend a mocking look. "Oh, I understand—marrying Megan Taylor means that you end up with the prettiest woman in town, who just also happens to own the only sawmill on your mountain. What a terrible sacrifice that would be for you!"

"For God's sake, cut it out!" Geoff growled. "I don't care

39

what she looks like or what she owns, I don't want to marry her. It's as simple as that, so let's just drop it, okay?"

"Okay, okay," Greg said agreeably, draining his beer glass and standing up. "It's your life."

"Exactly."

"Anyway, it's getting late, and I'd better get home to the best woman in the whole state, or she's going to be out looking for me—with her rolling pin in hand!"

Geoff shook his head. "You see what I mean? Wedded bliss is definitely not for me."

Greg wiggled his eyebrows meaningfully. "It has its compensations."

"I know, I know. And those compensations are exactly why you're suddenly in such a hurry to get home, aren't they?"

With a smug grin, Greg threw a coin on the table. "You bet. You really should try it sometime."

"Get out of here," Geoff ordered good-naturedly. "Go make your wife happy."

As Greg hurried out of the noisy, crowded saloon, Geoff leaned back in his chair and took another swallow of beer. "You really should try it sometime," he muttered, repeating Greg's parting words. Well, he had tried it . . . or at least, he almost had.

A vision of Francine MacGregor rose unbidden in his mind. Francine, with her golden-blond hair and cornflower-blue eyes. Francine, with her sweet, honeyed voice and tempting little body. Francine, whose every word of love had been a lie and whose every gesture and comehither look had been a calculated ploy to make him want her. And want her he had—with a passion that had completely blinded him to her true nature.

Thank God he'd awakened in time. He'd been annoyed when he'd received letters from several of Portland's top couturières, advising him that his fiancée had run up tremendous bills and then refused to pay, assuring the merchants that "Mr. Geoffrey Wellesley will settle my accounts right after the first of May."

But now, when he thought back on his anger, he knew that it hadn't really been Francine's presumptuous spending sprees that had killed his love for her. Rather, it had been her absolute lack of remorse. Even when he'd confronted her, she'd simply looked at him with those limpid blue eyes and said, "But Geoffrey, I *needed* those clothes. After all, I can't be married to a man of your influence and dress like a pauper!"

And when he'd coldly reminded her that they were not yet married, she'd simply shrugged and giggled, "Soon enough."

After that, his feelings had quickly eroded as he'd forced himself to take a long, objective look at their relationship. Little things that had in the past simply annoyed him suddenly took on new meaning: the fact that Francine never wanted to hear anything about his business—except how much money might be gained from a particular venture. Her stubborn refusal to marry him until he'd completed the magnificent house he was building for them. Her insistence that they take a three-month wedding trip to Europe, even when he'd repeatedly explained to her that he couldn't be gone that long during the height of the logging season. And most of all, her reaction to his amorous advances.

In his youth, Geoff had been handsome, impetuous, and hot-blooded. Even though the years had tempered these traits, he now possessed characteristics that were even more potently appealing. At thirty-four, he was still devastatingly handsome, but now he was also self-assured, charming, and successful—a combination that left even the most proper of ladies hard-pressed to deny him.

But not Francine.

For a while she had put up a front, welcoming his attentions, blushing modestly when he touched her, even as she threw him looks that made him shake with repressed desire. She never resisted when he kissed her, but she never really responded, either. Rather, she would remain complacent beneath his lips, steadfastly refusing to open her mouth to his seductively questing tongue, but smiling coyly and telling him how much she loved his caresses when he finally drew away in frustration.

As their courtship became more serious, Geoff worried that Francine's maidenly avoidance of his overtures might mask a true aversion toward the sensual side of marriage, but still he persevered, forcing himself to be patient and trying hard to believe her whispered promises of "how wonderful it would be" once they were married and she could give free rein to her passions.

The final blow had come two weeks before the planned date of their wedding, when to Geoff's astonishment, Francine announced that the nuptials had to be postponed. They had been touring the half-finished house he was building for them when she suddenly told him she'd decided they couldn't be married until the house was complete and Wallace B. Templeton, London's most famous interior designer, could be brought in to decorate it.

"We don't need Templeton," Geoff had argued. "There are lots of perfectly good decorators in San Francisco—and there's no reason why we can't be living in the house while they work on it."

Francine's voice had become glacial as she'd responded, "There's no one in San Francisco accomplished enough to decorate my home."

"Your home?" Geoff had retorted, his eyes narrowing. "Don't you mean *our* home?"

"Well, of course I mean our home," Francine had quickly prevaricated. Sensing Geoff's burgeoning anger, she had stepped forward, standing on tiptoe and giving him a placating kiss. "I'm only thinking of you, Geoffrey," she had cooed. "After all, you *are* the wealthiest, most successful man in the state of Oregon, and your house should be a reflection of your importance."

Geoff's expression darkened ominously. "Tell me something, Francine," he said quietly, "would you be marrying me if I *wasn't* the wealthiest, most successful man in the state of Oregon?"

His blunt question had given her pause . . . a pause that had told him all he needed to know.

Their disagreement had quickly escalated into a full-fledged screaming match, culminating with Francine's shouted admission that she'd never really loved him—that she thought him crude, vulgar, and completely inept at controlling his "nauseating masculine urges." The flash of pain that had crossed Geoff's eyes at her insulting words had done nothing to stem the torrent of abuse she was heaping on him, and she plunged on heedlessly, confessing that the only reason she'd agreed to marry him was to live in a beautiful house, wear beautiful dresses, and have a legion of servants to cater to her every whim.

By the following day, the whole town was abuzz with the news that Geoffrey Wellesley had broken off his engagement to Francine MacGregor. The startling turn of events was met by many different reactions—anger from Francine's family and friends, amusement from the town's many confirmed bachelors, and utter delight from the unmarried young girls whose hopes had been dashed when Geoff and Francine had become betrothed. Francine, for

43

her part, was so furious that she'd immediately packed her bags and left town.

It seemed the only person who was truly *upset* was Geoffrey himself. He was so devastated by Francine's cruel words of rejection that for the next three months he never left his logging camp, even to come to town to attend church services.

He had truly wanted to get married. He longed for a real home, with a wife and children to love. It was a dream he had secretly held for a long time—and one Francine had forever dashed with her sneered epithets that the only reason any woman would want a man so crude was his money.

Geoffrey pulled himself out of his melancholic reverie and slammed his now empty beer glass down on the planked table. "The damn Wellesley money," he growled. "It's more of a curse than a gift."

He shoved back his chair and stood up, reaching into his pocket and throwing several bills down. Having drunk far more than was his usual habit, he wove his way unsteadily out of the saloon and clumsily mounted his horse.

Luckily, the well-trained animal knew the way home and picked his way carefully up the rutted trail despite the lack of guidance from his rider. Geoff's mind began to clear as the cool mountain wind assailed him, but still he was surprised when his horse came to a sudden halt and he realized he was standing in front of his small cabin.

"You're a hell of a good nag," he complimented, giving the horse an affectionate pat as he slid off its back. Despite his inebriated state, he took a slow turn around the camp, making sure all the campfires were doused and the large, dangerous saws and other equipment were safely stored for the night.

When he was convinced that all was in order, he wearily

climbed the steps to his cabin and threw himself down on his hard bunk without even bothering to undress.

He figured he'd go to sleep immediately, especially considering the amount of liquor he'd consumed, but he didn't. After several minutes of staring at the ceiling, he closed his eyes and let his foggy mind drift back to his disturbing encounter with Megan Taylor.

Lord, but she was pretty, he ruminated. So little and curvy, it made a man's loins clench just to look at her. And that hair—that dark, soft, shiny hair. What would it feel like to thread your fingers through its silky thickness or bury your nose in its fragrant depths?

To Geoff's extreme annoyance, he felt the first stirrings of an erection. With a grunt, he turned over on his side, giving his meager pillow an irritated punch. "You should never drink rye, Wellesley," he chastised. "It always makes you horny."

Desperately, he tried to concentrate on tomorrow's cutting schedule, but after several minutes he finally gave up the struggle and got to his feet. Unbuttoning his tight denim pants, he pulled them off, releasing his stiff manhood from their painful confines.

Looking down ruefully at his jutting arousal, he muttered, "Look at you, you damn fool. You're like a sixteen-year-old kid! This is exactly why you can't even consider marrying her. Look what just thinking about her has done to you! Why, with that face and that body, you'd be addicted to her so fast, you'd never get any work done. Just forget her and let her marry Farnsworth, before you make yourself crazier than you already are."

With a determined jerk of his head, he again lay down and slammed his eyes shut. But it was to no avail. The vision of Megan as she had looked that day seated across from him in his shabby little office was like a fire in his blood. It was almost dawn before he finally fell into an exhausted doze, and even then, his last conscious thought was that there had to be some way he could help the girl extract herself from the odious marriage into which she had been sold.

Chapter 5

You couldn't have more appropriate weather for a funeral, Geoffrey thought dismally, pulling the brim of his hat down to shield his face from the incessant cold drizzle. Shifting his weight from one foot to the other, he grimaced at the sucking sound his boot made as he pulled it out of the mud he stood in.

"Yea, though I walk through the valley of the shadow of death, I will fear no evil . . ."

God, I hate that psalm, he mused. The mournful biblical passage reminded him of his parents' funerals several years before, when both had succumbed to the dreaded small-pox.

His eyes drifted away from the wet coffin with the soggy bouquet of roses lying across it and settled on the small, black-clad figures of Megan Taylor and her sister, Virginia Lombard.

Virginia was weeping openly, dabbing at her eyes with a small linen handkerchief and leaning heavily on her husband, Lawrence. Megan, however, was silent, her beautiful face set and emotionless, betraying none of the crushing grief that weighed down on her so heavily.

Geoffrey kept his head down in deference to the solemn

47

ceremony going on around him, but secretly, he was watching Megan's every move. She looked so small, so fragile and alone, standing a little apart from her sister.

What must be going through her mind, now that her father is dead? Geoffrey wondered. Frederick Taylor's death had been a shock, despite the fact that everyone in Wellesley had known he suffered from a serious heart condition. Even so, the massive attack that had taken his life had been so swift, so devastating in its finality, that the entire town had reeled with disbelief.

Geoff's covert gaze flicked over to George Farnsworth, who was standing behind Megan. What was the situation now regarding her contracted marriage to Peter? In the two months since Megan had approached him with her request that he marry her, Geoffrey had heard many rumors concerning her impending nuptials. For the first several weeks after their confrontation in his office, he had considered trying to intervene in some way, but as time had passed and he had heard nothing more from her, her dilemma had slipped to the back of his mind.

For the past several months, he had been completely immersed in the massive project of building a water flume to send his cut timber plummeting down the side of the mountain into the river far below, where it would then float naturally downstream to the Taylor mill.

Flumes were a relatively new concept in logging, and one that Geoffrey eagerly embraced, knowing that the construction of such a device would be a vast improvement over the current primitive method of timber transport— huge teams of oxen dragging the logs down "skid roads," a series of greased planks placed at close intervals down the side of the mountain.

So involved was Geoff in his project that his initial concern over Megan's welfare had long since faded. But now, seeing George Farnsworth hovering so near her as the minister intoned, "Ashes to ashes, dust to dust" and a clod of wet, mucky dirt was shoveled on to the lowered coffin, the immediacy of her situation again came to the forefront of his mind.

At one point, he'd heard that the marriage had been postponed indefinitely, since Meg was responsible for her ailing father's care, but now that Frederick Taylor was dead, Geoff couldn't help but wonder if plans for the wedding would accelerate.

"It's none of your business," he told himself. "She's a grown woman who can take care of herself." Still, as he glanced over at her forlorn little figure, he couldn't deny the feelings of sympathy that welled up within him.

His attention was drawn back to the present as the minister closed his prayerbook and said quietly, "Will you please join me now in the Lord's Prayer?"

When the small group had completed the simple prayer, the cleric added, "You are all invited to attend a reception at Lawrence and Virginia Lombard's home when our service here concludes."

After the final "Amen" had finally been voiced, the mourners quickly dispersed, hurrying off toward their wagons and the promise of a warm, dry house, with plenty of good food and hot cider to take the chill off.

As Geoff turned to leave, he noticed that George Farnsworth had stepped forward and solicitously offered Megan his arm, which, after a slight hesitation, she reluctantly accepted. Geoff's eyebrows rose in reaction to her obvious aversion to Farnsworth's possessive gesture, and for a moment, he contemplated stepping forward to join them. He quickly changed his mind, however, telling himself that it was not his place to intervene. The last thing he wanted to do was give Meg the idea that he wished to become involved in her personal situation. With a slight shrug, he turned away and strode over to his horse.

"Mr. Wellesley?"

Geoff turned to see Virginia Lombard holding up her hand to catch his attention. Walking over to where she stood with Lawrence, he swept his wet hat off his head and said, "Mrs. Lombard?"

"I just wanted to make sure that you're coming to the house."

"Actually, ma'am," Geoff demurred, "I have some things I need to do up at my camp . . ."

"Oh, please, Mr. Wellesley," Virginia entreated, "it would mean a great deal to us if you would come. Besides, with this terrible weather, there couldn't be much you can do today . . ."

"All right," Geoff conceded, not really understanding why Virginia Lombard was making a special point of asking him to the reception. "Perhaps I can stop for a few minutes."

"Thank you," she said gratefully. Casting him a wan smile, she turned away and stepped into the waiting carriage. Seating herself wearily on the hard leather seat, she looked out the window and said, "We'll see you there, then?"

"Yes," Geoff nodded, cursing the fact that he was now going to have to spend at least another hour in the depressing environment of a funeral reception. Lord, how he hated these rituals. But Virginia's plea had been so heartfelt that he just couldn't bring himself to say no.

Turning back toward his horse, he paused to watch George Farnsworth assist Megan into his plush carriage, noting the look of barely concealed distaste she threw at the older man as she settled her soggy skirts around her feet.

What in the hell could he be saying to her to make her

50

look like that? Geoff wondered. Then, irritated that he cared enough to be curious, he clapped his hat on his head and mounted. He settled himself on the wet, slippery saddle, frowning as he felt a small pool of water seep through the seat of his trousers.

"The last thing I want to do is go drink tea at some damn reception," he thought, grimacing as the icy water soaked through his underwear and hit his skin.

For a moment, he almost changed his mind and headed for home but then, remembering Virginia's hopeful face and envisioning Megan's small, stoic figure as she stood so griefstricken by her father's grave, he sighed in resignation and turned his mount in the direction of the departing wagons, bringing up the rear of the small parade headed back toward the center of town.

Geoff was appalled as he entered the Lombards' small house and saw the size of the crowd gathered there. Although the group at the graveside service had been small, it seemed everyone in Wellesley had decided to come to the reception. Why was it that people thought it necessary to throw a party after a funeral?

Thoughts of his parents' funerals again filled his mind. He remembered all the people who had crowded into his family's lavish Colorado home, each of them intent on offering personal condolences to him, his brothers, and his sister.

Maybe some people actually appreciated this public outpouring of grief. But he knew that for himself, all he'd wanted after laying his parents to rest was to return to his home and spend the remainder of the day sharing the bittersweet consolation of private memories with his family.

Five minutes, he told himself, as he peeled off his sodden

51

mackintosh. Just long enough to shake hands and drink a cup of tea. Then I can go home, get out of these wet clothes, and have a brandy.

Geoffrey ignored the many heads that turned in his direction as he walked down the hall toward the parlor. He was used to people staring at him. Not only was he the richest man in the area, he was also one of the most reclusive. Those two facts, combined with his incredible good looks, never failed to make people treat him like an object of curiosity every time he showed up in the town named for him.

Entering the crowded, stuffy parlor, with its drawn curtains and overwhelming smell of verbena sachets, Geoff glanced around, surreptitiously looking for Meg. He finally spotted her, standing a little to the right of her sister and listening with a tense expression to something George Farnsworth was saying.

Frowning, Geoff sidled closer to where they stood, trying to look nonchalant as he hovered near the refreshment table and shamelessly eavesdropped on their conversation.

There were so many people in the room that it was impossible to hear everything Farnsworth was saying, but the snatches of conversation that did reach his ears were enough to make him frown with suppressed anger.

"No reason to wait any longer . . . already sent Peter a telegram . . . wedding can take place within the month."

To Geoff's surprise, Meg said nothing in response to Farnsworth's stream of conversation. To the casual onlooker, it would appear that she was listening earnestly, but from Geoff's vantage point, he could now see that her eyes were vacant; he doubted that Farnsworth's words were registering at all.

To his surprise, he found himself wanting to break up the one-sided tête à tête. Setting down the cup of punch he was sipping, and skirting the small knot of people clustered around the table, he wove his way through the crowd until he stood next to Megan and George.

"I'll come to see you tomorrow and we'll work out the details," he heard Farnsworth saying.

"Not tomorrow," Megan interjected weakly. "Please, Mr. Farnsworth. I'm just not . . ."

"Now, no more of your arguments, young lady," Farnsworth interrupted, his expression hardening. "There isn't a person in the whole state who'd disapprove of your marrying soon, without waiting till you're out of mourning. Everyone knows that you need to get yourself settled, and now that Peter is returning, we can immediately proceed . . ."

Suddenly, Geoff could take no more of watching the man's high-pressure tactics, and he stepped forward. "Miss Taylor," he said, alarmed by Meg's exhausted, vacuous expression, "please allow me to offer my condolences."

Meg turned startled eyes on him, looking at him as though she had never seen him before. "Th . . . thank you," she stammered, her gaze sliding back to George, who was glaring at Geoff with unconcealed dislike. "I appreciate you coming today, Mr. Wellesley."

"I admired your father very much," Geoff answered automatically, his eyes narrowing slightly as he returned Farnsworth's icy stare.

Megan's brows drew together as she looked at Geoff in bewilderment. In the two days since her father had died, she had functioned like a person in a dream. The shock was so deep, her grief so intense, that even as she and Virginia planned the funeral, none of what she was doing really registered. Even George Farnsworth's cloying presence and constant reminders that it was now time for her to concentrate on her impending marriage to his son hadn't

53

pierced through the protective cloak of detached composure that she had drawn around herself.

But Geoffrey Wellesley's unexpected presence had changed all that. There was something about his huge, work-hardened hand clasping hers that had sent a tingling rush of warmth up her arm and, for the first time since she'd left her father's deathbed, she was truly aware of her surroundings. She looked around Virginia's parlor with an expression close to astonishment, realizing for the first time that there were more than fifty people crowded into the small room. She withdrew her hand self-consciously from Geoff's strong, warm grip, and raised her eyes to meet his. How strange, she thought, as she gazed into his handsome, chiseled face. The man who should have made her most uneasy had instead given her, with his kind words and warm handshake, a sense of reality and renewed purpose.

Maybe it was his huge physical presence, or just the knowledge that he was the one man who could intimidate George Farnsworth, that made her suddenly feel alive again. Meg had no idea why Geoffrey's interruption of her future father-in-law's latest diatribe had shaken her from the stultifying lethargy she was suffering, but she would be eternally grateful to him for his intervention. She was also relieved that her first encounter with him since the mortifying day he had turned down her marriage proposal had not caused her the embarrassment she'd expected. He seemed completely at ease in her presence, and his nonchalance allowed her to salvage some small bit of her devastated pride.

Meg's assessment of Geoff's current emotional state could not have been more incorrect. Far from relaxed and nonchalant, George felt a blend of guilt and a strange feeling of responsibility.

With a last nod and a smile that was almost apologetic,

he turned and walked away. When he reached the opposite side of the room, he leaned against the wall, looking back thoughtfully at Meg, who was being assailed with another torrent of verbosity from George.

"Why the hell doesn't the old bastard leave her alone, at least until the body is cold?" he muttered to himself. His lips thinning into a hard line of disgust, he stood staring at them for a moment longer. Then, suddenly, he came to a decision. Pushing away from the wall, he walked determinedly over to Virginia.

"Mrs. Lombard?" he said quietly, yet with a note in his voice that made Virginia turn away from the woman she was talking to and look at him curiously.

"Mr. Wellesley?"

"I'd appreciate a word with you, when you have a moment." He smiled apologetically at the woman whose conversation he'd interrupted. The lady flashed back a look of complete forgiveness, entranced, as women always were, by the Wellesley smile.

"Of course," Virginia responded, looking slightly flustered at his unexpected request.

Geoff threw another ingratiating but expectant look at the other woman, who finally picked up his cue and blurted, "Oh, well, yes. I'll . . . I'll talk to you later, Virginia."

Virginia nodded and turned back to Geoff with a puzzled look on her face. "You want to speak to me?"

"Yes," he said, casting another furtive glance in the direction of Megan and George Farnsworth. "I wonder if there is someplace we could go where we could talk privately for a moment."

Virginia's confusion deepened, but she nodded and inclined her head toward the kitchen. When the door was firmly closed behind them, she drew a deep breath and forced a smile. "Will this do?"

"Yes. First of all, let me express my sincere sympathies for your loss. My own father died two years ago, and I know what a difficult time this is for you."

"Thank you." Virginia nodded, surprised by his revelation. Geoffrey Wellesley kept his personal life so completely private that even though Virginia was aware that the wealthy and influential James Wellesley had passed away, she had never heard Geoff mention his loss.

"I'm not sure if you know that I'm aware of your sister's predicament," he continued softly.

"Predicament?" Virginia asked, at a loss for a moment as to what he was referring.

"Yes. Regarding Peter Farnsworth."

"Oh, of course," Virginia nodded, flushing with embarrassment. "Meg did tell me that she had spoken to you." She was surprised to see Geoffrey shift his weight from one foot to the other, as if the subject of Megan's proposal embarrassed him, too.

"I want to help her," he stated suddenly, causing Virginia's eyes to widen.

"You do?"

"Yes." He cleared his throat uncomfortably. "And I wonder if you might tell her that if it's convenient, I'd like to call on her tomorrow afternoon at two to discuss it."

"Tomorrow afternoon at two," Virginia repeated, her voice sounding dazed. "Yes, of course I'll tell her."

"If that's not a good time, have her send a message up to my camp and let me know what would be."

"I'm sure two o'clock will be fine," Virginia responded, the pitch of her voice suddenly rising.

Geoff looked at her in confusion, wondering what was

causing her sudden agitation. "Are you all right, Mrs. Lombard? Do you feel faint?"

"No," Virginia tittered nervously, circling her throat with a shaking hand. "No, I'm fine. I'll . . . I'll tell Megan."

Geoff nodded and turned to push the kitchen door open, gesturing her through it. "I have to leave now, ma'am, but again, please accept my condolences."

"Thank you so much," Virginia nodded, then added hastily, "for everything. You're very kind."

Geoffrey shook his head, brushing off her compliment. "I just don't like to see anybody forced into a situation they don't want to be in." Then, with a last, self-deprecating smile, he headed off toward the foyer, his massive shoulders seeming to fill the narrow front hall.

Virginia watched him until he disappeared out her front door, then sped over to where Megan stood. "Excuse me, Mr. Farnsworth," she said breathlessly, "but I need to speak to my sister for a moment."

Meg threw Virginia a look of grateful relief at finally being rescued from George Farnsworth. She excused herself with a murmured apology and quickly followed her sister back toward the kitchen. When they were alone in the big room, Virginia turned toward her with shining eyes.

"What is it?" Meg asked, astounded at Ginny's apparent excitement.

To her further astonishment, Virginia burst into a peal of girlish laughter. "You better sit down, little sister, because you are simply not going to *believe* what I have to tell you . . ."

"Did he actually say he'd decided to marry me?"

Virginia shrugged. "Not in so many words, but what else

could he have meant? I'm telling you, he's going to propose tomorrow!"

Meg shook her head and stared vacantly out the kitchen window, still not able to believe that Geoffrey Wellesley had changed his mind. "It just doesn't make any sense, Ginny. I haven't even spoken to the man since that awful day when I proposed to him, and suddenly he's decided to marry me? Why? What's changed?"

"I have no idea," Ginny admitted, "but this is no time to start analyzing his motivation. Just be ready to receive him tomorrow at two."

"Oh, I will," Megan assured her, smiling for the first time in days. "You can count on it."

It was very late that night before Megan finally went to bed. Despite her grief and exhaustion after the traumatic day, she had turned down Virginia's invitation to spend the night and had instead returned to the lonely solitude of her empty house.

Trying desperately to keep busy and avoid thinking about the last few days, she spent the evening going through her closet, trying to choose an appropriate dress to wear for Geoffrey's visit the next afternoon.

She looked wistfully at the rainbow of colors that hung in her huge armoire, regretting that her father's death precluded wearing anything but black. After repeatedly trying on the few somber-hued gowns she owned, she finally settled on a simple high-necked, long-sleeved black taffeta dress. The heavy fabric was really better suited to winter than May, but the stand-up collar was decorated with beautiful white tatting, and Meg felt that at least that simple adornment set off her porcelain skin and dark eyes to some advantage.

Carefully hanging the garment on the armoire door, she assessed it critically, deciding to steam it in the morning. She bathed and washed her hair, sitting by the window and brushing out the lustrous waves until they floated around her face like a dark cloud. The drizzle had finally stopped and the sky had cleared at sunset, allowing her to open the window and let the fresh breeze aid in the drying process.

As she methodically ran the brush through her thick locks, she let her mind drift, imagining what being married to Geoffrey Wellesley might be like. Of course, it wouldn't be a conventional marriage, since there would be no real intimacy between them, but still, the thought of having the handsome and much sought-after man escort her to social engagements and town events was titillating.

"Why, I'll be the most envied woman in Wellesley," she murmured. "I'll be *Mrs.* Wellesley!" The thought that she would actually be married to the man for whom the town was named caused a little shiver of anticipation to run through her, and for a moment, she almost wished Geoffrey's impending proposal had sprung from a more normal course of events. What might it have been like to have *the* Geoffrey Wellesley fall in love with her? To court her, woo her, and then, ultimately, propose to her because he *wanted* her for his wife?

With a wry little shrug, Meg shook off her silly schoolgirl fantasies. "This is much better," she told herself firmly. "The perfect situation. You'll have all the protection of being married to the most important man in town and still be free to run the mill and your life exactly the way you want to . . . with no interference from him."

With a little sigh, she set her hairbrush down and wearily climbed into her big, soft bed. "A much better situation," she repeated. But still, despite all the convincing arguments she could think of, she couldn't help but wonder what it might be like to have Geoffrey Wellesley *really* love her . . .

Chapter 6

Meg glanced at the large clock hanging in her front hall as she smoothed nonexistent wrinkles out of her dress. Two o' five.

For the hundredth time she peeked out the oval beveled window in the front door, and this time she was rewarded by the sight of Geoffrey Wellesley looping his horse's reins over her hitching rail.

"He's here!" she gasped, her heart pounding excitedly. "Just be calm. There's nothing to be nervous about." Dashing around the corner into the dining room, she leaned against the wall and willed her thundering heart to slow. Still, when his sharp rap on the door sounded, she jumped.

"Count to five before you go," she ordered herself. "You don't want him to think you're too eager." Taking a deep breath, she forced herself to slowly count to five, then glided around the corner and opened the door.

Geoffrey was dressed in a beautifully tailored dark-brown serge suit that set off his tawny skin and leonine good looks to perfection. He looked so handsome that for a moment, Meg just gaped at him in awe.

"Good afternoon, Miss Taylor," he finally said, sweeping his hat off his head and smiling.

"Good afternoon, Mr. Wellesley," she returned, a bit breathlessly. "Won't you come in?" As her eyes swept over him, she was amazed, as always, by his sheer size. Somehow, she mused, when he was outdoors, he didn't look so big. But when he stood in a normal-sized room with normal-sized people, he just seemed to fill it up.

Geoffrey looked at her expectantly for a moment, then gestured to a small three-legged table against the wall. "Could I put my hat here?"

"Yes," she blurted. "I'm sorry. Of course you can. Here, let me take it." She reached for his hat just as he set it on the table, then awkwardly drew her hand back when their fingers touched. "Oh, I'm so sorry!"

Why does she keep saying she's sorry? Geoff wondered. *And why is she so nervous?* Looking down at the flustered pink-cheeked girl, he could hardly believe this was the same woman who'd so boldly asked him to marry her only two months before. With a tentative smile, he said, "Perhaps we could sit down somewhere to talk?"

With a start, Meg closed the front door and threw her arm out toward the parlor. "Of course. Let's go in here."

Geoff nodded and followed her across the foyer, gazing around with interest at the well-appointed house. He had done business with Frederick Taylor for years, but this was the first time he'd ever been inside his home. Looking down, he glanced at the beautiful Aubusson carpet, noticing its fine texture and expensive weave. His eyebrow lifted in surprise, however, when, on closer inspection, he saw how worn it was in the center. Had Frederick been having financial problems? Was that the reason he had sold his daughter in marriage to George Farnsworth?

Intrigued, Geoff allowed his gaze to wander further,

noting, at once, several light patches on the silk wallpaper. It looked as if pictures had once hung there, but where were they now? Sold, maybe, to raise capital?

His speculations came to an abrupt end as they passed through the double doors leading into the parlor and Meg gestured toward a rose-colored velvet settee. "Please, make yourself comfortable, Mr. Wellesley."

Geoffrey sat down, unbuttoning his suit coat as he did. He fought back an urge to run his finger around the inside of his tight collar, annoyed that for two days now he'd been forced to squeeze his massive shoulders and thick, muscular neck into the uncomfortable confines of a starched shirt.

"Well," Meg smiled, sinking gracefully on to a settee opposite his and clasping her hands tightly in her lap. "You said you wanted to see me about something?"

"Yes," Geoffrey nodded, his eyes gliding away from her expectant gaze. Ever since yesterday afternoon, when he'd made his impetuous offer to try to help Meg out of her dilemma, he'd been trying to think of what to say once this moment was upon him. Now it was here and he still wasn't sure how to approach her.

Meg waited for him to continue, but when it became obvious he wasn't going to say any more, she finally broke the silence. "Would you like some tea? Or some brandy, perhaps?"

Geoffrey seized upon the momentary reprieve. "A brandy would be nice."

With a relieved smile, she rose from the settee and walked over to a beautifully carved sideboard upon which rested a crystal decanter and four snifters. Pulling the stopper out of the decanter, she poured a quarter of an inch of brandy into one of the glasses and carried it back to Geoff. "Here you are."

His lips twisted with amusement as he looked at the

meager amount of liquor in the large glass, but he inclined his head graciously. "Thank you, Miss Taylor."

"Why don't you call me Megan?" she offered, resuming her seat and her stiff pose.

Geoffrey swirled the shallow pool of brandy around the bottom of the glass. "If you'll call me Geoff."

Meg nodded and smiled again.

Another long silence ensued, and this time neither of them could think of anything to say. Finally, when they did speak, it was at the same time.

"I really appreciate you offering . . ."

"Maybe we should discuss your . . ."

Just as they'd started, they both stopped talking at precisely the same moment.

"Please, go on with what you were saying," Meg invited, her blush returning.

God, she's gorgeous when she blushes like that. "Well, as I told your sister yesterday, I have decided that I would like to help you with your, ah, problem."

"That's very kind of you," Meg murmured, her color heightening even more as she awaited his formal proposal.

Geoff took a long swallow of his brandy. "I don't know what the circumstances are surrounding your father's contract with George Farnsworth, but I hate to see anyone forced into being a party to an agreement someone else has made."

"As do I," Meg responded, becoming more and more excited as he finally neared his point.

"Anyway," he continued, setting down the empty snifter and leaning forward, his elbows braced on his knees and his hands clasped between them, "I don't know if it will help, but I thought I would go talk to Farnsworth."

"Well, of course that will help," Meg laughed. "Your going to talk to him will solve everything."

"Not necessarily," Geoff countered, wondering if the girl thought he was magic. "I'm afraid you're giving me too much credit."

Meg shook her head. "I don't understand. What could Mr. Farnsworth possibly do after you talk to him?"

"Unfortunately, he has every right to simply ignore me and proceed with his plans. He has all the contractual legalities on his side."

Meg smiled. "Contractual legalities won't mean much once we're married. There will be nothing he can do. We just have to make sure that if he won't be reasonable when you talk to him that we get married immediately, before he tries to stop us."

She paused to take a breath, not even noticing that Geoff was staring at her in stunned disbelief. "I don't mind not having a large wedding, if you don't," she said, her voice suddenly shy. "After all, I realize that ours will not be a . . . normal marriage, so a small, private ceremony is probably more in order, anyway . . ."

"Megan—"

"Speaking of the marriage, I think it would be a good idea if you and I drew up our own agreement stating the terms of our union. Things like your usage of my mill's services and the . . . the expectations we each have of the other regarding our . . . living arrangements."

"Miss Taylor—"

"I'm sure it will be a simple enough matter to have Sam Benedict draw up some sort of—"

"Miss Taylor!"

Meg stopped in mid-sentence and looked at Geoff in surprise. "Yes?"

"I think you're confused about what's going on here."

Meg looked at him blankly. "Confused?"

"Yes," Geoff nodded, rising and walking over to the

sideboard, where he poured a liberal portion of brandy into his snifter. Without turning around, he said quietly, "Did you think I came here today to accept your marriage proposal?"

Meg drew in a sharp breath and grabbed for the back of the settee, her head suddenly reeling.

Geoff turned around. "You did, didn't you?"

Quickly averting her gaze, Meg closed her eyes, willing herself not to faint. How could Virginia have so completely misunderstood Geoffrey's intent and put her in this humiliating position?

Steeling himself against the anguish he saw clearly imprinted in Meg's expression, Geoff walked back to where she sat and looked down at her. "Miss Taylor, I'm afraid there has been a misunderstanding. I didn't come here to discuss marriage. I merely thought that maybe I could help you by going and talking to George Farnsworth on your behalf."

Meg swallowed and pressed her lips together hard to keep her mouth from shaking. "That's not going to help, Mr. Wellesley," she said, forcing herself to meet his amber gaze. "Talking isn't going to solve anything."

"It might."

"It won't! The only thing that will prevent my being forced to marry Peter Farnsworth is for me to marry someone else. That's why I went to you in the first place."

"I know," Geoff said, trying hard to remain calm and desperately wishing he was anywhere but where he was. "But I can't do that."

"Why not?" Meg asked, throwing out her hands in a gesture of dismay. "I've already told you, I don't actually want *you*. I want only the protection of your name. I promise I'll make no demands."

For some reason, her words hit Geoff like a blow.

"Don't you see?" Meg continued, oblivious to the fact that she had just insulted him. "You won't have to really be a husband to me . . . not in any of the ordinary ways. I know that you don't want to be married, and neither do I. That's why this is such a perfect situation for both of us. We can continue to live our lives exactly as we have been. The only difference is that you'll save a great deal of money for the next several years and I'll be saved from marriage to Peter Farnsworth. What can be wrong with that?"

"What's wrong with it," Geoff said slowly, trying hard to be patient in the face of Meg's rising emotions, "is that one of us might actually meet someone someday who we *do* want to marry. What then?"

"That won't happen with me," she said positively. "I am never marrying—not for real, anyway."

"May I ask why not?" he questioned, suddenly curious as to why the beautiful girl had such an aversion to marriage.

"Because," she blurted, too distraught to come up with a discreet answer, "I will never allow myself to be at some man's beck and call. I've seen the lives my sister and my friends lead. Cleaning, cooking, sewing, washing, and having baby after baby after baby. That is definitely not for me."

"Don't you like children, Miss Taylor?"

"It's not that," she retorted. "I just refuse to be some man's convenient little playmate . . ." Suddenly she stopped short, seeming to finally realize who she was talking to. Her face suffused again with the becoming pink tinge.

"I see," Geoff said smoothly. "So, you don't like children."

"Not much," Meg murmured, so mortified by what

she'd just confessed that she wished the floor would open up and swallow her.

"Well, that's too bad, because I love them. So, you see, that's another reason why you and I couldn't marry. If and when I ever do, I want a whole houseful of kids."

"I don't think this is an appropriate subject for us to be discussing, Mr. Wellesley."

"Perhaps not," he smiled, amused by her sudden prim attitude. "But please believe me when I tell you that if there's anything I can do to help you, short of marrying you, of course, I'll be happy to."

"There's nothing," Meg said quietly, trying to gather up the shreds of her tattered dignity. "Unless you're willing to accept the terms of my proposal, my fate is sealed."

"I can't do that."

"Then, I think it's time for you to go."

"I think you're right," he agreed, setting down his glass.

Silently they walked toward the door. Meg reached it first, and with stiff, mechanical movements, picked up his hat and opened the door. "Good day, Mr. Wellesley."

Geoff took his hat from her shaking hand. "Miss Taylor . . ."

"Good day, sir!"

Blowing out a long, frustrated breath, Geoff clapped his hat on his head and walked out her front door, wincing when he heard it slam behind him.

Meg spent a terrible evening, calling herself every kind of fool for the humiliating scene she'd created in front of Geoffrey Wellesley. "I'll be lucky if he doesn't spread this all over town," she despaired, wringing her hands and pacing back and forth across her bedroom. "I'll probably be the laughingstock in every saloon and around every campfire from here to Oregon City. How dared he make Ginny believe he was going to accept my proposal, only to come here and calmly tell me it's out of the question."

Trembling with exhaustion and nerves, she finally crawled into bed, but even then, the blessed relief of sleep eluded her. "And you, you ninny," she chastised herself, "you spent half of last night lying here and fantasizing about what marriage to the great Geoffrey Wellesley would be like. How could I be such an ass?"

Appalled by her own profanity, Meg turned her face into her pillow and gave vent to long-suppressed tears. "If only he'd said he'd marry me," she wailed. "If only there were some way to talk him into it! *Now* what am I going to do?"

Geoff was spending an equally unpleasant evening, and even the half bottle of whiskey he consumed hadn't been able to erase the vision of Meg's distraught, embarrassed face when he'd told her he had no intention of marrying her.

"Why does she keep putting me in this spot?" he muttered, sitting at the small table inside his one-room cabin, his hand clenched around the neck of his whiskey bottle. "I don't *want* to get married, and especially not to some independent little wench who isn't even willing to give me a couple of kids for my trouble."

But despite his righteous indignation, Geoff still couldn't seem to hold his feelings of guilt at bay. "Trouble is," he hiccoughed, pouring himself another shot, "she's so damned pretty. If she wasn't so damned pretty and so damned sweet and so damned sexy when she blushes like she does, then I wouldn't feel so damned bad about turning her down."

But the truth was, Megan Taylor *was* pretty and she *was* sweet and she *was* sexy—and to Geoff's utter disgust, no amount of whiskey could make him forget that.

It was damned upsetting.

Chapter 7

"Boss, you better come now. We're just about ready to start floatin' that big boom down to the mill."

"On my way," Geoff said, throwing down his pen and rising from his cluttered desk. "Did you warn Miss Taylor that we're bringing a big load in today?"

"No," Ned responded, his brows snapping together with bewilderment. "I didn't know I was s'posed to. Thought you was gonna do that."

"Well, shit," Geoff swore. "How the hell did this happen? I told you to let her know way back on Monday."

Again Ned shook his head, knowing that Geoff had said nothing of the sort. Still, he could see that his boss was truly angry and thought better of arguing the point.

"I'm sorry, Geoff," he said contritely. "If you told me, I didn't hear it. But I'm sure it'll be okay. She'll be able to handle it."

"Handle it, hell. No mill is ready to handle this many board feet without some warning. Now I'm going to have to ride all the way down there and apologize for springing a job this size on her."

"Sorry," Ned muttered, turning away. He knew damn well that Geoff had never mentioned it was his responsibil-

71

ity to alert Miss Taylor about the huge amount of timber they were floating down the river to her mill today. But he also knew there was something odd going on between Geoff and Megan. At one time, Geoff had made regular trips down to the Taylor mill to discuss shipping schedules and cutting requirements. But for the past few months, ever since the day that Meg had ridden up to the camp to ask him to marry her, Geoff had avoided her like the plague, demanding that Ned handle all communication between the two companies. Ned had often wondered what had really transpired that day between his boss and the pretty Miss Taylor, but prudently, he had never asked.

Despite all the years he had worked as Geoff's assistant, they had never developed a personal friendship. Even on the many evenings they had sat in Geoff's small cabin and shared a bottle of whiskey, the boss never mentioned his personal life.

When news of his broken betrothal to Francine MacGregor circulated around Wellesley, Ned had been sorely tempted to ask what had happened, if for no other reason than to be able to defend Geoff to the many women in town who were angry with him for jilting his fiancée. But after the terrible night when they'd split up and Geoff had come back from town drunk and spoiling for a fight with anyone who so much as made eye contact with him, he had never mentioned Francine's name again.

There hadn't been too much to be curious about since that time . . . until now. But despite Geoff's attempt to lightly brush off Miss Taylor's proposal the day it happened, Ned suspected that more had passed between them than Geoff had let on. Obviously, something had occurred that had made him suddenly loath to face the girl.

"You want me to ride down and talk to her?" Ned

offered, hurrying over to where Geoff was saddling his horse.

"No. I'll take care of it."

"I didn't know she was even back at the mill, since her pa's funeral was just last week. Kinda figured she'd be takin' care of personal business or just sittin' around grievin' . . ."

"She's not the type to sit around grieving," Geoff snapped. "She's been back at the mill since two days after the funeral."

Ned's eyebrows rose in surprise at this revelation. How did the boss know so much about the lady's schedule? "I'll go, if you want me to," he offered one last time.

"Forget it," Geoff said, mounting his horse. "I said I'd take care of it, and I will. You just make sure that boom gets moving and that the river pigs don't let it jam."

Geoff wheeled his horse around and rode off down the trail, leaving Ned to stare after him with a curious, speculative expression etched on his homely face.

"Geoff Wellesley's here to see you, Miss Taylor."

Meg's head jerked up from the stack of accounts she was balancing. "He is?" she croaked, then quickly cleared her throat as she tried to cover the tremor in her voice.

"Yeah."

"Do you know what he wants?"

"Somethin' about a big boom he's bringin' in today."

"Well, tell him I don't have time to see him."

"But, Miss Taylor—"

"You heard me, Hank, I said to tell him—"

"I heard what you said to tell me," Geoff suddenly interrupted.

Hank Berkeley whirled around and gaped at Geoff,

73

amazed that the usually genteel and courteous man had followed him into Meg's office, uninvited.

"And I'm sorry if you're busy, Miss Taylor, but we're bringing in a load that's much bigger than normal, and I need to discuss schedules with you."

"I just told you, Mr. Wellesley, I don't have time to talk to you."

"Well, you better make some time," Geoff ordered, his face darkening with anger.

Meg's pen hit the desk with a sharp slap of annoyance and her lips thinned as she rose to her feet. "Please excuse us, Hank," she said softly, flicking her eyes toward the door in a gesture that told the man she expected him to leave.

Hank's bewildered gaze traveled between the two combatants. "But Miss Taylor—"

"The lady said to leave us!" Geoff barked.

Hank took a startled step backward, then with a quick nod, turned on his heel and disappeared out the office door.

"Now, listen here, Mr. Wellesley," Meg began.

"No, you listen to me, Miss Taylor! Just because you're mad that I won't go along with your crazy scheme of getting married, we still have to do business together."

Crazy scheme, Meg's mind screamed. How *dared* he call her plea for help a crazy scheme! A thousand stinging responses raced through her head; then, suddenly, her angry countenance relaxed into a smile of triumph.

"Oh, no we don't, sir."

"What are you talking about?"

When Geoff had first walked into Meg's office, she'd had no idea what she was going to say to him, but his last words had inspired the seed of an idea, and she eagerly seized upon it.

She sat back down, and in a voice as calm as if they were

74

discussing the weather, said, "As of today, the Taylor mill is no longer accepting shipments from Wellesley Timber."

Geoff's mouth dropped open. "What?"

"You heard me, Mr. Wellesley," she smiled, picking up her pen and turning back to her ledger book. "My company is no longer going to deal with your company, which means you're going to have to find yourself another sawmill. It's as simple as that."

"Don't be ridiculous!" Geoff snorted, his face flushing with outrage. "There *is* no other sawmill on this mountain and you know it."

"Precisely," Meg nodded.

An endless moment passed as Meg nonchalantly scratched figures into her ledger. Finally, Geoff sighed tiredly and said, "Okay. I understand that you're mad and that you want to punish me because I won't marry you, but let's get serious, Miss Taylor. Just how long do you think you can stay in business without my timber?"

Meg looked up and graced him with a serene smile. "Quite a while," she responded. "You are only one of many customers my mill services, but as you just pointed out, I own the only mill on this mountain. I'm sure I can survive without you a lot longer than you can without me."

Geoff flushed again, his golden skin taking on a bronze hue. "Are you telling me that you won't cut my timber unless I marry you?"

In actuality, Meg had not even thought of that possibility. All she'd really intended to do was humiliate Geoff into begging her the way she'd been forced to beg him. But now that he had unwittingly offered her the solution to all her problems, she grabbed at it like a drowning river pig grabbing at a floating log. Carefully formulating her words so as not to betray her excitement, she said coolly, "Exactly. Either you marry me, or you find yourself another mill."

"But," Geoff blustered, unable to believe that she still insisted on actually forcing his hand in this outrageous game they were playing, "that's blackmail!"

Meg pursed her lips with distaste. "What a nasty word, Mr. Wellesley. I really don't like it."

"Too bad," Geoff sneered. "That's exactly what it is."

Meg sighed dramatically. "Call it what you will, then, but until I see a wedding ring on my finger, your timber will remain uncut."

For the first time in years, Geoff was speechless. The success of Wellesley Timber had long been due to his brilliant negotiating tactics, but suddenly he found himself facing an ultimatum that he had no idea how to turn to his advantage. "You can't make me marry you," he insisted.

"You're right," Meg nodded agreeably. "I can't. Just like you can't make me cut your timber."

"Oh, yes, I can. Your father signed a contract with me for this year's production which states that Taylor Mill guarantees Wellesley Timber time, men, and equipment to cut at least ten million board feet."

"I know that, Mr. Wellesley," she smiled. "And I have the records right here as to how many board feet we've already cut." She ran the tip of her long, slender finger down the ledger page, coming to a halt near the bottom and sliding her finger across the page until she found the figure she was looking for. "Ah, yes, here it is. As of your last load, we have cut nine million, eight hundred seventy-two thousand, three hundred forty-three board feet for you this season. If my arithmetic is accurate, that leaves us obligated to cut roughly another one hundred twenty-seven thousand board feet the rest of this year." She looked up, smiling at him pleasantly. "Does the boom you're bringing in today fit within that margin?"

Geoff slammed his fist on Meg's desk in total frustration.

"You know damn well it doesn't," he snarled. "I just told you it's the biggest load we've had all year."

"Well, then," Meg said calmly, closing her ledger book and folding her hands on top of it, "I'm afraid we're not going to be able to accept it."

Geoffrey's hands clenched at his sides and the fury in his eyes was so terrifying that Meg shifted uneasily in her chair. *Don't let him know he's scaring you, or you'll lose all the ground you've gained! Brazen it out. You've got the upper hand, so just stay calm . . .*

"So, Mr. Wellesley," she prompted, pleased that her voice sounded calm despite her trepidation, "what's it going to be? Do my men leave the corrals closed and let your boom float by, or do you and I make an appointment to see Reverend Martin?"

"I don't believe this!" Geoff barked, scraping his hands through his long, chestnut hair in agitation. Whirling again toward Meg, he tried one last time to make her see reason. "Why do you want me to marry you? How happy do you think you'll be married to a man who doesn't want you?"

His harsh words made Meg's heart give a painful little thump in her chest, but her face remained impassive. "Happiness plays no part in this, sir. I have tried every way I can think of to make you understand my plight, but you refuse."

"That's not true!" Geoff thundered. "I offered to go talk to George Farnsworth for you."

"I know," Meg nodded coolly, "and I appreciated your offer. But as I explained to you before, that wouldn't work. I can assure you that I have tried to think of some other way that I might escape marriage to Peter Farnsworth, but unfortunately, I cannot come up with one."

"Just marry someone else!" Geoff shouted. "There are

77

hundreds of men in town who would love to be your husband."

"No," Meg answered, shaking her head. "No one else will do. You know how powerful the Farnsworths are. They would just buy off . . . or kill off . . . whomever I married, and I'd be right back where I started."

"Oh, come on, Miss Taylor! You think an awful lot of yourself, don't you?"

"What do you mean?"

"Do you honestly think Peter Farnsworth would kill a man just to have you?"

"Oh, it's not *me* Peter wants," Meg said, shaking her head and spreading her hand across her chest. "I mean, I'm sure that he would be delighted to have me around as a handy receptacle for his disgusting carnal appetites . . ."

Geoff's eyebrows shot up.

". . . but what he really wants is my *mill.*"

For a second, Geoff considered asking her what she knew about a man's "carnal appetites," but not wanting to digress from the subject at hand, he clamped down on his curiosity and said, instead, "The Farnsworths could build their own mill, if that's so damned important to them. God knows, they own enough land around here."

"That wouldn't do them much good when I hold all the contracts on the mountain. It's a lot more expedient just to bring me, and my mill, into the family."

Geoff paused for a moment, unable to think of another argument. He closed his eyes and clamped his teeth together, determined to try one last time to make Meg understand his feelings about her proposal. "Miss Taylor," he said slowly, "I have told you before and I will tell you again—I am *not* going to marry you. Period."

"All right," she sighed. "As you wish." She rose and stepped around him, leaning out the door of her office and calling to a nearby camp foreman. "Willie, when the Wellesley boom arrives, don't open the corrals. Just let it go by."

"Now, just a minute!" Geoff bellowed, lunging toward her and grabbing her arm. "You can't do that! I'll lose the whole load!"

"That's not my problem," Meg said, staring pointedly at his fingers until he released his grip.

"Big boom a'comin'," rang out a voice from upstream. "Open the corrals."

"What d'ya want me to do, Miss?" Willie called.

"What do you want me to do?" Meg parroted, looking at Geoff.

Geoff's eyes narrowed to glittering golden slits and a hard knot of muscle jumped in his jaw.

"Well?" Meg pressed.

"Ten o'clock Saturday morning," he snarled, grabbing his hat off the corner of her desk and slamming it on his head. "First Presbyterian Church."

Meg was so relieved that she thought she might faint. She had won. *She had won!*

"Ten o'clock will be fine," she nodded, then, again, leaned out the door. "Open the corrals, Willie."

The foreman nodded and quickly started shouting orders.

"You are going to regret this," Geoff warned softly.

"Maybe," Meg shrugged, "but nothing could be worse than Peter Farnsworth."

His face purple with rage, Geoff tore out of the small office and stomped off toward his horse.

"Mr. Wellesley?"

"What now?" he gritted, halting his headlong flight and turning back toward her.

"Please get your hair cut before the wedding, sir."

79

He stared at her for a moment, then, with a mocking little smile, he called back, "Go to hell, madam."

Meg drew in an offended little breath, but before she could think of a retort, he was on his horse and gone.

Oh, well, she shrugged, stepping back into her office and closing the door behind her, he's angry now, but he'll get over it.

She had no idea how wrong she was.

Chapter 8

"My God, Geoff, you're not going to get married wearing *that*, are you?"

Geoff looked down at his faded Levis and flannel shirt and shrugged. "Why not?"

Greg Stevens frowned impatiently and glanced at the grandfather clock standing in a corner of his parlor. "You know very well why not. Look, we still have a half-hour before the ceremony. Let's go see if we can stuff you into one of my suits."

"No," Geoff responded flatly. "I've worn enough suits for this woman. I'm not wearing another one. Besides, as soon as this thing is done, I've got work to do."

"Work! You can't be seriously considering going back to work. What about the honeymoon?"

Geoff threw his friend a jaundiced look. "There isn't going to be any honeymoon. You keep acting like this is a wedding, Greg. It's not a wedding. It's a ransom payment."

"What the hell are you talking about?"

"Think about it. You get blackmailed, you pay a ransom. That's all I'm doing. And once I put the ring on that little witch's finger, I'm gone. Back up my mountain and back to my work."

"And does the 'little witch' know this?"

81

"Well, we haven't discussed it, but I can't imagine her expecting anything else. She told me herself that she'd make no demands on me. The deal is that if I marry her, she'll cut my timber . . . and I'm marrying her."

"But that's *all*, right?"

"Damn right."

"Okay," Greg shrugged, "if that's the way you feel, then I guess it doesn't matter what you wear."

"No, it doesn't. Now, come on, let's get this farce over with."

With a sigh, Greg picked up his hat and followed Geoff out of the house, pausing to lock the door after him. He looked around for Geoff's wagon but saw only his horse tethered to the hitching rail. "Are you *riding* to the wedding?" he gasped.

"Sure."

"But how are you going to take Meg home afterward?"

"I'm not," Geoff said shortly, mounting his horse. "How she gets home is her problem."

"Geoff, this is ridiculous. You can't just abandon her at the church."

"Oh, can't I?" Geoff smiled snidely. "Watch me."

Without another word, he dug his heels into his horse's flanks and shot off down the lane in the direction of Main Street.

Greg watched Geoff disappear round the corner, shaking his head in disbelief. "This is a terrible mistake," he muttered, as he headed off toward his own wagon. "A terrible, terrible mistake."

"How do I look, Ginny?"

Megan whirled away from the mirror she was standing in front of and turned to face her sister.

"You look lovely," her sister responded, rising from a small stool and brushing a speck of lint off Meg's shoulder. "I just wish you could wear a real wedding dress. It doesn't seem right to get married in gray."

"It's not gray," Meg corrected, "it's ashes of roses. And I feel guilty even wearing this. I should be wearing black."

"Married in black, wish yourself back," Ginny prophesied.

"Oh, that's nonsense." With a heavy sigh, Meg turned back toward the mirror. "Besides, it's not as if it was a real wedding, so why should I wear a real wedding dress?"

Ginny frowned and resumed her perch on the stool. "I hope you're doing the right thing, Meggie. I'm just afraid that starting a marriage off by threatening the bridegroom bodes ill for the whole relationship."

Meg shrugged. "I did what I had to."

"But, what's going to happen . . . tomorrow?"

Megan eyed her sister wryly. "Don't you mean, what's going to happen tonight?"

"All right, yes. I do mean that and I'm worried, Meg. I know that you know what goes on between men and women in the privacy of the bedroom, but . . ."

Meg could barely contain her smile. "But what?"

"Well, it's just that it's always . . . hard . . . the first time, and if the man isn't gentle . . . I mean, if he doesn't have consideration for his bride . . ."

"Oh, Ginny," Meg laughed, no longer able to contain herself. "You're such a dear. You don't need to worry about my well-being because there isn't going to be any 'tonight' . . . or any other night."

"What?" Ginny gasped, her expression stunned.

"That's part of our agreement. No intimacies between us."

Virginia's eyes widened even further. "And Mr. Wellesley *agreed* to that?"

"He didn't exactly *agree,*" Meg admitted, "but that's only because we never discussed that particular issue specifically."

"Meg," Virginia's voice took on a distinct warning tone, "I think you're being a bit naive if you think Mr. Wellesley—"

"No, Ginny," Meg interrupted, "he isn't any more interested in that kind of relationship than I am. When I first talked to him, I assured him I'd make no demands on him and that there'd be no entanglements—except, of course, for putting on the pretense of being happily married for Peter's sake. Other than that, his life and mine will go on exactly as they always have."

"And what was his response?"

"Well," Meg hedged, "he said something about there *always* being entanglements, but I know there won't be. He'll see that he's wrong."

"Oh, Meg," Ginny sighed, "I hope you know what you're doing."

Meg pushed an errant strand of hair into place and smiled reassuringly at her sister. "Oh, of course I do. Now, we'd better go. It's nearly quarter to ten, and I don't want to be late."

"You're right, you don't," Ginny muttered, rising and following Meg out of the bedroom. "It's bad luck to be late to your own wedding, and Lord knows, you don't need anything else working against you."

"So, where the hell is she?" Geoffrey growled, looking down the street from where he stood in front of the church.

"Geoff, it's ten o'two!" Greg laughed. "Cut the lady a little slack."

"Yeah, well, how much slack has the 'lady' cut me?"

"Geoff . . ."

"I'll give her three more minutes. If she isn't here by five after, then I'm leaving and she can find herself another sucker. I'll just build my own damn sawmill, and to hell with her."

"That's not going to help you get this year's production cut," Greg reminded him.

"So what if I lose this year's contracts?" Geoff blustered. "I'll just pick up new ones next year. In fact, that might not be such a bad idea. Just let the damn things go . . ."

"Ah," Greg smiled in relief as he glanced down the street, "here comes the bride." Flicking his gaze back to Geoff, he frowned and added, "Take off your hat, for God's sake."

With a disgusted snort, Geoff pulled his battered hat off his head and reluctantly turned his eyes in the direction of the oncoming carriage.

"Meg, he looks mad," Ginny whispered, peering out the carriage window at the stone-faced man standing in front of the church. "And he's not dressed to get married, either."

Meg shot a quick look out the window and her heart sank. He had changed his mind.

All week she'd worried about the possibility of Geoffrey standing her up at the church. But now, seeing him in his work clothes, staring down the street at her carriage, she realized that he wouldn't do something that kind. He obviously wanted to personally inform her that he was jilting her—in public and at her most vulnerable moment—as she arrived in her bridal finery for the wedding.

"He doesn't look mad, Ginny. He looks smug."

85

"Smug? What does he have to be smug about?"

"He's going to jilt me—right here in front of you and Greg Stevens and Reverend Martin."

"Oh, no, Meg!" Virginia protested. "Mr. Wellesley is far too honorable to do something like that!"

"Oh?" Meg chuckled mirthlessly. "Then why is he dressed like he's on his way into the forest for a day's cutting?"

Virginia hesitated for a moment, then shrugged. "I don't know, but I don't believe for a second that he'd throw you over right here in front of the church. Why, anyone could just walk by!"

"Exactly," Meg nodded, gathering up her full skirt as the carriage came to a halt directly in front of the two men. "And that's probably what he's hoping for." With a resigned sigh, she opened the door to the carriage and stepped out into the beautiful spring morning. *Just pretend that nothing's wrong.*

"Good morning, Mr. Wellesley," she smiled, relieved that her voice sounded normal. "A lovely day, don't you think?"

Geoff's eyes swept over her long-sleeved, high-necked dress insolently. "A little warm for that get-up, don't you think?"

"Perhaps," she conceded, returning his appraisal with one of her own, "but it's hardly appropriate for denim and flannel, either."

Her gibe was not lost on Geoff, but before he could think of a suitable retort, Greg Stevens jumped in. "Why don't we go inside? I'm sure the reverend is waiting for us."

"Go inside?" Meg asked dumbly, looking expectantly at Geoff as she waited for him to tell her he'd changed his mind.

But Geoff said nothing. He merely looked at her as if he

thought she was the dumbest woman he'd ever met. "Did you think we were going to do this out here on the sidewalk?" he sneered.

"No," Meg stammered, trying desperately to regain her composure. "I just didn't think that you were going to—"

"Please, let's go inside," Virginia interrupted hurriedly. Reaching out, she clasped Meg's hand in her own, nearly dragging her up the church steps and into the cool, dark foyer. "Just act *natural!*" she hissed.

With a quick nod, Meg pasted a smile on her face and turned toward Geoff, who was still standing near the door. "Are you ready?" she asked brightly.

"Sure," he snorted. "I can hardly wait."

"Geoff," Greg whispered, "knock it off. You're acting like an ass."

Geoff threw his friend an angry glare, but clamped his mouth shut and stepped forward to greet Reverend Martin.

"Well, this is a most unexpected pleasure," the portly minister beamed, trying to mask his astonishment at Geoff's choice of apparel.

Turning quickly toward Meg, he added, "Is this . . . everyone, or are you expecting more guests?"

"This is it," Geoff answered shortly. "Do you suppose we could begin, Reverend? I have . . . other commitments today."

Reverend Martin tried unsuccessfully to hide his startled expression. Then, with a quick, jerky nod, he gestured the small party toward the front of the church. "Bride on the left, groom on the right," he directed, as they gathered near the altar. "Matron of honor to the left of the bride, and best man to the right of the groom."

He glanced warily at the strange little troupe as they took their appropriate places, then quickly flipped open his

87

prayerbook and began, "Dearly beloved, we are gathered here . . ."

Somewhere in the back of her mind, Meg knew that Reverend Martin was intoning the ancient words of the Christian wedding ceremony, but nothing he was saying really registered with her. The only thing she was truly aware of was Geoffrey's hostile presence next to her. She could almost *feel* the anger and resentment radiating from him.

It wasn't until Reverend Martin posed the inevitable question that would bind them together for life that Meg started listening to the proceedings going on around her.

"Do you, Geoffrey William, take Megan Elaine to be your lawfully wedded wife?"

Meg wasn't even aware that she was holding her breath until, after an interminably long silence, Geoff finally mumbled, "I do," and she let it out with an audible rush.

Reverend Martin also exhaled a relieved little sigh, and with a hopeful smile, turned to Meg. "And do you, Megan Elaine, take Geoffrey William to be your lawfully wedded husband?"

"I do," she answered quickly, her voice coming out in a strangled whisper.

Again the reverend sighed with relief, and quickly, before either half of this strange couple standing before him could change their minds, he finished up the service. Clapping his prayerbook shut with a resounding bang, he grinned at Geoff and said, "You may kiss the bride."

"No, thanks," Geoff retorted and, turning on his heel, he marched back down the aisle and out the front doors of the church, slamming them behind him.

"Why, I never . . ." Reverend Martin gasped, gaping at the three embarrassed faces in front of him. "What in the world is wrong with Mr. Wellesley?"

"Excuse me, please," Meg blurted. Whirling around, she raced up the aisle after her new husband.

"Megan, wait!" Virginia called. Throwing a distraught, apologetic look at the minister, she rushed off after her sister.

"Mr. Stevens, will you *please* explain what's going on here?" Reverend Martin demanded.

"Wedding day jitters," Greg answered smoothly. "A particularly bad case."

"But . . ." the reverend stammered, "they can't just run out of the church like this. They haven't even signed the marriage certificate yet. The marriage isn't legal until they do that."

"Oh, they'll be back to sign it," Greg assured the clergyman. Leaning forward, he whispered conspiratorially, "I think Mr. Wellesley may be just a little overly eager to start the honeymoon."

"Oh, I see," Reverend Martin nodded, hoping his face wasn't betraying his shock. "Well, ah, when you see Mr. and Mrs. Wellesley again, please tell them they must return as soon as possible and sign the marriage documents."

"I'll tell them," Greg promised. Then, fishing in his pocket, he extracted a wrinkled five-dollar bill, handed it to the reverend, and with a lame smile, fled up the church aisle after his departed friends.

By the time Meg reached the back of the church and burst through the large double doors, Geoff was already on his horse and starting down the street out of town.

"Mr. Wellesley," she called.

He didn't stop.

"Mr. Wellesley!"

With an irritated yank on the reins, Geoff pulled his

surprised mount to an abrupt halt and turned around in the saddle. "What do you want?"

He had stopped so fast that Meg, who was flying down the street after him, nearly ran into his horse's rear end. She threw out a hand to stop herself from crashing into the animal, but it was a moment before she regained her equilibrium enough to answer. When she finally spoke, her voice had a slightly breathless quality to it that Geoff found disturbingly appealing. "I just wondered . . . what time I should expect you?"

"For what?" he asked.

"For . . . for supper. I know you told Reverend Martin you had commitments today, but surely you'll be done by nightfall. I don't know what time you normally stop work, but if you'll tell me when you expect to be home, I'll have your meal ready."

For a long moment, Geoff just stared at her. Then, with a disbelieving shake of his head, he pulled his hat off and smacked it against his thigh, inadvertently sending a small cloud of dust whirling into Meg's face. "Lady, you just don't get it, do you?"

"Get what?" she coughed, turning her head to avoid the dust.

"Get the fact that I'm not coming for supper. Not tonight, or any other night."

"But—"

Geoff held up a hand. "Just be quiet for one minute and listen to me. You blackmailed me into marrying you by telling me you wouldn't cut my timber if I didn't. Well, I've married you, and by God, if you know what's good for you, those saws better be humming right this minute. Beyond that, madam, I want nothing to do with you. I don't want to see you, I don't want to talk to you, and I sure as hell

90

don't want to eat supper with you. Do you understand that?"

"Well, yes!" Meg retorted, thrusting her chin out defiantly. "Heaven knows, I don't want to spend time with you, either, but if we're going to convince—"

"No! We're not going to convince *anybody* of *anything!* Now, I've held to my part of this so-called 'bargain,' and I expect you to hold to yours. You promised you wouldn't make any demands on me, and lady, you damn well better stick to your word."

Slapping his worn hat back on his head, Geoff turned his horse away but immediately stopped again when he heard Megan's next words.

"Not one board foot of your timber will get cut until we have talked this out to my satisfaction, sir!"

Before she could draw another breath to continue, Geoff was off his horse and had her by the arm. "Now, you listen to me, you little bitch—"

"No," she shot back, wrenching her arm out of his grasp, "this time, *you* listen to *me.* Simply going through with the marriage ceremony does me absolutely no good. We have to make Peter Farnsworth think we are truly married—in every sense. Otherwise, he is going to go straight to an attorney waving that absurd agreement and screaming that he's been doublecrossed. I have no doubt that he, or his father, will try to have our marriage annulled on the grounds that it is not a true marriage and that it was perpetrated solely for the purpose of invalidating the prior agreement. I don't know if they can legally do anything, but it's a chance I'm not willing to take. I know I promised that I'd make no demands on you—and I won't. But I never expected that you'd think 'no demands' included our not living together—platonically, of course," she added hastily.

91

Geoff emitted a long sigh and stared at the distant mountains. He had to hand it to her—the woman had guts. There were few men in the town of Wellesley who would dare tempt his wrath, but this little woman, with her huge, dark eyes and rosebud mouth, berated him like he was a recalcitrant child. And despite his outrage at being forced into a marriage he didn't want, he couldn't help but feel a grudging respect for her audacity.

After an endless silence, he turned back toward her, and with a reluctant smile, said, "Six o'clock."

"What?"

"Six o'clock . . . that's when I figure I'll be done tonight."

Meg was so relieved she thought she might cry. "So, you'll do it? You'll pretend we have a normal marriage?"

"Do I have a choice?"

"Not if you want your timber cut."

Biting back a smile, Geoff shook his head and looked at the ground. When he finally raised his eyes, Meg was dumbstruck by the laughter she saw lurking deep in their amber depths. "I've got to admit, you're damn good."

"I beg your pardon?"

"I mean, you've won this round. At least for the time being, until I can get away to ride to Portland and see a lawyer myself."

Meg knew she should probably consider this last statement a threat, but she promptly put it out of her mind, too pleased by the fact that for now, Geoff was going to cooperate and she would be safe from Peter Farnsworth. "What would you like for supper?" she asked, a little shyly.

"Hell, I don't know," he shrugged. "I'll eat anything—as long as there's plenty of it and it's not fish. I hate fish. Why don't you make a steak? That's my favorite."

"I'll remember that," she nodded. "Six o'clock, then?"

"Yeah. Six." Again he mounted his horse.

"Goodbye, Mr. Wellesley."

Looking over his shoulder at her, he said, "You can call me Geoff if you want to."

Biting her lip to keep from shouting with triumph, Meg nodded. "Goodbye, Geoff," she repeated.

"Goodbye, Miss Taylor." And nudging his horse into a canter, he rode off down the street.

Virginia, who had been waiting impatiently on the church steps, now hurried over to where her sister stood, watching her new husband ride away.

"Where is he going?"

"I don't know."

"What were you two talking about? He looked like he was furious, and after the way he acted in the church . . . Oh, Meg, I just knew this wasn't going to work."

"Everything is fine, Ginny. He and I were just discussing what we're going to have for supper."

Virginia's jaw dropped. "Supper? You two were discussing *supper?*"

"Yes. Is that such a strange topic for married people to discuss?"

"Well . . . no, I suppose not," Virginia answered dubiously. "And just what are you going to fix?"

"Steak," Meg smiled. "The biggest, juiciest, most tender one I can find."

"Why, Meg," Virginia smiled, "if I didn't know better, I'd say you were trying to please that man."

Meg threw her sister an arch look. "Don't get any of your romantic ideas, Ginny. I'm only interested in pleasing

93

'that man' enough that he'll continue to help me keep Peter Farnsworth at bay. That's all."

"Of course that's all," Virginia said, a knowing little smile playing about her lips. "It never occurred to me that it would be anything more."

Chapter 9

The steak was ready. The potatoes were ready. The table was ready. So, where was he?

"Six-twenty," Meg muttered irritably, pulling back the lace curtain at the front door and peering surreptitiously down the street. "He said he'd be here at six. He's always late."

With an indignant huff, Meg turned away from the door and paced the length of the foyer. "Not that it matters," she told herself. "I don't really care if he ever comes." Even as she uttered the petulant words, she paused in front of a little oval mirror and checked to make sure her hair was in place.

It was. Every strand.

Taking a step backward, she checked her apron. It was straight and unwrinkled, the straps over her shoulders perfectly smooth.

She cocked her head to the side and again pondered whether she should have put on her red apron with the white lace. It was so much prettier than the plain white one she was now wearing. Besides, a white apron over a black dress put her in mind of a pilgrim wife, and that certainly was not the impression she wanted Geoffrey to have when he arrived.

"You're in mourning," she reminded herself. "You can't wear red. It would be disrespectful. And what do you care whether or not he thinks you're attractive?"

Marching down the hallway toward the kitchen, Meg pushed through the swinging door. "What do you care what he thinks?" she again scolded herself. "He doesn't even have the courtesy to arrive on time after you've spent the whole afternoon preparing him supper."

Angrily, she picked up a large wooden spoon and stirred the pot of mashed potatoes she'd left on the stove. The once light and fluffy mounds were quickly assuming an unappetizing gluey texture. Meg frowned as she stared into the pot, wondering what she could do to return the potatoes to their original consistency.

Setting the spoon down on the stove, she pulled open the door to the warming oven and stared at the large fried steak sitting inside. It still looked fine. Maybe not quite so juicy as it had been a half-hour ago, but still presentable. She closed the oven door and turned her attention back to the potatoes. If only she had some cheese or some heavy cream to stir into them. But she didn't. She hadn't had time to do much shopping this afternoon, and she'd not thought to buy anything other than the bare essentials.

At least dessert had turned out, she thought with satisfaction, glancing over at the perfect, golden peach pie cooling on a rack by the window. But that didn't help the potatoes.

Maybe a little butter would soften them, and a little paprika might make them look more appealing. Walking over to a small cabinet hanging on the wall, she opened the door, exposing several small jars filled with a fragrant array of spices.

Spices were so expensive and rare that many women

kept them in locked chests, considering them as valuable as cash. Meg had once heard that in some remote, rural areas, women used their precious stores of spices to barter for other goods. It was rumored that an ounce of tarragon could be traded for a full bolt of cloth or a hundred pounds of flour.

Meg was justifiably proud of the large selection of spices she'd acquired. There were bottles filled with dill and mint and bay leaves, as well as several more exotic flavorings, such as sweet basil and coriander. She ran her fingers lovingly over the small bottles, finally coming to rest on one containing a fine red powder.

Paprika. The extract of a pungent yet mild sweet pepper that added not only a pleasant tang to normally bland foods, but also a dash of color.

Uncorking the bottle, she shook the precious contents liberally over the pot, smiling in satisfaction as she watched the titian hues blend with the ivory potatoes and the pale yellow butter. "Very pretty, Megan," she complimented herself. "Even the chef at Miss Exton's Academy for Ladies couldn't have done better . . ."

For one of the few times in her life, Meg considered the possibility that perhaps the year her mother had forced her to spend attending the fashionable Eastern finishing school might not have been a complete waste of time, after all.

For several moments, she idly stirred the potatoes until she was suddenly startled out of her reverie by a sharp rap at the front door. *Dear God, he's here.* Quickly returning the vial of paprika to the cupboard, she headed for the front door. *Be calm, be calm,* she told herself, repeating the litany that seemed to be becoming a habit whenever Geoffrey Wellesley came to call.

Taking a deep breath, she pulled the door open, then

immediately swallowed her gasp of surprise as she took in his appearance.

As usual, Geoff was dressed in Levis and a flannel shirt, but they were different clothes than he had been wearing that morning. His shirt looked new, not faded from many rough washings, and tonight his sleeves were pulled down and neatly buttoned around his wrists. His boots were different, too. Instead of the heavy hobnail type that loggers wore to work, these were made of fine, soft leather that had been polished to a high sheen.

As Meg's eyes lifted past his massive shoulders to his chiseled face and thick chestnut hair, she realized she had never seen a more magnificent man. She had always thought him to be handsome, but tonight, standing in the soft glow of her porch lamp, Geoffrey Wellesley truly looked like the tawny lion he was so often compared to. There was something almost predatory about him—something not quite civilized. Meg couldn't define exactly what it was that set him apart from every other man she'd ever met, but whatever it was, it sent a ripple of excitement through her that made her feel slightly giddy.

"Won't you come in?" she murmured, stepping back and pulling the door wide.

Geoff looked at her curiously, wondering why she seemed so out of breath. It was the second time that day he'd noticed that breathless quality in her voice, and as it had before, the slightly husky sound sent a disturbing jolt of desire coursing through him.

"I know I'm late," he muttered, avoiding her eyes as he stepped into the foyer.

Meg looked at him expectantly, waiting for him to continue with an apology, but it didn't come. "I know I'm late," was as close as she was going to get. No remorse, no polite plea for forgiveness, just an acknowledgment of the fact.

"Supper is all ready," she announced, prudently deciding to ignore his tardiness. "Just go on into the dining room and sit down." She started for the kitchen, but was brought up short by the sound of his deep, rich voice saying her name.

"Megan?"

"Yes?" she asked, her cheeks unexpectedly pinkening as she turned to face him.

"Where is the dining room?"

A sudden little gust of nervous laughter escaped her. "To the left," she said, pointing. "First door."

Geoff nodded, his eyes following her as she continued on toward the kitchen. Why was she so nervous? Did she think he was going to throw her down on the dining room table and demand his conjugal rights? That arousing vision made his loins tighten again and he frowned, annoyed by the unwanted reaction.

He walked toward the dining room, pausing to peer around the corner before he entered the room. The table was set for two, but for some reason, Meg had elected not to place them at opposite ends. Rather, one setting was at the head of the table, and the other immediately to the right. The table was covered with a lace cloth, and the silver, china and crystal spread upon it were elegant and costly. A brace of candles sat in the middle, their wicks as yet unlit.

Geoff stared at the table in consternation. It looked like it was waiting for two lovers to enjoy an intimate meal together, and yet, he was positive that Meg had no more interest in him romantically than he had in her. Why had she gone to all this bother?

He was still mulling over this question when she pushed

through the kitchen door carrying a platter in one hand and a huge bowl of potatoes in the other.

Geoff glanced at the platter as she set it down on the table. Steak. He had asked her to make steak for supper, and she had. Was she actually trying to please him? And if so, why? He'd already married her. What else did she want from him that she was suddenly playing the role of a doting wife?

"Here we are," Meg smiled, seating herself and gesturing for Geoff to do the same. "I brought up a bottle of wine from the cellar. Will you open it?"

Geoff nodded and expertly inserted and twisted the corkscrew. Popping the cork out, he smelled the wine, then poured a small amount into each glass.

Meg took a deep breath and raised hers. "To friendship," she offered. "I know that ours has had a difficult beginning, but I hope that the . . . relationship . . . we forged today will be of value to both of us."

For a moment, she didn't think Geoff was going to join in her toast, but finally, with a nearly imperceptible shrug, he picked up his glass. Meg tipped hers toward his, but he ignored the gesture and took a drink, avoiding the customary clink of crystal. Putting his glass down, he reached for the platter, stabbing a large piece of meat and saying, "Exactly what do you *think* is going to happen now?"

"Well," Meg gulped, setting down her glass with suddenly shaking hands, "the first thing is that our marriage will be announced tomorrow morning, during Sunday services. I think it's important that we're there."

Geoff frowned. The last thing he wanted to do was be gawked at by every Presbyterian in town while suffering through one of Reverend Martin's interminable sermons.

"Will you go with me?" Meg prompted. "People might suspect something isn't normal if you're not there."

"How many board feet got cut today?" Geoff asked pointedly.

Meg sighed and put her fork down. "I don't know, but I can assure you the full day was spent on your timber. Now, will you go with me?"

"What happens after church?"

"I don't know," Meg said again, annoyed by his endless questions. "I imagine people will want to congratulate us, and there will probably be a few who will want to have a party for us."

"No," Geoff said adamantly, popping a piece of steak into his mouth, "no parties. I'm not that much of a hypocrite."

"But Geoffrey—"

"I said, no parties. Pass the potatoes, will you please? By the way, the steak is good."

"Thank you," Meg acknowledged. Deciding to let the subject of a party drop until things were a little more stable between them, she smiled sweetly and handed him the bowl.

Geoff stared at the potatoes for a moment, then looked at her doubtfully. "Why are these orange?"

"It's just a little spice I mixed in to give them color."

"Potatoes are supposed to be white. Why would you want to give them 'color'?"

"Oh, for heaven's sake," she snapped, completely fed up with him, "haven't you ever heard of adding a garnish to food to give it eye appeal? Where were you raised? In a barn?"

Very slowly, Geoff set down his fork. "As a matter of fact, madam, I was born into a very wealthy, influential family, and grew up on the largest cattle ranch in Colorado—in the house, not the barn, I might add. My parents, who immigrated from England after their marriage, are both descended from long lines of nobility and can trace their ancestry back to William the Conqueror. My mother had the reputation of being one of the most gracious hostesses in the entire country, and during my childhood I had the unique experience of regularly sharing meals with dignitaries from two continents. At one time, my family employed two chefs, one American and one French. Therefore, I believe I have eaten an unusually large number of rare and exotic dishes. But, never, ever, in all that time, was I ever served potatoes of any color other than white."

"Well, then," Meg countered, refusing to be intimidated by Geoff's unprecedented revelation about his illustrious family, "I'm very proud to be able to introduce as discriminating a palate as yours to something new."

Suddenly, Geoff began to laugh, a rich, rumbling sound that surprised him as much as it did Meg. She was truly incredible. There was nothing he could say that she couldn't somehow turn to her advantage, and as much as he hated to admit it, his respect for her wit and intelligence was growing by the minute. He was equally disturbed to realize that the more time he spent in her company, the more he liked her.

He didn't want to like her. Didn't want to be amused by her quick wit or aroused by her beautiful body. She had blackmailed him into marriage, threatened his very livelihood if he didn't move in with her, demanded that he attend church services and be seen in public with her, and now she was daring him, *daring him,* to eat her damned orange potatoes! Peter Farnsworth didn't know how lucky he was to have escaped this little witch. God help the poor fool who truly fell in love with her. She'd lead him a merry dance the rest of his miserable life!

"Okay," he chuckled, "you win. I'll try your orange

102

potatoes. But if I don't like them, I want you to promise me that tomorrow we'll have regular white ones."

Meg's heart leaped into her throat. Tomorrow! He was talking about what they were going to eat tomorrow! That must mean he was agreeable to moving into her house and carrying out the charade that they were well and truly married.

But then, it wasn't really a charade at all, was it? The realization that they were actually husband and wife in the eyes of God and man made a little shiver run down Megan's spine.

Geoff put a forkful of potatoes into his mouth, then, suddenly, let out a hoarse, strangled scream. "Jesus Christ! Water! Get me water!"

"What's wrong?" Meg demanded, jumping to her feet.

"Water! I need water!" Geoff clutched his throat as tears poured down his cheeks.

"Geoffrey, what is it?" Meg repeated, staring at the choking man in paralyzed horror.

"Hot!" he gasped, reaching for the bottle of wine and upending it straight into his mouth. He swallowed hard, then was immediately seized by another fit of coughing.

Racing around behind him, Meg began to pound him energetically on the back at the same time as she grabbed his left arm and held it over his head.

"Stop it!" he bellowed, jerking his arm out of her grasp and twisting away from the blows she was striking. "Jesus, I'm dying! *Get me some water!*"

Somewhere, through her panic, his words finally registered, and she streaked into the kitchen, grabbing a large tumbler off the shelf and filling it with water. Racing back into the dining room, she thrust it at him.

Gratefully, Geoff grabbed the glass, downing most of its contents in one long swig. Exhaling a shuddering breath, he turned on his wife in outrage. "Do you think this is funny? Is this your way of paying me back for not wearing a suit today?"

Meg took a startled step backward, appalled that he seemed to think she was behind his choking fit. "What are you talking about?"

"What's in those potatoes?" he thundered.

"I told you, it's a mild spice called paprika!"

"That's not paprika, lady. I've had paprika, and it doesn't taste like that."

"Well, I'm sorry you don't believe me," she retorted, her temper now flaring apace with his, "but I know what I put in the potatoes." Stepping up to the table, she swiped a finger through the mountain of mashed potatoes still sitting in the bowl and popped it into her mouth. Suddenly, her eyes widened and filled with tears. "My God," she gasped, reaching for Geoff's nearly empty water glass. "It's cayenne! I must have gotten them mixed up!"

Geoff neatly plucked the glass out of her hand before it reached her mouth. "It isn't so funny now, is it, Megan? Want me to pound *you* on the back?"

With an anguished look, Meg tore into the kitchen, furiously pumping water, then lowering her head to drink straight from the stream cascading into the sink. Even when her mouth and throat had finally cooled enough that she could again draw an even breath, she continued to stand at the sink, gripping its edge. Geoffrey thought she had done that to him on purpose. On purpose! How could he think so little of her that he'd believe she'd do something so despicable?

Tears of despair traced down her cheeks. He'd never believe the cayenne was a mistake. Why, she'd practically insisted he try her orange potatoes, so it was only natural he'd think she'd laced them with the hot pepper as a nasty joke.

"I'm sorry."

Meg jumped with surprise when she heard Geoff's quiet, contrite voice behind her. Straightening, she turned to face him, brushing tears off her cheeks with a quick swipe of her hand.

"I know you didn't mean to put cayenne on the potatoes. I'm sorry I accused you of doing it intentionally."

"I really didn't, you know," she blurted, her voice catching on a sob as all the events of the day suddenly overwhelmed her. Sliding down the wall till she was sitting on the kitchen floor, she looked up at him and whispered, "I just wanted to fix you a nice supper. You know, to sort of get things started off on the right foot between us. When you were so late, the potatoes got too thick, and I thought if I added a little butter and paprika, they'd look prettier."

Geoff stared down at the girl sitting at his feet on the floor and hated himself for causing her to look so miserable. "Here," he said, leaning down and helping her up. "Sit on this chair."

"Thank you," she sniffed. When she was again seated, she glanced up at him, her dark eyes still crystalline with tears. "You believe me, don't you?"

Geoff squatted down in front of her. "Yes," he nodded. "I believe you. Now, I think it's time we called it a night. It's late, we're both tired, and I have a long ride ahead of me."

"But," Meg protested, "you can't go. What about church tomorrow? And, anyway, I thought we'd agreed you'd move in here."

Despite his good intentions, Geoff's mouth tightened into an angry line. "We didn't agree on anything. You simply demanded that I move in."

"But you *have* to," she wailed, tears again spilling down her cheeks. "Otherwise, George Farnsworth won't believe we're married, and he'll make me . . ."

"For God's sake, don't cry again," Geoff ordered, wincing as he saw the fresh rush of tears. "I'll come back in the morning and take you to church."

"No! That's not good enough. If you don't sleep here, people are going to know we don't have a real marriage. I don't understand why you don't want to live here. Certainly my house is much nicer than that shack you live in."

Geoff swallowed hard, trying desperately to hold on to his composure. "I don't want to live here, lady, because it's not my choice to live here. Now, I said I'll be back to get you in the morning, and I will. At this moment, I refuse to agree to more than that."

Meg looked up at his set, angry face and decided not to press him further. "All right," she nodded. "Be here by nine-thirty."

"Nine-thirty it is," Geoff answered, then turned on his heel and hurried toward the front door.

"Geoffrey?"

He paused.

"Please don't hate me."

Geoff closed his eyes for a moment, cursing the fates that had placed him in this impossible situation. "I don't hate you, Megan," he answered quietly. "God knows I should, but I don't."

Chapter 10

Sunday church services started at ten, but Megan was ready long before that. She had slept poorly, her concerns over the next day's fateful announcement causing her to wake often. Finally, a full hour before dawn, she gave up her battle with Morpheus and rose.

She took a long bath, hoping that the warm water would soothe her jangled nerves and ease the knot of tension that was causing a painful ache between her shoulders. But when she hauled herself tiredly out of the tub, the ache was still there and her long soak had done little more than wrinkle her alabaster skin and cause her usually sleek, ebony hair to curl willfully around her face.

Glancing in the small mirror above the bureau in her room, she frowned in dismay at the purple shadows under her eyes and the white ring of tension circling her mouth. Would Geoffrey notice her ravaged appearance? And if he did, would he guess that it was mainly due to her worrying about how he was going to behave in front of her friends today?

"Lord, I hope he doesn't guess," she muttered aloud, picking up a powder puff and dusting it lightly across her nose. "If he thinks I'm worried that he'll embarrass me, he'll undoubtedly go out of his way to do just that!"

Pinning a cameo brooch to the collar of her black bombazine dress, Meg picked up her small reticule and walked slowly down the stairs. Nine-thirty. Geoff should be arriving any time—although, knowing his tendency for tardiness, she doubted that he would make an appearance any time before nine-fifty-five . . . and that was if he decided to come at all.

But Meg was wrong. At nine-thirty-three, there was a light rap on her front door. She hurried through the foyer, breathing a sigh of relief when she saw Geoff's wide shoulders silhouetted against the bright morning sun.

"Good morning," she said, smiling and pulling the door open. Another wave of relief washed through her as she saw that he was clad in a freshly starched white shirt and dark suit. "You look very nice this morning."

He grunted a nonreply to her compliment and pointedly did not return it. "Are you ready?"

"Yes," she nodded. "Just let me get my pocketbook."

"You don't need it," he shrugged. "I have money for our offering."

It was the first reference he'd ever made to them now being a couple, and for some reason, his casual words brought a strange, slightly queasy feeling to her stomach.

"All right. I'll just get my handkerchief, then."

He stood silently by the door as she picked up her reticule from a small table and searched for her handkerchief.

"Have you ever thought about having the inside of the house painted?" he asked.

"No," she answered, turning to face him and hoping that her face did not betray her astonishment, "not really. I probably could do it myself, but I'm so afraid of heights that I don't think I could climb a ladder."

She paused and looked at him expectantly, waiting for him to offer his services. Instead, he merely shrugged and said, "Well, it needs it."

Meg's breath came out in an offended little rush, and her voice took on a sharp edge. "I'll see what I can do."

Geoff's brows snapped together in surprise at her snippy tone, but he said nothing more. Instead, he glanced at his pocket watch and gestured toward the door. "Come on. It's quarter to ten. Let's get this over with."

Meg nodded curtly and swept by him, pinning a small hat into her hair as she walked outside. Taking a deep breath of the balmy morning air, she closed her eyes for a moment, determined to try to regain her composure. What was it about this man that could make her temper flare so quickly? She'd never been an overly sensitive woman. Unlike some of her friends, who could be reduced to tears by the slightest frown of disapproval from a man, Meg had always prided herself on retaining her dignity in any situation. Unflappable, her father had always called her. It was one of the characteristics that made her such a good businesswoman.

What was it, then, about Geoffrey Wellesley that could so quickly reduce her to a testy, sniping harridan? No other man had ever had such an effect on her, but then, she told herself, no other man had ever been her husband.

So, was this what their marriage was going to be? Was every conversation between them going to end with an argument, every casual exchange disintegrate into a contest of wills? Meg sincerely hoped not. Although she did not delude herself into believing that they would ever enjoy the easy intimacy of a true married couple, she had at least hoped that they might come to a level of understanding that would allow them to be friends.

Now, looking over at Geoffrey's dispassionate face as he

steered the wagon toward the church, Meg doubted that was going to happen. She had expected him to be angry about the forced marriage, had even anticipated that he might be belligerent toward her. But aside from his one small explosion the previous evening when he thought she'd purposely choked him on the potatoes, he seemed to have adopted an attitude of annoyed resignation. And somehow, his uncaring, disinterested mien bothered her more than his anger would have.

They pulled up in front of the First Presbyterian Church promptly at nine-fifty-five. As Geoff came around the back of the wagon to help her down, Meg noticed the many curious looks being thrown at them by the other members of the congregation. She could almost hear the murmurs of conjecture as women leaned toward their husbands and the town's maidens whispered behind their hands.

"Please take my arm," she whispered, as Geoffrey set her on the ground and turned toward the building.

His response was a withering glare and a muttered, "Give me a little credit, will you? I told you before, despite what you might think, I wasn't raised in a barn."

Meg's lips thinned at his shaming rebuke, but since it was accompanied by the offer of his arm, she ignored it.

The church was only about half full when they entered, and she was surprised when Geoffrey guided her into one of the back pews. "Why are we sitting way back here by ourselves?"

"Because when Reverend Martin makes the announcement, not so many people will stare at us if we're sitting way back here and they have to turn around."

Meg nodded at his logic, glad that he'd had the foresight to save them from the embarrassment of being openly stared at during the service.

The announcement didn't come until nearly the end of

110

the proceedings. Reverend Martin, who usually gave his sermon early in order to ensure maximum attention before the older members of the congregation started nodding off and the children started squirming, held off until just before the last blessing was given. Then, with a broad smile, he climbed the steps to his pulpit and said, "I have a very important and joyful announcement to make today. Geoffrey Wellesley and Megan Taylor were married yesterday in a private ceremony. I know all of you will want to stay for our social hour to offer them your congratulations. I am happy to inform you that Mrs. Martin has made a cake to celebrate the occasion."

There was a stunned silence as the congregation absorbed this unbelievable news. Then, as if on cue, every head in the church turned to stare at Geoff and Meg.

"Guess you were wrong, thinking that sitting in the back would make a difference," Meg murmured, as she smiled at their gaping audience.

"Guess I was," Geoff agreed, raising his voice to be heard over the excited buzz and scattered applause. "And we're not going to the social hour."

"What?" Meg gasped, concentrating hard on continuing to smile.

"We're not going."

"We have to," she insisted, gesturing in the direction of several matrons who were nodding their congratulations.

"Fine, then you go."

"I can't go alone!"

"Well, you're just going to have to, because I'm not." Clasping Meg's hand in his, he raised them briefly in a gesture of unity.

Meg's cheeks began to ache from the strain of her frozen smile. "You know, even from in here, I think I detect the sounds of the wood saws stopping."

"Don't threaten me, lady," Geoff gritted, leaning close to her ear in what appeared to be nothing more than a gesture of husbandly affection.

"Then don't even *think* about abandoning me during the social hour, or that threat will become a fact so fast your head will swim." Meg blushed becomingly as the female members of the congregation sighed with envy at Geoffrey's seemingly loving attention.

"Ahem!" Reverend Martin clucked loudly, bringing his flock's flagging attention back to him. Throwing the excited, flushed women in the group a reproving look, he said solemnly, "Let us pray . . ."

The moment the interminable service finally ended, Geoff grabbed Meg's hand and bolted out the church doors.

"Where are we going?" she asked breathlessly, as he hustled her down the steps.

"Nowhere, I guess," he answered, coming to an abrupt halt. "I just had to get out of there before everyone came pouring down that aisle and trapped us."

Meg looked at him speculatively. "You really hate this, don't you?"

"Yeah," he nodded, his tone slightly belligerent, "I really do. It's a lie, and I hate lies."

Meg felt a terrible wave of guilt engulfing her. "All right," she said finally, "you go ahead and leave. I'll stay here for the social hour by myself."

Geoff stared at the ground for a moment, then blew out a long, frustrated breath. "No, I'll stay, too."

"You don't have to, really. I'll cut your timber even if you don't. I'm . . . I'm sorry I threatened that inside. I

112

shouldn't have. You must think I'm the most conniving woman ever born."

As much as he'd have liked to have told her exactly what he thought of her, he was prevented from doing so by the sight of Reverend Martin's wife flying across the church lawn toward them.

"Oh, there you are!" she trilled, her plump cheeks pink from excitement and the exertion of running. "I'm so glad I found you. Now, just come over here, under these trees. I've set up a table for you to cut the cake, and I want to have you both in position to receive the rest of the congregation." She threw a distracted look over her shoulder, and seeing the crowd start to exit the church, added, "Hurry, now! They're coming!"

With a resigned shrug, Geoff looped Meg's arm through his and trudged after Mrs. Martin, taking up a position next to a rough wooden table upon which rested a large cake and several pots filled with coffee.

"This is very nice of you, Mrs. Martin," Meg smiled.

"Oh, I was happy to do it," the kindly lady responded. "It's not every Sunday we have cause for a special celebration, and I just love it when I can really, how do they say, put on the dog."

Geoff glanced down at the rickety wooden table covered by the inexpensive and worn muslin tablecloth and felt a surge of affection for the well-intentioned lady. "It looks lovely, Mrs. Martin."

"Thank you, Mr. Wellesley," she cooed, nearly beside herself with pleasure at the handsome man's approval.

Meg quickly looked away from her smiling husband, trying hard to conceal her surprise at his heartfelt words. Why, the charm was nearly *oozing* out of his pores! Never, ever, had he spoken to her in such a tone, and for some

113

reason she couldn't quite put her finger on, that fact rankled.

With an irritated switch of her shoulders, she shrugged off Geoff's light hand. "Where do you want us to stand, Mrs. Martin?"

"What?" the reverend's wife asked, still looking at Geoffrey dreamily. "Oh, it doesn't matter, dear. Just anywhere so people can shake your hand. We'll have a little receiving line and then, afterward, you can move behind the table and cut the cake."

Megan nodded and took a step away from Geoff.

"And don't forget, Mr. Wellesley," Mrs. Martin teased, blushing at her own boldness as she chucked him under the chin, "you have to feed the first piece to your bride."

Geoff smiled so indulgently that only Meg caught the double meaning of his next words. "I'll remember, Mrs. Martin. In fact, I'll be happy to give my bride a piece of her cake."

"This is such fun," Mrs. Martin tittered happily, then moved off to usher the first parishioners over to where Meg and Geoff stood.

"Please don't embarrass me when you feed me that cake," Meg entreated softly.

"I won't, although frankly, I'd like to ram it down your throat."

"Oh, you are terrible! And to think I once thought you were a true gentleman."

"And I once thought you were a principled lady," he shot back.

Their rapidly heating exchange cooled instantly as the first well-wisher rushed up to them. "Megan!" Sarah Ames shrieked, throwing her arms around her startled friend, "why didn't you tell us?"

"Well, I . . ."

"It all happened very quickly," Geoff smiled, effectively saving Meg from having to come up with a plausible excuse for their hasty nuptials.

"Ooh!" Sarah sighed, "how romantic!"

"Yes, it was, wasn't it, Megan?"

Meg shot a grateful look at her husband. "Very romantic," she affirmed.

A giggling group of young girls quickly joined Sarah, and for several minutes Meg accepted their good wishes, relying on Geoff to parry their probing questions. "Thank you for being so gallant," she whispered gratefully.

"I'm doing it for me, not you," he whispered back. "If these men think I allowed myself to be blackmailed into marriage, I'd never be able to effectively deal with them on a business level again."

"Oh, I see," Meg murmured, feeling vaguely disappointed.

After what seemed like an eternity, the crowd finally thinned as people moved off toward the shady trees to drink coffee and chat with friends. As was their habit, the town's matrons huddled together, their heads close as they speculated about what might be the *real* reason behind Geoff and Meg's hasty marriage.

"She's in the family way, that's the only explanation," Trudy Phillips announced boldly.

"Oh, Trudy, what a terrible thing to say about Megan. She's such a lovely, virtuous girl!" Beatrice Lennox defended.

"Virtuous, hah! No lady of virtue would work day in and day out running that sawmill—dealing with those lumberjacks and those rough timber buyers."

"But after her father got sick, she had no choice!" Beatrice insisted.

115

"A lady *always* has a choice, Beatrice. It should have been left to Virginia's husband, Lawrence."

"He's a banker! What would he know about running a mill?"

"More than Megan does, I'm sure." Trudy huffed. "At any rate, the only reason a couple would marry under such a cloak of secrecy is if they were trying to cover up an indiscretion. You mark my words, ladies—there will be a Christmas baby hanging in Geoffrey Wellesley's stocking."

Many hands were quickly clapped over mouths as the matrons of Wellesley tried in vain to conceal their scandalized laughter.

Margaret Edwards, a plump, pleasant woman in her late forties, turned to Trudy and smiled sagely. "Even if what you say is true, I, for one, can certainly see how even a girl as fine as Megan Taylor might succumb to that man's charms."

"Margaret!" Trudy gasped, her voice shrill with surprise, "how can you *say* such a thing? There's never an excuse for any young girl to 'succumb'! Shame on you for making excuses for Megan! And you, with a daughter of your own of marrying age . . . how would you feel if it was *your* daughter standing under that tree receiving wedding congratulations with a belly already swollen from tasting the forbidden fruit?"

Margaret grinned unrepentantly. "Oh, I think I might understand if the forbidden fruit she'd tasted belonged to Geoffrey Wellesley."

A new wave of shocked giggles rose from the cluster of women, causing Meg to look over at them curiously.

"I hope those ladies aren't talking about us," she fretted.

"You can just about count on the fact that they are," Geoff responded.

"But what could they be saying that they all keep laughing?"

"I don't think you want to know. God, I wish we could cut the cake and get out of here."

Meg glanced at him a bit warily and nodded. He'd been so gracious during the little reception that she didn't want to say or do anything that might alter his largesse. So far, she didn't think anyone suspected that they were anything other than what they appeared to be—a typical newly married couple, receiving the good wishes of their friends and anxiously anticipating the opportunity to be alone.

"Gather around, everyone," Mrs. Martin called. "It's time for the bride and groom to cut their wedding cake."

The chattering group of parishioners clustered around Meg and Geoff as Mrs. Martin ceremoniously handed a large knife to Meg. "If you would make the first cut, Mrs. Wellesley," she invited.

Meg smiled and bent to her task, cutting a small piece of the cake and picking it up daintily to offer to Geoff. With a sardonic smile, he bent his head and parted his lips, pulling the sweet confection from her fingers. To Meg's complete discomfiture, the sensation of his soft lips touching the tips of her fingers sent a rush of heat all the way up her arm. Hurriedly she withdrew her hand, picking up a square of linen and fastidiously wiping her fingers.

"Now you, Geoff," called a man from the back of the crowd. "Feed your wife a piece."

With a good-natured nod, Geoff picked up the knife and cut another small square, holding it up to Meg's mouth and cocking his brow at her insolently, as if daring her to touch his fingers with her lips.

Meg tried hard to be delicate, carefully nibbling at the edge of the cake so as not to make contact with his skin, but Geoff was having none of it. With a quick move, he pressed

117

the cake against her lips, forcing her to open her mouth wider and accept it, then slipping his fingers through her lips as she did.

Meg let out a little gasp as she felt his rough, calloused fingertips brush intimately across the inside of her lips, but her shock was nothing compared to his.

At his first contact with the warm, wet confines of Meg's mouth, a streak of desire shot through him that was so intense it almost knocked him off his feet. A heavy throb of excitement rocked him as lusty blood flowed into his loins and, immediately, he yanked his fingers away, taking a quick step backward and gaping at Meg in stunned astonishment.

"Kiss her, Geoff," the same man yelled, then to both Geoff and Meg's consternation, the chant was picked up by the entire congregation.

"Kiss her . . . kiss her . . . *kiss her!*"

The last thing Geoff needed at that moment was to be further stimulated by kissing the beautiful woman staring at him with her huge, questioning eyes, but he knew there was no way out of it.

Leaning forward, he grasped Meg lightly by the shoulders and planted a quick, chaste kiss on her lips.

"Ah, come on, Geoff!" the man chided. "That's wasn't nothin'. Let's see a *real* kiss!"

"God damn it, if that's one of my men, he's gonna be looking for a new job tomorrow," Geoff growled in Meg's ear. "Okay, lady, let's make this one look real so they'll quit their yammering." Tipping Meg's head back, he buried his fingers in her hair and lowered his lips to hers.

Meg had been kissed before, several times. Once when she was a teenager and Harvey Winston had taken her to a Fourth of July celebration, and then, several times by Robert McKnight, when they had briefly courted three

118

years before. But nothing she had ever experienced could have prepared her for the blazing inferno Geoffrey Wellesley's kiss ignited within her. It was as if the sensation of his lips covering hers sucked the strength right out of her limbs, leaving her feeling weak-kneed and shaky. A flash of heat coursed through her, and she could feel her nipples tingling where they touched his chest.

As if of its own accord, Meg's mouth softened beneath his and a little sigh of surrender escaped her as she threaded her fingers through the soft hair at the nape of his neck.

It was Geoff who finally pulled away. Reluctantly raising his head, he stared down at her, a hard, almost angry expression in his eyes.

"Now that's more like it!" a voice called.

"Better take her home, Geoff, before we have to call out the fire brigade," someone else shouted.

Geoff knew he should make some response to the randy comments being hurled at them. It was expected. Hell, there had been many times when *he'd* been the one shouting ribald comments at a newly married pair. But right now, he could think of nothing to say. Instead, he just kept staring at his wife, his eyes riveted on her slightly swollen lips and flaming cheeks. It was a long moment before he trusted himself to be able to speak and, when he finally did, his voice was hoarse and ragged.

"Don't ever do that again," he whispered, "or you just might get what you're asking for."

Then, turning back to the laughing crowd, he grinned triumphantly and yelled, "I know you'll excuse us if we leave now."

His outrageous statement was immediately answered by more shrieks of laughter and lusty catcalls. Quickly, he grabbed Meg's hand and pulled her toward Reverend and

Mrs. Martin, who were standing a little apart from the crowd, not knowing quite how to react in the face of such bawdy revelry.

"Thank you so much for everything," Geoff said, holding his hand out to shake the reverend's. "And to you, madam," he added, turning toward Mrs. Martin, "our sincerest appreciation for your thoughtfulness."

"Yes, thank you so much," Meg chorused, finally feeling like she could again draw a normal breath. "We'll . . . we'll see you next Sunday."

They were just turning back toward the church when suddenly Geoff came to an abrupt halt, nearly wrenching Meg's arm out of the socket as he pulled her hard against him.

"What's the matter?" she demanded. "Aren't we going?"

"Not right at the moment," he gritted, looking down the road.

Meg raised a hand to shield her eyes from the sun and what she saw made her draw in a quick, frightened breath.

Galloping recklessly toward them, his face a mask of rage, was George Farnsworth.

Chapter 11

"I want to talk to you, Wellesley!" George Farnsworth bellowed, jumping down from his horse before the winded animal had even come to a full stop.

"Let me handle this," Geoffrey warned quietly, shoving Meg behind him. "Don't say a word." Pasting a smile on his face, he waited for Farnsworth to approach him.

George Farnsworth marched aggressively up to Geoff, his face red and mottled with rage. "You're not going to get away with this, you know," he shouted.

"Good morning, Mr. Farnsworth," Geoff said pleasantly, his face betraying none of the anger building up inside him. "It's a good thing you got here when you did. The wedding cake is almost gone."

"Don't play games with me, you son of a bitch," Farnsworth hissed. "You've met your match this time, thinking you can cross me."

Geoffrey's smile faded. "Do you really want to discuss this in front of the whole congregation?" With a tilt of his head, he gestured to where the wedding celebrants were beginning to move toward them, curious as to what George Farnsworth was shouting about.

"I don't care *who* the hell hears me," Farnsworth thundered. "In fact, the more people who know about this dirty little scam of yours, the better. You think you're so high and mighty, with your big money and your big trees. Well, this is one time when you aren't going to come out the winner. I have an ironclad contract in my pocket signed by Frederick Taylor, promising Megan will marry my son, Peter. What do you think about that, Mr. Timber Baron?"

There were several audible gasps from the gathering crowd at Farnsworth's shocking words, and all heads quickly turned toward Geoffrey.

"I think," Geoff said very calmly, "this is just another example of the old adage that contracts are made to be broken."

George Farnsworth's face became even redder, if that was possible. "I know and you know that this marriage is a sham."

"A sham?" Geoff smiled. "I hardly think so, but if you don't believe me, just ask Reverend Martin over there. He performed the wedding ceremony for us yesterday."

"I certainly did," the reverend piped up, stepping out of the crowd and nodding vehemently at Frederick. "And in front of witnesses, too."

"You may have married them in words, Reverend," George snarled, "but I have it on good authority that that's all that happened yesterday."

"Whatever do you mean, sir?" Reverend Martin asked, clearly puzzled.

"What I mean," George explained, raking Geoff with an insolent look, "is that yonder groom spent his wedding night in his timber shack—alone."

Another shocked gasp rose from the crowd, and several mothers clapped their hands over their daughters' ears.

"You see?" Beatrice Lennox whispered to Trudy Phillips. "Megan couldn't be in the family way. They haven't even consummated their marriage yet!"

"Just because they didn't sleep together last night doesn't mean they didn't consummate things earlier," Trudy retorted. "Maybe since the deed's already done, Geoffrey just isn't interested in her anymore. Some men are like that, you know."

"Oh," Beatrice huffed, "that's utter nonsense."

"We'll see," Trudy smiled. "The next seven or eight months will tell the tale."

Beatrice frowned at her friend and turned her attention back to Geoff.

"Where I *slept* last night is of no consequence," Geoff chuckled, putting emphasis on the word "slept."

"Geoffrey, please!" Meg murmured, her face crimson with embarrassment.

Geoff glanced at her quickly, then turned back to George. "As you can see, it is embarrassing my bride to have our personal life discussed like this, so I'm afraid you'll just have to excuse us."

"You're going to be sorry you interfered with my plans," Farnsworth snarled, pushing his face close to Geoff's. "Very, very sorry."

"Don't threaten me, Farnsworth." Although Geoff's voice was soft, there was an unmistakable warning in his steely tone. With a last, quelling look at the older man, he guided Meg past him and back toward the church. "Come on, baby," he said loudly enough that everyone present could hear him, "let's go put the rumors of a chaste marriage to rest."

Meg gasped aloud at this outrageous statement and turned to give Geoff a piece of her mind, but then she felt the increased pressure of his fingers around her arm and prudently held her tongue.

"Why did you embarrass me like that in front of the entire congregation?" she demanded when they were well out of earshot.

"Would you rather have everyone know that our marriage *is* a sham?" Geoff asked.

"Well, no," she admitted, "I suppose not. But I don't think it was necessary to announce that you were taking me home to . . . to . . ."

"To make love to you?" Geoff asked, glancing at her crimson face and smiling at her discomfiture. "It may not have been *necessary*, but it certainly laid to rest any doubts old Farnsworth's statement might have planted in anyone's mind."

Meg sighed. "Yes, I suppose you're right, although I still don't think *he* believes us."

"I don't either," Geoff admitted quietly.

"Then what are we going to do?"

"About what?"

"About George Farnsworth, for heaven's sake! Geoff, I'm scared. Can he really have our marriage annulled?"

"Not if it's consummated, he can't."

"What?" Meg gasped, her eyes bulging. "What do you mean?"

"What I mean, lady," he responded, his voice strangely tense, "is that you're going to get your way. I'm moving in."

Consummated! God in heaven, was he serious?

The small knife Meg was using to peel potatoes stilled in her hand. And what if he was? What was she going to do to prevent it? Geoffrey Wellesley was, after all, her husband, and even though they had agreed to a marriage in name only, he was completely within his rights if he decided to change his mind and assert his conjugal privilege.

He didn't mean it, she told herself firmly. Geoff had no more intention of consummating their marriage than she did . . . and what good would it do even if they did? After all, this wasn't the Middle Ages, when wedding nights were witnessed and bloody sheets displayed the following morning. "Thank God *that* particular custom has been abandoned," Meg muttered aloud. How had women ever lived through the humiliation?

Idly, she began to pare another potato. At least now, a couple's wedding night was a completely private affair and only they knew for sure when and if a bride's deflowering had ever taken place. Unless, of course, she became pregnant.

Unless she became pregnant . . . the only way for everyone to know for sure that a couple was sharing a true marriage was for the bride to become pregnant . . .

My God, that was what she was going to have to do! The only way she'd ever truly be safe from George Farnsworth was to get pregnant. If she didn't, then he'd just continue to question the validity of her marriage and proceed with having it legally annulled.

The paring knife clattered into the sink as Meg suddenly realized where her thoughts were leading her. Instead of worrying about Geoffrey demanding his husbandly rights, she was going to have to encourage him to do so!

But how was she supposed to do that? Geoff had made it very plain that he wasn't interested in her in any romantic sense, and despite what he'd said in the wagon, she didn't truly believe he was serious about consummating their marriage; so how was she supposed to entice him into bed?

And how many times would she have to bear his attentions before she got pregnant? If she could somehow coerce

125

him into going through the process once, would that be enough to get herself with child?

She doubted it. Although she had never thought much about the physical side of marriage, she guessed that it usually took more than one effort to conceive a child. She'd heard too many rowdy comments from the loggers she dealt with to believe that men did it only three or four times in their lives. And besides, she knew the unmarried lumberjacks regularly mated with the prostitutes who worked at the Skid Road Saloon, and she'd never seen any of them pregnant.

Yet, she mused, it must be possible to get with child after only one encounter, because that's what had happened to her friend Jenny Thomas. Jenny had mentioned only one attack by Peter Farnsworth.

Meg bit her lip in vexation. Could she really bring herself to be intimate with Geoffrey Wellesley, even once? Unbidden, the memory of how his lips had felt on hers as he'd kissed her at the wedding party rose to her mind. She closed her eyes, seeing again the look of shock and tension on his face when he'd finally lifted his head. Had he experienced the same queer little thrill that she had? Was that what desire felt like?

Meg looked down at her hands, annoyed to see that they were shaking. Clutching one in the other, she squeezed hard, hoping the pressure would stop the trembling and at the same time remove the heady recollections of Geoffrey's kiss from her mind.

It was all so confusing! She wasn't in love with Geoffrey Wellesley, and yet the mere thought of his kiss made her head reel. She had no desire to lie with the man, and yet the mere thought of how his shoulder muscles had felt under her hands made her tremble uncontrollably.

But, she asked herself again, how did one go about

asking a man to take one to bed? She couldn't very well walk up to him and say, "Geoffrey, I'd appreciate it if you'd make love to me enough times that I get with child." Could she?

"Of course not!" she muttered aloud. "Don't be a ninny. He'd just tell you that you had no right to make any more demands on him, and then ask you how many board feet got cut today."

But how else was George Farnsworth going to be convinced that their marriage was real?

Meg shook her head and rubbed her tired eyes. Maybe she'd ask Virginia's advice. If there was anything Virginia knew about, it was how to have babies.

With a decisive nod, she again picked up her paring knife. That was it—she'd ask Virginia. Ginny always had the answer for everything.

"So, you're movin' in with her, are ya?"

Geoffrey glared at his foreman, Ned Johnson, and threw two flannel shirts into a worn valise. "Yeah, and I don't want to hear anything about it from you."

"I ain't sayin' nothing," Ned laughed, holding his hands up in mock defense. "I just hope you realize that by movin' in with her, you're gettin' yourself into this for life."

"I've always known I was in it for life," Geoff growled.

Ned's eyebrows lifted with interest. "No kiddin'? I thought maybe you was just gonna stay married long enough to get Farnsworth off Miss Taylor's tail and get your timber cut."

Geoff paused and turned to look at Ned in surprise. "What made you think that?"

"Oh, nothin' much. Just the fact that you don't care about the little gal, you got no interest in bein' married to her, you got blackmailed into this mess, you hate livin' in town, you . . ."

"Okay, okay, I get the point. And you're right. I hate everything about this situation, but the fact remains, I'm married, for better or worse, till death do us part. And, short of murdering my bride, I don't see any way out of it."

"I see," Ned chortled, "so you *are* plannin' on beddin' the girl."

"Now, what the hell has that got to do with anything? Not that's it's any of your damn business."

Ned chuckled, thoroughly enjoying Geoff's obvious discomfort. "Hell, Geoff, even *I* know that if two married people ain't sleepin' together, they ain't really married and they can get out of it if they want. I just figured that's the way you was gonna handle this."

"Well, I'm not," Geoff snapped, turning back to his packing. "There's . . . advantages to being married to Miss Taylor."

"Yeah, and I know what they are," Ned grinned.

"Shut up, Ned. You don't know anything."

"Oh, don't I? Then, why don't you tell me about the advantages of bein' married—other than the obvious ones which, with that pretty little gal you just got hitched to, are considerable."

Geoff sighed, wondering, not for the first time, why he put up with the crusty old lumberjack's constant meddling. *Because he's the best logging foreman in the state*, he reminded himself.

"If you must know, Miss Taylor and I have agreed to a marriage in name only. The advantage for her is that she will be protected from Peter Farnsworth."

"And for you?" Ned prodded.

"For me, the advantage is that I will no longer have to

fight off every greedy, ambitious mother in this town with an unmarried daughter."

"So, you're *not* gonna sleep with her?"

"You're just not going to let this go until I give you an answer, are you, old man?"

"Nope," Ned responded cheerfully.

Geoff shook his head, amazed by his employee's audacity and even more amazed at himself when he realized he was actually going to answer him. "No, I'm not going to sleep with her."

"Why not?" Ned asked instantly.

"Why not?" Geoff gasped. "What the hell do you mean, why not?"

"Why not?"

"Because it would make things about a hundred times more complicated than they already are, that's why not!"

"She's your wife," Ned said slyly. "And a by God pretty one at that. Damn it, Geoff, if I had a little gal like that waitin' for me every night when I came out of the forest, you can bet I'd be climbin' into her bed, and to hell with 'complications.' "

"Well, I'm not you," Geoff said, snapping the valise closed.

"You're right about that, boy. What you are is a whole lot younger and a whole lot randier."

"I've had enough of this conversation, Ned," Geoff said flatly, hefting the valise off the bed and starting for the door, "and I don't want to hear that anything we've said here tonight has been repeated to the other men, you got that?"

Ned drew himself up like an offended rooster. "You know damned well you don't have to worry about that."

"Good," Geoff responded, nodding curtly. "Then I'll see you in the morning."

"Okay, boss," Ned grinned. "See you tomorrow morning."

Ned watched Geoff stride out of his small cabin and mount his horse, an amused smile on his weathered old face. "If you can still walk tomorrow mornin', that is . . ."

Chapter 12

"You don't have to knock," Meg smiled, pulling open the front door to admit her husband. "After all, this is your home now, too."

Geoff gave her a slightly quizzical look, but said nothing except, "Where should I put my clothes?"

Meg's eyes widened with surprised offense at his curt manner. "Upstairs, the first door on the left."

With a noncommittal nod, Geoff proceeded up the staircase, wondering exactly whose bedroom he was going to find through the "first door on the left." When he reached the second level, he paused a moment, looking down the hall as if he could ascertain which bedroom was which from that vantage point. Then, with a little shake of his head, he turned into the first bedroom.

The chamber was obviously set up for guests. Although it was large and airy, with a bank of windows looking out over the backyard, there was an austerity about it that bespoke no particular ownership. The top of the bureau was bare, as was the surface of the night-stand. Glancing to his right, Geoff saw a large armoire and walked over to it, pulling the doors open. It was empty.

The fact that Meg had chosen to place him in a guest

bedroom spoke volumes. "Guess the master doesn't get to sleep in the master's chamber," he muttered.

Opening his suitcase, he started pulling out his belongings and throwing them haphazardly on the bed. "So, I'm to be treated as a guest, am I?" he growled, becoming more angry by the moment as he continued to stew over Meg's choice for his bedroom.

Finally, he tipped the valise over and shook the rest of its contents on to the bed. Then, planting his hands on his lean hips, he took a step backward and gazed irritably around at the barren room. "We'll just see about that, *Mrs.* Wellesley."

Flinging the case aside, Geoff strode out of the room and down the hall, pausing before each door to look into the other bedrooms.

There were three more that looked much as his did, and it wasn't until he reached the far end of the hall that he found what was obviously the master suite. Pushing open a set of double doors, he stepped into a huge chamber, smiling with satisfaction as his eyes swept the luxurious room. A thick cream and blue carpet covered the floor, and heavy velvet drapes of the same azure hue hung at a wide bay window. Skirting the massive tester bed, Geoff bent a knee on a padded windowseat and looked outside. Just as he'd expected, there was a magnificent view of the mountains.

"Yup," he nodded decisively, "this is my room."

Turning, he walked out of the beautiful room and headed back down the hall toward the guest chamber. He gathered up the pile of clothes on the bed and retraced his steps, reentering the master suite and dumping them on the bed. Starting down the hall again to collect the remainder of his belongings, he paused, reaching for the doorknob of the only room he hadn't already inspected. He hesitated a moment, knowing he had no right to peek into what had to be Megan's room, but unable to contain his curiosity, he cast a furtive look down the hall, then cracked the door and stuck his head in.

The room was exactly what he'd expected: neat, innocent, and decidedly feminine. The floor was covered with a large Aubusson rug, the swirls of pink and white flowers giving the illusion of stepping into a spring garden. There was a small dressing table against one wall, its top littered with delicate bottles of scent and a sterling silver hairbrush, comb, and mirror set. Silently Geoff padded across the carpet, lifting the stopper out of one of the bottles and inhaling the perfume's delicate scent.

"Smells just like her," he murmured, his eyes unconsciously closing as he breathed deeply of the tantalizing fragrance. Replacing the bottle on the dressing table, he turned, his eyes drifting past a carved white pine armoire and coming to rest on the small brass bed.

It was covered by a pale pink lace coverlet of the same shade as the rug, rolled neatly over a plump mound of feather pillows. A rosebud-sprigged nightrail was thrown casually across the footboard.

It had been a long, long time since Geoff had been in a lady's bedroom and, for some reason he couldn't name, the lure of the gauzy nightgown was irresistible. Walking over to the bed, he ran his hard, callused hand lightly over the filmy material, smiling slightly as the soft fabric flowed between his fingers.

Suddenly he realized what he was doing and dropped the nightgown as if it was on fire. "Get the hell out of here," he ordered himself. "This room isn't for you . . . and neither is she."

Turning on his heel, he quickly left, pulling the door closed behind him. He'd taken no more than two steps down the hall when he saw Meg appear at the top of the stairs. Heaving a gusty little sigh of relief that he hadn't been caught in her room, he smiled at her engagingly.

"Getting settled?" she asked, glancing into the bedroom she'd assigned him and then looking back at him in surprise. "Where are your things?"

"I decided I don't want that room."

"What?" she asked in astonishment. "Why not?"

"Because I like this one better." He thrust his thumb over his shoulder, gesturing toward the master suite.

"You can't have that room," Meg gasped. "That's my father's room!"

"Was."

"I beg your pardon?"

"Was your father's room."

"Well, yes," Meg conceded.

Geoff instantly regretted his hard words as he saw a look of sorrow cloud her eyes, but knowing now was the moment to establish his position in the household, he plunged on. "And would you agree that that room was designed for the master of the house?"

"Y . . . yes."

He shrugged elaborately. "Well, then?"

"But . . ."

"Yes?"

"But it's right next to *my* room!" Meg blurted.

Geoff looked at her for a moment and a glint of amusement sprang to his eyes. "So?"

"I just don't think it's appropriate—"

"Now, wait a minute," he interrupted, preparing himself for their first domestic showdown, "I'm your husband, you're my wife. There is nothing inappropriate about us having adjoining chambers."

"Well, normally, no. But in our situation . . ."

"I'm not sleeping in the guest room, Megan. Either I take up residence in the master chamber or I don't take up residence at all. Which is it going to be?"

"Oh, you're impossible!" Meg gritted, taking several steps toward him, her hands clenched at her sides. "You have no consideration, no manners, no . . ." She stopped in mid-sentence, suddenly realizing that not an hour before she'd been plotting how best to seduce her new husband. Now, here he was, telling her he wanted to move into the chamber next to hers, and she was adamantly resisting him. *What's wrong with you, you ninny? This is exactly what you should want him to do!*

"All right," she said abruptly. "Go ahead and move into my father's room."

Geoff was astonished by her sudden about-face, but he was careful not to allow his expression to betray his surprise. "I'm glad you see it my way," he said quietly, when he finally found his voice again.

Meg shrugged, trying hard to conceal the consternation she knew was rampant on her face. "I don't care where you sleep," she said, pleased that her voice sounded far more nonchalant than she felt.

"Good. Then I'll just go in and finish unpacking." Brushing past her, Geoff headed back down the hall.

Closing the bedroom door behind him, he leaned against it, shaking his head in bewilderment. "Now, what was that all about?" he asked the empty room. "First she says she doesn't want me in here, then she says she doesn't care . . . Women! If I live to be a hundred, I'll never understand them."

With a dismissive shrug, he scooped up a pile of shirts and shoved them into a bureau drawer, wondering why he didn't feel more elation over his small victory. But for some

135

reason he couldn't quite name, he wasn't altogether sure that he'd really won anything.

Dinner was a stilted affair. After their brief altercation in the hall, they seemed to have little to say to each other, and although Geoff ate heartily, Meg picked disinterestedly at her chicken, wishing the meal would end so she could escape to the solitude of her bedroom.

"I won't be home every night," Geoff announced abruptly.

"Oh?" she responded, looking up from her plate.

"No. In fact," he added, suddenly seeing an unexpected out to having to play the dutiful husband seven nights a week, "I'll probably be here only on the weekends."

"The weekends! Why just the weekends?"

"Well," he hedged, thinking fast, "during the week, we start felling at dawn and we work till sundown. Doesn't make much sense to come all the way down off the mountain just to sleep."

"But what about George Farnsworth? He's going to think it's strange if you come home only a couple nights a week. It will look like . . . like . . ."

"No it won't," Geoff interjected quickly. "Farnsworth knows the hours lumberjacks work. He would probably think it strange if I *did* come home every night."

"Oh, yes," Meg retorted sarcastically, "he might think that you're actually so much in love with your wife that you want to spend your evenings at home. We certainly wouldn't want him to think that!"

"For God's sake, Megan," Geoff snapped, throwing his napkin down on the table, "I'm not going to ride down that mountain every damn night just so Farnsworth will think we're having sex."

136

Meg's eyes widened to the size of dinner plates at Geoff's use of *that* word. No gentleman ever said that word—especially in the company of a lady!

"I beg your pardon, sir," she huffed, her napkin hitting the table with as much vehemence as his had a moment before, "but you will not use such obscene language in front of me."

"What obscene language?" Geoff asked, genuinely confused.

"You know very well what I mean. That word you just said."

Geoff's brow furrowed for a moment, then a wide grin spread across his handsome face. "You mean *'sex'*?" he needled.

"Geoffrey, I'm warning you, stop saying that!"

To Meg's complete amazement, he burst out laughing, a low, rich sound that made goose bumps prickle up her arms.

"What's so funny?" she demanded.

"You. You're funny."

"Why?"

"Because you're such a paradox."

As always, Meg was astounded by Geoff's vocabulary, but she refused to let him see how impressed she was. Instead, she calmly speared a piece of chicken and said, "Oh? And why do you say that?"

"Because you come up my mountain with both guns loaded and demand that I marry you. When I say *no*, you blackmail me into it. Then you demand that I move in with you so George Farnsworth won't get suspicious. Now, ordinarily speaking, those actions would denote a pretty bold woman, and up until tonight, I thought you were. But suddenly, you're showing me a whole new side of your personality. First, you get upset just because I'm going to sleep in the room next to yours, and now you tell me that it offends you to hear the word 'sex' spoken in your presence. I guess I never expected you to have a puritanical streak."

"I don't have a puritanical streak," Meg protested hotly. "It's just that gentlemen and ladies do not discuss . . ."

"Sex?" Geoff provided helpfully, his brandy-colored eyes dancing with deviltry. "You're right. Gentlemen and ladies *don't* discuss it. They just do it."

"Oh!" Meg sputtered. "You're terrible!"

"I know, I know," he laughed, holding up a hand. "No consideration, no manners. I've heard it all before."

"Well, it's true!"

"What did you *expect* to find when you came looking for a husband in a logging camp?" he asked, surprised at how much he wanted to hear her answer.

"I expected to find the smartest, most influential, and most powerful man in three counties," Meg answered tartly. "I expected to find Geoffrey Wellesley!"

Geoff's smile faded. "And instead you found an uneducated, inconsiderate lumberjack, right?"

"Yes . . . no . . . oh, I don't know. I just know that this isn't turning out at all like I thought it would."

With a slow, wry smile, Geoff rose and walked over to her, bending down and tracing a finger lightly down her cheek. "Things seldom do, Mrs. Wellesley. Things seldom do."

Meg turned over in bed and gave her pillow an irritated punch. *Now what am I going to do?* she thought dismally. *How am I ever going to seduce the man after I told him it offended me to hear the word "sex"?* Even mentally voicing the forbidden word made her gulp with shame.

138

She knew she shouldn't have reacted as she had to Geoff's goading, but she just couldn't help it. Men and women of quality *didn't* discuss that subject and they certainly didn't use that word! Meg still couldn't believe that Geoff had dropped it into their conversation as casually as if he was talking about the weather. But then, Geoffrey Wellesley was different from any man she'd ever known.

What did you expect to find when you came looking for a husband in a logging camp? For some reason, Geoff's softly spoken words kept replaying in her mind.

But, Meg mused, staring at the ceiling with a slight smile curving her lips, he wasn't an inconsiderate, ill-mannered lumberjack. Rough? Yes. Shockingly frank? Absolutely. But there was another, intriguing quality about her new husband that he had shown her tonight . . . an innate gentleness that she'd seen deep in his eyes when he'd run his finger down her cheek. He kept it well hidden beneath his brash exterior, but it was there, nonetheless.

A little shiver ran through her as she thought again of how his finger had felt against her skin. He was so handsome, so big and hard and golden, that just thinking about him made her breath catch in her throat.

And tomorrow, she had to set about seducing him. The very thought made her shift nervously on her soft mattress. Finally she sat up, lighting a candle.

She couldn't do it. She just knew she couldn't. But she *had* to—it was the only way she'd ever be truly safe from George Farnsworth. Her marriage alone wasn't going to be enough to stop him. He'd made that perfectly clear at the church today. She *had* to get pregnant. And the only way to do that was to make Geoffrey want her. But how?

"Subtly," she whispered to herself. "You have to be subtle, or he'll laugh in your face and make some snide comment about what ladies do and do not do." If only she knew how a woman went about tactfully letting a man know that she wanted him to . . . Meg closed her eyes and swallowed hard . . . have sex with her.

"Ginny," she murmured. "Ginny will know." The thought of her older sister's calm reason immediately made her feel better. But, her sense of well-being was short-lived when she suddenly heard the unmistakable sound of someone turning over in bed in the next room. For a split second, Meg felt a rush of fear at the unexpected noise, but she relaxed again when she realized it was just Geoffrey.

"Just Geoffrey," she giggled, her mind conjuring up scandalous images of what he must look like reclining on her parents' bed.

What did he wear when he slept? Her father had always worn a linen nightshirt that hung down well below his knees, but somehow Meg couldn't picture Geoff in such amusing garb. But, if he didn't wear a nightshirt, what *did* he wear?

"You shouldn't be thinking about such things," she told herself firmly. "It's not fitting for a lady to even wonder." Despite her stern reprimand, her traitorous imagination continued to churn as she visualized Geoffrey bare-chested. As far as what he might be wearing on the bottom half of his body, she wouldn't even allow herself to contemplate.

"Stop this!" she chided herself. "The man wears *something* to bed. No one sleeps . . . naked!"

Quickly, as if to hide her own embarrassment, she reached over and snuffed the candle, scooting back down into the depths of her bed and clapping her hands over her flaming cheeks.

"Of *course* he wears something," she assured herself. And even if he didn't when the weather was warm and he was alone, surely he would if she was with him . . . wouldn't he?

140

Meg lay for a long time staring at the ceiling as thoughts of Geoffrey clothed and unclothed tumbled scandalously through her mind. "This is crazy!" she told herself. "There must be some way to find out for sure. That's the only way I'll quit thinking about it."

Then a thought occurred to her: *tomorrow* . . . maybe she'd be able to find out tomorrow morning, after Geoff left for the logging camp. After all, she rationalized, he'd need fresh water in his washing pitcher, and she would probably have to make his bed, since he undoubtedly wouldn't bother. And while she was in his room, she could just sneak a quick look into his bureau drawer . . .

Meg giggled at her own nonsense. If anyone had told her a month ago that she'd be losing sleep over Geoffrey Wellesley's sleeping apparel, she'd have told them they were out of their minds. But that was before he'd smiled at her and run his finger down her cheek. Somehow, that provocative moment in the dining room had changed everything.

Chapter 13

Meg opened her eyes and stared groggily out the window at the dark sky. What time was it, and what had awakened her in the middle of the night?

From somewhere downstairs, she heard the sound of someone opening a door. Geoffrey! He must already be up.

Throwing back the covers, she swung her legs over the side of the bed, yawning expansively as she tried to focus on a small clock on her night-stand.

Four-thirty-five.

Meg squeezed her eyes shut, then opened them wide as she tried to clear her foggy vision. She must be reading the clock wrong. No one got up at four-thirty in the morning! She gazed at it again, amazed to see that the time had not changed—except that it was now four-thirty-six.

"Good Lord," she moaned, rubbing her eyes. "He *does* get up in the middle of the night." Tiredly, she stood up and staggered over to a small stand upon which sat a pitcher and basin. She splashed some water in her face and picked up her hairbrush, trying to coax some semblance of order into her loosely plaited hair. Pulling on her robe, she walked out of her room and down the stairs.

Geoff was just shrugging into his jacket when he looked

up and saw Meg's bare feet at the top of the staircase. He paused, one arm shoved halfway into a sleeve, and watched the provocative way the bottom of her robe gapped open, displaying her shapely calves through the gauzy material of her nightgown. His eyes swept upward, taking in her slightly disheveled hair and limpid, sleepy eyes. Immediately he felt a familiar tightening in his loins.

No woman should look that good at four in the morning. Her thick ebony hair was practically begging to be unbraided, and the drowsy expression in those dark eyes of hers was enough to set a man on fire.

"What are you doing up?" he asked crossly, pointedly turning away as he fumbled with his jacket buttons.

"I thought I'd make you some breakfast before you left."

"I already had some bread. Just go back to bed. There's no reason for you to be up yet."

"I'm sorry, Geoff," Meg said contritely. "If I'd known you were leaving so early, I'd have gotten up and made you a real breakfast."

"Don't worry about it," he said curtly, thinking that the last thing in the world he needed was to see Meg in her current state of dress doing something as intimate as cooking his breakfast. He'd probably never make it up the mountain! Just the sound of her voice saying his name caused the erection he was fighting to strengthen, and he was afraid that if he didn't get out of the house fast, he was going to do something that an hour from now he'd regret mightily.

"I've got to go," he announced, hurrying over to the front door.

"Will you be home tonight?" she asked softly.

He paused, careful to keep his back to her. "I told you I was only coming here on weekends."

"I know, but I thought maybe . . ."

"I'll see you Friday," he growled, jerking the door open and rushing out of the house.

Meg frowned in confusion at the unnecessary vehemence with which he'd closed the door, then stepped forward and peered out the beveled window after him. He disappeared around the side of the house, heading for the shed where his horse was tethered.

For a long moment, she stood by the door, wondering what she'd said to annoy him so. Then, with a dejected sigh, she turned and went back upstairs, wishing the gods had been kinder than to saddle her with a man who was surly in the morning.

Geoff walked into the small shed and carefully closed the door behind him, leaning against the rough wall of the structure and blowing out a long, shaky breath. Shoving his hand down the front of his denims, he tried in vain to adjust his straining erection to a more comfortable position. Damn it! Why had he chosen to wear such tight pants today?

His horse nickered a welcome and he glared at the animal with a jaundiced expression. There was no way in hell he was going to be able to sit in a saddle until he calmed down a little.

"Damn woman," he growled, walking over and jerking his bridle off a hook on the wall. "Why in hell did she get up?" Another vision of Meg in her light, summerweight bathrobe swam before his eyes, and he groaned. "Quit thinking about her," he commanded himself. "Think about all the trees you have to fell this week, think about all the drunk lumberjacks who won't show up for work this morning, think about anything except your curvy little wife parading down the staircase in her nightgown and bare feet."

A little shiver ran through him as he thought again about

144

the sight of Meg's bare feet as she'd paused at the top of the staircase. Was there anything in the world sexier than a barefoot woman with tousled hair? Maybe, but if there was, Geoff couldn't think of it.

"What I need is a little something to take the edge off," he muttered. Maybe he'd ride over to Oregon City tonight. There were plenty of pretty girls at Lulu's, and for a few coins, he could sate his lust without anyone in Wellesley being any the wiser. He smiled, remembering his last trip to Lulu's in March, when several of her girls had offered to sate his lust for *no* coins.

March. Was it really three months since he'd been there? "No wonder you're horny, Wellesley," he chided himself. "You're living like a monk!"

With a decisive nod, he made up his mind—a night spent with one of Lulu's comely, undemanding, but highly accomplished girls would be just the thing to make him forget about the conniving, gorgeous little vixen who was now sharing his name—but not his bed.

"Hell, you wouldn't take her, even if she offered," he told himself firmly, wishing he could believe it. "You think she's been trouble before? You don't even know the *meaning* of the word until you start something like that with her."

No, far better to stick with Lulu's . . . maybe he'd even go again on Thursday night. If he had a woman tonight and again on Thursday, surely that would see him through the weekend.

Wouldn't it?

Of course it would. After all, he was thirty-four years old, not seventeen! Twice in three days would certainly be enough for him to be able to spend the weekend with Meg without disgracing himself like some randy kid.

Geoff sighed and slipped the bit into his horse's mouth.

Now, all he had to do was figure out how to make himself believe that.

Meg accepted with a wan smile the cup of coffee Virginia handed her. As was their custom every Tuesday afternoon, the sisters were seated at Ginny's kitchen table, sharing coffee, a plate of cookies, and their innermost secrets.

"What's the matter, honey?" Virginia asked, leaning over and plucking her baby daughter out of her cradle. "Are you still upset over the ruckus George Farnsworth caused after church Sunday?"

"Yes," Meg admitted, "but at least now that I'm sure the Farnsworths aren't going to give up even though I'm married, I know what I have to do."

"You're going to ask Mr. Wellesley for the money to pay the debt on the mill," Virginia said positively.

"No! I can't do that, Ginny. I just *can't*. I feel bad enough that I've involved him in all this by forcing him to marry me. I won't ask him to pay my debts."

"But, Meg!" Virginia protested. "If you don't pay the debt, George Farnsworth is going to proceed legally with trying to have your marriage annulled. And Lawrence thinks there's a possibility he can do it. Something about prior agreements negating later contracts or something like that."

Meg shook her head. "There's not a court in the land that would declare my marriage invalid if I . . ."

"If you what?"

"If I have a baby."

Virginia gaped at her sister in stunned amazement. "You're going to get pregnant?"

"I don't have any choice," Meg wailed. "I can't ask

146

Geoffrey for the money to pay off the Farnsworths, and the only other way to void that contract is to make my marriage unbreakable. A baby would do that."

"You're right," Ginny mused, looking down at the baby she held and smiling. "A baby would do it. If there's anything that binds two people together for life, it's creating a child together."

"Oh, God," Meg moaned. "I don't want to be bound to Geoffrey Wellesley for life!"

Ginny smiled wistfully. "Like you said, you don't have a choice. But don't worry. It won't be so awful, and having a baby is the most wonderful thing in the world."

Meg frowned. "I know you feel that way, Ginny. I just hope I'll feel the same once I've . . . done it."

"You will," Virginia assured her, reaching out and giving Meg's arm a motherly pat. "I promise, you will."

Meg hesitated a moment, toying with the handle of her coffee cup. "The problem is," she murmured, "in order to get a baby, I have to . . . have to . . ."

"I know what you have to do," Virginia smiled, saving Meg from having to complete the embarrassing sentence.

"But I don't think I can," Meg blurted.

"Of course you can. It's something every married woman has to face, and we all get through it. You will, too."

"But it's different for you, Ginny. You love Lawrence and he loves you. I'm sure that when that's the case, the rest just comes naturally."

"Well, mutual love helps," Virginia conceded, "but I don't know that it ever comes 'naturally'—at least, not for a woman."

Meg's eyes widened. "What do you mean? I thought that when two people were in love, they wanted to . . ."

"*Men* want to," Virginia corrected gently. "Most of the

147

women I know, myself included, could happily live the rest of our lives without it, but the compensations more than make up for the unpleasantness." Again she gazed down at her baby.

A look of genuine horror crossed Meg's face. "Oh, Ginny, is it really terrible?"

"No," Virginia said quickly. "It's not terrible. It's just that when God devised his great plan for procreation, he seemed to be thinking more about men than women. But we women have devised all sorts of ways to make it more tolerable."

"Like what?"

"Well," Virginia whispered, looking around to make sure that none of her children were lurking about, "what I find works best is to think about other things while it's going on."

"What kinds of things?"

"Oh, nice things—like a pretty spring day, a new hat, just about anything that takes your mind off what's actually happening. Then, it's not so bad."

"It hurts, doesn't it?" Meg asked quietly.

Virginia shook her head and rose from her chair to put the sleeping baby into a nearby cradle. "Not really. Well, I take that back. Like I told you the other day, it hurts the first time. But once you get used to it, it doesn't anymore. Especially if you just lie still, close your eyes, and let your mind drift."

"Merciful heavens, it sounds awful," Meg groaned.

"Now, Meggie, don't feel that way. It's not *awful*. If it was, the human race wouldn't have endured all these thousands of years."

Meg looked doubtful. "There's something else I've been wondering," she began.

"Yes, dear, what is it?"

When Meg didn't answer, Ginny reseated herself at the table and said, "Come on. Don't be embarrassed. Answering questions you can't ask anyone else is what I'm here for."

Meg shot her older sister a grateful look. Whatever would she do without Ginny? "How often do you have to . . . well . . . *submit* to a man in order to have a baby?"

Virginia tapped a finger against her teeth thoughtfully. "That depends. Some women, like me, get into the family way quite easily. For others, it doesn't seem to happen as fast."

"Do you think once will be enough?" Meg asked hopefully.

Virginia frowned and shook her head. "I doubt it. I know that happens sometimes, but usually it takes a few more tries than that."

"Do you have to do it *every night?*" Meg whispered, not sure she wanted to hear Ginny's answer.

"Good heavens, no!" Ginny giggled. "God forbid! I don't know about other people, of course, but once a week is about as often as Lawrence, well, you know. And it's generally on Saturday night."

"Why Saturday night?"

"I don't know," Virginia shrugged. "It just seems like Lawrence gets in the mood on Saturday nights. For some reason, I think a lot of men do. That's good, though, because then on Sunday morning, all the women whose husbands have been . . . *affectionate* the night before can go to church and pray that they'll be granted a baby for their efforts." Smiling, Ginny gazed fondly over at Angela. "And sometimes those prayers are answered."

"Is being in the family way awful, too?"

"No, not at all! In fact, it's wonderful—unless, of course, you're sick every morning the first few months. I've heard

149

that's very unpleasant, but I've never had the problem." Leaning forward conspiratorially, she added, "Pregnancy is especially nice for women who don't enjoy their husband's, ah, attentions, because once you're in the family way, many men don't make any demands on you until after the baby is born."

"So, you have nine months that you don't have to . . ."

"Exactly," Ginny smiled. "Of course, being in the family way doesn't mean you *can't* be intimate if you want to. Why, I've heard of women who continued to have relations with their husbands right up until the end!"

Meg shuddered. "What an odious thought!"

"I agree, but apparently, it is possible."

"But, what would be the point in that?" Meg questioned. "If the woman is already in the family way, why would she continue to do something whose only purpose is to get her into the condition she's already in?"

Ginny chuckled at her sister's logic. "It's like I told you before—men like doing it just because it feels so good for them. So, if a woman is unlucky enough to have a very demanding husband, I imagine she would feel she has to continue to participate just to please him."

"Thank heavens that won't be an issue with me."

"Why not?"

"Well, once I get with child, I *never* have to do it again."

Virginia looked at her sister skeptically. "I don't think you can count on that, Meggie. Once men get used to the pleasure they get from the marital bed, I don't think they give it up real easily. Even the most sensitive husbands expect to start right up again a little while after the baby is born."

Megan looked appalled as she considered the possibility

150

of having to endure Geoffrey Wellesley's lust every Saturday night for the rest of her life.

Virginia correctly read the terrified expression on Meg's face, and quickly sought to assuage her fears. "You know," she said casually, pouring them each another cup of coffee, "there are some rather nice things about the whole process that I haven't told you about."

"Really?" Meg said, brightening. "What?"

Virginia smiled. "Well, sometimes, afterward, Lawrence feels real affectionate and he hugs me and kisses me and rubs my back. It's a wonderful way to go to sleep."

"But, that's only sometimes?"

"Well, yes," Ginny admitted, "because most of the time he's too tired afterward to stay awake very long."

"Then what does he do?"

Virginia cleared her throat uncomfortably. "He just turns over and goes to sleep. But," she added, holding up a finger, "even when he does that, there's a certain sense of contentment I always feel."

"Why?"

"Because I know the whole thing makes him happy, and I feel happy knowing that I've made him happy."

Meg covered her face with her hands. "Well, I think the whole thing sounds terrible. I'm just afraid I won't be able to go through with it."

"Yes, you will," Virginia said positively. "We all do what we have to, and you will, too."

Meg's eyes narrowed into dark slits of fury. "You know, I could just *kill* that damned Peter Farnsworth for putting me in this position!"

"Meg!" Virginia gasped, astounded by her sister's rash statement—and her unprecedented use of an obscenity. "You should never say something like that. You know you don't mean it!"

"Well, I'm sorry if I've shocked you, but I swear I could do it. That's how furious I am that I've been forced into this impossible situation. None of this is my fault, yet I'm the one who has to suffer through submitting to a man I don't love and bearing a child I don't want."

"You'll want the baby once you have it," Ginny soothed. "And, as far as the situation you're in, there's nothing you can do about it. Just keep telling yourself that once your encounters with Geoffrey Wellesley have borne fruit, your problems will all be over and you won't have to worry anymore. *And* you'll have a beautiful, precious baby as a reward."

For a long moment, Meg sat chewing her lip, pondering all Virginia had told her and dying to ask the one question that had been plaguing her all day.

"What's the matter?" Virginia asked, knowing her sister had something else on her mind.

Meg's cheeks flushed with embarrassment. "What do you . . . *wear* when you're doing this?"

Virginia looked at her in surprise. Why would that particular question seem to embarrass her so much? She'd already asked many others which were much more personal. "You wear your nightclothes, silly."

Meg breathed a huge sigh of relief. "You mean you don't have to be . . . naked?"

"Good Lord, no! Lawrence and I have *never* been naked in bed together—or anywhere else, for that matter. I undress behind the changing screen, and so does he. And when we go to bed, the lights are always out and we're always under the covers."

"Then how do you . . ."

Virginia held a hand up to stay Meg's next, obvious question. "You just pull your nightgown up to your hips

152

and so does he . . ." Now it was her turn to trail off in embarrassment.

Meg grimaced as she thought back on her fruitless early morning search of Geoff's room. As soon as he'd left, she'd flown up the stairs and searched every inch of the master suite—even the sitting room. But to her extreme dismay, she'd found nothing that even came close to resembling a nightshirt. She'd found his pants hung neatly in the armoire, and shirts, underwear, and shaving supplies in the bureau drawers, but that was all. She'd even checked his bed when she made it, but there had been no sign of any sleeping apparel mixed in with the sheets and blankets. He had either gone to bed with nothing on . . . or had slept in his clothes.

Meg had spent the rest of the morning trying to convince herself that maybe Geoff had simply forgotten to include a nightshirt when he'd packed to come to her house and that, probably, when he came back on Friday, he'd have one with him. But for some reason, she just couldn't quite make herself believe that. He'd remembered to pack a book to read. She'd seen it sitting on the night table. A man who would remember a book would certainly remember his nightshirt!

Turning back to her sister, who was now standing at the counter, slicing a loaf of bread in preparation for supper, she said softly, "I have one more problem to deal with that you've never had."

"What's that, sweetie?" Virginia asked, her knife poised in mid-air.

"Geoffrey doesn't want to have a real marriage with me. He and I agreed that our marriage would be in name only, and he hasn't shown any signs of wanting that to change. How am I going to convince him that I want him to . . ."

Virginia giggled and walked back to the table, handing Meg a piece of warm, fragrant bread. "You mean, how are you going to *seduce* him?" she whispered, bending down and breathing the scandalous word in Meg's ear.

"Oh, Ginny, don't call it that!"

"I'm sorry," Virginia relented. "I know how hard this whole ordeal has been for you. But I can assure you, this is the easy part. There are many ways a wife can show her husband that she'll accept his advances."

"Subtle ways?" Meg asked hopefully.

"Of course, subtle," Ginny responded, surprised Meg would ask. "Only one type of woman would go about it in an overt fashion—and those women usually aren't dealing with their husbands."

"So, what do I do?"

"Well, the most important thing is to keep a clean house."

Meg snorted with disbelief. "A clean house? What does that have to do with anything?"

Virginia smiled knowingly. "A clean house will always win your husband's approval, and an approving husband is an affectionate husband."

Meg looked at her sister dubiously, finding it hard to picture Geoff becoming amorous because there was no dust in the parlor.

"What else?"

"Good food served on time at a pretty table."

"You're joking!"

"No, I'm not. In fact, I have a book I should lend you that says exactly the same thing. It's called *Buckeye Bride*, and Lawrence's mother sent it to me from Ohio when we first got married. It's full of recipes and helpful hints for new brides. It explains how to make butter, how to do laundry properly, how to clean carpets, things like that. I'll

154

see if I can find it before you leave, and you can take it with you."

Meg fervently hoped that Virginia would forget about the book. The last thing she wanted to do was feel obligated to read some boring tome about how to get your bed sheets white. How to get your husband in between those sheets was what concerned her.

"Anyway," Virginia continued, warming to her subject, "this book states that the biggest reason that men stray from their wives is gastric distress, and it promises that a woman who's a good cook will find a contented and faithful husband sitting at her table every night."

Meg could tell that Virginia was absolutely serious about the veracity of this book's teachings, but still she couldn't contain her mirth. Clapping her hands over her mouth, she gave way to her amusement, finding it nearly impossible to sober even when Ginny glared at her in obvious offense.

"I'm sorry," Meg gasped, when she could finally speak again. "Really I am, but the thought of gastric distress being the major cause of marital infidelity is the funniest thing I've ever heard!" Again, she gave in to a fit of laughter.

"I'm only trying to be helpful," Ginny said coldly. "After all, you did ask."

"I know I did," Meg nodded, biting down hard on the inside of her lip. "And I'm not making fun of you."

"Make fun if you want," Ginny snapped, "but I've been happily married for ten years, and that book is responsible for a great deal of my success."

"I'm sure it is."

"I know you still don't believe me," Virginia accused, truly offended by Meg's patronizing attitude, "but I can tell you, little sister, that I have employed many of the book's

155

suggestions, and never once has *my* husband left on a Monday and said he's not coming back till Friday night!"

All traces of amusement fled from Meg's eyes. "I'm sorry, Meggie," Virginia said, instantly regretting her harsh words. "I didn't mean to say that. You know I'd never say anything to hurt your feelings. But don't laugh about the value of a clean house and a well-cooked meal. It has sweetened my husband's temper more than once."

Meg nodded, not doubting for a minute that prissy Lawrence Lombard could probably be coerced out of a bad mood by a sparkling privy. "I appreciate everything you've told me, Ginny," she said earnestly. "Really I do. Is there anything else I should know?"

"One last thing," Virginia smiled, reaching over to pick up the baby who'd begun fussing. "Always, *always* look pretty for your husband. All the good food in the world won't win his affection if you look like a sloven when he comes home at night. Tidy hair, a clean apron, and a welcoming smile are just as important as a perfectly cooked pot roast."

Virginia had finally said something about men that made sense to Meg, and she cringed inwardly. What must Geoffrey have thought of her when he saw her this morning in her bathrobe and bare feet? Lord, he probably wouldn't come home for a month!

"Thank you, dear," Meg said, rising from the table and giving her sister an affectionate hug. "You have helped me so much, I just can't tell you."

"Just a minute," Ginny said, handing the baby to Meg and turning toward a bank of cupboards over the sink. "Let me see if I can find that book."

"Oh, don't bother," Meg demurred, "I really do have to run. I'll get it next time."

"Okay," Virginia agreed, retrieving the baby. "I'll find

156

it tonight and have it ready for you next time I see you."

The two sisters sauntered toward the front door, pausing when they reached it to share one last hug.

"Thanks again," Meg said, stepping out on to the front porch.

"Anytime, sweetie," Ginny smiled, waving. "And, Meggie?"

"Yes?" Meg answered, turning back and looking at her expectantly.

"Good luck."

Chapter 14

"Mrs. Wellesley, your husband's here."

With a startled little gasp, Meg lifted her hand to her throat. "He is?" she croaked.

"Yeah," Hank nodded, puzzled by her reaction. "They're floatin' another big boom in today, and I guess he came down to talk to you about it."

Meg blushed, astutely guessing that the word was already out that Geoffrey had spent the previous night at the logging camp instead of at her house. "Tell him to come in," she smiled, determined not to let Hank see how much Geoff's unexpected arrival was disconcerting her.

Hank nodded and turned away. "Go on in, Mr. Wellesley," he called. "Your wife's waitin' on ya."

Her heart pounding in anticipation, Meg stood up, self-consciously smoothing her slim skirt along her hips.

"Hi, Meg."

Meg's breath caught in her throat as she turned to face her husband. "Good morning, Geoff," she returned. "How are you?"

"Fine," he nodded, his eyes sweeping the alluring sight of his wife in the form-fitting skirt. Her high-necked, starched white blouse was tucked neatly into the waistband, causing the garment to hug her full breasts. It was a long moment before Geoff finally dragged his eyes away from his appreciative perusal. Swallowing, he said, "We're bringing in a new load today."

"I know," Meg nodded, "Hank told me."

"Are you ready for it?"

"Yes. The load you brought in last week is all finished and ready to ship. In fact," she added, turning to run a finger down a ledger sheet on her desk, "in the past four days, we've cut . . ."

"It doesn't matter," Geoff interjected hurriedly. "I didn't come to get a board foot tally."

"Oh?" Meg said, looking up curiously from the ledger sheet. "Then what can I do for you?"

Geoff hesitated, having no answer to that question. He really had no reason for coming this morning, except that, for some reason even he couldn't explain, he'd wanted to see Meg. But now that he was here, she was acting as if they were nothing more than business associates, and her aloof demeanor made him feel like a tongue-tied kid.

Hell, last time I saw her she was standing barefoot in her night-gown, with her hair down, and now she's acting as if we don't even know each other.

"Well," he stammered, "as I said, I just figured that I'd, uh, check and make sure you can handle the new load before I bring it in."

Meg looked at him speculatively, not believing his lame excuse for a minute. But if he was lying to her, as he appeared to be, then why *was* he here?

"That was very considerate of you . . ." she answered pleasantly, her eyebrows rising as she looked over his shoulder and saw the boom arriving even as they spoke. *Check and see if we're ready for it, indeed!* "But it looks like it's already here."

159

Geoff whirled around, hot color creeping up his neck as he realized he'd been caught in his lie. "Guess the men were so anxious to get it started that they decided not to wait for me to give them the go-ahead," he muttered, his embarrassment obvious. "They must have just figured you'd be caught up by now."

Stepping out of Meg's office, he shielded his eyes against the bright June sunshine and started shouting orders at the men who were trying to corral the floating timber.

Meg stood in her office door, smiling with satisfaction. To think that she had the great Geoffrey Wellesley blushing like a schoolboy with his first flirtation! It was enormously satisfying after all the humiliations she'd endured in the last few weeks.

"Everything all right?" she asked, walking down the office steps to stand beside him.

"Yeah," he nodded, "they're bringing it in just fine."

"Your men always do a good—"

Her words were abruptly cut off by a shout from one of the lumberjacks standing precariously on top of the floating boom. "Hey, boss," the man yelled, grinning and waving his hat, "why don't you give your bride a little kiss?"

The man's rough suggestion was quickly embraced by the other men riding the huge float of logs. "Yeah! Come on, Geoff, let's see you kiss her!"

Geoff drew in a sharp breath. "Quit horsing around and get that boom in here," he yelled back, his voice brooking no further nonsense.

"Aw, come on!" the men shouted, "What's one little kiss? We just want you to show us how it's done!"

Geoff turned toward Meg, throwing her a beseeching look. "I'm sorry," he apologized, "but now that they've come up with this harebrained idea, they probably won't stop till we . . ."

"It's all right," Meg laughed merrily, caught up in the rough men's good-natured exuberance. "It's easier just to do it than argue with them about it."

With a grateful smile, Geoff turned her so that their profiles were in full view of the men on the boom and bent his head. Meg watched his whiskey-colored eyes close as his lips hovered above hers, then, with a little sigh, she closed her own.

The suggestive whoops and catcalls of the men seemed to fade into the distance as Geoff's mouth touched hers. He kissed her gently for a moment, then gathered her closer and placed a hand on the side of her face, his thumb stroking her soft skin as his fingers threaded into her hair.

Meg's lips softened and unconsciously parted, her every sense tingling as she felt the soft rush of Geoff's breath enter her mouth. Their embrace became more intimate as Geoff began to move his mouth seductively over hers, tracing his tongue along the inside of her lower lip.

Meg emitted a shocked little gasp at his boldness, but despite the fact that they were standing on her office steps in full sight of at least fifty gaping men, she didn't stop him.

Taking a step backward, he suddenly became aware of his men hooting and clapping. Loath to let them see how his wife's kiss had affected him, he quickly turned and executed a mocking bow for the cheering audience.

Meg turned crimson as the men became even more raucous, and clapping her hands over her cheeks, whirled around and fled back into her office.

Geoff clumped into the small room behind her. "Think that convinced them?"

"Convinced them?" she choked out, appalled by how her voice was shaking. "Convinced them of what?"

"Nothing," Geoff said quickly, cursing his wayward tongue.

"Well, you must have meant something," Meg argued, nervously shuffling the papers on her desk. "What are you trying to convince your men of?"

"I just took a ration of teasing last night, that's all."

Meg looked up at him in bewilderment. "What were they teasing you about?"

"For not going back to your house for the night," Geoff muttered, studying the floor as if he'd suddenly found something fascinating on the toe of his boot.

"What?"

Geoff looked up, frowning that she was obviously not going to let him off the hook. "For not going back to your house last night," he repeated loudly. "Look, it was nothing, so just forget it. I've got to go."

"Did your men think you *should* have come back to my house last night?" she pursued.

"Yeah. Now, I've really got to go. I'm testing the new flume today. I'll see you."

Meg nodded, unable to conceal the triumphant gleam in her eyes. Geoff's men obviously agreed that he should be spending his evenings with her instead of at his camp. "See you, Geoff."

He certainly did give a girl a lot to think about, Meg mused, toying with a pencil as she stared idly out the window of her office. She had a spectacular view of the river rolling slowly by, framed by a vista of snowcapped mountains, but Meg saw none of it. Her mind was entirely focused on the vision of Geoffrey Wellesley's lips as they'd hovered above hers just before that kiss.

That kiss . . .

Meg sighed dreamily as she indulged herself in sweet remembrance. What was it about the man's kisses that made her feel so . . . giddy? After all, she wasn't some giggling schoolgirl. She'd been kissed before . . . and by two different men! But as she thought back on those earlier experiences, Harvey Winston's and Robert McKnight's kisses had shown very little similarity to the way Geoff kissed, except, of course, for the fact that they had all placed their lips over hers.

But it was what Geoff did with his lips *after* pressing them to hers that made the difference. Where Harvey's and Robert's lips had been cool and dry, Geoff's were warm, soft, and slightly moist. Also, Harvey and Robert had kept their lips still while kissing her, but Geoff moved his, running them softly across her own and enticing her to play some sort of erotic game that was as frightening as it was thrilling.

Virginia had told her that Francine MacGregor had once confided that she detested it when Geoff kissed her because it made her feel naked. At the time, Meg had looked at her sister in bewilderment, not understanding how having a man touch his mouth to yours could make you feel like your clothes had suddenly disappeared. But now, having experienced Geoffrey Wellesley's kisses herself, she understood completely. Obviously she and Francine had experienced the same sensations from Geoff's caresses. The only difference was that Meg definitely did *not* hate it. Whereas Francine had found Geoff's intimacies unpleasant, Meg found them exciting—and just a little bit sinful.

"What does that say about you?" she asked herself wryly. Even Virginia, who was totally devoted to Lawrence, had intimated that the marriage bed and all that went on in it was the least pleasant aspect of her marriage. Ladies were supposed to tolerate a man's desires, not enjoy them! And the thought that the two times Geoff had kissed

163

her had made her yearn for something more . . . something she couldn't even define . . . frightened her even as it titillated.

Perhaps the most gratifying conclusion she reached as she pondered Geoff's kiss was the fact that he'd obviously been affected by it, too. She had felt his breath quicken, had felt him unconsciously press her closer to him as the caress had deepened. He wasn't immune to her any more than she was to him, and that thought was heartening in light of her planned seduction.

"But a kiss is only the beginning," she reminded herself. She had no doubt that if she put her mind to it, she could probably entice him into kissing her with very little resistance. But even though she had no experience with seduction, she was sure it took more than one kiss to raise a man's desires to the point that he'd want to bed her.

A little shiver ran down Meg's spine as those words repeated themselves in her mind. *Bed her* . . . She was actually going to have to get into his bed and *give* herself to him. And before she did that, she was going to have to figure out some way of tempting him enough that he wouldn't throw her out once she did.

Meg shook her head, convinced that she would never be able to go through with this mad plan. But she had to. It was the only way she'd be safe. She *had* to.

Geoff sat on the ground next to his grazing horse and stared off at his mountain. "You may own your own mountain, Wellesley, but if you don't quit kissing that little witch you married, pretty soon you're not going to own your own soul."

As it had a hundred times during the last hour, his mind drifted back to the kiss he'd shared with Meg that morning.

What the hell was it about her that excited him so much? He'd kissed scores of women, maybe even hundreds—from chaste pecks on the lips when he was fifteen and terrified, to full-blown erotic feasts with the girls at Lulu's, who'd begged him to stay even after his time was up.

So, what was it about *this* girl that made him feel like he was going to explode every time he touched her?

Francine hadn't made him feel that way—and he'd been in love with her, hadn't he? He was far from sure about how he felt toward Megan, but he sure as hell knew he wasn't in love with her! Not like he'd been with Francine.

Francine . . . Even after all this time, just the thought of her made his stomach knot. Almost without realizing it, he swung his gaze to the south. Far off in the distance in a rolling meadow at the base of his mountain stood the eerie skeleton of the house he'd started to build for her. He squeezed his eyes shut, blotting out the sight of the lonely, abandoned structure. He'd been so happy when he began building it . . . so excited for the life he planned to start in that house. A life of love and companionship and children and contented old age that he'd thought to share with the beautiful blond girl who'd ultimately betrayed him.

"I should tear the damn thing down," he growled to himself, opening his eyes and taking another look. The city council was right. It was an eyesore, and it should be destroyed. Destroyed . . . just as his dreams had been. "Damn her," he cursed. "Damn her for ruining everything."

But had she, really? Or had Francine actually *saved* him heartache by revealing her true character before the wedding? His brothers certainly seemed to think so—all of them. Miles, Stuart, Eric, even Seth had written him to tell him that despite how he felt at the moment, his broken engagement wasn't a tragedy. That in fact, the only real tragedy would have been a loveless marriage.

"So, here you are," Geoff muttered, picking a blade of coarse mountain grass and rolling it between his fingers, "six years later, trapped in a loveless—and *this time* sexless—marriage."

At least if he'd married Francine, he might have gotten some regular lovemaking out of the deal. But then, he remembered the last epithet she'd thrown at him that terrible night when they'd broken their betrothal. He grimaced, remembering her pretty face contorted into a mask of rage as she confessed that his "disgusting masculine urges" nauseated her.

Geoff's brow knitted in painful consternation. What was it about him that women of good quality found so objectionable? Whores certainly liked him well enough, but that probably didn't count. Whores liked any man with the right amount of coin. But still, more than one of the girls at Lulu's had told him that he was different from other customers . . . that he was a real gentleman. So, why didn't nice women seem to agree? *Was* he crude and vulgar in his romantic advances? Obviously, Francine had thought so, and now Meg had made him agree to a marriage in name only, even when she was the one who had initiated the union.

It was a question that had nagged at him for a long time. In his mind, he didn't see that he was far different from his six brothers—and they were all married to women who seemed to be crazy about them.

Well, *almost* all of them, he corrected. Adam wasn't, but then, he was still in law school back East and hadn't really had time to think about marriage yet.

But even Eric was married. Shy, uncommunicative, artistic Eric, whose dreamy personality had always bewildered his brothers—almost as much as the immense size of his masculine attributes had always awed them.

"The Hose Man." Geoff smiled, thinking fondly of his older brother even as he voiced aloud his outrageous nickname. Eric might have bought a wife through a mail-order bride advertisement, but Kirsten had quickly fallen in love with him, and after four years of marriage, they already had three children.

Geoff sighed, thinking enviously about his brothers' successful alliances and ruing his own bad luck. He supposed he really should send them telegrams and let them know that he'd married. They would all, no doubt, be delighted to hear his news.

"Delighted," Geoff mused. Delighted would probably mean that they'd want him to take Meg for a visit, or worse yet, pack up their wives and come to visit him. Then what would he do? How would he explain his situation to Stuart, who was so in love with his wife, Claire, that he couldn't even say her name without getting pie-eyed? Or Nathan, who nearly smacked his lips with anticipation every time anyone even mentioned his wife, Elyse? They'd never understand why he'd allowed himself to be blackmailed into a passionless marriage. He didn't understand it himself.

Lying back in the grass, Geoff stared up at a bank of clouds that was gathering to the west. There would be rain tonight, but that was hardly unusual. It rained almost every night, although this spring had been considerably dryer than normal.

His mind drifted back to Megan. Why *had* he married her? In the final analysis, he hadn't really had to. Although it would have been a financial drain if she had carried out her threat and banned him from cutting his timber, with his enormous resources he could have borne the loss and hardly even noticed it. So why hadn't he just told her to go to hell and take her sawmill with her?

For the first time since agreeing to the marriage, Geoff allowed himself to ponder this question. Of course, there was the obvious answer that by wedding Meg, he was safe from all the other marriage-minded women in Wellesley. But he'd managed to effectively hold them at bay for years, and he could have continued to do so. In his heart of hearts, he knew that wasn't the real reason he'd allowed himself to be coerced.

So, why?

Because she makes you feel like you can't swallow every time you look at her, that's why.

Geoff frowned at his own admission, wishing that Meg didn't have the effect on him that she did. But there was no denying that he wanted her. Every time he closed his eyes, the vision of her bare feet and long, slim legs coming down the stairs rose to haunt him.

But what difference did his attraction to her make when she had made it very clear that she had no interest in him? Of course, he *could* insist . . .

His eyebrows rose in speculation as he thought about that possibility. After all, Meg was his wife, and he was certainly within his legal rights to claim conjugal privilege . . . Maybe bedding her was exactly what he needed to do to get her out of his system. But what would her reaction be if he demanded she submit to him?

Good God, man, you're as bad as Farnsworth. She married you so she wouldn't be forced to bed a man she didn't care about, and here you are, contemplating exactly the same fate for her.

Still, if Meg was half as sensual as he suspected she was, it might be worth risking her ire to have one night with her.

Geoff snorted, disgusted by his own lusty thoughts. "Forget it, Wellesley," he muttered. "Just leave things the way they are and everyone will be better off."

He rose, dusting off the seat of his pants and picking up his horse's trailing reins. Mounting, he guided the animal back on to the rutted path leading to his camp.

Maybe he'd drop over at Meg's tonight, just to prove to himself that he could spend an evening with her without becoming sexually aroused. Besides, he liked her cooking, and if he got there at suppertime, maybe she'd have enough prepared that they could eat together.

The thought that tonight was the night he'd planned to go to Lulu's flitted through his mind, but he cast it aside. He really didn't feel like riding all the way to Oregon City for just one night. Better to wait until he could spare a couple of days. Then he'd go and make a real holiday of it.

Satisfied with that decision, he kicked his horse into a canter. He had a lot of work to get done today, and he had to leave time to take a bath and shave. After all, even though he planned on paying his wife nothing more than a casual call, he didn't want to arrive on her doorstep smelling like a mule.

Chapter 15

Meg stood in the center of the kitchen and looked around, beaming with satisfaction. Even Ginny wouldn't be able to fault the shining cleanliness of the room. She had spent most of yesterday and all afternoon today dusting, sweeping, and scouring the house until the old rooms fairly gleamed from her efforts.

She had left the massive stove until last, knowing that it was the most odious task and dreading having to actually tackle it. But now, even though she was covered with a thick layer of soot and grime, the stove sparkled.

Walking over to the sink, Meg glanced at her reflection in the spotless windowpane, smiling at the black smudges on her cheeks and across her forehead.

"You look like a chimney sweep," she giggled, then turned to throw a pail of dirty wash water out the back door. Putting the empty pail under the shelf in the pantry, she returned to the sink, pumping enough water to scrub the stove black off her hands and arms. Then she gave the big room one last approving glance and headed for the staircase, pulling off the dirty dust cap she was wearing.

She was just traversing the front hall when she heard a knock at the door. "Now, who could that be at this hour?"

she grumbled, reluctant to answer the summons in her current filthy state. Figuring, however, that it must be Virginia paying an unexpected late-afternoon call, she walked over to the door, eager to show her sister the results of her travails.

Taking a peek through the sheer lace curtains which covered the oval window, she gasped in dismay.

It wasn't Virginia. It was Geoff.

She took a quick step backward, trying to determine whether Geoff had already seen her or if she could possibly get away with pretending she wasn't home. "I have the worst luck!" she fumed. "I spend two days scrubbing this house because Ginny tells me it will impress him and now here he is, with me looking like I've been down in a coal mine. That should impress him for sure!"

"Meg? Open the door. It's me, Geoff." His voice filtered through the door and Meg groaned, knowing he had seen her.

"Just a minute," she called, picking up the hem of her apron and scrubbing furiously at her dirty face. Unfortunately, this exercise did little except to smear the smudges of stove black, making her face look even dirtier. Heedless of this fact, she quickly smoothed the apron back over her dress, patted her straggling hair, and with as much dignity as she could muster, opened the door.

Geoff stared at her for a moment, too stunned to speak. Then he burst out laughing. "What in the hell have you been doing?"

"Why do you ask that?" she asked haughtily.

Stepping into the foyer, Geoff laid his hat aside and took her by the shoulders, steering her toward the oval mirror. "That's why," he grinned as she gazed in horror at the wide streaks of black painting her cheeks. "Are you going out on the warpath?"

Meg thought she might cry. Although she'd worried that she might disgrace herself trying to carry out her planned seduction of her reluctant husband, even she had never dreamed of a situation as humiliating as the one she found herself in now.

"No," she mumbled. "I'm not going out on the warpath. I was cleaning the stove, and I *didn't* expect company."

Geoff ignored her pointed reproach. "Cleaning the stove? At six o'clock in the evening?"

"Well, yes," Meg answered defiantly. "I didn't get started till after I got home from the mill, and it took longer than I expected."

"But why were you cleaning it? Did you spill something on it?"

"No! It just needed cleaning. Stoves do now and then, you know."

Geoff shrugged. "I always just figure that whatever is on there will eventually burn off."

Meg made a face that plainly told him what she thought of that theory.

"Personally," he continued good-naturedly, "I think women spend far too much time cleaning and scrubbing. There are so many other ways to spend time that are a hell of a lot more fun than cleaning stoves or scrubbing floors."

Good Lord, just what other ways did he mean? "Perhaps you're right, but a clean house is a happy house." *There, that platitude should make Virginia proud.*

Geoff looked at her like she'd just sprouted a second head. "Who the hell told you that?"

"No one told me," Meg retorted, suddenly feeling very foolish. "It's just something that . . . that every woman knows. Just like the fact that good marriages are the result of good cooking."

"And good sex," Geoff added. Instantly, he wished the

172

floor would open up and swallow him. *What in hell had he been thinking to say such a thing in front of her?*

A long, uncomfortable silence fell as both of them wondered what they could possibly say to smooth over Geoff's outrageous gaffe. Finally Meg cleared her throat and in as nonchalant a tone as she could muster, said, "Why are you here? I thought I wouldn't see you again until Friday."

"Well," he hedged, realizing for the second time that day that he had no excuse for his unexpected appearance. "I was in town anyway, and I just thought I'd drop over and see how you're doing."

Meg looked at him in bewilderment. "I'm doing fine," she answered. "What are you doing in town?"

"Oh, ah, well, I had to pick up some supplies."

"At six o'clock at night?" Meg asked, arching a disbelieving brow as she parroted his words. .

"Yeah, um, I was out of . . . flour."

"I see," she answered, her mind working furiously as she tried to determine what had really precipitated this unexpected visit from her erstwhile husband. "I wish I could offer you some supper, but as you can see," she threw her arms out in a gesture that encompassed her disheveled state, "I'm not cooking this evening. I haven't even restoked the stove since I cleaned it."

"That's okay. Thanks anyway," Geoff nodded, surprised at how disappointed he was that they wouldn't be having supper together after all. "Now that I know that everything's . . . okay with you, I guess I'll just be on my way."

"Everything's fine," Meg smiled. "I'm just sorry that I couldn't offer you something to eat."

"Don't fret about it. I have my flour now, so I can make some biscuits or something when I get back to camp."

Meg looked at him sympathetically. Was it possible that he had stopped by hoping for a meal? And wouldn't it be just her luck that that would be exactly what he was looking for on the one night she hadn't cooked? "Geoff," she said hurriedly as he walked toward the door, "do you want me to fix you a sandwich or something?"

"No," he demurred, picking up his hat and putting it on. *Lord, did the woman think he was a charity case, coming here looking for a handout?* "Just go back to your cleaning . . . or whatever it is you were planning to do now. I'll see you Friday."

"All right," Meg nodded, opening the door. "About seven?"

"Yeah. About seven."

With a farewell nod, Geoff ducked out the door and hurried down the sidewalk.

"Geoff?"

"Yeah?" he answered, turning back.

"Why don't you buy a new hat?"

"A new hat?" he repeated, looking up at the misshapen brim of the one he was wearing. "Why?"

"Because that one is a wreck."

"Naw," he grinned. "It's not a wreck. It's just broken in properly. Takes a long time to get a hat to fit as comfortably as this one does."

"It's a wreck," Meg repeated firmly.

"Do you really think so?" Reaching up, he plucked the disreputable hat off his head and stared at it fondly.

"Absolutely."

"Well, I'll think about it."

"You do that," Meg smiled, turning away to reenter the house.

"Hey, Meg?"

"Yes?"

"See you Friday."

"Right. Friday."

"Oh, and Meg?"

174

"Yes?"

"Take a bath."

Shooting him a cheeky look over her shoulder, she replied, "You buy a new hat and I'll take a bath. How about that?"

"It's a deal," Geoff grinned. He turned and headed off down the street, leaving his soot begrimed wife smiling after him.

Meg lowered herself into the big brass tub and laid her head back along its rim. Plucking a soft cloth and a bar of rose-scented soap from the small table next to her, she thoughtfully began working up a lather. "Well, Ginny," she muttered to the empty kitchen, "guess not every man is impressed with a clean house."

Oh, *why* had Geoff shown up tonight? She wanted so much to impress him. No, she corrected. *Needed* to impress him. Lord, but didn't she have the worst luck! The one night he decides to appear uninvited, and she answers the door, looking like Cinderella in the old children's story. All she'd needed were a few ashes clinging to the end of her nose to make the picture complete.

Meg sighed, stretching the tired muscles in her shoulders. She couldn't remember when she'd been so fatigued—and all for nothing. Her cleaning marathon of the last few days had obviously gone unappreciated by her husband.

He doesn't care about an immaculate house. He wants a good meal, some company while he eats it and, afterward, some good . . .

Meg's thoughts trailed off. She couldn't voice the word Geoff had so casually spoken, even to herself. So how was she supposed to seduce the man?

Groaning with frustration, she raised an arm and

scrubbed energetically at a smear of soot that had caked in the bend of her elbow. What did she know about how a woman went about tempting a man? Nothing except that, obviously, Virginia's suggestions weren't going to work. But if Ginny couldn't help her, who could? "No one," she said aloud, plunging the cloth into the sudsy water. "You don't know a single soul in this whole town who can tell you what to do. You're just going to have to figure it out yourself."

If *only* she hadn't made him sign that agreement stating that their marriage would be in name only, then she could have just gone to him, explained her continued fears about Peter Farnsworth and asked for his cooperation. But since it was she who had insisted on the agreement, she couldn't do that. Somehow, their bedding just had to . . . happen. At least, that's what Geoff had to think.

Idly, Meg soaped her neck and chest, then dipped the cloth under the water and raised it again to rinse. She looked down.

Breasts. Men liked breasts. At least, she'd always been told that a lady never displayed them because they were a wicked temptation—even to the most God-fearing of gentlemen.

Meg stared at the plump, round globes. What was it about this particular part of the female anatomy that men found so alluring? For her part, she'd always considered them a nuisance, especially full, lush ones like hers. They necessitated the altering of standard dress patterns, they made her uncomfortably hot in the summer, when good taste still dictated that they be corsetted and concealed, and about once a month, they became so painfully tender that she couldn't even comfortably sleep on her stomach. So, what was so great about them?

She had no idea, but she did know that on several

occasions, she had caught Geoff surreptitiously looking at hers. It must be some male peculiarity, she decided. But possibly, it was a peculiarity she could use to her advantage. She had heard tales that the saloon girls down on Riley Street wore shockingly low-cut dresses just to show off their breasts in hopes of generous tips. Of course, she'd never seen a saloon girl's attire close up since the ladies of Wellesley would never venture near Riley Street, but their scandalous dress was often the topic of whispered discussions among the town's matrons.

"If only I could see one of those dresses, maybe I could alter one of mine to look more like it. I bet that would attract him . . ."

But how? She couldn't very well just walk into a saloon and ask one of the soiled doves if she could examine her dress!

Meg cocked her head, her washcloth dangling forgotten from her hand. Surely there must be *some* way she could get a look at one of them. Perhaps she could sneak downtown after dark one night and peek through a saloon window. It would take only a second, and if she was very careful, she could surely get away with it without being seen.

With a decisive nod, Meg dropped the cloth into the rapidly cooling water and stood up, cupping water in her hands to rinse the soap off her legs. That was exactly what she would do. Tomorrow night. She'd dress all in black and make sure she stayed in the shadows. In fact, she could wear her mourning bonnet with the black veil. That way, even if she was seen, no one would be able to tell who she was.

She stepped out of the tub, well pleased with her plan. Picking up a linen towel, she dried herself, then walked over to her pier glass. Holding the towel against her breasts, she lowered the edge until a half-inch of cleavage was visible. Right there, she decided, gazing at the expanse of bare, swelling flesh. Right there is where the top of the bodice should be. Low enough to be tempting but, high enough not to be *too* obvious.

"Geoffrey Wellesley," she giggled, flinging the towel away and reaching for her nightrail. "You're not even going to know what hit you."

Like a robber about to perpetrate a crime, Meg crept along the side wall of Rhonda's Place, the most notorious of all of Wellesley's notorious saloons. She was sure no one could see her, plastered as she was against the side of the building, but still she paused and held her breath when she heard the heavy clump of boots coming down the boardwalk.

"Come on, Geoff, let's just stop at Rhonda's for a quick one before we go back to camp."

Meg gasped. Geoff! My God, could her luck really be so terrible that she was going to run into her husband? How would she *ever* explain why she was skulking around the alley next to Rhonda's?

Of course, there might well be more than one "Geoff" in Wellesley. Perhaps the man being spoken to was not her husband, but just some man with the same name. The next voice she heard immediately dashed that hope.

"Okay, but just one. You know I don't like this saloon, and besides, it's late and I want to start on that virgin stand first thing in the morning."

It *was* him, Meg thought with a little squeak of panic. But with her luck, she should have known it would be. Please don't let him look this way, she prayed, squeezing her eyes shut. *Please!*

For a change, luck was with her, and the two men passed

her hiding spot without a glance. Meg slumped against the wall in profound relief when she heard the noisy squeak and bang of unoiled batwing doors slapping together.

"He didn't see you," she whispered. "You can still get out of here." But even as she mouthed the words, something stopped her. If it would aid her cause just to see what saloon girls wore, wouldn't it be even more advantageous to see how they treated Geoff . . . and how he reacted?

She took a step away from the building and looked both left and right, hoping to see a side window. There was none. "I can't peek through the front window," she moaned. "He's sure to see me." Despite her concealing veil, she was still unwilling to take the risk that Geoff might recognize her.

Quietly, she walked around the back of the shabby building and rounded the corner to the other side. To her delight, she spied a small window set into this side of the building. "Perfect," she breathed.

Tiptoeing up to the dirty glass, she peeked inside. The image was hazy, due to the veil in front of her face and the thick layer of dirt on the window, but still, as she gazed into the crowded, smoky room, she could see Geoff and his foreman, Ned, sitting at a table. With a smile of triumph, she angled herself to the right of the window, where she had an unrestricted view.

Several girls passed by the window, carrying trays of beer mugs and bottles of whiskey. All of them were dressed in similar clothing; knee-length dresses with full skirts and deeply scooped necklines that displayed an indecent amount of cleavage. The dresses were mostly red, although one brunette was clad in deep purple trimmed with black lace. Even with her blurred vision, Meg could tell that the dresses were made of cheap materials—mostly imitation satin.

Her gaze was drawn over to a particularly buxom blonde who had obviously spotted Geoffrey and was making a beeline for his table. The girl's face was coated with makeup, her smiling lips a wide red slash against her heavily powdered white cheeks. Rings of kohl circled her eyes, giving her the appearance of a happy raccoon.

Why would anyone want to make herself up like that? Meg wondered. *Does she actually think that's attractive? More important, does he?*

By now, the girl had nearly reached Geoff's table, her sashaying walk speaking volumes to the man who looked up and smiled at her.

He must think she's pretty, Meg gasped, appalled that her husband would show such a lack of taste. *Just look at that smile. He's never smiled at me like that!*

The blonde bent over, her large breasts nearly spilling out of her daring décolletage. Meg quickly looked at Geoff to see his reaction, but for the moment at least, he had turned away, seeming to be more interested in something his companion was saying than in the girl's suggestive pose. Finally, he looked back at the girl and said something to her. She straightened, her look of disappointment so obvious that Meg snickered with satisfaction. After conversing briefly with the other man, she turned and headed back for the bar.

Meg's eyes shifted over to her husband, who was now leaning back in his chair and pulling a cigarette out of his pocket. Before he could even lift it to his mouth, another saloon girl suddenly appeared, swinging around the back of his chair and planting herself in his lap. The girl held up a match, expertly flicking it to life with her fingernail.

Geoff turned toward the girl sprawled on top of him, preventing Meg from seeing his frown of annoyance at the woman's boldness. From her vantage point, all she saw was his head dip as he touched the tobacco to the match, then raise again as he took a deep drag. The girl shook out the match and leaned provocatively toward him, saying something and ruffling his hair. Geoff nodded and smiled.

"Well," Meg snapped, *"now* you know the kind of woman he likes."

With a contemptuous snort, she whirled away from the window and stomped around the back of the building. Stalking off down the street toward her house, she jerked her shawl more tightly around her, furious at the jolt of jealousy she'd felt when she'd seen the saloon girl throw herself into Geoff's lap.

"I could never do that. Never! A modestly low-cut dress, maybe, but I could never wrap myself around him like that! If that's what tempts him, then I'll just take my chances with Peter Farnsworth!"

But even as she voiced the hated man's name, a shudder ran through her. She slowed her agitated pace, her expression behind the concealing veil becoming thoughtful.

You'd better think about this. You're either going to have to get into Geoffrey Wellesley's bed now, or face the possibility of having to get into Peter Farnsworth's later.

Meg pushed through the gate at her front yard and trudged up the sidewalk, heaving a long, resigned sigh. She was right back where she'd started. She'd never succumb to Peter. She'd die first. And the only way to prevent that eventuality was to get herself with child by Geoffrey Wellesley. And if that took acting like a common trollop, then so be it. She had to do what she had to do.

Chapter 16

It was Friday afternoon and Meg stood in front of the pier glass in her bedroom, assessing her reflection and frowning.

She had spent the better part of the last two days ripping apart and redesigning a midnight-blue watered-silk dress that her father had given her for her birthday two years before. The previously high-necked garment now clung provocatively to her shoulders, its new, scooped neckline revealing a far greater expanse of flesh than she had anticipated. A line of cleavage at least two inches long was visible, and the creamy skin of her throat and shoulders was completely bared.

"It's too low," she fretted aloud. "He's going to think I look like a strumpet."

You might as well look the part, a little voice deep inside her niggled. After all, what you're planning for tonight is a strumpet's plan, isn't it?

Meg bit her lower lip and gave the revealing bodice a hard tug upward. How was she going to do what had to be done this evening? She knew her entire future hinged on tonight's performance, but if she was this embarrassed just gazing at herself in the mirror, how would she ever find the nerve to put her mad plan into action?

"You'll do it," she told herself firmly, giving her carefully arranged corkscrew curls a vehement shake. "You have to, so you will."

Nervously, she raised a hand and pressed it firmly against the swelling upper curves of her breasts, trying to push the ripe flesh down into the bodice. But she hadn't left enough material to contain the full, lush globes, and her efforts were for naught.

"Just don't take a deep breath," she reminded herself, glancing in trepidation at the clock on her night stand.

Six-fifty-five. He would probably be here any minute. For the first time since she'd known him, Meg prayed that Geoff would exercise his usual bad habit of being late. But even as this feeble hope flitted through her mind, she heard the front door knocker being pounded against its brass plate.

"Lord save me, he's here!" she gasped, unconsciously dragging in a huge draught of air. She felt her breasts swell as her lungs expanded and quickly looked down, appalled to see that her startled gasp had accomplished exactly what she'd feared. Her breasts had lifted to the point that the dusky tops of her nipples were very nearly visible above the edge of the bodice. "Don't take a deep breath," she whispered breathlessly. "Don't take a deep breath! And, for heaven's sake, *whatever* you do, don't bend over!"

Meg descended the staircase, hoping desperately that her wobbly legs wouldn't give out before she reached the foyer. She paused for a moment, then, with a last plea for courage, pulled open the door.

"Good evening, Geoff," she smiled, praying that the darkness would conceal her trembling lips.

"Hello, Meg. How do you like my . . ." His eyes dropped to her chest. ". . . New hat."

"Oh, did you buy a new hat?" she asked weakly.

183

"Yeah," he responded, suddenly remembering himself and dragging his eyes back up to her face. "Thought I'd take your suggestion."

"Well, come in and let's have a look at it."

"It's a Stetson," he said numbly.

"Really . . . I've always heard they're the best."

Taking a quick step backward, Meg swung the door wider and waited for Geoff to enter the house. A long moment passed as he continued to stand on the porch, crushing the brim of his new hat in a white-knuckled grip.

"Are you all right?" she finally asked.

"What? Oh, yeah, I'm fine." He still didn't make any move to enter the house, but instead remained standing where he was, his eyes fixed on some point just past her shoulder.

"Don't you want to come in?"

"Well, ah, sure." With a smile that Meg could have sworn held a trace of embarrassment, Geoff stepped into the foyer.

"Let me take your hat."

He held it out to her and as she turned away to lay it on the hall table, his eyes again glued themselves to her cleavage. *Where has she been hiding those all this time*, he wondered irreverently.

Last time he'd seen her, she'd looked like a chambermaid, and tonight here she was, dressed like a courtesan! Christ, the momentary peek he'd had of her bare legs had been enough to give him an erection that had lasted a week. How in the hell was he going to control himself now that she'd decided to display this . . . feast?

"It's really beautiful, Geoff."

"What is?" he asked dumbly. *Quit staring!*

"Your hat," she smiled. "Your new hat."

"Oh, yeah. It's not as comfortable as my old one, though."

"You probably just need to wear it for a while."

"Right."

Their inane conversation petered out, and despite his good intentions, Geoff's eyes once again drifted downward.

Seeing the path his gaze was taking, Meg nervously clapped a hand over her chest and said, "Well, we certainly don't have to stand here in the foyer. Let's go in and sit down. Supper is almost ready, so I hope you're hungry."

"I am. Starved, in fact." *And if you only knew for what, you'd run up those stairs and lock yourself in your bedroom.*

They walked into the parlor and perched stiffly on the edge of the settee.

"So," Geoff ventured, "did you have a good week?"

"Yes. It was busy, though, what with your load and a big one from the Santana Company."

Geoff nodded. "Mine was busy, too. We broke into a new stand up toward the northeast point. Is that a new dress?"

Meg blinked in surprise at the unexpected change in subject and a wave of color washed over her cheeks. "No," she said carefully, "I've had it for a couple of years."

A couple of years! If she'd had it that long, she must have worn it before. But where? And with whom? He was certain that if she'd worn it out in public, he'd have heard about it from someone. Probably from everyone.

"It . . . looks nice on you," he stammered. Turning away as if to look at something outside the front window, he bit down hard on his lower lip. *Settle down, for God's sake! You're squirming around like a kid who's never seen a bosom before.* Why hadn't he gone to Lulu's this week? If he had, maybe he wouldn't be acting like a fifteen-year-old on his first date.

185

"Thank you," Meg murmured. "I think supper should be ready by now. Shall we go into the dining room?"

"Absolutely," Geoff agreed, nearly jumping off the settee, "let's eat."

They walked into the dining room and Geoff sat down, while Meg continued on to the kitchen. As the door swung closed behind her, she gripped the edge of the sink and let out a long, shaky breath.

This wasn't going to work. Geoff wasn't attracted, he was merely embarrassed by her indecent display.

"You have to try harder," she told herself firmly. "After supper, ask him if he wants a cigarette and when he says yes, do what you saw the saloon girl do." For the past two days, she'd been practicing how to light a match with her nail. She'd nearly burned her thumb off in the process, but finally, this morning, she'd gotten the hang of it and had successfully lit three matches in a row.

"Matches," she muttered. "Get a match so you're ready." Hurrying over to the stove, she pulled a match out of the box and stuffed it into her scanty bodice. She took several deep, calming breaths, then again shoved her straining breasts back into the dress. Picking up the plates of food, she took a last glance at her reflection in the kitchen window, and with a tremulous sigh, walked back into the dining room.

"Here we are," she said, trying hard to force a note of gaiety into her voice. "I hope you like pork roast."

"I do," Geoff nodded. He'd spent the few moments Meg had been in the kitchen frantically trying to adjust his persistent erection into a more modest position, then had drunk an entire glass of cold water in an attempt to calm himself. He'd considered pouring the water *over* his erection, knowing that would kill it, at least for a while, but had abandoned the idea when he realized he'd never be able to

186

come up with a discreet explanation for having wet trousers.

Meg seated herself and started to daintily pick at the food in front of her, far too tense to enjoy her meal.

Geoff was suffering much the same fate. Meg had set her place directly across from him, and every time he looked up, his eyes were immediately drawn to the swell of femininity she was so overtly displaying.

She has the most beautiful breasts I've ever seen, he mused, working hard to swallow a tiny bite of meat. *But she needs a necklace to set off that gorgeous skin. An emerald solitaire would be perfect.*

Meg gave up the pretense of eating and pushed her plate away.

"Aren't you hungry?" Geoff asked.

"Aren't you?" she returned, gesturing to his nearly untouched plate.

"Guess not. It's real good, though," he added quickly. "Maybe I'll have the rest for breakfast tomorrow or something."

"Would you . . ." Meg swallowed. "Would you like to smoke a cigarette?"

Geoff looked at her curiously. He didn't even realize she knew he smoked. "Yeah, as a matter of fact, I would, but why don't we go out on the porch, so I don't stink up your house?"

"No!" Meg said quickly. *Good God, she couldn't very well jump into his lap out on the front porch!*

Geoff raised a questioning brow.

"I mean, I think it's starting to rain."

"Is it?" he asked, turning around in his chair and looking out the window. "Doesn't look like it to me. The window isn't wet."

"Oh, just go ahead and have it in here," she said, a note of desperation creeping into her voice.

"Whatever," Geoff shrugged. Reaching into his pocket, he began fishing around for a cigarette.

Okay, this is it! Leaping out of her chair, Meg flew around the table.

"What the hell?" Geoff exploded, his breath coming out in a loud whoosh as all one hundred and ten pounds of his wife landed on his stomach. "Megan, what are you doing?"

"I thought I'd light your cigarette for you," she gasped, her voice breathless with fear and excitement.

Geoff's eyes widened in astonishment and then nearly bulged out of his head as she plunged her hand down the front of her bodice and extracted the match. With a smile that she hoped was properly seductive, she held the match in front of his face and snapped its head against her thumb-nail. Nothing happened. She giggled nervously and tried again. Still the match remained unlit.

"Megan," Geoff said, shifting beneath her as he tried to extricate her knee from his groin.

"Now, just wait a minute. I can do this. I know I can."

Dropping the forced smile, she pressed her lips together in an expression of ferocious determination and tried again. This time the match flared to life with a loud hiss. "There!" she crowed triumphantly, waving the match precariously close to Geoff's nose.

"Hold it still, for God's sake!" Grabbing her hand to steady it before she set them both on fire, he touched the flame to his cigarette. Taking a quick puff to ignite the tobacco, he blew the match out. "Thanks."

"You're welcome," she answered, distraught that her voice came out in a terrified squeak instead of the seductive purr she was going for. Trying desperately to appear as though she sat in men's laps every day, she tossed the spent

188

match on to the table and wrapped her arm around his shoulders. "So, Geoffrey, how is everything?"

Geoff's eyes narrowed as he tried to figure out what was behind Meg's outlandish behavior. He felt her wind her fingers into the hair at the nape of his neck and give his head a hard shake as goose bumps skittered down his spine. "Megan," he said softly as she bent her head to lay it on his shoulder. "Megan!"

Meg raised her head and looked at him adoringly. "Yes, Geoff?"

"What's going on here . . . and quit batting your eyes at me. It's not working."

"Whatever do you mean?" she simpered, summoning every bit of willpower she had not to jump off his lap and run.

"I mean, what is this nonsense all about?"

"What nonsense?" She blinked flirtatiously.

"Okay, enough is enough." Scooping one arm under her legs and the other around her shoulders, he lifted her off his lap and stood up. "You want something from me, and I want to know what it is."

"I don't know what you're talking about," she protested innocently. "I'm just acting like a wife."

"You're not acting like anybody's wife I know," Geoff snorted. "And anyway, you're not really my wife. Not that way, at least."

Meg's composure crumpled. "That's the problem," she whispered. *"You* know I'm not really your wife, *I* know I'm not really your wife, and pretty soon, George Farnsworth is going to know it, too."

"Oh . . ." Geoff murmured, the truth finally dawning on him. "So, that's what this is all about."

Meg nodded miserably.

"Come in here and sit down," he said gently, taking her

by the hand and leading her back into the parlor. "Now, tell me what's going on. Has George Farnsworth been threatening you?"

To her horror, tears sprang to Meg's eyes. "No, but don't you see? He will if I don't have a baby."

"A baby!"

"Yes. It's the only way he's going to accept our marriage as real. I have to have a baby." Meg looked down, unable to meet Geoff's eyes, but what she saw horrified her even more than their current discussion. Sometime, during her attempted seduction, she must have taken the dreaded deep breath, because her breasts looked like they might, with the slightest provocation, pop right out of the tight bodice. Quickly, she turned away and yanked the bodice up, praying that Geoff hadn't noticed.

He had, of course, but he was trying hard to do the gentlemanly thing and ignore it.

"Having a baby isn't a good idea, Meg. It would just make everything more complicated."

"No, it wouldn't," she argued, turning back toward him. "Things wouldn't have to change between us at all. I'll raise the baby by myself. All you have to do is . . ."

"Provide stud service?" Geoff asked coldly.

"Don't be so crude."

"Crude! Who's being crude? All evening, you've been displaying your more than ample charms to me, climbing into my lap, draping yourself all over me, and then admitting that you want me to give you a baby, and I'm being crude? I beg to differ, Miss Taylor."

"The name is Mrs. Wellesley, if you don't mind!" Meg shot back.

Geoff blew out a long breath and slumped back on the settee. He didn't want to be reminded that she was his wife. What he wanted was to argue against this insane idea. To rail against her logic and tell her she was crazy. But he couldn't—because she was right. Eventually, if Meg didn't turn up pregnant, George Farnsworth was going to find grounds to question their marriage. Even if they could discreetly spread the rumor that she was having trouble getting with child, people were bound to be skeptical—especially considering her sister's prowess at begetting children. And if the truth be known, it didn't sit well with him to have people whisper that maybe *he* wasn't up to the task.

But a baby! A baby was the tie that bound people together for life. Once children were involved, the strings of marriage became so intertwined that there was no way ever to untangle them.

Would that really be so terrible? Even though he'd been coerced into the marriage, Geoff had never intended to divorce Meg, so would it really harm anything if they were bound together by a child? And he wanted a family so badly . . .

Pondering this, he looked around the shabby parlor, with its worn furniture and threadbare carpet. Just this week, he'd retained the services of one of those new interior decorating firms that had sprung up in Portland after the war. He'd intended to tell Meg tonight that Mr. Benjamin B. Spoffard would be arriving soon to begin talking about plans for new paint, wallpaper, carpets, and furniture. Would it be so difficult to add a nursery to those plans?

Glancing over at his pretty wife with her tear-glazed eyes and outrageous floozy's dress, Geoff suddenly realized what an important part of his life she'd become in the past few weeks. There was something about her that made him want to take care of her, protect her, make her smile. And above all, he wanted to remove the fear that she had for that goddamned George Farnsworth. Suddenly, everything seemed very clear. A child would accomplish it all.

191

"Come on," he said softly, reaching over and taking one of her icy hands.

"Where are we going?"

"Upstairs."

A startled little breath caught in Meg's throat. "You mean we're going to . . . right now?"

Geoff chuckled. "You want a baby, don't you?"

"Yes . . ."

"Well, this is the only way I know how to get the job done."

Meg drew a deep, shuddering breath, heedless of the fact that again her breasts threatened to burst their confines. "All right," she said decisively, standing up. "Let's get it over with."

Geoff's quickly rising passions flagged like someone had thrown a bucket of ice water on him. "For God's sake, Meg, you sound like you're taking the last walk to the guillotine!"

"Do I?" she tittered nervously, pulling her hand out of his. "I'm sorry, I don't mean to." In vain, she tried to smile.

Oh, this is great, Geoff thought irritably. He had no experience at all with nervous virgins and didn't have the slightest idea what to say to wipe that look of impending doom off her face.

"Tell you what," he suggested. "Why don't you go upstairs and . . . get ready. I'll lock up down here and join you in a few minutes."

Mutely, Meg nodded, then turned on her heel and fled.

Geoff stood in the parlor and watched her terrified flight up the stairs. What the hell was wrong with her? Here he was, willing to give the girl what she wanted, and she suddenly looked like a rabbit caught in a hunter's snare.

What does she think I'm going to do, ravage her on her pallet? His

ENJOY ALL THE PASSION AND ROMANCE OF...

Heartfire Romance

Heartfire

ROMANCES from ZEBRA

After you have read HEARTFIRE ROMANCES, we're sure you'll agree that HEARTFIRE sets new standards of excellence for historical romantic fiction. Each Zebra HEARTFIRE novel is the ultimate blend of intimate romance and grand adventure and each takes place in the kinds of historical settings you want most...the American Revolution, the Old West, Civil War and more.

SUBSCRIBERS $AVE, $AVE, $AVE!!!

As a HEARTFIRE Home Subscriber, you'll save with your HEARTFIRE Subscription. You'll receive 4 brand new Heartfire Romances to preview Free for 10 days each month. If you decide to keep them you'll pay only $3.50 each; a total of $14.00 and you'll save $3.00 each month off the cover price.

Plus, we'll send you these novels as soon as they are published each month. There is never any shipping, handling or other hidden charges; home delivery is always FREE! And there is no obligation to buy even a single book. You may return any of the books within 10 days for full credit and you can cancel your subscription at any time. No questions asked.

Zebra's HEARTFIRE ROMANCES Are The Ultimate
In Historical Romantic Fiction.
Start Enjoying Romance As You Have Never Enjoyed It Before...
With 4 FREE Books From HEARTFIRE

TO GET YOUR
4 FREE BOOKS
MAIL THE COUPON BELOW.

FREE BOOK CERTIFICATE

GET 4 FREE BOOKS

Yes! I want to subscribe to Zebra's **HEARTFIRE HOME SUBSCRIPTION SERVICE.**
Please send me my 4 FREE books. Then each month I'll receive the four newest Heartfire
Romances as soon as they are published to preview Free for ten days. If I decide to keep
them I'll pay the special discounted price of just $3.50 each; a total of $14.00. This is a
savings of $3.00 off the regular publishers price. There are no shipping, handling or other hidden
charges. There is no minimum number of books to buy and I may cancel this subscription at any time.
In any case the 4 FREE Books are mine to keep regardless.

NAME _____

ADDRESS _____

CITY _____ STATE _____ ZIP _____

TELEPHONE _____

SIGNATURE _____

(If under 18 parent or guardian must sign)
Terms and prices subject to change.
Orders subject to acceptance.

ZH0494

Heartfire Romance

GET 4 FREE BOOKS

HEARTFIRE HOME SUBSCRIPTION
SERVICE
120 BRIGHTON ROAD
P.O. BOX 5214
CLIFTON, NEW JERSEY 07015

frown deepened. *Christ, this was her idea, so what does she have to be so scared about? I'm the one who should be scared.*

With a sigh, he moved around the house, checking windows and locking doors. He dawdled as long as he could over the simple tasks, and when, finally, there were no more windows to check, he blew out the lamps and headed up the stairs.

He paused at the door to the guest room Meg had originally assigned him, then, with a shrug, entered the empty chamber and began peeling off his clothes. He remembered a story his older brother, Eric, had once told him about his first time with his wife, Kirsten. Eric had recounted that his greatest concern had been that the intimidating size of his erection would frighten her.

"No worry there," Geoff snorted, looking down at his disinterested manhood. "With her attitude, you'll be lucky if you can get it up at all, much less scare her with it."

With a resigned shrug, he peeled off his shirt and clad only in a pair of light, linen underwear, picked up a candle and padded down the dark hall to the master bedroom.

Cracking open the door, he held the candle in front of him and peered into the black room, not even sure Meg was in there. "Are you ready?" he whispered.

"Yes," came a petrified squeak.

He frowned, hating the fear he heard in her voice, but closed the door softly behind him and walked over to the bed. Holding the candle aloft, he peered down at her.

She was lying on her back, her hair plaited into a prim braid that she had carefully tucked into the neck of a high-necked, long-sleeved nightgown. Her eyes were squeezed shut so tightly that her whole face looked pinched. The sheet was pulled up nearly to her chin, and her hands were clutching the edge of it so hard that her knuckles were white.

"You think I'm going to attack you, don't you?"

There was a long pause, and when Meg finally answered, her voice was shaking so much, he could hardly understand her. "No, I don't think that."

Geoff set the candle down and slowly lowered himself until he was sitting on the edge of the bed. "I'm not going to hurt you, sweetheart," he whispered, leaning over and nuzzling her neck. He placed his hand on the side of her face, stroking her cheek until she looked up into his soft, whiskey-colored eyes. "Kiss me, Meg."

Meg turned her head away. "Please, Geoff, do I have to?"

"Have to?" he cried, leaping to his feet.

Knowing that she'd insulted him, she quickly amended her hasty words. "It's not that I don't like your kisses, but please, can't we just get this over with?"

"No, damn it, we cannot just 'get it over with.' "

"Why not?" Meg asked, bewildered by his sudden anger. "I thought men liked to do this."

"Men do, but . . ."

"But you don't?" she supplied helpfully.

"Oh course I do! But not like this."

"I don't understand," she said, sitting up and staring at him in confusion. "What's wrong?"

Geoff finally lost the battle to hold on to his temper. "What's wrong," he gritted, "is that you initiated this, and now you're lying here in your grandmother's nightgown, looking like a lamb who's about to be slaughtered."

"Oh, so it's my nightgown you're worried about," Meg smiled, vastly relieved that his anger was over something so insignificant. "I promise it won't get in your way. I have it pulled up to my hips, just like Virginia told me."

"Your sister told you this is the way married women

make love? Just pull their nightgowns up and 'get it over with'?"

"Yes," Meg nodded. "And she should know. She has five children!"

Geoff chuckled mirthlessly. "Well, I guess old Lawrence Lombard is a better man than I."

"What in the world are you talking about?" Then a terrible thought occurred to her, and before she could catch herself, she blurted, "You have some sort of . . . problem, don't you?"

Geoff's face darkened with outraged offense. "No, I don't have a 'problem'! I just don't make love to women who look like they belong in a convent cell instead of my bed. Especially when that woman is my wife."

"Well, how do you think a wife should look?" Meg demanded, her own temper igniting.

"I think she should be naked, and smiling, with her hair down and loose. I think she should look like she wants me."

"From what I've heard, what women want is babies, and this is the price one has to pay to get them."

Geoff was so furious that he was shaking. "That may be the case with some women, and it may be okay with some men. But it's not with me. If my wife wants a baby, she's going to have to want me first."

"That's never going to happen," Meg said positively.

"Then a baby is never going to happen, either."

Turning on his heel, Geoff marched out of the room and back down the hall to the guest chamber. He yanked on his trousers, but his hands were shaking so badly he couldn't push the buttons through the holes. With a low growl of frustration, he grabbed his shirt and boots, wanting only to get away from his icy, unresponsive wife. He tore down the stairs and out the front door, but paused when he reached the porch, realizing that he couldn't very well ride all the way back to his camp bare-chested and barefoot.

Stuffing his arm into the sleeve of his shirt, he shrugged it on to his shoulders, then bent over and pulled on his boots. "Do I have to kiss you?" he mimicked, all the hurt and rejection he'd felt when Meg had uttered those words again washing over him.

"No, you don't have to kiss me, lady," he answered himself. "You don't have to kiss me, you don't have to talk to me, you don't have to even see me again."

Straightening, he stomped his heel into his boot and strode down the porch steps, heading for the back of Meg's house to collect his horse.

He was so angry, he didn't even notice the man who stood lurking in the bushes, a satisfied smile painted on his handsome face.

Chapter 17

The sharp knock at the front door made Meg nearly jump out of her skin.

Geoff, she thought, her heart pounding. It had to be. Who else would come calling at this time of night?

In the week that had passed since their altercation in the bedroom, Meg had neither seen nor heard from her husband. The days had dragged, though she had desperately tried to keep herself busy at the mill. And the nights . . . the nights were even worse when, lying sleepless, she would find herself replaying the embarrassing fiasco over and over in her mind.

"If my wife wants a baby, she's going to have to want me first . . ."

It was those words that haunted her night after night. Geoff wanted her to want him and, in truth, she knew she did. She loved it when he touched her . . . loved the hot, tingly sensation she felt deep inside when he kissed her.

Why had she acted like such a ninny when they'd attempted to consummate their marriage last week? Because she'd been scared.

Everyone said that sex was something a woman had to endure, and since the little she'd experienced thus far had been so pleasant, something about the actual act must be terrible. Otherwise, why would women feel that way?

The worst part of her dilemma was that there was no one she could turn to. She couldn't talk to Ginny again, since her sister had already made her feelings on the subject very plain, and she wasn't close enough to any of her married friends in town to ask such personal questions.

She wished Geoff would come to see her. Wished they could put last week's embarrassment behind them and start over.

"If my wife wants a baby, she going to have to want me first . . ."

How many times had those words spun through her mind in the past week? And when had she realized that she *did* want him? Certainly she hadn't wanted him when the moment was upon them. But sometime, in the week that had passed, she'd begun to realize how much he meant to her. Despite his anger over their marriage, he had acquiesced to most of her wishes, even agreeing to give her a child when she'd asked him. And then she'd allowed her maidenly fears to ruin everything, telling him she'd never desire him and leading him to believe that she expected his intimate attentions to be little more than rape.

No wonder he'd left in a rage.

But now, it looked like she might get a second chance. He was obviously standing at her door, and this time, she was determined he would not leave angry. In fact, if all went as she hoped, he wouldn't leave at all.

With a little shiver of anticipation, Meg set her sewing aside and rose from the settee. Walking quickly into the foyer, she drew a deep, calming breath and opened the door—then immediately slammed it closed again.

It wasn't Geoffrey Wellesley standing on her porch.

It was Peter Farnsworth.

* * *

Meg slid the bolt home a split second before Peter tried to force the door open from the other side. Taking several steps backward, she raised a shaking hand to her lips. For a long moment she stood paralyzed, then she saw his shadow disappear from the other side of the oval glass.

Was he gone? Would he give up that easily? Did she dare open the door and check? *Oh, God, Geoff, where are you?*

With a gasp, Meg remembered that the she'd left the back door unlocked. Whirling around, she raced toward the kitchen, but she was too late. She burst through the swinging door at the precise moment that Peter stepped into the house.

"Good evening," he said, as pleasantly as if she'd invited him over for a cup of coffee.

"Get out of my house," she hissed. "Right now—before I call the sheriff."

"Now, why would you want to do that, Megan?"

"Don't call me Megan."

"Pardon *me*," Peter said with exaggerated politeness. "I repeat, why would you want to call the sheriff, *Miss Taylor?*"

"You're still wrong," Meg retorted with a bravado she was far from feeling. "The name is Mrs. Wellesley."

"Ah, yes, I heard that you'd reneged on your father's word and married Geoffrey Wellesley." Peter threw his hat down on the table, then pulled a chair out from the table and straddled it. "An unfortunate mistake, my dear. It makes everything so . . . complicated."

"What are you talking about?" Meg asked, her composure slipping a notch. "There's nothing you can do. I'm married, and that's all there is to it."

"Not quite," Peter smiled, his boyish blond handsomeness belying the sinister note in his voice. "Your father signed a contract stating very clearly that in return for monies received, you'd become my wife. And never doubt it, Megan. You *will* live up to his promise."

"You're crazy!" she blurted rashly. "There's no way you can make me marry you. Haven't you heard a word I've said? I'm already married!"

"A minor—and very temporary—inconvenience, I assure you."

Meg's heart slammed against her ribs, but she forced herself to remain expressionless. Somehow, she had to stay calm and brazen this out. Summoning up a bright, confident smile, she said, "Oh, I think Geoffrey might have something to say about that."

"If you don't cooperate with my plans, Geoffrey Wellesley might not have anything to say about anything."

"Is that a threat, Peter?"

"Certainly not," he protested, throwing her a hurt look. "Would I threaten the woman I love?"

"Love?" Meg snorted. "Like you *loved* Jenny Thomas?"

Peter's plaintive expression disappeared, replaced by an icy hostility. "I'll let that pass this time, Megan, but don't mention it again. Do you understand? She has nothing to do with you and me."

"There is no you and me!"

"But of course there is. I'm going to make you my wife, we're going to live together in my father's house, we're going to have children together, and then, we're going to get old together."

Meg sat down at the table. "Peter, listen to me," she pleaded, switching tactics in a desperate attempt to make him see reason. "I'll pay you the money I owe you. My mother left me some jewelry. I'll sell it and give you every cent."

"No matter how many jewels your mother had, they won't be enough." Peter smiled blandly.

"Maybe not," Meg admitted, "but the mill is turning a good profit now. You and I can come up with some agreement where I can pay back the rest over time."

"Oh, Meg, Meg," Peter sighed as if dealing with a not very bright child. "When are you going to get it through that pretty little head of yours that I don't want your money? Even if you pay back every dime your father borrowed, it won't make any difference. I want you, and I mean to have you."

Meg swallowed hard as the terrifying reality of Peter's intentions sank in. "Well, you can't have me," she said boldly. "I'm married to Mr. Wellesley, and you're just going to have to accept that fact."

Peter shot her a smile that made a chill run down her spine. "I don't have to accept anything, darling. As I just told you, your marriage to Wellesley is nothing more than a minor setback. It will all be cleared up in just a few months. In fact, my father expects that we should be able to marry by Christmas."

"Well, your father is wrong!"

Peter dropped all pretense of civility and leaned forward until his face was just inches away from her own. "My father is never wrong. Everyone knows that your marriage to Wellesley is a sham. Why, he doesn't even live here with you. Marriages of that kind are easily annulled in the face of prior legal agreements."

"Where Geoff lives has nothing to do with anything," Meg argued desperately. "He and I simply agreed that it would be easier for him to spend the weeknights up at his camp and come home only on the weekends. In fact, he should be arriving any minute."

Peter chuckled nastily. "You're either a bad liar, Meg, or

201

you're the only person in town who doesn't know that your loving husband is in Portland this weekend."

"What?" Meg gasped, her astonishment evident. "How do you know that?"

Peter smiled smugly. "I saw him leave. He took the eight-forty train this morning, and old Ward Prescott, down at the depot, told me he won't be back until Tuesday. You didn't know, did you?"

"Of course I knew," she blustered. "I just didn't realize that my husband's private business affairs were looked upon with such interest by other people."

"It's no good, Meg. Those big brown eyes of yours have given you away."

"I don't know what you're talking about."

"Oh, yes you do. You didn't know a thing about Wellesley's plans, and he obviously doesn't care enough about you to bother to tell you. And that tells me that your relationship isn't quite so cozy as you want me to believe. Now, come on—why don't you just admit the marriage is a sham, get an annulment, and we can have a fall wedding, instead of having to wait till after the cold weather sets in."

"We are *not* going to have a fall wedding," Meg gritted, "or a Christmas wedding, or any other kind of wedding. And as for my relationship with my husband, it is absolutely none of your business."

Peter sighed, a long, dramatic exhalation that made Meg long to slap him. "I told Father you were going to be difficult. I guess that he and I will just have to go back to our original plan."

"You do that," Meg challenged, heedless of the danger she might be putting herself and Geoffrey in, "but in the meantime, I want you out of my house."

To her astonishment, Peter nodded agreeably and stood up. "All right, I'll go. I didn't come here tonight to upset you. I just came to let you know that I'm back and that plans are proceeding on schedule."

"Get out!" Meg blazed, leaping up from her chair and wrenching the door open. "And don't come back. The next time I see you skulking around here, I *will* call the sheriff. I swear I will."

Nonchalantly, Peter picked up his hat and sauntered toward the door. "See you soon, my dear," he cooed, reaching out and chucking Meg under the chin. "Real soon."

With a last smile, he stepped out into the cool night air. Meg could hear his smug laughter long after she'd slammed and locked the door behind him.

She was up before the birds on Saturday morning. After a quick breakfast, she went out and saddled her mare, then headed for Geoff's timber camp.

Peter *must* have been lying last night, she assured herself. Geoff wouldn't go away for four days and not tell her. Surely, when she reached his camp, she'd find him there.

But what if she didn't? If she went to his camp and he really *was* gone, her lack of knowledge would be all over town by supper time tonight. She could only imagine what delight the gossips would have if they found out that after only two weeks of marriage, Mrs. Wellesley didn't know where her husband was. Not to mention the credence it would give Peter's suspicions about their lack of intimacy.

Suddenly unsure of her mission, Meg pulled back on her horse's reins, bringing the mare to a stop. Maybe she should rethink this reckless flight up the mountain. But, she warred with herself, she needed to talk to Geoff; needed to tell him that Peter was back, needed to warn him of the evil man's threats.

Meg sat on her horse for several minutes, gazing off at the panoramic vista before her and wondering what to do. Damn Geoffrey, anyway, for putting her in this position. If he lived with her like a normal husband, she wouldn't be facing this impossible quandary.

And if you treated him like a normal husband, maybe he would live with you. She frowned at her own admission, realizing that although there was probably a thread of truth in her self-castigating thoughts, there was nothing she could do, at least at that moment, to rectify her wifely shortcomings. Determinedly, she put the matter out of her mind, intent on concentrating instead on how to handle the immediate situation.

Perhaps it would be better if she sent a message up to the camp. That way, if Geoff wasn't there, she wouldn't be faced with the embarrassment of having one of his men tell her so. But still, she mused, shifting in her saddle, everyone in town would probably hear the tale that Mrs. Wellesley was sending messages to her husband when he was a hundred miles away.

Meg shook her head dejectedly and turned her horse back toward town. It was too big a risk to take! She just couldn't hand Peter and George Farnsworth the weapon of knowing that her marriage was exactly what they suspected it to be. She'd have to wait until Tuesday, when Geoff came back from Portland—if he'd even gone there, of course. But even if he hadn't, by Tuesday she'd be safe in sending a message to him. Until then, she'd just have to bide her time—and hope that Peter Farnsworth kept his distance.

At least she could get the letter she'd written to the jeweler in Portland sent off. Although Peter had said the previous night that repaying the loan didn't matter, Meg clung desperately to the hope that if she presented George

Farnsworth with a sizable check, he could somehow stop Peter from carrying out his awful threats.

Tears welled in her eyes as she thought of selling the beautiful family heirlooms her mother had so lovingly bequeathed to her. But she knew she had no other recourse, short of asking Geoff for the money—and that she would never do.

With the steely resolve that was so much a part of her character, Meg nudged her horse into a canter, never slowing her pace until she reached the post office.

It was Monday afternoon, following the longest weekend of Meg's life. She had spent nearly the entire time at home, venturing out only to attend church on Sunday. She'd hardly slept at all. Instead, she spent the interminable nights lying fearfully in her bed, her ears straining to hear the slightest sound. In her feverish, exhausted mind, every sigh of the night breeze sounded like a door opening, every creak and groan of the old house a footstep.

She had not gone to the mill at all, sending a brief note to Hank pleading a vague, womanly ailment that she knew would excuse her with no questions asked.

Meg glanced up at the clock, noting it was close to three. Carefully, she folded the note she had written to Geoff and placed it in an envelope. She had gone over to her nearest neighbors, the Bensons, this morning and asked Mrs. Benson if her twelve-year-old son, Emo, could deliver a note to Geoff's camp that afternoon. Judith Benson had raised her eyebrows in surprise at Meg's request, but had quickly masked her curiosity and assured her that Emo would be delighted to earn the quarter Meg was offering for the task.

True to Judith's word, Emo appeared at her front door promptly at three. He listened dutifully as Meg described whom he was to give the message to, then accepted the quarter with a huge grin, promising he wouldn't dawdle on the way to the camp.

Meg closed the door after the boy, content that he would do her bidding. She had spent a long time composing the note, trying to impart the urgency with which she needed to see Geoff without alarming him. If Peter was watching them, as Meg suspected he was, she didn't want to give him the upper hand by making Geoff's arrival at her house look like anything other than a normal, loving reunion between newlyweds.

"Please, God," she murmured fervently, sinking down on the couch and leaning her head back wearily, "make him put his pride aside and come. Please!"

Meg jerked awake at the sound of someone beating on her front door. She hadn't even realized she'd been asleep, but when she looked out the window, she saw that the sun was peeking over the horizon, heralding a new day.

For a moment, she looked around in confusion. What was she doing in the parlor? The last thing she remembered was eating a light supper, then sitting down and trying to concentrate on a book of poetry. She had a vague recollection of nodding off over her book, but had she actually slept the whole night sitting up on the sofa?

Again the fist hammered against the front door. Meg leaped off the couch, wincing painfully when her cramped muscles protested her sudden movements. "I'm coming, I'm coming," she called, as the knocking became even more insistent. But when she reached the foyer, she paused, suddenly fearful of who might be on the other side of the door.

"Who is it?" she called nervously.

"It's Ned Johnson," came a gruff shout.

"Ned?"

"Yeah, your husband's foreman."

Geoff's foreman? Why in the world would he be at her door at seven o'clock in the morning? With a little shiver of apprehension, Meg threw the bolt and opened the door. It took only one glance at the old man's distraught face to know that something was very wrong. "What is it?" she demanded without preamble. "Has something happened to Mr. Wellesley?"

"Yeah," the man nodded. "There's been an accident . . . You have to come right away, missus."

"An accident? What kind of accident? The train? Was there a train wreck?"

"No. Not the train. Geoff got back last night. The accident happened this morning."

"This morning?" What could have happened this morning?

"Yeah. Geoff was fixin' to come down to see ya, soon as the sun was full up, but he said he wanted to get a couple of hours' work in on that flume of his first. I told him he shouldn't be workin' out there 'fore the light was good, but he wouldn't listen."

Meg's head began to reel as she imagined the worst, and blindly, she groped for the door. Anyone who had been raised in a logging town had heard hundreds of horror stories about lumberjacks being chewed up alive by the giant, spinning saws or crushed to death by an out-of-control log hurtling down a hill.

"What happened?" she whispered.

"Nobody rightly knows, ma'am. It appears Geoff was working on the flume and a log got loose and came down the flume and hit him."

"Got loose? How could a log 'get loose'?"

207

"Well, that's the puzzle of it. They can't."

"Then how did it happen?" Meg prodded.

Ned threw her an uneasy look. "Somebody musta pushed it."

"Oh, my God!" Meg gasped. "You mean someone was intentionally trying to hurt Geoff?"

"Kinda looks that way," Ned nodded.

"Is he . . . is he dead?"

"No, no, he ain't dead," Ned said quickly, "but his left hand got crushed pretty bad. The doc's with him now."

Meg blanched, causing Ned's eyes to widen with alarm. "You ain't gonna faint or nothin', are ya, missus?"

"No," she answered, wishing she felt as sure of that as she sounded, "I'm fine. Are you sure he's going to live?"

"Oh, yeah, he's gonna live, all right, but I think you'd better come anyway."

"Of course," Meg nodded, recovering herself. "Did you bring a wagon?"

"No, I rode. A wagon takes too long to get up the mountain. You got a horse, ain't ya?"

"Yes." Meg glanced down at her rumpled gray dress. "But I can't ride in this. You go out and saddle my mare, and I'll run upstairs and change."

Ned nodded a quick agreement and headed off for the carriage shed.

Meg sped up the stairs and into her room, unbuttoning her dress as she went. Was someone actually trying to *kill* her husband? They must be. Why else would they purposely have sent a log down the flume when he was working on it? But who would do such a thing?

Suddenly she paused, her hand involuntarily clutching her throat. Peter . . . it had to be. He *had* meant those threats he'd uttered the other night—and he'd wasted no time in putting his nefarious plans into action. But how could she prove it?

She *had* to talk to Geoff. Somehow, they had to come up with a plan to keep him safe. When Peter found out that Geoff was still alive, he'd undoubtedly try to kill him again—especially now that Geoff was injured and helpless. With a crushed hand, Geoff probably wouldn't even be able to use a gun.

Meg recalled that Ned had said Geoff's left hand was crushed, and desperately, she tried to think which hand Geoff favored. She thought he was right-handed, but she'd never really paid much attention.

He has to be right-handed. I'd have noticed if he favored his left. Left-handed people always look so awkward when they eat. That thought made her feel a little better, but still, the reality of Peter's deadly intentions made her stomach knot sickeningly.

She had to get to Geoff as quickly as possible. With renewed fervor, she released the tapes on her petticoats and shimmied her dress and undergarments over her slim hips. Racing over to her armoire, she grabbed a heavy twill riding skirt and clumsily stepped into it. She yanked on a blouse, then tore out of the bedroom and back down the steps, fastening buttons and tying ribbons as she ran.

Ned was already back on the porch waiting for her. Meg paused in the foyer long enough to tuck in her blouse and pull on her riding boots, then joined him.

"Let's go!" he commanded.

The man's dictatorial attitude was highly improper, considering that he was speaking to his employer's wife, but Meg was too distraught to take him to task over his rudeness. Instead, she answered his order with a quick nod and mounted her prancing horse.

"You know how to handle that mare?" he asked, dubious, as she flung herself into the saddle.

"Don't worry about me," she retorted. "Just try to keep up." And digging her heels into her horse's sleek flanks, she took off down the street like a shot, leaving the gaping Ned to follow in her dusty wake.

Chapter 18

Never in the history of Wellesley had anyone ridden from town to the timber camp as fast as Meg did that day. For years afterward, men argued over Ned Johnson's claim that the lady had made the hour long trip in forty-two minutes, and though many a wagering man had tried to duplicate her time, none ever had.

But Meg wasn't thinking about setting speed records as she spurred her horse unmercifully up the rough mountain trail. She was thinking only of getting to her husband—as fast as possible. The ride seemed interminable, and when she finally arrived at camp, she didn't even notice how close her beloved little mare was to collapsing from exhaustion. She merely leaped off the trembling animal and heedlessly pushed her way through the large knot of men who stood outside Geoff's cabin.

Bursting through the open door, she looked around frantically for her husband, then nearly fainted from relief when she saw him propped up in his narrow cot, looking at her in vague surprise.

"Hi, Meg," he greeted, his voice weak and slightly slurred.

"Oh, Geoff!" Racing over to the cot, she dropped to her

knees, her eyes quickly assessing the stiff bandage wrapped around his left hand. "Are you in pain?"

To her complete astonishment, he threw her a lopsided smile. "I'm kinda numb."

"Numb?"

"From the alcohol," came a clipped voice behind her.

Craning her head around, Meg noticed Dr. Emerson standing at a small table, shoving a stethoscope into his black bag. With a subtle jerk of his head, he summoned Meg from Geoff's bedside.

"Is it bad, Doctor?" she asked when she reached his side.

The doctor nodded. "Your husband's hand is badly injured, Mrs. Wellesley. Three of his fingers are crushed, and I don't know how many bones are broken. Unfortunately, the bones in the hand are so small, there's not much I can do for him. I've wrapped it in bandages to keep it immobile, and we just have to hope it will heal correctly. I can't guarantee that he'll ever have full use of the hand again, though."

Meg closed her eyes and swallowed. "What can I do for him?"

"Actually, you're going to have to do just about everything for a while. He was lucky that it was his left hand that got hit, but he's still going to have to have help eating, dressing, and bathing. He's also going to be in a lot of pain when the whiskey wears off."

"You mean, he's drunk?" Meg gasped, turning back to glance at Geoff, who was now lying against the pillows with his eyes closed.

The doctor nodded. "I had to dull the pain enough to examine him. And if you take my advice, you'll keep him in that condition for the next couple of days. It will allow him to sleep, and he needs to rest. In addition to his hand injury, his arm is badly bruised and he wrenched his shoulder, so it's very important that he remain quiet and let everything heal."

"What about some laudanum? Wouldn't that help?"

The doctor shook his head adamantly. "I don't believe in laudanum. It's too addicting. Just give him a shot of whiskey when he wants one. It's much better for him."

Meg nodded somberly at the doctor's instructions. "Would it be all right to move him to my house? I can take better care of him there."

"Yes, that shouldn't hurt him, as long as you're careful of his shoulder. I'll come by your place tomorrow morning to check on him. If he shows any signs of worsening or starts running a fever, send me a message immediately."

Meg promised she would, then saw the doctor to the door, thanking him profusely for his assistance. After he had departed, she turned back to the men who were still hovering around the bed and mustered up her best no-nonsense tone. "All right, men, here's what we're going to do. You, sir," she said, pointing to a great bear of a man with a huge red beard, "go find the best wagon you have and bring it around. We're going to move Mr. Wellesley to my house."

"What?" the men gasped in unison, looking at her like she'd lost her mind. "You can't do that. He needs to stay quiet."

"I'm not here to argue with you, gentlemen," Meg said firmly. "Now, you there, in the red shirt, what's your name?"

"Davidson," the man answered, whipping a battered cap off his head and stepping forward. "Matt Davidson."

"Well, Mr. Davidson, I'd appreciate it if you would go find a small featherbed to put in the wagon."

"Featherbed?" the burly lumberjack guffawed. "I'm sorry, ma'am, but we're fresh out of featherbeds."

213

The other men joined in his laughter and Meg colored with embarrassment. "All right, then, just bring some heavy blankets and some pillows. You do have those, don't you?"

"Well, sure, but I don't see no reason to be movin' him down to town."

"I don't really care what you think," Meg interjected flatly. "I appreciate the fact that you're concerned about my husband, but believe me, no one is more concerned than I. Now, I am going to move Mr. Wellesley to town, and if you are unwilling to help me, I would advise you to return to your regular duties. That goes for the rest of you, too," she added, her determined gaze sweeping over the men.

None of them moved, but several cast uneasy glances in Ned Johnson's direction. Ned couldn't remember when he'd seen anything funnier than the sight of seven giant lumberjacks being brought to heel by one little woman.

"Are there any questions?" Meg asked.

Seven heads swung back and forth.

Meg nodded with satisfaction. "Good. Then, let's get to work."

As one, the men started moving out of the cabin, sidling past Meg as though they thought she might strike them. Stepping into the morning sunshine, they joined the large group of men waiting outside.

"Is the boss okay?" one of the river rats asked.

"Yeah," answered the man who'd been instructed to fetch the wagon. "Hell, a few broken bones is the least of his problems. It's that woman he married that's scary."

"And to think that just last week I was envying him, crawlin' into bed with her every night."

"Crawlin' into bed with her might be fine," another man

214

chuckled, "but facin' her in the mornin' would be some-thin' else altogether."

"You see, boys," said Matt Davidson, "that's why I like whores. They offer the same pleasures as wives, and you don't gotta take none of their sass."

There was a general rumble of agreement, but it quickly faded to silence when Meg stepped out on to the porch. "Have you gotten that wagon yet?" she called, directing her words to the bearded giant to whom she'd assigned the task.

"I'm just goin' now, ma'am," he answered contritely. "It won't take but a second."

The other lumberjacks looked over at the object of Meg's displeasure, their jaws slack with astonishment.

"Never thought I'd see old Jasper knuckle under to a little gal that way," one of them laughed.

"Lord, but she *is* scary, ain't she?"

"Mebbe, but did you see the way she kissed the boss over to her mill the other day? I tell you, boys, it about set my hair on fire. You gotta figure, a woman who kisses like that is gonna be a handful every other way, too. But damn! If she always kisses like that, it just might be worth it."

The trip back to Meg's was made without incident, thanks to the generosity of several of the lumberjacks who took it upon themselves to pour enough whiskey down Geoff's throat to completely knock him out.

Two men rigged up a crude stretcher and accompanied Meg back to her house. When they finally reached their destination late that afternoon, they rolled Geoff's uncon-scious body on to it and carried him inside.

"Where do you want him, ma'am?" Matt Davidson asked. Despite the embarrassment he'd felt when Meg had taken him to task in front of the other men, he was one of the men who had insisted on escorting her.

Geoff had given him a job years before, when he had first come to Oregon after a stint in prison for killing a man in a barroom brawl. Matt had never forgotten his employer's kindness in giving him a chance when others had turned him away. There was very little he wouldn't do for Geoffrey Wellesley, and even though he felt that his boss's new wife needed a sound whipping to remind her of her place, he was determined to be polite and accommodating.

"Upstairs, please," Meg said, responding to his question. "If you'll follow me, I'll show you which room."

The two brawny lumberjacks struggled up the stairs with their equally brawny patient. By the time they reached the door to the master suite, they were staggering under the weight of their load.

"Just put him on the bed there," Meg directed. "I can handle it from here."

The men did as she bade, then leaned against the wall of the bedroom, panting from their exertions. Meg let them rest a moment, then saw them back to the front door. She paused a moment in the foyer, thanking them both for their help. "Please feel free to visit any time," she invited. "I know Mr. Wellesley will be happy to see you as soon as he's feeling better."

"If you don't mind, ma'am," Matt said quietly, "I think I'll just spend the night out here on the porch."

Meg's eyebrows shot up in question. "I don't think that's necessary, Mr. Davidson. I'm sure I'll be able to handle everything from here."

"If you don't mind my saying so, ma'am, you wouldn't be able to handle whoever it was that tried to kill him if the scum decides to come back tonight to finish the job. I think

I'll just stick around until the boss is healed up enough to look out for hisself."

Meg stared at the big man for a moment, then nodded. "Thank you," she whispered. "I'm very grateful."

With an embarrassed grunt, Matt Davidson sat down on the top step. "Just go about your business, missus," he directed. "Nobody's gonna bother you tonight."

With a nod, Meg went back into the house, knowing she'd never felt safer in her life.

"I don't want any more damn whiskey, Meg. I want something to eat."

Meg looked down at her irascible husband and determinedly held out the glass. "Your dinner is all ready, but Dr. Emerson said you should have whiskey for the pain."

Geoff shoved himself up into a sitting position. "Right now, the pain in my head is a lot worse than the pain in my hand."

Meg smiled patiently. "I'm glad to see you so cranky. It's a sure sign you're feeling better."

"No, I'm not," Geoff complained. "My head is killing me."

"Oh, come on," Meg cajoled. "Men always like to have a whiskey before dinner. Why not tonight?"

"Because I've had nothing but whiskey for two days, and I don't want any more. I want *food.*"

"All right," Meg sighed, putting the glass on the night stand. "I made you some vegetable soup. I'll go get it."

"I don't want soup. I want a steak, and some potatoes, too. *Without* hot pepper in them," he added, throwing her a jaundiced look.

"Fine," she gritted, her patience with his ill temper wearing thin. "If you want steak, I'll fix steak." Turning, she started out the door.

"Hey, Meg?"

"What now?" she sighed, not bothering to turn around.

"Thanks."

Meg smiled and continued on her way.

She returned a half-hour later, carrying a tray laden with steak, potatoes, green beans, and chocolate cake. "This should fill you up," she announced, setting the tray on his lap and tucking a napkin under his chin. Perching on the edge of the bed, she picked up a fork and speared several beans, lifting them to his mouth.

"What the hell are you doing?" he asked, looking down at the fork poised in front of his lips.

"What does it look like I'm doing? I'm feeding you your dinner."

"I don't need you to feed me!" he retorted, irritated that she seemed to think he was completely helpless. "My right hand is fine and that's the one I eat with." As if to prove his point, he lifted his uninjured hand and flexed his fingers.

"All right!" Meg snapped, throwing the fork down. "Be my guest."

Geoff picked up the fork and shoved the beans into his mouth. "God, you're cross. You have a lot to learn about being a nurse."

"And you have a lot to learn about being a patient!" Meg shot back, standing up. "I'll be back in a while to get the tray. Enjoy your meal."

"You're leaving?" Geoff asked, his mouth full of potatoes.

218

"Yes, I'm leaving." And before he could think of a reason to ask her to stay, the door slammed behind her.

"Thanks a lot, lady," he growled. "Leave me lying here hour after hour by myself. A man could die up here and you'd never notice!"

Angrily, he stared down at his steak, then realized that with only one useful hand, he couldn't cut it. "Oh, this is just great!" he fumed. Feeling terribly sorry for himself, he drove his fork into the middle of the big piece of meat, lifting the whole steak off the plate and taking a bite off one side. The force of his teeth pulling against the meat caused it to slip off the fork so that suddenly the entire steak was dangling out of his mouth. Leaning forward, he dropped the meat back on to his plate and lifted the napkin to wipe off his greasy chin.

"Meg!"

Working hard to hide a smug smile, Meg opened the door. She had been standing just outside, knowing that as soon as Geoff tried to tackle the steak, he was going to need her. "Yes?"

"I can't cut the meat."

"You can't?" Her voice fairly dripped honey.

"No, I can't, damn it."

"Would you like me to help you?"

"Yeah," he muttered.

"What? Did you say yes? I couldn't hear you."

Geoff threw her a killing look, then suddenly his expression softened and he began to laugh. "Yes, I would appreciate you helping me, if you wouldn't mind."

With great effort, Meg managed to keep her voice solicitous. "Of course not." Again she traversed the room and settled her hip on the edge of the bed. Picking up the fork and knife, she daintily cut the whole steak into bite-sized pieces. "Would you like me to feed it to you?"

"No, I can handle it . . . but thanks."

She started to get up, but Geoff held out a restraining hand. "Don't go. Stay and talk to me while I eat."

A little jolt of pleasure rippled through her. "All right," she nodded, rising and moving to a chair next to the bed. "How *is* your hand, Geoff?"

"It hurts like hell," he admitted. "My shoulder, too. When that log came at me, I had my back to it and I just didn't have time to get out of the way."

"Didn't you hear it in time to move?"

"Yeah, I heard it, but I was trying to get my tools out of the flume."

Meg looked at him curiously. "You'd risk injury to save a few tools?"

"They're not just any tools," Geoff defended. "They're handmade, and very precise. I had my brother Stuart send them to me all the way from Boston. I didn't want to lose them."

Meg nodded, even though she still didn't really understand how anyone could consider a tool, handmade or not, more important than their well-being.

"What I can't figure out," Geoff said thoughtfully, pausing with a piece of steak halfway to his mouth, "is who sent that log down the flume, and why."

"I think I know," Meg murmured.

Geoff's eyes lifted to hers in surprise.

"It's what I sent you the message about," she continued quietly. "Peter Farnsworth is back from Texas."

The fork clattered noisily to the plate. "Are you saying that Farnsworth is trying to kill me? What makes you think that?"

Meg's voice was strangled when she answered. "He came here the other night . . . and he made some threats."

Haltingly, she filled him in on some of the details of her

220

confrontation with Peter, but pointedly omitted her desperate offer to try to repay the loan. Geoff still didn't know anything about the money her father had borrowed from George Farnsworth, and Meg was afraid if he found out, he'd feel bound to pay it back. She was guilty enough about the horrible situation she'd dragged him into, and she couldn't bear having him think her motives had been his money. She wouldn't accept Geoff's money if he offered it, so it was pointless to bring it up. Besides, Peter had made it clear that he intended to pursue her even if the debt was paid off.

Geoff listened silently to her abbreviated version of the facts, looking down several times at his broken hand. When her words finally trailed off, he said only, "I think it's time I paid Mr. Farnsworth a little visit."

Meg drew a startled breath and unconsciously wrapped her fingers around his arm. "Please don't do anything foolish, Geoff. The man is crazy. He won't stop at anything to get what he wants. He never has."

Geoff covered Meg's hand with his own, giving it a comforting little squeeze. "Don't worry. This time he's not dealing with Jenny Thomas."

"You . . . you know about that?"

Geoff nodded. "I always suspected there was more to that story than anyone knew. Jenny's older brother Hal worked for me for a while. I met her a couple of times when she came up to the camp to see him. Used to bring him pies. She seemed like a nice girl—a little giggly and nervous, but certainly not the type to kill herself over some man."

Meg looked away. "You're wrong about that," she whispered. "Jenny *did* kill herself."

Geoff drew in a startled breath. "How do you know?"

221

"She sent me a letter telling me she was going to. I received it the day after her death."

"My God, Meg, did you tell the authorities?"

Meg shook her head.

"Why not?"

Very slowly, she lifted her eyes. "Jenny was going to have Peter's baby. That's why she killed herself. But I didn't think there was anything to be gained by everyone in town knowing that."

"That bastard," Geoff growled. "An innocent little girl like that. And he wouldn't do the right thing by her?"

Meg faltered. How could she bring herself to tell Geoff the intimate details of this tragedy? She'd had a hard enough time telling Virginia.

"What's the matter?" he asked, alarmed by her tortured expression. "Is there something more you're not telling me?"

In a nearly inaudible voice, Meg murmured, "Peter raped Jenny, got her with child, then refused to acknowledge it. Jenny couldn't bear the shame, so she killed herself."

Geoff's whiskey-colored eyes darkened with rage. "That son of a bitch. And now he thinks he's going to have *my wife?*" With an abrupt movement, he set the tray aside and flung back the blanket.

"What are you doing?"

"I'm getting out of this damn bed and going to see Farnsworth."

Meg shot out of her chair and placed a staying hand on her husband's chest. "Geoff, you can't do that! You're not well."

"I'm fine, damn it. You act like I'm dying when all I've got is a broken hand. Now move out of the way, Meg. I have to get dressed."

But Meg stood her ground. "Geoffrey, please, listen to me. We have no proof of anything, and if you go over to the Farnsworths' now, there's no telling what could happen. If Peter gets violent, how will you protect yourself? Until your hand heals, how can you fight back? Please don't go. I don't think I could bear it if you got hurt again because of me."

It was her last words that stopped him. For a long moment, he stared down at her upturned face. Then he slowly sat back down on the edge of the bed, pulling her down next to him and wrapping his uninjured arm around her shoulders. "What do you mean, because of you?"

Meg covered her face with her hands and started to cry. "This is all my fault," she sobbed. "If I hadn't forced you to marry me, you wouldn't be involved in any of this."

Geoff lifted his bandaged hand to the side of Meg's face, gently guiding her head down to his shoulder. "You're right," he murmured, placing a gentle kiss next to her nose, "if you hadn't forced me to marry you, I wouldn't be involved. But, the fact is, I did marry you, and no one threatens what is mine."

Meg raised tear drenched eyes to his. "But you can't confront him tonight. You're hurt, and the doctor said . . ."

"Shh," Geoff crooned, his mouth close to her ear, "I know what the doctor said, and you're right. This isn't the time."

"Oh, Geoff, I'm so sorry about all this," Meg choked. "What I did to you was terribly wrong. I know that now, and I won't fight you if you want to have our marriage annulled. I didn't realize Peter was so set on having me that he'd come after you. I feel so guilty . . ."

"When did I say anything about an annulment?" Geoff whispered.

"But . . ."

"Shh."

Before she could protest again, Geoff's mouth covered hers. His lips were soft and warm . . . intoxicating in their sensuality as they enticed her own to open and allow his tongue entrance. Meg felt a deliciously familiar shiver run up her spine, and with a small, surrendering sigh, her lips parted beneath his.

Geoff gathered her closer, deepening his kiss as he gently laid her back on the bed. Lazily, his fingers moved from her cheek to her neck, then trailed lower, skimming across the upper swells of her breast.

Meg was aware of the path his hand was taking, but she was of no mind to stop him. Instead, she twined her arms around his neck, threading her fingers into his thick, russet hair and arching her back.

Her subtle invitation was not lost on Geoff, and with a low moan, he lowered his hand and cupped the lush globe, sweeping his thumb back and forth across her nipple until he felt it harden and peak. His excitement mounting, he twisted his body, throwing a leg over hers and pressing his swelling erection against her thigh.

Meg could feel his heated arousal, even through the layers of her skirt and petticoats. She was surprised that the sensation didn't frighten her at all. Instead, she experienced an overwhelming need to move closer so she could feel its insistent pressure against the very core of her. Mindlessly allowing herself to sink into the heady swirl of first desire, she shifted her hips.

With a strangled gasp, Geoff broke the embrace. Meg had said she wanted a baby and God knew, it would be easy enough to grant her her wish. But not like this. Not sprawled on the edge of a rumpled bed with her petticoats shoved up to her waist.

When they finally made love—and after tonight, he knew it was inevitable—he wanted it to be perfect. So perfect that Meg's mistaken idea that lovemaking was the price a woman had to pay for the reward of gaining a child would forever be laid to rest.

With greater willpower than he'd ever dreamt he possessed, Geoff disentangled their legs and sat up.

Meg was so surprised by his abrupt abandonment of her that for a long moment she just lay on the bed and stared up at him. Then, suddenly realizing that she must look like a wanton, she scrambled off the bed, careful to keep her back to him as she nervously patted her disheveled hair into place.

"I'll . . . I'll take your tray now, if you're finished," she said, mortified that her voice was shaking as badly as her hands. *Why had Geoff stopped his lovemaking? Was she so unappealing in her inexperience that he didn't want her?*

"Yeah," Geoff rasped, his own breath still coming in quick, harsh pants. "I'm done."

Avoiding his eyes, Meg scooped the tray off the bed and hurried toward the door. "If there's anything else you need tonight, just call," she said, shooting a quick glance at him over her shoulder. "I'll be in my room."

"Thanks, but I'm fine," Geoff nodded. The door closed behind her and he flopped back on the bed.

Sure you're fine, he thought ruefully. "You're also nuts," he chided himself aloud, "stopping like that in the middle of everything. She was ready, you were ready, and you stopped because the sheets were rumpled?"

With a sigh, he shook his head, still not quite believing his own behavior. God knew, rumpled sheets had never bothered him before.

But somehow, tonight had been different. Meg wasn't just some girl to be taken for a moment's pleasure. She was his wife, and even though he didn't love her, he cared too much for her to initiate her with a quick tumble on the edge of a bed. Better to wait until the moment was right.

With a wry smile, Geoff plucked at his long johns, pulling the clinging material away from his still throbbing shaft. Now his only problem was to figure out how to make that moment happen—and how to control himself until it did.

Chapter 19

For the next several days, Geoff played the dutiful convalescent, limiting his activities to those which he could easily handle with one hand and spending the bulk of his time resting.

To Meg's dismay, he said nothing about their lusty encounter on the bed, a fact that she interpreted as proof of her original suspicion that he had probably kissed a hundred women in just such a passionate manner and had found her to be woefully lacking. When, after two days, the subject still had not come up, she figured he had simply put the incident out of his mind and she vowed to do the same.

She couldn't have been more mistaken. Despite Geoff's seeming nonchalance, he had thought of little else, spending hour after hour staring sightlessly at the novel Meg had given him to read, while he invented and discarded a hundred different plans to tempt his wife into his bed. By the morning of the third day, he still hadn't come up with a workable idea, and his inability to think of a viable seduction was taking its toll on his temper.

"I'm tired of sitting around in my wrapper," he complained over breakfast. "I want to take a real bath and put on some clothes."

"All right," Meg nodded agreeably. "I'll fix a tub after we're done eating. Would you mind bathing in the kitchen so I don't have to carry the buckets upstairs?"

"You don't have to carry the buckets at all," he responded irritably. "You're not my slave. Just show me where everything is and I'll pump and haul the water myself."

"I'll be glad to help you," she protested, wondering what she could have said that had put him in such a rank mood. "You bring the water in and I'll get the tub ready."

Geoff grunted a reluctant agreement and the two of them returned to their eggs.

After breakfast, Meg heated several kettles of water on the stove, adding them to the buckets Geoff poured in the big, copper tub until his bathwater was pleasantly warm. "There, that should do it," she smiled, placing a bar of soap and several towels on a small stool. "Are you sure you can manage alone?"

"You gonna help me if I can't?"

"Well, yes," she stammered, blushing to the roots of her hair. "I suppose so."

Geoff instantly regretted his rudeness and in a contrite voice, murmured, "I'll be fine. I've been taking baths for years."

Meg smiled at his joke, then hurried out of the kitchen. She started to close the door, then changed her mind and pulled it open a few inches. "Just in case he really does need me," she told herself, all the time praying he wouldn't.

She heard a splash and knew he had sat down in the tub. Then everything was quiet. The silence lasted so long that she became concerned and was just about to call out to him to when she heard a soft thud and then a muffled curse. Without thinking, she stepped forward and peeked through the crack in the door.

228

Nothing could have prepared her for the sight of Geoffrey Wellesley, the most sought-after man in the state of Oregon, sitting naked in the tub. As she gaped at the sheer physical perfection of him, he leaned over the tub's high side, stretching out his uninjured arm in an attempt to reclaim the soap which he'd obviously dropped and sent skittering across the floor.

Meg couldn't catch the little gasp of awe that escaped her as she watched the wet, gleaming muscles in his shoulder grow taut with his effort. She clapped a hand over her mouth in horror, paralyzed with fear that he might have heard her. He hadn't, but it was a several seconds before she finally dared exhale.

Stop this! You shouldn't be watching him. It's utterly shameful to stare at a naked man. But despite the words of self-recrimination that flew through her mind, she didn't move, finding it impossible to tear herself away from the mesmerizing sight of her magnificent husband in all his tawny, naked splendor.

Her eyes drifted down to where crystalline drops of water beaded in the curly, flaxen hair covering his chest—a chest so muscular and bronzed that just looking at it made her yearn to run her fingers across its rocklike planes.

Heedlessly, she moved a step closer, positioning her eye in the crack of the door to allow herself greater visibility. Her efforts were promptly rewarded by the unhindered view of Geoff getting to his knees and leaning over the side of tub as he grabbed for the elusive bar of soap. The sight of his massive back and long, sleek hip and thigh made Meg suddenly feel that there wasn't enough air in the world to allow her to take a deep breath.

She swallowed hard, her breath coming in harsh little rasps as something warm and tingly unfurled deep inside

229

her. Covering her mouth with shaking fingertips, she leaned against the wall, feeling weak and shaky and hot.

Walk away. Walk away!

But she didn't walk away. She wanted to . . . she really did. It was the only decent thing to do. But she just couldn't seem to make herself do it. Instead, she stepped back up to her vantage point, her tongue unconsciously sweeping along her lips as she watched her husband, the soap finally retrieved, sink back into his bath.

Geoff leaned his head back against the rim of the brass tub and sighed contentedly. God, but a real bath felt good. After days of sponging himself off in the small basin in his bedroom, he couldn't think of anything that could possibly feel better than soaking his sore, injured muscles in the warm water. Except, of course, for one other thing . . . But that one thing and how to attain it were frustrating him beyond all reason.

What was he going to do about Meg? In the past few days, they'd spent a lot of time together, and Geoff had to admit, he couldn't have asked for a better nurse. She was considerate, efficient, and patient. The only problem was, he didn't want Meg for his nurse—he wanted her for his lover—and he didn't have the slightest idea how to make her stop treating him like a patient and start treating him like a man.

Wearily, he closed his eyes, idly running his hand across the surface of the water. Meg's whole attitude toward him had become almost maternal, and after the kiss they'd shared on Thursday night, it was damn irritating.

How had Stuart handled his wife, Claire? She had been his nurse, too, during the war, when Stuart was injured and held prisoner in a Confederate hospital. Stu had told him several amusing stories of his early relationship with his ravishing redheaded wife, but had never mentioned any-

230

thing about Claire treating him like a mother hen fussing over a chick.

Maybe he should write Stu a letter and ask him for his advice. After all, if there was any man on earth who knew how to seduce a woman, it was Stuart Wellesley.

A slight sound over by the door caught Geoff's attention, and he lazily opened his eyes. What was that sticking through the crack in the door? It looked like a scrap of fabric.

Suddenly, his heart slammed against his ribs as he realized he was looking at the hem of a drab gray dress. The same color as the one Meg had been wearing that morning.

She was watching him take his bath.

Geoff closed his eyes, not wanting her to know that he'd caught her at her little game. He could barely contain his smile. So his little wife wasn't as disinterested in him as he'd thought. The mental vision of Meg peeking at him from the other side of the door was highly arousing, but for a change, Geoff didn't try to control the erection he felt surging to life just under the water.

So, you want to see a man just as God made him, do you, sweetheart? Well, far be it from me to deny you.

He stood up.

And Meg nearly fainted.

Geoff heard her audible gasp and knew that his provocative move had achieved the desired effect, but he forced himself not to look at the door. Rather, he picked up the soap and bent over, casually running the bar up his legs. In this position, he could raise his eyes enough to check and see if she had run away from his boldly masculine display.

She hadn't. The hem of her full skirt was still visible, and he knew she was still looking at him.

Straightening, he turned so that he was facing directly toward her line of sight and idly ran the soap up his thighs, moving inexorably closer to the place where he hoped she was focused.

She was—and the sight of her fully aroused husband was so stimulating that her knees almost buckled.

Meg had seen a naked man before—or at least, she'd seen a statue of one during a trip to an art museum in Portland. But the statue hadn't come close to having the breathtaking masculine attributes her husband was now displaying. Although its male organ had been clearly visible, it had looked small and limp, nestled cozily between heavily muscled alabaster thighs.

Geoff's manhood was anything but small and limp. Rather, it was thick and hard, and much, much bigger—standing out from his body with a bold, pulsing aggression that was almost frightening in its primitive maleness.

"Love's great weapon," Meg whispered, remembering a phrase she'd once read in a scandalous French novel. She closed her eyes for a moment, trying hard to draw a deep breath. When she finally found the courage to open them again, she was met by the arresting sight of Geoffrey's hand sliding up and down his stiff shaft as he washed himself. Although Meg knew that he was only bathing, there was something incredibly erotic about his hand's movements. To her complete shock, she realized that she wished it was *her* hand gliding so passionately over that jutting, satiny length.

Just thinking about touching Geoff in such an intimate manner made something deep inside her begin to pulse, and she gasped out loud, shocked by her body's primitive response to her husband's silent call.

In the quiet of the kitchen, Geoff heard Meg's shaky, indrawn breath and quickly made a decision—one that would affect the rest of his life. Bending over, he hurriedly sluiced water over his loins. Then, without hesitation, he stepped from the tub and started across the kitchen.

Meg saw him throw one leg over the edge of the tub and took a quick step backward, intending to flee from her guilty position before he toweled off and reentered the hall. But she managed only three steps before the kitchen door suddenly flew open and Geoff appeared—naked, dripping, and magnificently aroused.

Meg didn't have time to utter a sound before he was all over her—his hot, sexually charged body pressing against hers, his mouth passionately plundering. Her response was immediate. With a small cry of surprised delight, she circled his neck with her arms and opened her mouth, welcoming his invading tongue. She felt the moisture from his chest soaking through the bodice of her dress, making her nipples tighten. Instinctively, she rubbed her wet, tingling breasts against him, silently cursing the fabric that separated their scorching flesh.

"Do you want to really be my wife?" he rasped, breaking their torrid kiss and staring hard at her.

"Yes, I do," she answered honestly. A shiver of anticipation coursed through her at the blaze of desire that ignited in his amber eyes. "Do you want to really be my husband?"

"Yes, I do." The hoarse need in his voice was like an aphrodisiac, and again Meg lifted her lips for his kiss.

But Geoff didn't kiss her. Instead, he placed his forefinger beneath her chin and silently waited until she again opened her eyes. "Are you sure, Megan?"

"Yes."

"Good," he nodded, scooping her up into his arms and heading for the staircase. "*Now*, the vows have truly been spoken."

He carried her up the stairs as easily as if she were a

child, but stopped halfway down the hall and set her on her feet.

"Is something wrong?" she asked. "Am I too heavy?"

"No," Geoff panted, pulling her up hard against him. "I just can't wait any longer to kiss you again."

Meg started to respond, but her words were trapped by Geoff's mouth descending on hers. His kiss was hot and lusty, searing in its demand, and she loved it.

"Did you kiss Francine like this?" she gasped, when he finally released her enough that she could speak.

Geoff raised his head and gaped at her in stunned astonishment. "Why do you want to know that?"

"Because," Meg said breathlessly, "she told Virginia she didn't like your kisses."

"No, I never kissed Francine like this."

Meg giggled and brushed her lips provocatively along his. "Maybe that's why she didn't like it."

"I doubt it," he growled, lowering his head again. The last thing on earth he wanted to talk about at this moment was his cold, calculating ex-fiancée.

"Well, personally, I think . . ."

"Quit talking about Francine, and kiss me," he demanded. Wrapping his arm more tightly around her, he stepped forward, pinning her between the wall and his big, muscular body. Meg could feel his hard arousal pressing insistently against the front of her dress, and unconsciously, she spread her feet, wanting to feel it against the very center of her.

Geoff immediately reacted to her body's invitation, lowering his hands and pressing her hips tight against his. "You're . . . making me crazy!" he panted, and again swept her up in his arms, continuing to kiss her even as he carried her down the hall.

They entered the master bedroom and Geoff laid her

234

gently on the bed. His body was so hot with desire that he felt like he was going to burst into flames, but he knew he had to go slowly. Meg deserved more than a quick coupling that would most certainly leave her unsatisfied and disappointed. Despite the fact that this moment had come with neither candles nor champagne, as he'd planned, Geoff was determined to make her first sojourn into passion's pleasure as special as he knew how.

"You're beautiful, do you know that?" he whispered.

"Thank you," she blushed, feeling suddenly shy, now that the moment was at hand. "So are you."

Geoff smiled. "Dressed or undressed?"

With a boldness that surprised even her, Meg reached up and lightly brushed her fingers across his still damp chest. "Both, but undressed is better."

Well pleased with both her answer and her caress, Geoff ran the backs of his fingers down her soft cheek. "You know that if we do this, we're voiding our agreement."

"I know."

"And that doesn't bother you?"

"No."

He leaned over her, bracing himself on his uninjured arm. Lowering his head, he kissed her eyelids, then slowly moved his lips over to the sensitive skin near her ear. "Are you doing this because you want a baby, or because you want me?"

Meg turned her head till her lips brushed his. "You," she said simply. "I want you."

Casting her a look that made her feel like she might melt, Geoff slowly began unbuttoning her dress. Meg didn't protest, but closed her eyes and allowed herself to drift in the thick, warm pool of love's first awakening.

When her dress gaped open to the waist, he reached up and quickly untied the ribbon on her light chemise, drawing in a long, shuddering breath as he feasted on the sight of her lush breasts. Meg opened her eyes, suddenly frightened by the intensity in his hot, lusting eyes.

Geoff felt her stiffen. "Don't be frightened," he murmured. "I'm not going to hurt you."

Meg nodded and relaxed, closing her eyes again and smiling as she felt the tingling sensation of his rough fingers against the delicate skin of her breasts.

His warm breath on her face was like a caress as he again bent to kiss her. His mouth's first touch was gentle, but when she parted her lips beneath his, he responded with a passion that threatened to steal the very breath from her lungs.

Still kissing her, he slipped his arm behind her neck and raised her to a sitting position, peeling her dress off her shoulders and skimming the material down her arms until she was free of the bodice's tight confines. Slowly, he lowered her back to the bed and stood up.

"Raise your hips," he directed softly, and when she complied, he skimmed her skirts and petticoats off, tossing them carelessly on the floor behind him. Meg felt a quick tug at her feet, then heard two soft thuds as her shoes joined her clothing. She lifted her eyes and found him standing next to the bed, looking like some great, naked god. "I feel like a beggar at a banquet," he said softly.

A maidenly blush spread over her as she watched her husband blatantly peruse her nude body, but she resisted the temptation to cover herself with her hands. "Should I take my stockings off?" she whispered.

Geoff shook his head. "No, leave them on. I don't think there's anything in the world quite as exciting as a woman wearing only her stockings."

With the innate sensuality of a woman born to be a lover, Meg raised her knees and crossed one slim leg over the other. "And I, Mr. Wellesley, don't think there's anything in the world quite as exciting as watching you take a bath."

Geoff threw her a slow, seductive smile. "You won't be saying that in an hour, sweetheart," he promised, lying down next to her and pulling her over on top of him. "I'm going to show you something that's a lot more exciting than bathing."

Meg shivered. Stretched out full length atop his massive body, she could feel his pulsing erection nestled intimately between her thighs, pressing against the threshold of her womanhood with a heated intent that even in her innocence she understood.

"I love the way you feel against me," he whispered, skimming his hand up her body until his fingers reached the side of her full breast. "Every night when I was in Portland, I'd lie in bed and imagine what this would be like."

"You did?" Meg asked, bracing herself on her elbows and looking down at him in wonder. "You thought about me when you were in Portland?"

"Oh, yeah," he chuckled, taking advantage of her new position to slide his tongue sensuously down the cords of her neck. "I also think about you when I'm sitting in my office trying to tally the day's production, or when I'm eating beans and bacon with the men, or when I'm working on the flume, or when . . ." He paused, his brows drawing together in startled recollection. "You know, I was thinking about you when that damn log came down the chute."

"That's terrible!" Meg cried, stiffening her arms and lifting herself off his chest. "I thought you didn't get out of the way of that log because you were trying to save your tools."

"I *was* trying to save my tools," he grinned, "but I wouldn't have left them lying in the chute if I hadn't been daydreaming about doing this . . ." And raising his head, he buried his face in the softness of her breasts. Cupping his hands around her bottom, he nudged her upward, causing her to lift her breasts until his mouth closed around her taut nipple.

Meg let out a little shriek as a jolt of desire shot from her breasts straight down to the core of her being. "What are you doing to me?" she gasped.

"Making love to you," he responded hoarsely, rolling her over and seizing her mouth in another consuming kiss.

Meg reached up and ran her fingers lightly over his chest, surprised to hear his groan of pleasure as her fingers skimmed his flat nipples. "Does that feel good?" she murmured against his lips.

"Oh, God, yes. Everything you do feels good."

Meg smiled, reveling in her newfound feminine power. She threaded her fingers through his thick hair, then arched her back and rubbed her nipples provocatively against his. "How about this?" she purred.

Geoff suddenly shot to his knees, gulping in a great draught of air. "You've got to slow down, sweetheart."

Meg looked at him in bewilderment. "I'm sorry," she stammered. "I didn't know . . . I thought you'd like that."

"Oh, God," he moaned, his eyes riveted at the point where the sheer black stockings clung to her slender thighs, "I *do* like it. That's the problem—I like it too much. That's why we've got to slow down a little."

Meg didn't really understand what he meant, but she was vastly relieved that he seemed concerned that his desire for her was too great, not too little. "What do you want me to do?" she murmured.

He closed his eyes, thinking of about two thousand

things he'd *like* her to do—none of which would do anything to slow things down. "I want you to just lie still," he rasped. "Don't touch me for a minute."

Meg grimaced doubtfully, not sure that she could keep herself from touching him if he started working his magic on her again. "But I thought you told me the other night that you *wanted* a woman who wouldn't just lie still."

"Yeah," he muttered. "I know I said that. I just didn't realize how closely you were listening."

"All right," Meg sighed, "if you want me to lie still, I will." Obediently, she dropped her hands to her sides and closed her eyes.

Geoff threw a beleaguered look at the ceiling, thinking he must have lost his mind to make such an insane request. But then he looked down at his impassioned, throbbing manhood and knew that if he didn't, he'd never be able to control himself long enough to give Meg the pleasure she deserved.

Still kneeling, he lowered his head and kissed the sensitive skin on the underside of her breast, then trailed a moist path downward with his tongue, finally pausing with his mouth against the soft skin of her abdomen.

Despite her resolve, Meg shifted restlessly beneath him, incapable of lying completely still as Geoff's mouth wove its intimate path down her body. Unconsciously, her thighs parted and she opened herself to him in ultimate invitation.

Geoff smiled in unabashed male exultation at his wife's response to his sensuous attentions. Languidly, he trailed his forefinger down her belly, pausing when he reached the soft down at the juncture of her thighs before continuing on his seductive quest.

He glanced up and found Meg staring at him, her eyes wide with a combination of desire and apprehension. He held her gaze, binding them together in a silent lover's communion as his finger dipped into her hot, wet depths.

Meg's eyes flared wide at this first, tentative invasion and Geoff immediately withdrew, not wanting to frighten her. She moaned at the loss of the exquisite friction, then nearly bucked off the bed when his knowing fingers touched her sensitive little bud. "Please," she gasped, her head flailing back and forth on the pillow, *"please* let me touch you!"

Geoff's battle was lost. Eagerly he moved over her, gently pushing back the hair at her temple. "Kiss me," he whispered.

With a breathy little sigh, Meg put her hands on either side of his face and raised her lips to his. Geoff covered her mouth with his own, silently cursing the pain he knew he was about to cause her. Then slowly, carefully, he entered her.

He winced as he broke through her maiden's barrier and heard her little cry of pain. Lifting his head, he looked deep into her questioning eyes. "It'll get better now," he promised softly.

She nodded, blinking away the tears that had sprung to her eyes.

With an iron will, Geoff clamped down hard on his rampaging lust, forcing himself to lie still and allow her time to recover. His sensitivity was rewarded a few seconds later, when the cloud of pain vanished from her eyes. "Is that it?" she asked in a small, disappointed voice. "Are we through now?"

Gathering her closer, he buried his head in the hollow of her neck. "No, sweetheart," he chuckled, his heart bursting with an emotion he couldn't even name, "we've hardly even begun."

"Good," Meg smiled. "Good."

Uttering a quick prayer that his starved passions wouldn't get the better of him, Geoff started gently rocking, introducing his wife to love's ancient dance. Meg responded with several clumsy rotations of her hips, making him smile. He reached down and carefully guided her movements until they melded with his own. "Like this," he murmured.

"Oh, that feels wonderful."

A shudder ran through him at her softly voiced words, and gradually, he increased his pace.

Meg's eyes widened at the sudden fervor of his lovemaking. Then, from somewhere deep inside her, a pressure started to build—an exquisite, expanding bubble that felt like it might burst at any moment.

Geoff felt it, too, and deepened his thrusts. Together they slowly climbed toward love's pinnacle, breathlessly reaching the summit at the same moment and hurtling simultaneously over the other side as they shared passion's great gift.

Long moments passed before either of them spoke. Finally, Geoff broke their intimate contact and rolled to his side, taking Meg with him. His eyes were warm and gentle as he lightly stroked her flushed cheeks. "I didn't hurt you, did I?"

"No," she demurred, "not much, anyway. Besides, Virginia told me there was pain the first time."

"And what about the other things Virginia told you?" he asked quietly.

Meg smiled and gave him a quick, saucy kiss. "She was wrong."

Geoff laughed and wrapped his arms around her, hugging her close. "So it wasn't exactly like Virginia told you it was going to be?"

"Not exactly," Meg responded wryly. "Actually, though, there's probably just one main difference."

"Oh? What's that?"

"Virginia married Lawrence Lombard, and I married you."

Geoff grinned, suddenly very pleased with his wife and his marriage. For a long time they lay contentedly wrapped in each other's arms until Meg broke the silence with a little giggle. "Geoff?"

"Hmmm?"

"May I watch you take a bath again someday?"

"Baby," he laughed, turning her toward him and kissing her soundly, "next time, you can *give* me a bath."

Chapter 20

"I have to go up to my camp this morning."

Meg turned over and smiled languidly at her husband. "You can't," she drawled, reaching out and running a tapered finger down his chest. "You're not well yet."

Geoff snorted his opinion of that statement and firmly removed her hand from where it now rested well below his waistline. "If I can do what we've been doing for the past three days, I think I'm well enough to go to work for a few hours."

"Do you really have to?" Meg purred, ignoring his frown of warning as she again dipped her hand beneath the sheet.

"Yes, I really do," he answered, but his voice had lost much of its conviction. "And I don't have time for . . . Meg! Stop it!"

"Stop what?" she asked innocently, her hand closing around his already swelling shaft.

"Stop *that*," he ordered weakly. Flipping the sheet back, he reached down and covered her hand with his own. "*Now* look what you've done."

She smiled. "It just sort of happened."

243

"Yeah," he grunted, trying hard to conceal his own smile. "Just like it's 'sort of happened' every couple of hours for the last three days."

"If you really want me to stop," she sighed, "I will." She removed her hand and got to her knees to provocatively brush her breasts across his chest. "I'll just do this instead."

Geoff squirmed with pleasure as she lowered her head and flicked his nipples with her tongue. "My God," he groaned, "is this the same little girl who lay stiff as a board in this bed two weeks ago and asked me to just get it over with?"

Meg giggled. "Speaking of 'stiff as a board' . . ."

Again her fingers encircled his pulsing erection, gently caressing the sensitive underside.

"Lady, you are a wicked one," he growled, pulling her head up to give her a searing kiss. "You just can't get enough, can you?"

"No," she smiled. "I think I'm addicted. But since you aren't interested, you might as well get on your horse and go to work."

"Yeah, right," he answered wryly, looking down at his hard, thick length. "Like I'm going to be able to ride with that."

"Well, in that case, you're in luck, Mr. Wellesley," she teased. "I just happen to know how to cure your problem." Again, she moved down his body, her tongue tracing a wet little path down his chest.

Geoff groaned in surrender, then held his breath as Meg's head moved downward past his navel. "What are you planning to do down there?" he rasped.

"Something I read about in a French novel," she answered, her voice muffled against his abdomen.

For a long moment, his breath caught in his throat.

Then, suddenly, he released it in a cry of pure, primal ecstasy as Meg's mouth closed over him. "Jesus Christ, what kind of books do you read, lady?"

Meg smiled, her tongue swirling around the hot, wet tip of his throbbing manhood. "I was trying to bone up on how to be a good wife."

"Yeah, well, you learn real quick."

"Thank you," she murmured, and lowering her head farther, she took him fully into her mouth.

Geoff moaned and clenched his teeth together in an effort not to explode. "Megan. Megan, stop! Please, sweetheart, I can't take anymore."

Meg looked up into his passion-hardened face and knew he spoke the truth. With a smile full of promise, she crawled up the length of his body, threw her leg over his hips, and sat down.

Geoff was so stunned that for a moment he just stared up at her. Then she wiggled her hips and threw him a sassy wink, reminding him that she was waiting.

It was all the encouragement he needed. Grabbing her around the waist, he propelled her up and down, faster and faster, until they exploded together.

Meg collapsed on his chest, both of them panting and sated. After a long, exhausted silence, she finally lay down next to him, snuggling her head against his shoulder.

"You are one amazing little woman," he chuckled, "and I'm so done in I may never move again."

Meg smiled in pleased satisfaction at his words of praise. "But, Geoff, you *have* to move."

"Why?" he groaned.

"You said it yourself. You have to go to work today!"

* * *

Geoff walked over to the big, carved armoire and pulled out a light jacket. "What are you going to do while I'm gone?"

Propping her head up on her hands, Meg smiled with contentment. "I don't know. I suppose I really should go out to the mill. I haven't been there in over a week."

"You don't sound very excited."

"I'm not."

"Then don't go. I want to talk to you about that anyway. I'd really prefer you not work out at the mill anymore."

Meg opened her mouth as if to protest, but Geoff stayed her words with a raised hand. "Now, don't get your back up about this. You can still oversee everything and keep the books. I'd just rather have you do it at home. Besides, Greg Stevens is out of work since the Riley Mill had that fire, and he's a terrific manager."

"But the cost, Geoff . . ."

"Hang the cost. We can afford it, and Greg needs the job."

Meg felt a little thrill of pleasure at Geoff's use of the word "we." "Actually," she admitted, "I *would* rather stay home." Quickly she amended her words to add, "As long as I don't lose control over what's going on at the mill."

"You won't," Geoff assured her. "You'll just run things from a distance. Okay?"

Meg nodded her agreement and he threw her an approving grin. "Since we settled that so easily, I'll talk to Greg about starting right away."

"It sounds wonderful," Meg sighed, pleased that her husband was lifting the yoke of responsibility from her shoulders. "And to celebrate, I'm going to make you a really good supper, for a change." She giggled. "I swear, all we've eaten for three days is cold meat and cheese and bread . . ."

"And each other," Geoff finished with a leer.

"Geoff!" she giggled, staring at him in scandalized astonishment. "I don't *believe* you said that."

Geoff grinned unrepentantly, adroitly ducked the pillow that came hurtling his way, and lunged for the bed. Grabbing Meg's naked body against him, he buried his face in her breasts. "You taste better than anything I've ever eaten."

"Well, I should hope so! She squirmed out from under him and leaped to her feet. "Now, get out of here," she ordered, backing away as he followed her off the bed.

"Give me a kiss and I'll go."

"No," she answered tartly. "If I do that, you'll never leave."

"You may be right," he laughed, and pinned her to the wall with his big body. Reaching around, he cupped her bottom in his hands, pressing her hard against his hips and groaning with renewed desire as he massaged her warm, firm flesh.

"Stop it," Meg warned, ducking away from him, "or you're not going to be able to ride again."

"You sure are in a hurry to get rid of me," he complained. "You got a date with somebody else?"

"Oh, absolutely," she taunted. "Now that I've found out how much fun lovemaking is, I've decided to give it a try with every man in Wellesley—just to make sure you're as good as I think you are."

Geoff grinned at the compliment. "You're wasting your time. I guarantee you're going to be disappointed."

Meg sashayed over to him, looping her arms around his neck and lifting her lips for his kiss. "You know, I think you're probably right. Guess I'll just tell all those other men that I've changed my mind."

"Good idea," he murmured, bending his head and kiss-

247

ing her. "Just make sure you don't change your mind about me."

"That's something that will never happen."

It was a full hour before Geoff finally left the house.

Geoff pulled his horse up in front of the large white house and dismounted, throwing the reins over the hitching rail. Striding aggressively up the walk, he stepped on to the porch and knocked on the front door.

Thank God Meg had bought his story about going up to his camp to work. Not that he'd really lied to her. He *had* gone to the camp, but he hadn't stayed for the two or three hours he'd intimated he would. Instead, he'd had a quick meeting with Ned Johnson, reviewed the past week's production sheets, then quickly departed and returned to town.

It was time he and Peter Farnsworth had a little talk.

As he glanced down at his bandaged hand, Geoff's eyes narrowed with tightly controlled anger. There was no doubt in his mind who was responsible for his accident, but that wasn't the main reason he was standing on the Farnsworths' doorstep. He would deal with Peter later regarding that situation—after he'd had a chance to gather some hard evidence against the man.

Today he was here solely to issue a warning—to let Peter know, in no uncertain terms, that if he ever threatened Meg again, he would pay with his life.

Geoff did not consider himself a violent man. But the thought of Farnsworth forcing his way into her house and confronting Meg with veiled threats of what he would do if she did not keep the promises her weak, misguided father had made threw him into a towering rage.

He was here to make sure it wouldn't happen again. The

marriage was consummated and Meg was his, period. He would brook no further interference from Peter, Peter's father, or anyone else.

Receiving no answer to his first summons, Geoff raised his hand and knocked again, more loudly this time.

The door opened immediately, as if someone had been standing there all along and had just now decided to respond. George Farnsworth, looking pale and apprehensive, stood on the other side.

"Good morning, Wellesley."

Geoff ignored the greeting. "I'm here to see your son," he said flatly.

"Peter isn't here."

Geoff stared in silence at the old man, attempting to weigh the truth in his nervous words.

"He's not!" George reiterated. "He left this morning for San Francisco. He'll be gone for several weeks. A vacation, you know . . ."

"How nice for him," Geoff gritted, "and how timely, too."

George shook his head, trying hard to adopt a look of bewildered innocence. "I'm afraid I don't know what you mean."

"I'll just bet you don't. All right, if you say he's gone, I'll believe you. Just give him a message for me when he gets back."

Farnsworth nodded. "Of course . . ."

"Tell him the next time he threatens my wife, he's a dead man."

George's eyes widened at the steely thread running through Geoff's voice. "Now, see here, Wellesley," he blustered. "Just who do you think you are, making threats like that?"

Geoff smiled, a mirthless grimace that made George pale

even further. "Who am I, Mr. Farnsworth? I'm the man who has every intention of killing that slimy bastard you call a son if he's foolhardy enough to go anywhere near my wife again."

"You think you're above the law, don't you?" George challenged.

"I'll tell you what I think. I think there's not a jury in the state of Oregon that would convict me for ridding the world of a rapist."

George drew a strangled breath and his eyes bugged out so far that Geoff thought he might be having an apoplectic attack. "Get off my porch and off my land!" the old man choked.

"Just make sure you give Peter the message," Geoff spat. Without another word, he turned and walked away, leaving George Farnsworth gaping after him.

"Hell, yes, I'd love to manage Taylor Mill!"

Geoff leaned back in his chair and grinned at Greg Stevens, relaxing for the first time since he'd left George Farnsworth an hour before.

After his brief, unsatisfying confrontation with Peter's father, he'd started for home, but had changed his mind and stopped at the Rosamonde Saloon, deciding he needed a drink to calm himself down before he faced his wife.

He'd pushed through the saloon's batwing doors and headed for the bar, but had stopped short when he'd heard Greg calling out an invitation to join him at a small table.

After sharing a couple of beers, Geoff had broached the subject of Greg managing Meg's mill and was immediately rewarded by his friend's enthusiastic response.

"I thought you'd be interested," Geoff nodded. "And I

can't think of anyone I'd rather have looking after Meg's affairs."

"So you convinced her to stay home, huh?" Greg chuckled.

"Actually, it didn't take much convincing. Turns out she doesn't like being at the mill any more than I like having her there."

"Does this new desire for togetherness mean things are going better between Mr. and Mrs. Wellesley?"

Geoff signaled the barkeep to bring them another round. "Yeah," he nodded. "Much better."

"I'm glad to hear it, Geoff. I was beginning to worry about the two of you."

"You and me both, buddy, but since I got hurt, Meg and I have spent a lot of time together and we've worked a lot of things out."

Greg smiled knowingly. "So you don't regret being forced into the marriage?"

Geoff pondered the question for a moment, surprised at just how much his feelings had changed in the last two weeks. "No," he said thoughtfully, "I don't regret it. I mean, I was mad as hell at first—"

"You had every right to be," Greg interjected.

"But now," Geoff continued, pausing to light a cigarette, "well, she's sort of grown on me."

Greg laughed and slapped his friend on the back. "Women have a way of doing that, especially when they're as pretty as Meg."

"She *is* pretty, isn't she?" Geoff nodded, a faraway look on his face. "Pretty, and funny, and . . ."

"Affectionate?"

Geoff chuckled and took a drag on his cigarette, blowing out a long, satisfied stream of smoke. "Yeah. Affectionate."

"I'm happy for you, Geoff. I really am."

"Thanks," Geoff acknowledged. "I'm happy for me, too. I've waited a long time to find the right woman, and even though I didn't exactly *find* Meg, everything seems to be turning out just fine."

"That's all that matters."

The two men sat is silence for a moment, contentedly smoking and drinking their beers. Finally, Greg took a deep breath and asked the question that had been bothering him ever since Geoff had sat down. "What about this thing with Farnsworth?"

Geoff's mellow expression disappeared. "There's nothing I can do about that for now. I went over to his house this morning to straighten him out, but his father informed me that he's *vacationing* in San Francisco and won't be back for several weeks."

"Vacationing?" Greg sneered. "More likely, he's hiding out, waiting for you to cool down. I figured he was the one responsible for your 'accident.' "

Geoff nodded. "I know he is. I can't prove it, of course, but I'd bet my life on it. That's not what I went to see him about, though."

"Oh?" Greg asked curiously. "Has something else happened?"

"Yeah. Apparently, Farnsworth paid a call on my wife while I was in Portland."

"Jesus Christ!" Greg blurted, slamming his beer glass down on the table as his own ire rose. "Did anything—"

"No," Geoff said quickly, "nothing happened, except that he scared the hell out of Meg by telling her that if she didn't dump me and marry him, he'd see to it that I met a sudden and violent end."

"Well, shit, Geoff," Greg growled, "Farnsworth's not the only one who can stage a fatal 'accident'! Let's just kill the bastard. The world would be a better place without him, anyway."

Geoff grinned at his friend, grateful for his loyalty. "That's exactly what I told his father I would do if Peter ever went near Meg again."

"Do you think the old man believed you?"

"Yeah, I think so. Whether it will have any effect on Peter remains to be seen, though."

Greg tipped his head back, draining the last of his beer. "You need any help with the bastard, you just let me know."

Geoff nodded. "Thanks. I appreciate the support. Now, let's have another beer and talk about how much pay that new job of yours is worth."

Chapter 21

"Meg?"

No answer.

"Meg, I'm back."

Still no answer. Frowning, Geoff walked through the foyer and stood at the bottom of the stairs. "Meg!" he called up to the second floor. "Are you up there?"

No answer.

"Where the hell is she?" Pushing through the swinging door, he strode through the kitchen and out to the back porch. "Meg, you out here?"

No answer.

A little prickle of apprehension made the hair on the back of his neck stand up, and hurriedly, he retraced his steps back into the house, looking around for a note.

There was none.

Suddenly, George Farnsworth's words floated through his mind. *Peter left this morning for San Francisco . . . a vacation, you know . . .*

"Jesus Christ!" Geoff swore, his heart pounding with fear as he raced up the stairs. Tearing into the master bedroom, he glanced around wildly, looking for anything that might indicate that Meg had packed a bag.

There was nothing. No drawers hanging open, no clothes strewn around, and her valise was sitting on the floor of her armoire, where she always kept it.

"Don't panic!" Geoff ordered himself. "She's probably just over at Virginia's."

Bolstered by that thought, he thundered back down the stairs and out the front door, leaping on to his horse and taking off down the road toward the Lombards' house like all the demons in hell were after him.

Bounding up Virginia's front steps, he pounded ferociously on the front door. It opened almost immediately and he looked down to see a small child staring up at him, her eyes wide with curiosity.

"Is your ma here?" Geoff demanded, heedless of the fact that his size and loud voice might scare the child.

The little girl nodded mutely.

"Will you go get her, please?"

Again the child nodded and took off for the back of the house, leaving him standing on the porch.

"Mama, mama, there's a big man outside!"

Virginia had heard the pounding on her front door and was already on her way into the foyer, wiping her hands on a dish towel. "Oh, Mr. Wellesley," she greeted, relief evident in her voice, "it's you. Won't you come in?"

"No thanks, Mrs. Lombard," Geoff responded, trying hard to keep his voice calm so he wouldn't needlessly scare her. "Have you seen my wife?"

"Today?" Virginia questioned, looking surprised.

Geoff nodded.

"Why, no. I haven't seen Meg since Saturday. Is something wrong?"

"I don't know," Geoff said truthfully. "I came home a little while ago and she wasn't there."

Virginia smiled. The anxious tone in Geoff's voice was

clearly a sign that the romance she had hoped for so fervently must finally be budding. "I'm sure there's nothing to worry about," she said calmly. "Meg probably just walked downtown to do a little shopping, or maybe she went out to the mill."

Geoff shook his head. "She's not downtown. I was just there, and I'm sure I'd have seen her."

"Is something wrong?" Virginia questioned again, suddenly feeling apprehensive herself.

"I hope not. It's just that Meg told me this morning when I left that she was going to stay home today, and now, I can't find her."

"There must be a logical explanation," Virginia insisted. "Surely nothing could happen to her in broad daylight."

"You're probably right. It's just that Peter Farnsworth left unexpectedly on the morning train . . ." Geoff's voice trailed off.

"Merciful heavens," Virginia gasped, her fingers clutching at her throat. "You don't think he . . ."

"No, I'm sure it's just a coincidence," Geoff interrupted quickly, wishing he felt as positive as he sounded. "I'll just keep looking. Thanks for your time." Turning, he started down the porch steps.

"Mr. Wellesley?" Virginia called after him.

"Yes?"

"Please let me know the minute you find her."

"I will, Mrs. Lombard."

Virginia watched Geoff vault into his saddle and tear off down the street, then closed the door and leaned her head against it. "Please, God, make her be at home when he gets there. Please!"

* * *

Geoff stopped briefly back at the house, just in case Meg might have come home. He poked his head in the front door and called her name, but wasn't surprised when she didn't answer.

Remounting his horse, he rode over to the Wellesley depot, hoping to ask old Ward Prescott, the ticket agent, if he'd seen his wife board the southbound train that morning. But again his efforts were thwarted. When he arrived at the train station, the old building was deserted and dark.

"God *damn* it!" he cursed, hitting his uninjured fist against the wall of the building in angry frustration. "Megan, where the hell *are* you?"

The only place left to look was the mill. He didn't really believe Meg was there, since they'd just talked about it this morning, but he headed out toward the river anyway, not knowing what else to do.

The ride took only twenty minutes, but in that time, Geoff made the decision to catch the train to San Francisco the following morning. He didn't know how much good it would do, since it would be almost impossible to find the couple in the huge, bustling city even if they *were* there, but he knew he couldn't just sit here and wait. He had to do something. At least in San Francisco he could hire a detective agency to assist him in his search.

He rode up to the mill office and was greeted by Hank Berkeley, Meg's foreman. "Afternoon, Mr. Wellesley," the old man said pleasantly, bobbing his head in welcome. "Come to fetch your wife?"

Geoff's heart slammed against his ribs. "Is she here?"

"Yup. Right there in her office. Why? Did you think she was lost?"

"Something like that," Geoff muttered. He drew a deep breath and let it out again. Now that he knew Meg was

257

safe, he was suddenly very, very angry. Why hadn't she left him a note, telling him where she was going? *Why?*

Quickly he dismounted and dropped his horse's reins to the ground, not even bothering to tie him.

"Oh, Mr. Wellesley," Hank said, oblivious to the other man's forbidding expression, "I've been wantin' to ask ya—"

"Not now," Geoff growled, striding up the office steps.

"But, sir, I need to—"

Geoff swung around and glared at the hapless old man. "Didn't you hear me? I said, *not now!*"

Hank took a startled step backward. "Sorry . . . I didn't mean to . . ." His words trailed off as he watched Geoff again turn away and disappear through the office door, slamming it mightily behind him.

Meg nearly jumped out of her skin as the door to her office banged open. "Geoff!" she cried, clapping her hand against her chest, "Sakes alive, you nearly scared me to death!" Then, seeing the anger on his face, she asked quickly, "What's wrong? What are you doing here?"

Wordlessly, he rounded the corner of her desk, pulling her out of her chair and clutching her to him in a desperate embrace. "Where the hell have you been?" he demanded, his voice hoarse.

"Why, I just decided to come out here and—"

Her words were cut off by his mouth descending on hers in a scorching kiss.

"Geoffrey!" she gasped, pulling her mouth away and trying to loosen his bone-crushing grip. "What is *wrong?*"

Geoff's words tumbled out incoherently as he continued to kiss her eyes and cheeks and neck. "Farnsworth . . . San Francisco . . . thought he'd taken you . . ."

"What? You thought Peter Farnsworth kidnapped me?" She felt him nod against her neck.

Suddenly he raised his head. *"Why* didn't you leave me a note telling me where you were going?" he demanded angrily. "I came home, and you weren't there, and . . ." He cut off his own words as he grabbed her again, covering her mouth with his own.

"I'm sorry!" Meg apologized, when he finally released her lips. "I thought I'd be home before you were."

Lacing his fingers through her hair, he tipped her head back until their eyes met. "Don't ever do that again," he commanded, giving her a little shake. "Do you understand me? Don't *ever* do it again!"

"All right!" she nodded frantically. "I said I'm sorry. It never occurred to me you'd be worried."

Geoff made no move to release her and Meg's eyes widened as she heard her hairpins dropping to the ground with sharp little tinkles. "Why are you taking my hair down? Geoff, stop it!"

"Shut up and kiss me," he ordered, the fire in his eyes quickly turning from anger to passion.

"Not here!" Meg gasped, trying to wiggle away from his rocklike chest. "I'm done with my work here, and we can go home . . ."

"No," he said, his hands sweeping downward to cup her full breasts. "I don't want to go home yet."

"But, Geoff, this is insane!" Horrified, she looked down to see his fingers flying down the buttons on her bodice. "Stop this right now!" she demanded. "What in the world are you thinking of?"

Geoff grabbed her hand and placed it over the swelling bulge in his denims. "That's what I'm thinking of," he grinned.

"Well, stop thinking of it!" She wrenched her hand away from his heated arousal. "We can't do this here. Someone might see us!"

"No one's going to see us," he panted, racing over to the window and pulling down the shade. He lunged for the door, yanking the curtain across the window and snapping the lock into place. "See?" he said, returning to where Meg stood gaping at him and pulling her back into his arms. "No one can see us and no one can get in."

"Geoff, this is crazy," she protested, still not able to believe that he really intended to make love to her with fifty men not more than a stone's throw from the door.

His grin widened. "I know. One time a couple of years ago, my brother Seth made love to his wife, Rachel, on the desk in her office."

"And, did they get caught?" Meg asked, her eyes suddenly dropping to his midsection as he began unbuttoning his Levis.

"Yeah," he answered, pulling the denims down his lean hips. "But that's because they forgot to pull down the shades. Some old maid saw them through the window."

"Then what happened?" Meg asked vacantly, her eyes riveted on his erection.

Geoff saw where her eyes were focused and quickly divested himself of his pants. "The old bitch told everyone in town," he drawled, walking toward her, nude from the waist down. "It was a real scandal."

"How awful for them," Meg murmured, reaching out and wrapping her fingers around his throbbing length.

Geoff groaned. "Yeah, it was." Moving a step closer, he spread open her gaping bodice and dipped his head, pulling a ripe breast into his mouth as he worked her dress up her thighs.

"We have to be very quiet so none of the men hear us," Meg warned, as her fingers fumbled frantically with the ties on her pantalettes.

Geoff nodded and brushed her hands away, hooking his

fingers into the waistline of her drawers and ripping them all the way down the front.

"Geoff!" Meg gasped. "That wasn't necessary. I could have done it."

"But not fast enough," he leered, pulling the ripped pantalettes down until they lay at a pool at her feet. He picked her up and sat her on the edge of her desk, wrapping her long, slender legs around his waist so they were facing each other, she sitting, he standing.

Meg threw her head back and closed her eyes, shivering with anticipation as she felt Geoff's rough fingers skim up the inside of her thighs. Reaching down, she resumed her intimate caresses.

Geoff lowered his lips to hers, toying with her excited nipples as his tongue dipped erotically in and out of the soft interior of her mouth. Then, suddenly, he could wait no longer. Grasping her by her hips, he propelled her forward and entered her.

Meg let out a little shriek of surprised pleasure and braced her hands behind her on the desk, thrusting her hips forward to meet her husband's passionate assault. Nothing she had ever experienced had excited her as much as the raw sexuality of this frenzied coupling, With a deep, throaty moan of ecstasy, she answered his every thrust, moving with him until they came together with a lusty shout.

For an endless moment, they stayed as they were, panting and spent. Then, slowly, Geoff withdrew as Meg unwrapped her legs from where they still gripped his loins and collapsed backward on to her desk. He smiled and bent over her, gazing deeply into her dreamy, sated eyes.

"I almost went crazy when I thought you were gone," he whispered, kissing her.

"I promise I'll leave a note next time," she whispered

261

back, and raised a limp hand to lightly stroke his thick, russet hair. "I really did think I'd be home before you were. You must not have stayed at your camp very long."

"No," he said, shaking his head. "I didn't."

"How come?" she yawned. "Is your hand bothering you?"

"No. I just checked on a few things, ran a couple of errands, and then came back home."

"Missed me, huh?"

"More than you know."

Meg was very pleased with that answer. Raising her head, she gave him a soft kiss and sat up. "Let's go home, Mr. Wellesley."

Geoff's eyes flared. "Haven't you had enough for one day?"

"I don't know," she shrugged coyly. "Is twice enough for one day?"

Geoff grinned and bent down to run his tongue tantalizingly across her nipples. "I think three times a day is better," he murmured, inhaling deeply of the sexy, spicy scent of her skin. "Sort of like eating."

Meg pushed him firmly away and hopped down from her desk. "Eating is something we should definitely think about doing."

"Yeah. I'm starving. How about if we stop at the Palace Cafe on the way home and get some supper? That way, you won't have to cook."

"Oh, I don't know," Meg replied, stretching luxuriously. "I'm so tired, I'm afraid I might fall asleep right in the restaurant."

Geoff smiled into her sleepy eyes. "Okay, sweetheart, we'll go home. There's always cold meat and bread and cheese."

Meg smiled and dragged a tapered nail across the rock

ribbed expanse of his abdomen. "That's becoming my favorite meal."

Hank Berkeley leaned against the wall of Meg's office and chewed on a blade of grass. To the casual observer, he appeared to be merely whiling away the late afternoon, enjoying the waning sunshine and relaxing after his day's work. In reality, however, he was guarding the door.

He'd been concerned when Geoff had first arrived, bewildered by the big man's seeming anger and worried that it might be directed toward his beloved employer.

Hank had worked for the Taylors for thirty years, had known Meg from the time she was a tiny girl being dandled on her father's knee, and he was not about to let anyone hurt her—even if that someone was Geoffrey Wellesley.

When Geoff had rushed into Meg's office and slammed the door angrily behind him, Hank had immediately taken up a post near the back window, standing far enough away that he couldn't be seen, but close enough to give him a shadowy view of what was going on inside.

What he'd seen had soon changed his worried frown into a satisfied smile. He'd watched Geoff grab Meg and pull her close, nearly suffocating her in his frenzy to kiss her. Curious to see what Meg's response would be to her husband's lustful overtures, Hank had remained near the window until he saw her reach down and intimately caress him. With a gusty little sigh of relief, he'd finally walked away and taken up his current position near the door. "So he's not mad, after all," he muttered happily to himself. "He's just got his blood up for her."

Hank tried hard not to listen to the fevered sounds sifting through the rough boards of the office walls, but he was unable to repress his smug smile when he heard Meg's scream of pleasure, followed almost immediately be Geoff's answering, triumphant shout.

When the storm inside the little shack finally died down, he pushed away from the wall and sauntered away, well pleased with what he'd overheard.

He headed down toward the river, pausing when he saw Luigi Padroni, an Italian immigrant who had recently joined the Taylor Mill staff, striding energetically toward Meg's office.

"Miss Taylor, ah, I mean, Mrs. Wellesley, is she in her room?" Luigi asked, in his heavily accented English.

"Yeah . . ." Hank answered hesitantly.

The burly Italian nodded his thanks and continued on toward the shack.

"Wait a minute," Hank called, running a few steps to catch up to him. "You can't go in there now."

"Why not?"

"Because *Mr.* Wellesley is with her."

"So?" Luigi shrugged.

"So," Hank answered, throwing the man a meaningful look, "they can't be bothered just now. Understand?"

Luigi looked at him in confusion for a moment, then a huge grin spread across his face. "Oh yes, now I understand. So, it is like Mrs. Phillips predicts?"

"What are you talking about?" Hank asked, shaking his head.

Luigi laughed. "You did not hear? That old woman, she's told everyone in town that Mr. Geoffrey Wellesley is going to find a bambino in his Christmas stocking!"

"She said that, huh?" Hank chuckled.

"Oh yes, many times."

"Well, I'll tell you somethin', Luigi. This time the old bat might just be right."

Chapter 22

"How is your hand feeling?" Meg asked one Saturday morning, as she and Geoff sat down to breakfast. Geoff's hand had healed with remarkable speed, and the previous day, Dr. Emerson had removed the last of the bandages.

"Pretty good," Geoff acknowledged, flexing his fingers. "Except for the stiffness in my little finger, I'd never know I'd been hurt. The doc says even that will probably go away with time."

"I'm so glad," Meg smiled. At least *some* of the guilt she felt about Geoff's accident had been lifted with the knowledge that he hadn't sustained any permanent damage.

"Do you have anything special planned today?" Geoff asked casually.

"No," she responded. "Nothing special. Do you have something in mind for us to do?"

"Yeah. I want to show you something, but it will take the whole morning, and you need to dress in old clothes."

Meg looked at him in surprise. "Are we going to get dirty?"

"You never know," Geoff answered, wiggling his eyebrows.

Meg giggled at his outrageously lecherous look, already

thinking about what she might wear that would be practical, yet easy to get off. She blushed, just thinking about what Geoff must have in mind.

The past four weeks had passed in a blissful haze. She and Geoff had been together almost constantly, spending the long, lazy summer days getting to know each other. During the evenings they took long walks, strolling hand in hand through the verdant summer greenery as they talked about their childhoods, their families, and their dreams and hopes for the future.

On rainy days, they stayed home, reading aloud, playing chess, or puttering around the house together as Geoff made minor repairs to long-neglected furnishings and fixtures.

Their newfound camaraderie made each new day an adventure, filled with the promise of new pleasures as they discovered how much they had in common.

And the nights . . . Never would Meg have believed she could find such rapture in a man's arms. Geoff was the perfect lover—at times so virile and demanding that their encounters lasted only a few minutes. At other times, he made love to her with such slow, sensuous sophistication that she thought she might die before he granted her release from the sweet torture he wrought upon her receptive body. But whatever his mood, he was always tender and considerate as he tutored and guided her in the subtle art of making love.

As the days passed and their intimacy grew, Geoff also encouraged her to explore the carnal side of her nature, whispering words of encouragement and delight when she boldly responded to his scandalous suggestions.

Meg had never realized it was possible to find such fulfillment in another person's company and, as the halcyon month of July drew to a close, she was happier than she'd ever been in her life.

Geoff never mentioned Peter Farnsworth, although Meg suspected the evil man was never far from his mind. Several times he had left the house alone, returning hours later wearing a look of grim determination that Meg found somehow frightening. But despite the lurking threat, she cherished the days they spent together—laughing, talking, and falling in love.

Meg had long since admitted to herself that she was in love with her husband. Regardless of the bizarre circumstances that had brought them together, she realized that in Geoff, she had truly found her life's mate. Basking in the warmth of his growing affection, she seemed to blossom, her newfound happiness evident in her every smile and gesture.

It was nearly ten o'clock before they were ready to leave. Meg stepped out on the porch and watched with surprise as Geoff led their horses from the shed.

"Are we riding?"

"Yeah, I thought we would. Is that okay?"

Meg smiled and gestured to the split skirt she was wearing. "It's perfect."

They mounted and headed out of town, taking the trail which led to Geoff's land.

"Are we going up to your camp?" she asked, as they trotted along companionably.

"No, but where I'm taking you is in the same direction," he answered vaguely.

"Why all the mystery, Geoff? Where are we going?"

"You'll see," he laughed, and nudged his horse into a

canter, effectively cutting off the possibility of further conversation.

"You're mean," she called after him, then gave the lie to her words by throwing him a broad smile when he turned around and looked at her.

They came over a rise and Geoff pulled his horse to a halt, waiting for Meg to catch up.

"Why are we stopping?" she asked as she joined him.

"Because this is what I wanted to show you." With a sweeping gesture, he motioned to the valley below.

Meg's eyes followed the path of his arm, then widened with astonishment as she noticed what he'd obviously brought her out there to see. "Your house is gone!"

"Yup," he nodded. "All except the foundation."

"But why did you tear it down?"

"Because I want to start it over," he said softly, "and I thought you might like to have a hand in designing it."

Meg's eyes slowly swung over to meet his and the look that met her was so soft and full of love that for a moment she thought she might start to cry. "Oh, Geoff . . ." she breathed.

He reached over and took her hand, raising it to his lips and kissing it. "I love you, Meg," he whispered. "I want us to build this house together and then move in and build our lives together. I want to fill it up with children and grandchildren and spend my old age sitting on the front porch with you. But I need to know if that's what you want, too."

"Oh, yes," Meg answered, her throat thick with the joyful tears she was trying so hard to contain, "it's exactly what I want."

Before she even realized his intent, Geoff was off his horse and wrapping his hands around her waist to lift her off hers. "Kiss me," he murmured when she was on the ground. "Kiss me and tell me you love me."

268

"I do," Meg sighed, her eyes filling. "Oh, Geoff, I love you so much . . ."

They kissed, a long, heart pounding caress full of love and promise and excitement.

Geoff finally broke their embrace and sat down, pulling her down next to him and wrapping his arm around her shoulders. "Just look at that land, sweetheart, and all of it . . ." he paused and pointed, "all the way from the edge of those trees over there to that rise over there . . ." He swung his arm in a huge arc, pointing to a spot in the shadowy distance far to the west, "is mine. It'll be the perfect place to raise a family."

Meg nodded, so full of emotion that she couldn't speak. When she finally did find her voice, it was shy and a bit tentative. "Geoff?"

"Yes?"

"How long will it take to build the house?"

"Not too long. I've already made up some rough plans. If you approve of them, I'll hire a crew and get started right away. We should be able to move in before the snow flies."

"Good," Meg smiled.

Placing his finger under her chin, Geoff tilted back her head until their eyes met. "Are you so anxious?"

"Well, yes," she murmured, ducking her head and blushing.

Geoff looked at her curiously. "Megan, what is it?"

She looked up at him, her eyes filled with light and happiness. "I just want to be in and settled before our baby is born."

"What?" Geoff shouted, his voice booming across the valley and echoing off the surrounding hills. "A baby? Already? But, sweetheart, how do you know? It's only been a few weeks."

Meg nodded, blushing again. "I guess a few weeks is all

it takes," she giggled. I wasn't going to tell you till I was absolutely sure, but I've already missed my woman's time." If possible, her face turned an even deeper shade of crimson. "And Virginia said I have all the signs."

"The signs?" Geoff gasped. "What signs? Are you sick? My God, girl, what the hell are you doing riding a horse? Why didn't you tell me?"

"I'm fine," she laughed, pushing playfully at his massive shoulder, "and I'm only queasy when I first get up."

"You shouldn't be riding," he repeated. "What if you fell?"

"I won't fall. I'm the best horsewoman in the county and you know it."

"That doesn't matter. Anybody can take a fall. Now, we're going to walk these horses home and you're not getting back up on one until next spring. Do you understand me?"

"Oh, you're being so silly. I never took you for the overly protective type."

"You're damn right, I'm overly protective," he muttered, laying her back in the coarse mountain grass and bending close to gaze into her eyes. "That's my baby you've got in there, and I'm not taking any chances with him . . . or you."

"Him?" Meg teased, pushing back a lock of hair that had fallen over his forehead. "What if it's a her?"

"Him . . . her . . . it doesn't make any difference. The point is that you have to take care of yourself now, and if you won't, I will."

"Does this mean no more lovemaking for the next eight months?" Meg asked, pursing her mouth in an innocent little moue.

Geoff frowned. "I don't know. I guess we'll have to ask Doc Emerson about that."

"Oh, you're so funny!" Wrapping her arms tightly around him, Meg pulled him down on top of her and buried her head in his neck. "Virginia already told me that it's perfectly safe to make love—right up until the end."

"I don't know," Geoff answered doubtfully. "I still want to ask Doc Emerson."

"Geoffrey Wellesley," Meg protested, pushing him away, "if I had known you were going to be such a fool about this, I wouldn't have told you."

Bracing himself on an elbow, Geoff smiled down at his beautiful wife. "You're right," he said softly, "I am a fool . . . when it comes to you. Now, come on, let's walk down this hill—*slowly*—and I'll show you the existing foundation and you can tell me how big you want this place to be. Then, we're going to go back to town, you're going to take a nap, and I'm going to go wire all my brothers with the news."

"Oh, Geoff, do you really think you should tell them this soon? I mean, so many things could go wrong. Maybe we should wait another month or so."

"Nothing's going to go wrong," he assured her, taking her hand and starting down the hill. "Not with me here, looking after you. Besides, I think I set a new record, and I want them all to know about it."

Meg looked over at her swaggering husband and a little frown furrowed the space between her eyes. "What do you mean, a record? Are you and your brothers in some sort of contest to see who can have the most children the fastest?"

"No," Geoff hedged, wishing he hadn't said anything. "It's nothing like that."

Actually, it was *exactly* like that. As each of the Wellesley brothers had gotten married, there had arisen a good-natured rivalry as to who had sired his first child the fastest. And now Geoff, the oldest so far to marry, could finally mark his entry into the competition by boasting that his wife must have gotten pregnant during their first night together. He couldn't wait to show his brothers up after the years of ribbing he'd taken about his advancing age and how, if he didn't get married soon, he'd probably be too old to sire children at all.

"If it's not a contest, what exactly is it?" Meg pursued.

"It's nothing," Geoff laughed. "Forget I mentioned it. I just know how happy all my brothers will be to know I'm going to be a father and I can't wait to share the news."

Meg smiled, delighted that Geoff seemed so pleased. When she'd first suspected she was pregnant, she'd been worried that he might be upset she'd conceived so fast. After all, they'd hardly even begun their life together, and now, in just a few short months, they'd be adding a child to the relationship. Obviously, she'd worried for nothing.

When they reached the bottom of the hill, they paused a moment, catching their breath and looking around at the spectacular panorama. "Are you really happy about the baby?" Meg asked softly.

Geoff drew her into his arms and kissed her, rubbing his palm against her still flat stomach. "Sweetheart, everything about you makes me happy."

Meg leaned back against him, smiling with sublime contentment. "I love you, Geoffrey Wellesley."

Bending his head, he kissed her ardently. "And I love you, my precious wife."

Chapter 23

Geoff walked into the Palace Cafe and looked around for his brother-in-law. He'd been surprised to receive the brief note from Lawrence Lombard asking him to join him for lunch, but had quickly sent the bank messenger on his way with an affirmative response.

Geoff didn't know Lawrence well, but on the few occasions they'd met, he'd found him to be somewhat of a pompous know-it-all. Still, he *was* Meg's sister's husband, and Geoff had no reason to turn down his invitation for lunch.

Spying Lawrence sitting stiffly at a table at the back of the cafe, Geoff nodded a greeting and walked over to join him.

"Afternoon, Lombard," Geoff greeted, thrusting out his hand.

"Ah, Mr. Wellesley," Lawrence returned, rising, "so good of you to join me."

Geoff frowned. Obviously, their new, familial relationship had done nothing to relax Lawrence's formal demeanor. Seating himself, Geoff picked up the menu laying in front of him. "What's good today?"

To his surprise, Lawrence laughed. "Oh, come now, you know nothing is *good* here."

Geoff joined him in his mirth. "Yeah, but when it's the only restaurant in town, that's bound to make everything taste a little better."

"The waitress recommends the meatloaf," Lawrence advised him, "so that's what I'm having."

"Sounds fine to me," Geoff nodded, slapping his menu shut and tossing it back on the table. "There's not too much anybody can do to ruin meatloaf."

"Oh, if I know this place, they'll find a way."

Geoff chuckled, surprised by the other man's humor. Lombard wasn't really so bad after all, when he wasn't trying to impress people with the importance of his position at the Wellesley Bank.

"So," Geoff said, motioning to the waitress to bring him a beer, "any particular reason you wanted to have lunch?"

Lawrence sobered. "Actually, yes. I mean, not that we need a reason, now that we're related, but there is something I think we need to discuss."

Geoff nodded, but remained silent as the waitress put his beer on the table and took their order. She sauntered away, then turned to throw Geoff an enticing look over her shoulder.

"Does that happen to you often?" Lawrence asked.

Geoff shifted uncomfortably in his seat, a bit embarrassed that his prudish brother-in-law had noticed the girl's attempt to lure him. "Yeah, sometimes," he muttered.

Lawrence sighed. "It never happens to me."

Geoff was so surprised by Lawrence's wistful tone that he didn't know whether to burst out laughing or feel sorry for the man. Clearing his throat, he said, "You were about to tell me why you wanted to have lunch."

Lawrence straightened, trying to think of a delicate way

to broach the subject of Peter Farnsworth with the formidable Geoffrey Wellesley. In truth, Lawrence had always been in awe of Geoff, as most of the men in Wellesley were. After all, he had everything: money, good looks, and power. A daunting combination in any man, but Geoff carried his charm and success so nonchalantly that it was downright intimidating. No man with that much money and that much power should be so casual.

It had taken more than two weeks for Lawrence to screw up enough courage to extend his brother-in-law this invitation for a private tête à tête, and when he'd received Geoff's acceptance, he hadn't known whether to be flattered or terrified. Especially considering what he wanted to talk to him about. But Lawrence Lombard knew his family duty.

Unable to come up with a subtle way to ease into the conversation, he decided just to plunge right in. "I thought you and I should talk about how to repay the debt to Farnsworth."

Geoff froze, his beer halfway to his mouth. "What debt?"

Lawrence swallowed hard. This was something he'd not anticipated. Was it possible that Wellesley didn't know about the massive amount of money the Taylors owed the Farnsworths? Was that why he'd taken no initiative to pay it?

"I figured Megan would have explained the family's financial situation to you by now," he said, his voice heavy with trepidation.

Geoff set down the beer glass. "Well, she hasn't, so why don't you tell me what this is all about. *What debt?*"

Lawrence blinked, stalling for time, but there was no way out of it. He was going to have to tell Geoffrey Wellesley that, as Meg's husband, he owed the Farnsworths either the deed to the mill or fifty thousand dollars. Drawing a deep breath, he said quietly, "A long time ago, Frederick Taylor borrowed a great deal of money from George Farnsworth. Apparently, Mr. Taylor was never able to pay Mr. Farnsworth back, and for many years, nearly until the time of Mr. Taylor's death, in fact, Mr. Farnsworth let the payments slide. He merely continued to add interest to the amount owed, but never pressed Mr. Taylor for it. Then, when he heard that Mr. Taylor was dying, he demanded that either the loan be paid in full, the deed for the mill signed over to himself and his son, or . . ."

". . . Or Meg marry Peter and bring the mill into the family that way," Geoff finished.

"Yes," Lawrence nodded.

"So," Geoff continued, his voice tight, "Meg, in order to keep her mill but save herself from having to marry Peter, decided to blackmail me into marrying her instead, figuring that once we were married, I would repay the loan."

"Oh, I don't think that was her motive," Lawrence blustered.

"Never mind," Geoff snapped, cutting off any further defense of Meg that Lawrence might try to mount.

"Geoffrey, please . . . oh, pardon me. May I call you Geoffrey?"

Geoff nodded dully.

"Virginia and I own twenty percent interest in the mill. The other eighty percent was willed to Meg."

"That hardly seems like an equitable inheritance," Geoff noted.

Lawrence shrugged and said without rancor, "I suppose that because of my position at the bank, her father felt that Virginia was well taken care of. At any rate, I have arranged to borrow the necessary funds to pay Virginia's portion of the indebtedness. As for the rest . . ." He trailed off lamely.

"How much do I owe?" Geoff asked, his voice curiously flat and devoid of emotion.

"Forty-two thousand," Lawrence croaked.

Geoff nodded curtly and rose. "You'll have my draft within the week. As you know, I don't keep that kind of money in your bank, but I will wire Portland immediately."

Lawrence looked up into Geoff's shuttered face. "I hope you won't hold this against me."

To his complete astonishment, Geoff laughed, a cold, humorless bark that made the hair stand up on the back of Lawrence's neck.

"No, Lombard, I don't hold a thing against you. You're certainly not the one to blame."

"It's not Megan's fault, either," Lawrence said desperately.

Geoff threw the man an icy look. "That's between her and me, isn't it? Thanks for lunch." And flipping a dollar on to the table, he turned on his heel and strode out of the cafe.

Lawrence watched Geoff leave, then gazed down at the money sitting on the table. "He didn't even eat," he murmured, shaking his head. "He left a whole dollar to pay for a twenty-five-cent meal and didn't even eat."

Geoff mounted his horse and rode as far and as fast as he could, never slowing his reckless pace until the exhausted animal finally stopped of its own accord.

He looked around, surprised to see that he was several miles out of town, not far from the site where his new house was being constructed. Wearily, he climbed down from his shaking, blowing horse and sat down in the grass, dropping his head into his hands.

Just like Francine. *Just like Francine.* Those three words

had pounded through his head ever since Lawrence Lombard had told him the news that had so completely shattered his world.

"You stupid, gullible idiot!" Geoff cursed aloud. "She doesn't care about you. She never did. She only cares about your money!" He threw his head back and stared up at the dreary, cloud-laden sky, his face a mask of pain and betrayal and rage. "She's no different from Francine—just a whole lot more sophisticated in her methods."

A million images of Meg flashed through his mind—her sunny smile across the breakfast table, the funny way she wrinkled her nose when she pretended he was shocking her, the dark, fathomless depths of her eyes as they lay in each other's arms after making love, her shy, slightly embarrassed expression when she'd told him he was going to be a father . . .

"God damn you!" he cried in a voice thick with misery. "Why don't you love me for myself? Why is it always the money?"

Lord, how he wished he was poor. There wasn't a single man among all his employees who wasn't happier than he was—and all because of money. None of them ever had to worry that a woman was interested in him only for what he might buy her, or that a man wanted to be his friend solely for the influence he might be able to exert on his behalf.

How wonderful it must be not to always have to be wary of other people's motives. To know your wife married you because she loved you. *You.* Not your bank account.

It had always puzzled Geoff that none of his brothers seemed to feel the same as he did about their wealth. The Wellesley family was one of the richest in the country, and after their parents' tragic and untimely deaths several years before, all eight children had inherited more money than they could spend in ten lifetimes. The rest of his siblings

278

seemed to enjoy their staggering wealth. Only Geoff had a problem with it.

Maybe, he thought bitterly, that was because he was the only one who was fool enough to fall in with people who exploited him for it. Even his brother Eric, with his kind disposition and gentle heart, had never seemed to suffer the problems Geoff did.

And now he was married to a woman who was the most artful exploiter of all—and she was going to have his baby. Geoff squeezed his eyes shut and shook his head. She'd wanted the damn forty thousand so badly that she'd prostituted herself for it. Night after night she'd lain in his arms, seducing him with her soft voice and her silken body—and all for forty thousand dollars.

"Well, now you have it, you lying, deceiving little bitch!" he snarled. "I'm just sorry I promised Lombard a bank draft. It would have been more appropriate to leave the cash on the night stand."

Slowly, he heaved himself up and stood looking out at the site where his house was going up for the second time. "How many times are you going to start that thing and then tear it down before you finally wake up?" he asked himself bitterly.

But right now, the house was the least of his concerns, and quickly he turned away. The real question was how he was going to handle the rest of his life, now that he knew Meg didn't care about him. His first impulse was to confront her—to shout and rail and tell her exactly what he thought of her. And then leave. Walk out of her precious, shabby house and never return.

But even as he thought about how good it would feel to abandon the scheming little witch who'd so duped him, he knew he couldn't do it. Meg was his wife, his responsibility. He couldn't just walk out.

Geoff's jaw tightened as he thought again of her duplicity. God knew he'd been furious when she'd blackmailed him into marrying her, but he was able to overcome that, once he realized how desperate she'd been for his protection. And with everything they'd shared in the past two months, he might even have been able to put this little shocker behind him, if only she'd just told him the truth.

Considering the way he'd come to feel about her, all she'd have had to do was ask and he'd have given her anything. My God, forty thousand dollars was a pittance. He'd have given her ten times that much if she'd just told him the truth.

That thought gave him pause. How *had* Meg intended to get the funds she needed? Had she, perhaps, gone to Lombard and asked him to intervene on her behalf? Geoff shook his head, discounting that theory almost as fast as he'd formulated it. Lawrence had been too conspiratorial, too *manly* with his invitation for the private lunch meeting, and too shocked when he realized that Geoff didn't know about the debt. No, Meg hadn't sent Lombard to serve as her extortionist. Of that, at least, Geoff was sure.

"She must just be biding her time till she finds the right moment," he growled. "In bed, probably."

He chuckled mirthlessly. If that was her plan, she was going to have a long wait. There would be no more "bed" for them. Meg wanted his money, and she could have it—every miserable cent. He would pay her debts, he would build her the most opulent house in the state, he would buy her everything she laid her eyes on. But from now on, his money was all she would have of him. As far as he was concerned, the marriage would go back to the original rules.

No entanglements . . . hadn't those been her words?

280

Well, now she was going to get her wish. No more love . . . no more relationship . . . no more anything.

He had allowed his heart to rule his head for the last time.

Chapter 24

Geoff barely made it through the front door before Meg raced into the foyer, her eyes bright with excitement. "Mr. Spoffard is here!"

"Mr. Spoffard? Who the hell is Mr. Spoffard?"

"Shh!" she warned, casting a look backward and covering her lips with her finger, "he'll hear you."

"I repeat," Geoff whispered loudly, "who is Mr. Spoffard?"

"For heaven's sake, Geoff, he's the man you told me you'd hired to decorate the house. Don't you remember?"

Geoff closed his eyes, groaning inwardly. The last thing he needed in his present state of mind was to have some prissy curtain-and-rug salesman tromping around the house taking measurements and talking about brocade. "Yeah, I remember. Well, you go ahead and talk to him."

Meg looked at him in utter astonishment. "You aren't going to see him?"

Geoff shrugged and started up the stairs. "Why should I? Decorating is woman's stuff."

"But," Meg sputtered, hurrying after him and laying a hand on his arm, "it's your house, too. Don't you care about what I choose?"

Geoff shrugged off her hand, finding it almost impossible to be in such close proximity to her without giving rein to his temper. "Actually, I couldn't care less."

Meg's mouth dropped open at his unexpected rudeness. "What in the world is wrong with you?"

"Nothin'," he muttered, and continued on up the stairs.

Meg watched in complete bewilderment as Geoff disappeared up the steps, then turned and slowly walked back to the parlor.

"Please excuse the delay," she apologized. "Mr. Wellesley just came in, and I thought perhaps he would be able to join us, but unfortunately, he has, ah, something else that requires his attention right now."

"I understand," Mr. Spoffard replied, smiling benignly. Benjamin Spoffard was a small, thin man in his late forties, with a receding hairline and penetrating gray eyes. He had made a fortune in the past ten years, furnishing and decorating the mansions of the newly rich western gold miners and timber barons, and he had long come to realize that money didn't denote breeding. He was accustomed to hearing the wives of these self-made millionaires make excuses for their husbands' boorish manners.

But somehow, he had thought Geoffrey Wellesley would be different. First of all, the Wellesley fortune wasn't new, and second, the telegram he'd received from the man requesting his services had been polite and literate. Obviously, however, he'd been wrong in his initial assessment. Mr. Wellesley was apparently just as gauche as most of his nouveau riche counterparts in this godforsaken part of the wilderness.

With a last little apologetic shrug, Meg sat down on the edge of the worn settee, folding her hands in her lap and looking at Mr. Spoffard expectantly.

Spoffard drew a small black book out of the case he had

brought, and producing a pencil, said, "Now, madam, suppose we start with you telling me exactly what it is you envision for your home."

"I'm not exactly sure," Meg admitted, her eyes straying back to the staircase. "Some new carpets for the first floor, perhaps, and fresh paint everywhere."

"Ah, yes," Mr. Spoffard nodded, looking around at the dingy walls with poorly concealed distaste, "I would most certainly agree that paint and wallpaper are in order. I have a sample of some lovely silk paper that just arrived from Paris. I think it would do very nicely in your foyer."

He pronounced the word "foy-yea," and Meg could barely control the smile that threatened at the little man's pomposity. "I would like to see it," she remarked, straightening her spine and adopting a equally haughty mien.

"Now, what else?" Spoffard prompted, scribbling furiously in his little book. "What about furniture? Certainly this room needs to have all the pieces replaced, or at least recovered. And from what I can see of the dining room," he leaned forward, squinting into the dining room myopically, "I would guess that you need, at the very least, a new table and chairs, and a breakfront."

"Oh, I don't know about that," Meg said uncertainly. "I hadn't really thought about replacing the furniture, since my husband is building us a new house and I don't know how long we will be living here."

Spoffard's eyebrows rose almost to the level where his hairline should have been. "A new house?" he asked excitedly. "So you will be needing my services on another house after this one is completed?"

Meg could almost see the dollar signs spring up in his eyes. "That's a possibility," she nodded coolly, "depending, of course, on how satisfied I am with your services on this assignment."

Spoffard cleared his throat, knowing he had overstepped his bounds. The girl might be young and sweet, but she was nobody's fool. "Yes, well, all right, then, let's get back to the matter at hand. I feel very strongly that if you and Mr. Wellesley are going to sell this home, you will want to put everything to rights in order to get the best price."

"I agree," Meg nodded, "but I don't think it's necessary to bear the expense of replacing the furniture, considering . . ."

"Oh, for Christ's sake, Megan, quit quibbling about the money and replace the damned furniture!"

Meg looked up in horrified embarrassment as Geoff strode into the room, a glass of whiskey in his hand. "Mr. Spoffard," she said quickly, forcing herself to close her mouth and quit gaping at her husband, "may I present my husband, Mr. Wellesley. Geoffrey, this is Mr. Benjamin Spoffard."

Geoff nodded and grunted a greeting. "Don't listen to her about the money, Spoffard. Replace everything, get the place looking as good as it can, and hang the expense."

"A capital attitude, Mr. Wellesley!" Spoffard exclaimed ecstatically. "It's rare to find a man so generous when it comes to matters of the household."

"I'm sure my wife will attest to the fact that I am the epitome of generosity," Geoff said, throwing her an icy look. "Isn't that right, *dear?*"

Meg was so flustered by Geoff's unprecedented rudeness that she didn't even respond. What in the world was wrong with him this afternoon? "Mr. Spoffard," she said quietly, "I wonder if you would excuse Mr. Wellesley and me for a moment? I need to ask my husband a . . . question."

"Absolutely," Spoffard beamed. "Take your time. Take your time."

Meg rose and threw a damning glare at Geoff. "May I see you in the kitchen for a moment, please?"

He opened his mouth as if to deny her request, but seemed to change his mind. Shrugging, he followed her out of the parlor.

As soon as the kitchen door swung closed behind them, Meg whirled on him, her eyes blazing with anger. "What in heaven's name is the matter with you this afternoon?" she demanded. "You are behaving abominably!"

"Am I?" Geoff said coldly, taking a long drink of his whiskey.

"Yes, you are. And why did you tell that man to replace all the furniture? You know we're moving to the new house in a few months and none of it will fit there. Why would we replace it now?"

"Why not?" Geoff shrugged elaborately. "I can afford it."

"That's not the point," Meg snapped. "It's an utter waste when we're going to sell the house anyway."

"I've decided not to sell it," Geoff announced.

"What? You mean we're going to keep the house, even though we're not going to be living here? Why?"

"No, we're not going to keep it. I'm going to give it to Lawrence and Virginia—furnishings and all, so I want it to be nice."

"Give it to Lawrence and Virginia!" Meg gasped. "But they already have a house . . ."

"That place they live in is hardly better than a cracker box, and this was Virginia's home as well as yours. Why not let her have it?"

For a long moment Meg just stared at Geoff, unable to credit his generous words with his angry, set expression. "Please tell me what's wrong," she entreated.

"Nothing's wrong. I just decided to give the house to

286

your sister, that's all. Lawrence and I had lunch today and he . . . told me something so valuable that I feel as if I owe him."

Meg's brows furrowed as she tried to imagine what Lawrence could have told Geoff that he would consider that important. "All right," she sighed, "if you want to give the house to Lawrence and Virginia, that's fine with me. But I hardly feel that I should be picking out furniture for Virginia's home."

"You're absolutely right," Geoff nodded, swigging down the rest of his drink and heading for the cupboard to pour another. "Why don't you set up another appointment with old Spoffard in there and have Virginia come over at the same time. That way, she can pick out her own stuff."

Meg nodded, but her expression was dubious. "I don't know how Lawrence and Ginny will feel about accepting all of this. They're not a charity case, you know."

"Of course they're not, but why shouldn't they accept it? After all, I can afford it."

Meg's eyes narrowed. Why did Geoff keep talking about money? She had never heard him mention it before, and yet this was the second time in five minutes that he had said, "I can afford it." She definitely wanted to get to the bottom of whatever it was that was causing him to act so strangely, but first, she had to get rid of Benjamin Spoffard.

Pushing through the kitchen door, she walked back into the living room, reseating herself on the settee and turning her attention on the decorator. "If you don't mind, I would like to postpone looking at fabrics and colors. Mr. Wellesley has decided that we aren't going to sell the house, after all. Rather, we're going to give it to my sister and her husband, and I would like to have her make the selections, since she will be the one living here."

Benjamin Spoffard blinked with surprise, but quickly

recovered. "Of course, madam. That only makes sense. I wonder, though, since I'm already here, if I might look around the house. It will help me to determine what might fit in specific rooms so that when I meet with your sister I can make appropriate suggestions."

"Of course," Meg nodded graciously. "If you'll just follow me, I'll be happy to show you around."

They quickly circled the first floor, then climbed the stairs to the bedrooms. Meg was talking when she and Spoffard turned the corner into the small guest room, but she halted in mid-sentence when she found Geoff standing by the bureau, stuffing shirts into a drawer.

"Geoff?" she said, her eyes flicking from the bureau to his face and back again. "What are you doing?"

"Rearranging some things," he muttered, then slammed the drawer shut and strode out of the room without another word.

"Mrs. Wellesley, if this is a bad time . . ."

"No!" Meg blurted, turning back to Mr. Spoffard with a smile that was much too bright. "Not at all. This is one of several small bedrooms on this floor. If you'll follow me, I'll show you the others and then we'll look at the master chamber."

The tour was completed in record time, but it couldn't be over soon enough to suit Meg. When Spoffard had finally packed up his things and Meg had closed the front door after him, she leaned against it and breathed a long sigh of relief. Then, she resolutely marched up to the second floor, determined to have it out with her irascible husband. To her astonishment, she again found him in the guest bedroom.

"What *are* you doing?" she demanded, by this time totally out of sorts with him.

288

"I told you," he answered, not turning around, "I'm rearranging my things."

"But why are you putting them in here?"

"Because I'm going to start sleeping in here."

"What?" she gasped. *"Why?"*

Geoff gripped the edge of the bureau, fighting the nearly overwhelming temptation to tell her what he'd found out. It would feel so good, so *damn* good, to yell and shout and vent his anger and pain.

But he didn't. It wouldn't change anything, and at this point, he was so tired and overwrought that he didn't think he could stand the ugly scene he knew his accusations would spawn.

Better just to make an excuse. He had already decided that since Meg was pregnant, he wasn't going to leave her, so he might as well try to make their new "arrangement" as bearable as he could.

"I'm afraid I might kick you in bed," he said vaguely, "or hurt the baby some way. So I've decided to move in here."

Meg felt a tremendous wave of relief wash over her. He wasn't mad, after all. He was just being overly cautious because of her condition.

"Oh, Geoff," she laughed, stepping forward and throwing her arms around him, "I told you before, you're not going to hurt me—and the baby's fine. Why, it's still so little, you couldn't possibly do anything to hurt it."

Geoff stood frozen, making no attempt to return Meg's exuberant embrace. "Even so," he said quietly, unwrapping her arms from around his waist and taking a step backward, "I'll feel better sleeping in here."

Meg looked at him, then looked down at her arms that he'd so pointedly removed from around his body. "You're scaring me," she said quietly. "What have I done that has made you so angry?"

"Quit asking me that," he snapped, scooping a pile of socks off the bed and tossing them in a drawer. "I keep telling you, nothing is wrong."

"You're lying," Meg accused. "Something is very, very wrong, and I want to know what it is. Please, Geoff, don't shut me out. I'm your wife!"

"Yes," he said tiredly, shoving the last of the bureau drawers shut, "you are that. For better or worse, till death us do part. Now, if you'll excuse me, I'm going to go to bed."

"Going to bed? Now? Are you sick?"

"No, I'm not sick."

"But it's only a little past seven," she protested as he propelled her into the hall. "We haven't even had supper yet."

"I'm not hungry."

"But Geoff—"

"Good night, Meg."

With an insolent click, the bedroom door closed in her face.

Chapter 25

"Ginny, it's not just that Geoff doesn't sleep with me any-more, it's that he doesn't even touch me! If I so much as place my hand over his, he pulls away like I'm a leper."

Meg accepted the handkerchief her sister offered and daintily blew her nose. The sisters were sitting in Meg's parlor, after having spent the afternoon with Mr. Spoffard looking at fabric swatches and paint samples and wallpaper patterns.

The day after Geoff moved out of their bedroom, he had gone to Lawrence and offered him the house. Meg had no idea what had transpired during that conversation, but the Lombards were very definitely intending to accept Geoff's incredible gift.

The meeting today with Mr. Spoffard was the third that she and Ginny had had in the past week, and Meg ada-mantly hoped it would be the last. With all the problems in her marriage, the last thing she cared about was whether Ginny should choose robin's-egg blue or sky blue for the second nursery.

As far as Meg's new house was concerned, she had absolutely no idea how the building was proceeding. Geoff never mentioned it, and neither did she. Of course, this wasn't really surprising, since, for the last two weeks, they had barely spoken to each other on any subject. Geoff had taken to leaving for his timber camp well before dawn, often not returning until late at night, after Meg was in bed.

At first, Meg had tried to draw him out, asking him over and over what had caused the startling change in his attitude toward her. But his constant refusal to answer, coupled with the dark, forbidding looks he threw her every time she asked, finally made her give up. He obviously didn't want to tell her what was bothering him, and she refused to beg him for answers.

As the days passed, they spent less and less time together, and on the few occasions when they did happen to both be home, they pointedly ignored each other.

"Meggie," Virginia said quietly, her heart breaking over her younger sister's unhappiness, "are you sure you're not imagining some of what you're telling me? I know whenever I'm in the family way, I often blow little problems way out of proportion. That's something that just seems to happen with pregnancy."

Meg shook her head and dabbed at her eyes with the soggy handkerchief. "I'm not imagining it, Ginny. Geoff hardly even looks at me anymore. It's almost like . . . like he hates me for something."

"Oh, darling," Virginia crooned, pulling Meg into her motherly embrace. "What could he possibly hate you for?"

"I don't know," Meg sobbed. "Maybe he really doesn't want the baby, after all. Everything seemed to start going wrong after I told him about it."

"Nonsense. You said yourself that he was overjoyed when you told him. And he must have wired his brothers to share the news, since you received all those telegrams back from them. Now, would he have done that if he wasn't excited about being a father?"

Meg shook her head. "I wouldn't think so, but if it's not the baby, what could it be?"

"Maybe it's exactly what Geoff says it is. Maybe he's just being cautious with your well-being so that nothing happens to the baby."

"Oh, hogwash," Meg sniffed. "He's not going to hurt the baby by *talking* to me, and that's something he's completely stopped doing!"

"He's always so polite and friendly when he's over at our house," Virginia noted. "If you hadn't told me about your . . . problems, I'd never know there was anything wrong."

Megan sat up, looking at her sister in surprise. "Geoff's been over at your house? When?"

"Several times. He comes to see Lawrence. I'm not sure why, but I would imagine it's about the house. A couple of times he's brought papers with him, so I assume that's what they're discussing."

"And are you privy to these discussions?"

"No. They always go into the parlor and close the doors."

Meg looked at her sister in exasperation. "Don't you find that odd, Ginny, considering Geoff's really giving the house to you?"

Virginia shrugged. "I have no experience with business, Meg. It makes perfect sense to me that Geoff would talk to Lawrence."

Meg looked at her sister speculatively. "I think there's more going on here than just the house. I just wish I knew what it was . . ."

"And *I* think you're making mountains out of molehills," Virginia chided gently. "You wait and see. As soon as the baby is born and you're moved into your beautiful new home, things will be just as they were before."

"Do you really think so?" Meg asked hopefully.

"Absolutely," Virginia assured her, patting her hand. She rose and picked up her reticule. "Now, I'd better run. Are you and Geoff going to the church dance Saturday night?"

Meg shook her head. "I don't think so. He hasn't said anything about it."

"Have you mentioned it to him?"

"Well, no."

Virginia laughed and shook her head. "Maybe you should, little sister. You might just find yourself at the dance with a very handsome escort."

Meg raised her eyebrows thoughtfully. "Perhaps you're right. I just might do that."

"Let me know," Virginia smiled, pinching Meg's cheek fondly. "If you and Geoff decide to go, we can all ride over together."

Meg purposely waited up for Geoff that evening, and when he finally arrived home about eleven, she was sitting in the parlor, reading a book of poetry.

"Good evening," she smiled, rising to greet him as he stepped into the room. Determinedly, she walked over to where he'd paused near the door and placed a soft kiss on his cheek. "How was your day?"

"Fine," he answered, backing away as if he feared he might catch something from her. "What are you doing up?"

"Waiting for you," she murmured, her eyes clouding at his obvious rejection. "I see you so seldom anymore . . ."

Unable to meet her tortured gaze, Geoff turned away and walked over to the breakfront, pouring himself a liberal draught of whiskey. "I'm real busy up at the camp," he explained, his back still to her. "You shouldn't stay up this late. You need your sleep."

"Oh, for heaven's sake, Geoff," she huffed, her disappointment changing to frustration. "I'm pregnant, not dying!"

Slowly, he turned around and a melancholy note slipped into his voice. "How *are* you feeling, Meg?"

"I'm fine," she answered, determined to keep her voice even. This was the longest conversation they'd shared in the last two weeks, and she was determined not to ruin the moment by losing her temper. "A little sick when I first get up, but that passes."

"I know you're having a hard time in the mornings. I've heard you."

Meg colored, embarrassed that he'd heard her retching. "It's nothing. Ginny says it's completely normal."

Geoff looked at her for a long moment, trying hard to conceal the yearning in his eyes. "Is there . . . anything I can do?"

Yes! Meg screamed silently. *You can hold me. You can kiss me and tell me you love me. You can explain what I've done to make you angry so I can apologize and we can get it behind us . . .*

Out loud, she said, "No. I don't think there's any remedy for what ails me, except time."

Geoff nodded and set down his glass. "Well, I guess I'll turn in . . ."

"Geoff!" Meg wailed. "Please don't go to bed yet!"

He turned, looking at her quizzically. "Is there something else you want to talk about?"

"Yes!" she said, frantically searching her mind for anything that would prevent him from going upstairs and closing his bedroom door against her. "There's a . . . dance Saturday night at the church. The fall dance. You know the one. They have it every year."

"Yeah," he nodded. "What about it?"

"I'd like to go."

"I don't think so, Meg. I have too much work to do. The flume is almost ready to start testing, and . . ."

Meg's temper finally snapped. "Oh, to hell with your damn flume! You can't work on it after dark, and you know it. You just don't want to take me to the dance."

Geoff eyes flared angrily at her accusation, but he clamped down hard on his temper. "You're right," he said quietly, "I don't."

Meg was staggered by his flat refusal to accompany her, but she was determined he wouldn't see her pain. "Well, fine, then! I'll go by myself."

"No, you won't," Geoff said, his voice brooking no argument.

But Meg was having none of it. "Oh, won't I?" she taunted. "Just watch me."

"Don't do this, Megan. You're not going to the dance alone, and that's the end of it."

"You have no right to tell me what I can and cannot do," she screamed.

"I have every right!" he shouted back. "I'm your husband, and I say you're not going!"

"Husband?" she spat bitterly. "Since when have you ever acted like a husband?"

His voice was deceptively soft when he answered her. "Maybe I'd have been a better husband if I'd been allowed to choose my own wife."

"Oh!" Meg gasped, his cruel words hitting her like a blow. "You're horrible! I wish I'd married anyone but you."

"I wish you had, too," he barked, grabbing his whiskey glass and swilling down the contents in one great gulp.

A great silence descended as the two adversaries stood glaring at each other. Finally, Geoff broke the painful silence. "Go to bed, Megan."

"I'm going," she retorted and headed for the door. She paused a moment, turning back to throw him one last look. "And I'm also going to the dance. With you, without you, it makes no difference. I'm going."

With a swish of her full skirts, she was gone.

The designers of the First Presbyterian Church had had the foresight to build a basement under the structure which offered the townsfolk a hall for civic gatherings. Everything from town meetings to wedding receptions were held in the cavernous room, and twice a year, at Valentine's Day and at harvest time, the city council sponsored a town dance.

The dances were considered to be the social highlight of the year, and everyone, from lumberjacks to storekeepers to saloon owners, attended. The cost of admission was a quarter, used to offset the expense of refreshments, decorations, and a band imported all the way from Eugene. All the attendees cheerfully paid this fee, knowing that they'd get more than their money's worth in food alone.

The long-awaited event was already well under way when Lawrence, Virginia, and Megan finally arrived on Saturday night. Two of Virginia's children had colds, and after Meg arrived at the Lombard house, it had taken the better part of an hour to get all five children settled into bed.

Unfortunately, the lengthy delay had given Meg ample time to regret her stubborn decision to attend without her husband, and by the time Lawrence finally found a spot to park the wagon, she had decided not to participate in the festivities after all, but simply to walk home.

"I won't hear of it," Virginia snorted, when Meg told her she'd changed her mind. "You're not going to walk home in the dark with every rowdy from the camps in town tonight. Now, come on. We're going in and you're going to have a wonderful time."

"I really don't want to," Meg argued. "It was stupid of me to come here without Geoff. I know that now."

"Nonsense," Virginia sputtered, taking her sister firmly by the arm and propelling her toward the church's open doors. "You're with us."

"But what will everyone think?"

"No one will think anything. Everyone knows how busy Geoff is with his flume and all."

"They're still going to wonder," Meg insisted.

"Who cares? Even if they do, do you think anyone would dare say anything to you? After all, you're Mrs. Geoffrey Wellesley."

"Right. It's just too bad that *Mr.* Geoffrey Wellesley doesn't think about that anymore."

Virginia looked over at her sister sympathetically and sighed. "I know this is hard for you, Meggie, but you've come too far to turn back now. Please, come in with us for a few minutes. Then, if you still want to go home, Lawrence will escort you."

Megan nodded reluctantly. "All right, if you promise Lawrence will take me home if I want to go."

"Of course I will," Lawrence interjected solicitously. "Now, come on, ladies. Let's go in before all the food is gone."

The three of them entered the big hall and Meg could actually hear her name being whispered as every woman in town took note of the fact that Geoff was not with her.

"Oh, this is awful!" she moaned, leaning toward Virginia. "They're all talking about me."

"Never mind," Virginia placated, nodding her head in greeting as they threaded their way through the large

298

crowd. "Just smile and act like everything is perfectly normal."

Taking a deep, bracing breath, Meg plastered a smile on her face and began returning the many greetings being called to her. It seemed to take an eternity before they finally reached the relative sanctuary of the refreshment table.

"Sandwich?" Virginia offered, gesturing to a large tray of cold meat sandwiches sitting on the table.

Meg shook her head. "No, I couldn't eat a thing." She stared at the sandwiches for a long moment, her heart twisting with pain as she thought of how many of those she and Geoff had eaten nestled intimately together in their big bed.

She stayed close to Lawrence and Virginia while they drank punch and chatted with the guests. Then, Lawrence leaned over and said something to Ginny which made her nod and turn to Meg. "Sweetie," Virginia whispered, "Lawrence would like to dance with me. Would you mind?"

"Of course not!" Meg answered, embarrassed that her presence was preventing the couple from enjoying themselves. "You two go right ahead. I'll just sit down on that bench." She pointed at a long, low bench against a wall.

"You're sure?" Virginia quizzed.

"Absolutely. Now, go. Scoot."

With a grateful smile, Virginia looped her arm through Lawrence's and the two of them headed out on to the dance floor. Meg walked over to the bench and sat down, fanning herself with her handkerchief. The room was crowded and stuffy, and she sincerely wished she could leave.

Several of her old school friends approached her, pausing in their dancing to offer congratulations on her marriage and ask about the house Geoff was building.

After about half an hour, Virginia and Lawrence danced by and Ginny leaned over to whisper, "Is everything all right?"

"Yes," Meg whispered back, "but everyone in town seems to know about the new house."

"Doesn't surprise me," Ginny shrugged, then allowed Lawrence to dance her away again.

Another few minutes passed and Meg was finally beginning to relax a little when it happened. A movement to her left caught her eye and she looked up to see Peter Farnsworth heading toward her.

Drawing a terrified breath, Meg looked around wild-eyed, trying to find some means of escape. There was none. She was hemmed in on every side. She leaped to her feet and headed for the door, dodging the whirling dancers as best she could, but the sheer number of people on the floor prevented her from making much progress. She'd taken no more than ten steps when Peter caught her by the arm.

"Good evening, Megan," he said smoothly. "May I have this dance?"

"No!" she blurted. Her startled words came out much more loudly than she'd intended, and she immediately felt twenty pairs of curious eyes turn toward her. "Thank you for the invitation, but I don't care to dance."

"Of course you do," Peter responded, his voice as loud as hers had been. "You're far too beautiful a girl to be left sitting on a bench, and since Mr. Wellesley isn't here to attend you, I'll be happy to take his place."

Peter's outrageously forward comment made several of the women closest to them gasp. Meg closed her eyes, wishing the floor would open up and swallow her. "I just told you, Mr. Farnsworth, I don't care to dance."

300

"And I just told you, *Miss Taylor*, that you do."

His intentional use of Meg's maiden name brought about another round of shocked gasps. Several couples stopped dancing.

My God, he's going to make a scene right here in front of the whole town, Meg thought desperately.

Before she could think of anything to say that might deter him, Peter whipped his arm around her waist and swung her into a waltz. He was holding her much more tightly than was appropriate, and when Meg finally collected herself enough to react, she braced her forearms against his chest, determined to put some space between them.

"Stop trying to push me away," Peter ordered softly, his wide, happy smile belying his steely command, "or I'll kiss you right here in front of the whole town. That should make a few old bats swoon."

"You wouldn't!" Meg gasped, instantly ceasing her struggles, since she knew there was no doubt he would.

"That's better," he smiled. "Now, tell me, how have you been? I haven't seen you lately, even though I've been tempted to call on you several times."

"How I've been is none of your business," she hissed, stiffening her shoulders so he couldn't pull her any closer. "And I told you before, if you come to my house again, I'll call the sheriff."

Peter sighed. "You certainly make courting difficult, Miss Taylor, and I . . ."

Suddenly, from the corner of her eye, Meg saw a huge hand reach over her shoulder and give Peter a mighty push, causing him to spin away from her and careen off the edge of the refreshment table. Meg whirled and looked up into the blazing eyes of her outraged husband.

"Her name is *Mrs. Wellesley*," Geoff snarled at the staggering Peter, "and your dance is over, Farnsworth."

"Why, you son of a bitch," Peter yelled, finally regaining his balance and charging at Geoff like an enraged bull.

But Geoff had anticipated him and neatly sidestepped, smashing a fist into the center of Peter's face and sending the smaller man sprawling to the floor.

Several women screamed, and with an abrupt, discordant squeal, the music stopped. Men quickly pushed their wives and sweethearts behind them, then formed a circle around the combatants.

"Get the bastard, Geoff!" one lumberjack shouted encouragingly.

"I heard him tell your wife he wanted to call on her," another one added, hoping to incite Geoff to take another swing at the cowering man on the floor.

But Geoff was back in control and simply leaned over and yanked Farnsworth to his feet by his shirt front. Pushing his face close to Peter's bleeding nose, he growled, "The next time you put your filthy hands on my wife, I'll kill you. Understand?"

Peter's head wobbled dizzily.

"Do you understand?" Geoff thundered, giving the reeling man a hard shake.

Weakly, Peter nodded, holding his hands up in a lame attempt to protect himself.

With a disgusted sneer, Geoff shoved him away. Peter staggered backward, then hit the wall behind him and slowly sank to a sitting position, his head drooping to one side and his eyes closing.

Geoff swung around and held out his hand to Meg. "Come on. We're going home. Now." His expression dared her to defy him.

But Meg was in no mood to argue with anything her

hero might demand. With a quick nod, she took his hand and, together, they moved toward the exit. The crowd, still stunned by the unexpected violence they'd witnessed, parted silently to make way for them.

They climbed the stairs and walked out of the church's double doors. Geoff paused and took a deep, calming draught of the cool night air. "Are you all right?" he asked quietly, turning to look at her in the darkness.

"I'm fine," she murmured. "And you?"

Geoff nodded and they continued, still holding hands, across the big churchyard together. Meg had no idea why Geoff had suddenly appeared at the dance or what he must be thinking of her now. At this moment, she knew only that he had saved her yet again from the ever-present threat of Peter Farnsworth, and she wanted very badly to thank him.

She never got the chance. They stopped near his wagon, and just as she opened her mouth to speak, he grabbed her, crushing her in a desperate embrace and burying his head in her neck. "My God, when I saw that bastard with his hands on you . . ."

"Shh," Meg begged, tears streaking down her face as she turned her head to gently kiss him. "I'm sorry I defied you, Geoff. I'm so sorry . . ."

Suddenly, his lips were on hers and words were forgotten. They kissed long and passionately, feeding a hunger that had built to ravenous proportions during the weeks of their estrangement.

When Geoff finally raised his head, he was gasping and his voice was rough with long-repressed desire. "Not here, sweetheart," he whispered, his entire body shaking with need. "Let's go home."

Chapter 26

It was fortunate for the Wellesleys that the horses knew their way home.

Their trip started reasonably enough. Geoff helped Meg up on to the wagon's high seat, then climbed up himself and clucked to the horses, turning them in the direction of her house. But the reins soon went slack in his hands as he pulled his wife into his muscular embrace and starting kissing her. From that point on, it was up to the horses to find their barn, for their master was far too involved in his own pleasure to give them any guidance.

Even when the faithful beasts reached their small shed, they stood for a full five minutes, stamping their hooves and shaking their harness before the man in the driver's seat noticed that they'd reached their destination.

"We're home," Geoff said hoarsely, pulling his lips away from Meg's breast.

"We are?" she asked, looking around in surprise.

Geoff grinned at the provocative sight she made, sprawled across his lap with her bosom bare and her dress hiked high up her thighs.

One of the horses nickered and turned its head to throw Geoff a baleful look. Taking pity on the poor beast, he planted one last kiss on Meg's mouth and said, "Don't go away. It'll just take me a minute to put these horses up."

She nodded and sat up, making a feeble attempt to cover herself with her hands.

"Don't do that," he ordered, grinning at her as he quickly unhooked the harness buckles. "I can't remember when I've ever enjoyed unhitching a team so much."

Meg smiled and abandoned her halfhearted attempt at modesty. Raising her arms, she pulled the few remaining pins from her hair. The movement made her full breasts lift and jut forward, presenting Geoff with a heartstopping pose that reminded him of a Rubens painting.

Unabashedly ogling Meg's beautiful body, he dropped the wagon's traces and gathered up the trailing reins, clucking to the horses impatiently as he led them off toward the shed.

Meg's gaze swept over Geoff's retreating figure with just as much appreciation as he had shown her. His long, lean legs, his massive shoulders, the way the muscles of his back rippled as he walked . . . She shivered, hardly able to believe that through the unlikely intervention of Peter Farnsworth, she had suddenly reclaimed her husband's interest. Of course, there were still problems they needed to settle between them, but all of that could wait. Right now, all she could think about was how long it would take Geoff to finish with the horses so they could resume their love play. A scandalous idea suddenly dawned deep in her brain, and with a naughty little smile, she climbed down from the high wagon seat and slipped, unseen, through the shed door.

Geoff led the big, plodding draft horses into the shed and gave each of them a hearty slap on the rump, encouraging them into their stalls. The animals needed little prodding.

They were tired, hungry, and as anxious to reach their soft straw beds as Geoff was to reach his featherbed.

With a quick ripple of muscles, he hefted two flakes of hay into their mangers, added a large portion of oats, and grabbed the water buckets. Hurrying outside, he dipped them into the trough, filling them both with one swipe through the water. He glanced over at the wagon, disappointed to see that Meg was gone. Maybe she went inside to get ready for bed, he thought hopefully. He grinned and picked up his pace as he headed back to the shed.

When he finally had the horses fed, watered, bedded, and rubbed down, he closed the stall doors with a satisfied slam and started out of the shed. He only got halfway down the aisle, though, before he was stopped by the sound of Meg's soft, husky voice floating through the dimly lit building.

"In a hurry, Mr. Wellesley?"

Jerking his head around in the direction of the sound, he peered into an empty stall. There, reclining in the straw, was his wife—clad only in her black stockings and red garters.

Entranced, he moved forward, stepping into the stall and gazing down at Meg in awe. "My God . . ."

She smiled languidly and slowly got to her knees. "I never thought you were going to finish with those horses," she purred.

"Me either." He took another step forward and dropped to his knees, his eyes riveted on her bare breasts.

The light from the single kerosene lamp cast a warm, mellow glow over them as Meg raised her hand, tracing the edges of his sculptured lips with a fingertip. "I heard you rubbing the mare down," she whispered, her other hand deftly slipping the buttons on his shirt through the holes, "and all I could think about was having you do that to me."

Leaning forward, she pushed his shirt over his shoulders and off his arms. "Mmm," she sighed, rubbing her breasts lightly against his muscular chest, "that's nice."

"Nice," he repeated, his head falling back and his lips parting.

Meg continued to rub against him for a moment, then leaned back and murmured, "Stand up."

Geoff was shaking so badly that he wasn't at all sure he'd be *able* to stand up, but suspecting what she might have in mind, he forced himself to get to his feet. Quickly, he leaned down and yanked off his boots and socks, then straightened again and looked down at where she still knelt in front of him.

Meg smiled up at him, her eyes holding a look that was tantalizing and full of promise. Raising a slender hand, she brushed it provocatively against the stiff material of his denims, her fingers tracing the pronounced outline of his straining arousal. "These are too tight to be comfortable," she whispered, pursing her lips in sympathy. "I think we should take them off."

"Good idea," Geoff moaned, burying his fingers in her hair.

With a deliberate slowness that made him want to scream for mercy, Meg worked her way down the placard of his denims. "There," she cooed, as she released the last button, "now see if this doesn't feel better." Skimming her hands up to his waistband, she worked the jeans down his hips, pausing to throw him a hungry look as she freed his impassioned manhood.

"You're beautiful when you're like this," she smiled, raising her hands to stroke his thick length. "So soft and yet so hard. Like satin over steel."

Her husky voice and caressing hands were quickly bring-

307

ing Geoff to the brink of his control. "Megan," he rasped, his voice rough with lust, "Megan . . ."

Tipping her head back, her eyes swept up the length of his magnificent body until they reached his handsome, chiseled face. "I think you must be the most beautiful man God ever created," she whispered reverently. And, leaning forward, she took him into her mouth.

Geoff threw back his head and emitted a long, low groan of pleasure, then looked down, thinking he'd never seen anything as arousing as the sight of his wife loving him so intimately. "Sweetheart," he moaned, knowing he couldn't last much longer, but loath to end the erotic torture. "Baby, I have to . . ."

Meg raised her eyes, still stroking him with her tongue. "I know you have to . . . so do I."

With a throaty moan, Geoff dropped back to his knees, curling his arm around her shoulders and pulling her against him so the entire length of their bodies touched. His hard length slipped between her thighs, making her shiver.

"Oh, Geoff," she murmured, rotating her hips so she could better feel him between her legs, "it's been so long . . ."

"I know," he nodded, shifting his hips so that just the tip of his manhood entered her. "I've missed you so much." Tightening his arm around her to cushion her fall, he pressed her back into the straw, his shaft slipping deep inside her as they fell.

With a little sigh of ecstasy, Meg started to wrap her stocking-clad legs around his hips, but to her dismay, he withdrew from her. "Don't go!" she cried, clutching at his shoulders in an effort to bring him back. "What's wrong?"

"Nothing's wrong," he smiled, his words coming in short little gasps, "you're just not ready yet."

"But I am," she protested, wiggling under him as she tried to get closer to his jutting shaft.

"Not as much as you're going to be," he promised.

"But Geoff . . ."

"Shh," he crooned, kissing her down the length of her body. "Just relax."

Meg let out a plaintive little mewl, but obediently released her grip and let her arms fall limply to the straw. Her eyes drifted closed as Geoff's lips reached the soft down between her legs. He blew on her gently, causing goose bumps to rise all over her body. "Oh . . ." she sighed, "that's so nice."

The word "nice" suddenly went from a breathy sigh to a sharp scream as Geoff's tongue dipped inside her.

"Geoff," she shrieked, "Geoff, you shouldn't . . ." But her shocked protest died in her throat as her body suddenly began convulsing in reaction to the pure eroticism of Geoff's lovemaking. His tongue flashed in and out, touching her in places she didn't even know existed, then settling over her tiny, hidden bud. As he toyed with this most sensitive part of her body, Meg felt the familiar pressure building deep inside her and let out a long, keening scream of pleasure as she found her heaven.

Geoff continued his intimate lovemaking until the pulsing waves within her ebbed, then moved up next to her, smiling down into her dreamy eyes.

"I think I just might die," she sighed, her eyes drooping languidly.

Geoff grinned. "I thought you might like that."

"How do you even *know* about things like that?"

Geoff was not about to answer that question. "Just instinct, my love."

Meg smiled, not believing him for a second. "Come here and kiss me, my instinctive Mr. Wellesley."

Mr. Wellesley was all too happy to comply. Stretching out on top of her, he lowered his mouth and gave her a searing kiss. Meg could taste herself on his lips and smell her own musky essence against his skin. She shivered, her excitement renewed just thinking about the intimacies they'd just shared.

Geoff's unrelieved erection was hot and hard against her thigh and she reached down and wrapped her fingers around him, looking up at him questioningly.

"I'll be okay," he murmured, answering her unspoken question.

"I know you will," she smiled, and shifting her hips, she guided him deep inside.

Geoff was starved for her and it took every bit of willpower he possessed not to explode immediately, but he held on until he felt Meg's body start to pulse around him. Finally, knowing she was ready, he surrendered to his basest instincts and let himself go.

Their cries of mutual pleasure echoed through the barren confines of the shed, making the draft horses prick up their ears and look at them curiously as they munched their hay. From the far end of the aisle, they heard a loud crack as a hoof kicked the side of a stall.

"What was that?" Meg gasped, looking apprehensively over Geoff's shoulder.

"It's my stallion," he panted, his voice muffled against her hair. "He can smell us and it's exciting him."

"I understand," Meg nodded, inhaling deeply. "The smell of you always excites me, too."

Geoff looked at her in astonishment, hardly able to believe his proper little wife would admit to such primitively sexual urges. "Believe me, sweetheart," he chuckled, "it's not *my* smell that's exciting him. It's *yours.*"

Meg blushed and turned her head away, embarrassed

now by her confession. "We should probably go in the house," she murmured.

"I suppose," Geoff nodded, sitting up and shaking the hay out of his thick hair. He stood, then turned back toward her, intending to offer her a hand. But he paused, his breath catching in his throat as he looked down at her lying in the straw; her hair tousled and full of hay, her lips swollen from his passionate kisses, her breasts flushed and rosy from their lovemaking. His eyes dropped lower and he smiled as he gazed at her long, slim legs, still encased in those sexy black stockings.

"You are one incredible sight," he drawled. "And you'd better get up or we might never make it out of this barn."

"You're one incredible sight yourself," Meg returned, her eyes sweeping the length of him where he stood above her.

Her lusty perusal made the hot blood of desire again rush to Geoff's loins. "Oh, no you don't," he laughed, reaching down and pulling her to her feet. "Don't you start drooling over me again till we get back into the house."

"Drooling!" Meg gasped. "I've never drooled over a man in my life!"

"Well, you drool over me," Geoff teased. "Every time you look at me."

"I do not! That's just wishful thinking on your part."

"No, it's not," he chuckled, pulling her arm away from where she'd wrapped it around her breasts and backing her toward the wall. "It's the absolute truth. But it's okay, because you make me drool, too."

Meg's back hit the wall, forcing her to stop her retreat. "Geoff, I do not drool over you," she insisted stubbornly.

"No?" he whispered, taking her hand and wrapping it around his stiffening shaft. "Then, maybe this is what puts that look in your eye."

311

A shiver ran the entire length of Meg's body as she felt him harden in her hand. "You're ready again?" she asked, her voice trembling with excitement.

"It's the stockings," he chuckled. "They do it every time."

Meg grinned with delight, thrilled with her husband's seemingly insatiable passion for her. "If this is the effect they have, I may never take them off."

Geoff groaned his approval of that suggestion and pressed heated kisses all the way from her neck down to the tip of her trembling breasts. "Good idea, as long as you don't put anything on over them."

"I'm sure that would turn a few heads at the general store," Meg giggled. Her tinkling laughter suddenly turned into a pleasured moan as Geoff ran his hand down the length of her body, then dipped a finger into her creamy depths.

For several moments they caressed each other, their breath quickening as renewed desire tangled them in its sensuous web. Then, without warning, Geoff suddenly cupped Meg's bottom, lifting her off the floor. "Put your legs around my waist," he directed.

Meg did as he bade, then let out a little shriek of surprise as he thrust deep inside her.

"My God, Geoff, against a wall?"

"Fun, isn't it?"

"Oh, yes!" she screamed, her legs clenching around him as a blinding climax overtook her. Geoff's lusty shout of satisfaction followed almost immediately, then he sagged against her, breathing hard.

Meg dropped her legs, and together they sank back down into the straw, so exhausted they could hardly move.

"I'm so tired," Meg sighed when she could finally speak again.

"Me too. Let's go in and go to bed."

Meg shook her head. "I *can't* put all those clothes on again. I just can't."

With great effort, Geoff stood up. "Forget it. We'll leave everything here until morning."

"I can't walk back to the house naked!"

"You don't have to walk. I'll carry you."

"You can't walk back to the house, naked."

"Sure I can. Who's going to see me? It's after midnight and there's no moon. Even if somebody does pass by on the street, they'll never see us."

Under ordinary circumstances, Meg would have never agreed to such an outrageous suggestion. But the past two hours had hardly been ordinary, and she was too happy and exhausted to argue.

"Are you sure you can carry me?"

Geoff snorted. "The day I can't carry a little slip of a thing like you is the day they'll put me in the ground."

"You sound just like a lumberjack," she laughed.

"I *am* a lumberjack," he retorted, "and proud of it." Leaning down, he scooped Meg out of the straw, his arms trembling slightly with the effort. "But, I have to admit that lumberjack or not, you have just about done me in."

Meg looked up into his tired face. "Put me down, Geoff. I can walk."

"Not a chance. If I put you down, I couldn't do this." And, burying his face playfully in her breasts, he carried her across the yard.

Meg smiled in sublime contentment, sure that nothing in the world could be more romantic than being carried nude across the yard by this great handsome beast of a man.

Again she wondered if it was the altercation with Peter Farnsworth that had reawakened Geoff's passion for her. Sometime, they really did have to talk about the trouble between them and get things settled. She needed to know what she had done to make Geoff so angry, if for no other reason than to help her keep from ever doing it again.

But tonight was not the time for that discussion. Tonight was for lovemaking; for kissing and caressing and fondling. For rediscovering the beauty of each other's bodies and the wonders of physical communion. Everything else could wait . . .

Geoff lay awake long after Meg had fallen asleep. They'd made love one more time after they'd gone to bed, a slow, gentle, luxurious encounter that had lasted for more than an hour.

It was past two o'clock when Meg had finally drifted off, her head nestled into the hollow of Geoff's neck, her soft breath fanning the hair on his chest as she slept.

But despite the long hours of love they had shared, Geoff still couldn't sleep. Instead, he lay quietly thinking, trying to come to terms with his feelings toward his wife.

How could she show such passion toward him if she didn't care about him? No woman, no matter how artful an actress, could feign the pleasure Meg had so obviously found in his arms tonight. Her kisses, her fevered responses to his most intimate caresses, her breathy sighs of pleasure and contentment as they lay wrapped in each other's arms . . . all her reactions to his lovemaking showed a depth of feeling that far transcended physical release. Even now she lay snuggled against him, her hair spread across his chest, her hand lying possessively across his abdomen as she slept. These were not the actions of an accomplished courtesan; these were the gestures of a wife truly in love with her husband.

Carefully, he turned his head and gazed down at her

serene face, and from somewhere deep inside him, a little voice screamed the words he refused to consciously voice.

You still love her.

Geoff drew a deep breath, the truth of his admission rocking him to the very core.

He'd thought he was over her, thought he'd wiped her out of his mind these past few weeks as night after night he'd lain in the small guest-room bed and brooded over her perfidy.

Even tonight, when he'd seen her desperately trying to extricate herself from Peter Farnsworth's odious grasp, he'd thought he understood his feelings toward her. Granted, he had wanted to kill the man with his bare hands, but he'd attributed that to simple possessiveness. Meg was his wife. His and his alone, and even if he didn't love her, he would never allow another man to touch her. But it wasn't until right now—after the passionate hours he'd spent in her arms—that he realized his feelings ran much deeper than that.

Despite her deceit, despite her lies, despite everything he had tried so hard to hate her for, he still loved her—and knowing that meant that nothing that had gone before mattered anymore.

Chapter 27

Megan awoke to the heady sensation of Geoff toying provocatively with her right breast. "Mmm," she sighed, opening her eyes and looking at him. "That feels wonderful."

"Good morning, sweetheart," he smiled, nuzzling his way up her body until he covered her mouth with a warm, welcoming kiss. "Do you know it's past ten?"

"It is?" she asked dreamily, as he went back to his provocative play. "We should probably get up, shouldn't we?" She stretched luxuriously while Geoff moved back down her body, trailing a path of warm kisses over her slightly rounded stomach.

"How's that baby in there?" he asked, placing his ear on her abdomen as if hoping to hear an answer from within.

"Fine," Meg giggled, pushing at his shoulders and trying to wiggle out from under him. "And, for once, I'm not feeling sick this morning."

"Lord, am I glad to hear that," he muttered, grasping her hips in his big hands to stop her squirming. His kisses trailed lower . . .

"Geoff, we don't have time for this now! It's late, and I have a million chores to attend to today." Again she tried to slip out from under him, not realizing that her squirming was doing nothing but exciting him further.

"Forget the damn chores," he rasped, his tongue dipping sensuously in and out of her navel. "This is much more important."

"But," she protested breathlessly, "don't you have to go to work?"

"No." His voice was muffled against her inner thigh. "It's Sunday."

"That's right," Meg sighed. "We should be getting ready for church."

"I think we're going to miss church," Geoff grinned, getting to his knees and gesturing down at his throbbing arousal.

"We have to go to church!" Meg said stoutly. "You're just going to have to put that away."

"Yeah, and I know where."

"Geoff, you're terrible!"

"You won't think so in a minute," he promised, and bracing himself on his arms, he entered her.

Meg let out a little shriek, surprised at how ready she was for him. "How did you know I was . . ."

"I've been awake a long time," he confided, "and you know what they say in church about the sin of idle hands . . ."

Meg giggled at his irreverent comment, but her laughter soon turned to moans of ecstasy. Geoff's lovemaking was furious and passionate, and after only a few lusty thrusts, they reached a blinding climax.

When the tremors finally stilled, Geoff rolled to his side, taking her with him and holding her close.

"Now, that's the way to start the morning," he chuckled.

Meg nodded, sighing with contentment. "I didn't know

317

it was possible to do this so often in so short a time. Don't you ever sleep?"

"Sure, I do—a little. Seems like a waste of time, though, when you could be making love instead."

"You're insatiable, do you know that?"

"Only with you, sweetheart," he whispered, kissing her gently near her temple.

They lay quietly for a long time, drowsing in each other's arms. Finally, in a hesitant voice, Meg said, "Why have you been so angry with me lately? What did I do?"

She felt him stiffen next to her. "I don't want to talk about it," he said firmly, breaking their embrace and getting out of bed.

"But, Geoff, we need to talk about this. You know we do. Something upset you to the point I almost lost you, and I want to know . . ."

"It doesn't matter anymore," he interrupted, throwing her a quelling look. "I've gotten over it, so let's just forget it."

Meg sat up, sweeping her hair out of her face and looking at him determinedly. "No. We're not going to forget it—and *I* haven't gotten over it. I almost died thinking you didn't care anymore, and I don't want it to happen again."

"It won't."

"It could, if we don't get things settled between us."

"Things *are* settled between us. The last twelve hours should have convinced you of that."

"No," Meg said stubbornly. "The only thing the past twelve hours proved is that you still desire me. The problem, whatever it is, is still there."

"No, it isn't."

"How can you say that?"

"Because the reasons I was mad don't matter anymore."

318

"But they do! And I don't even know what those reasons were. I think you owe me some sort of explanation."

Geoff turned toward her, his eyes blazing. "I owe you? Oh, that's rich, Megan."

Meg blinked, taken aback by his angry vehemence. "Regardless of what you seem to think," she said softly, "I *don't* know why you were angry, so please tell me."

"I *don't* want to talk about it," Geoff repeated. "And I can't believe you want to dredge it up again."

"And I can't believe that after the last twelve hours, you still don't care enough about me to get this out in the open and behind us."

Geoff clenched his jaw in frustration, pacing over to the window and looking out at the bleak, drizzly morning. How the hell had they gotten embroiled in this? Ten minutes ago they were kissing. What had happened?

"Geoff!" Meg said, her voice demanding his attention. "Tell me."

"All right!" he barked, whirling to face her, his fists clenched at his sides. "Since you're determined to prolong this, I'll tell you. It was the money."

"Money?" Meg asked blankly. "What money?"

"The money you planned to extort from me when you blackmailed me into marrying you."

Meg drew in a sharp breath. "What in the world are you talking about?"

"Don't play dumb, Meg. I found out that the other provision of your father's agreement with Farnsworth—the one you didn't bother to tell me about—was that if you didn't marry Peter, you either had to turn the mill over to him or pay him forty-two thousand dollars."

"Forty-two thousand dollars!" Meg gasped, her head reeling. *Was it possible her father owed that much?* "Who told

319

you Papa owed Mr. Farnsworth fifty-two thousand dollars?"

"Lawrence told me," Geoff shouted.

"Lawrence! Lawrence told you I married you so you'd pay my father's debt to the Farnsworths?"

"In so many words, yes!" Geoff spat, jerking on his underwear and denims. "He invited me to have lunch with him, but his real motive was to ask me when I was going to pay off your part of the loan."

"I can't believe this!"

"I'm sure you can't," he sneered. "You probably weren't expecting old Lawrence to let the cat out of the bag, were you?"

Meg's eyes ignited with anger. "There was no cat, Geoff."

He looked at her for a long moment as if trying to assess the truth in her words. "Look," he said, a chilling resignation creeping into his voice, "I've paid the debt and I've gotten over the resentment I felt about it, so please, let's just forget it. But don't insult me by trying to make me believe that you didn't marry me for my money."

"But I didn't!"

He threw her a furious look.

"Okay," Meg admitted, meeting his icy gaze squarely, "I confess that I knew there was a payoff clause in the agreement, but I never intended to ask you for the money."

"Right," Geoff snorted. "You just planned to save up some grocery money and pay it back yourself, right?"

"Of course not," she snapped, her own anger igniting that he still didn't believe her. "What I planned was to sell my mother's jewelry and use that money as a preliminary payment, then use the profits from the mill to pay the rest."

"Forty-two thousand? Your mother must have had one hell of a jewelry collection!"

"She did," Meg returned.

"So, did you sell it?"

Meg looked down at her tightly clenched hands. "I wrote a . . ."

"Did you sell the jewelry?"

Meg's head jerked up and she stared at him coldly. "Not yet."

"That's what I thought," Geoff laughed mirthlessly. "Why part with your jewels when it was so much easier to con some rich sucker into marrying you?"

Tears of outraged offense sprang to Meg's eyes. "That's not it at all. I just haven't had time to go to Portland—"

"Of course not," Geoff interrupted, his voice clearly disbelieving. "You've been far too busy decorating houses!"

Meg's mouth dropped open. "How dare you accuse me of that? You were the one who contacted Mr. Spoffard, not I!"

Geoff blew out a long, agonized breath and stared down at his bare feet. "You're right. I did send for Spoffard. I had no right to accuse you of that."

"Oh, Geoff," Meg wailed, tears running freely down her cheeks now. "Spoffard doesn't matter. I know I forced you into marrying me, and my reasons were far from honorable, but I can't stand to have you think it was your money I was after. I've heard that's what Francine wanted, and I . . ."

"It's what every woman wants from me!" Geoff shouted, his anger again boiling over. "Francine, you, and every other woman in Wellesley. But I've told you before and I'll say it again. It doesn't matter anymore. We're married, for better or worse, and I've come to terms with that. You have my name, you have my protection, you have my money. What more do you want?"

"I want you to believe me!" Meg sobbed.

Geoff shook his head. "That's asking too much. Why can't you just take what I'm offering and be content with it?"

"Why?" Meg shrieked, throwing back the blankets and hurtling herself off the bed. "I'll tell you why. Because I love—"

The sound of a man's voice yelling Geoff's name, followed almost immediately by a thunderous banging at the front door, caused Meg's words to die in her throat.

"What's that?" she gasped.

Geoff shook his head and hurried over to the front window.

"Wellesley!" came another shout, this one even louder than the first.

Geoff threw open the window and looked down. "What the hell is it, Parker?" he yelled back. "For Christ's sake, quit beatin' on my door!"

"You gotta come quick," the man bellowed. "Someone set fire to your flume, and it's spreadin' so fast, it looks like it's gonna take your whole forest!"

Chapter 28

"Help! We need help!"

The twenty or so townsfolk gathered at the Wellesley General Mercantile stared in astonishment at the distraught lumberjack with the smoke-blackened face.

"I thought the fire was under control," a man yelled from the back of the store.

"Yeah, I heard the drizzle had just about put it out."

Dan Parker gaped at the people in the store like they had lost their minds. "What's the matter with you people? Hasn't anyone bothered to look outside for the past two hours? The fire ain't under control, it's spreading like a son of a bitch!"

Several women gasped at the lumberjack's curse, and quickly he muttered, "Pardon me, ladies, no offense intended. But the wind has shifted and the fire is movin' toward town. If you men don't get out and help us fight it, you're all gonna lose your homes and maybe your lives. As it is, three men are already dead and a whole passel more are injured."

"Moving toward town!" Trudy Phillips screeched, running to the store's front window and looking out in the direction of the billowing smoke. "My land, he's right! Come on, everyone. We have to go help!"

"I didn't mean for the ladies to come, ma'am," Parker said quickly.

"Nonsense," Meg intervened, stepping forward from where she stood near the ribbon counter. "There's no reason why we can't help. Some of us might not be strong enough to haul buckets, but we can certainly tend to the injured."

"She's right," Trudy nodded, throwing Meg the first approving glance she'd ever received from the old harridan. Rounding on the rest of the women in the store, Trudy immediately started to spout orders. "Norma, Ethel, Lydia, go round up your men, your neighbors, and anyone else you can find. You men there," she added unnecessarily, since everyone was already heading for the door, "go hitch up your wagons and get up to that mountain as fast as you can. Megan, in your condition, you shouldn't be anywhere near the fire, but if you feel up to it, you could go door to door and spread the word."

Meg blushed crimson as every person in the store paused to turn and gape at her. How in the world did Trudy Phillips know she was pregnant? She hadn't told a soul except Virginia and Dr. Emerson, and she was absolutely certain Geoff hadn't. "I'll be happy to," she nodded, deciding the best way to diffuse Mrs. Phillips' tactless statement was simply to ignore it.

The store quickly emptied as people scattered in all directions. Meg hurried out with the rest of the crowd, stopping only briefly to catch Dan Parker by the arm. "Is my husband all right?" she asked, terrified of what his answer might be.

"He was the last time I saw him," Parker assured her.

"Now, don't upset yourself, Mrs. Wellesley. It ain't good for a lady in the family way to get riled."

Meg bit back a sharp retort, silently cursing Trudy Phillips' big mouth. She nodded her thanks and quickly headed for home, stopping at every house along the way to alert her neighbors of the impending disaster and encourage them to get out and help.

By the time she reached her house, the streets of Wellesley were teeming with people. Wagons careened down Main Street laden with ropes, buckets, and medical supplies. Men flew by on horses, galloping pell-mell toward the road leading to Geoff's mountain. Little children stood in fenced front yards, squalling over being left by their mothers in the care of elderly neighbors whom they'd never seen before.

Meg rushed through the front door and straight into the kitchen, throwing open cupboards and tossing liniment, bandages, baking soda, and butter into a large bag. Then she tore out to the back porch, grabbing all the buckets she could find. She briefly considered going out to the shed and trying to find some rope, but decided against it. It would take too much valuable time and she wasn't sure she could carry it anyway.

Racing back outside, she ran down the street, rounding the corner on to Main and flagging down the first wagon she saw. "Will you give me a ride?" she yelled up at the startled driver.

"Sure thing, Mrs. Wellesley," he responded, working hard to control his excited horses. "Throw that stuff in the back and climb in."

Meg did as he bade, barely settling in the seat before he whipped up the team, sending them into a frenzied gallop toward the edge of town.

"I'm Deke Slater," he yelled, making a fumbling attempt to doff his hat.

"How do you do?" Meg yelled back, holding on to the lurching wagon seat for dear life.

"Does your husband know you're comin' up here?"

Meg looked at the man in surprise, shocked at such a forward question from a complete stranger. "No, he doesn't," she answered truthfully.

"Oh-oh," Deke grinned. "I bet he's gonna be plenty mad when he sees you, what with you bein' in a delicate condition and all."

Meg looked away in embarrassment. Was there anyone in town who *didn't* know she was pregnant? She'd never seen this man before in her life, but even he knew. When she found out who had spread this most personal of secrets, she intended to give them a piece of her mind they wouldn't soon forget!

"Have you lived in Wellesley long, Mr. Slater?" she shouted.

"Naw, just a few days. Moved here from Sacramento. I was hopin' to get on with your husband, but he ain't hirin' right now. Figured if I helped him put out his fire, mebbe he'd find a place for me, though. What d'ya think?"

"You'd have to speak to him about that," Meg hedged, unwilling to make any promises on Geoff's behalf.

"Been tryin' to do that for the past week, ma'am, but he's a hard man to find. Never seems to be up at his camp. I even came by your house a coupla nights ago, but no one was home."

Meg turned away again, thinking that must have been the night that she and Geoff had been at the dance and then in the barn. Little wonder the man hadn't been able to find them. Turning back toward him, she shouted, "After this fire is out, I'm sure Mr. Wellesley is going to

326

need more help. Why don't you go up his camp one morning next week and tell him I sent you."

Deke Slater looked over at Megan and grinned from ear to ear. "Thank you mightily, ma'am. I'll do that."

The smoke thickened as the winding snake of wagons neared the camp and Meg looked around in horror as she saw the extent of the damage the fire had already wrought. It was much worse than anyone in town had realized.

"Christ almighty," Deke muttered. "I *guess* they need help."

Meg nodded grimly, then was seized by a fit of coughing.

"Here," Deke said, whipping off his neckerchief and handing it to her. "Put this over your face. You shouldn't be breathin' this smoke."

Meg didn't argue. Nodding gratefully, she tied the bandanna around her face and started to climb down from the wagon.

"Wait a minute," he ordered. "I'll help you."

"I'm fine," Meg assured him.

"Please, Mrs. Wellesley, let me help you. If you tripped on that step and fell, I'd never forgive myself—and your husband would sure never give me a job. In fact, as much as I've heard about how excited he is over this baby, he'd probably kill me."

Meg was horrified by the man's seemingly endless knowledge about her personal life, but she halted her descent, waiting patiently as he hurried around the back of the wagon and lifted her down.

"Thank you, Mr. Slater," she said, when she was safely on the ground. "Now, if you'll just hand me that bag and those buckets, I'll—"

Her words were cut off by the unexpected arrival of Ned Johnson. "What are you doin' here, missus?" he gasped, throwing the hapless Deke an accusing glare.

327

"I've come to help tend the injured."

Ned shook his head apprehensively. "Geoff ain't gonna like this, what with you bein' in the family way. You should be home restin'."

Meg gritted her teeth in utter frustration. If one more person mentioned her "condition" . . . "I think that's my business, don't you, Mr. Johnson?" she said coldly. "Now, if you'll just tell me where the men are who have been hurt, I'll go see what I can do to help."

"Over there," Ned pointed, still shaking his head. "Near Geoff's office."

Meg nodded curtly and headed off.

As she hurried away, Ned turned to Deke, who was standing in the wagon bed, tossing shovels over the side. "Who are you, mister?"

"Name's Deke Slater. I'm a topper, and a good one. I just moved here from Sacramento, lookin' for work. I'd like to get on with your crew."

"Well, you made a big mistake bringin' Mrs. Wellesley up here, specially if you want a job from Geoff. He's crazy about that little girl, and he's gonna be mighty upset once he gets wind that she's up here in the middle of this."

"Well, hell," Deke spat, planting his hands on his hips. "What was I supposed to do? She chased my wagon down Main Street, yelling at me to stop and give her a ride. I tried to tell her that her husband wouldn't want her here, but she wouldn't listen."

"Yeah," Ned sighed, grudgingly acknowledging the other man's dilemma. "She never does."

Deke shrugged philosophically. "It's probably better for her to be up here than sittin' at home frettin' about it."

"Maybe," Ned said doubtfully, "but I don't think Geoff's gonna see it that way."

Deke jumped down from the wagon bed. "Okay, I've got my stuff out now. Where do you want me to start?"

"There's a crew over there, tryin' to build a firebreak," Ned pointed. "Why don't you go join 'em?"

As Deke raced off, Ned took off his cap and wiped his soot-begrimed forehead with the back of his sleeve. Dejectedly, he looked around, wondering how a handful of people with buckets were ever going to control the blazing inferno surrounding them. Already hundreds of acres had been destroyed, and with the wind picking up the way it had the past hour, there was no telling how far the fire would spread. "If I ever get my hands on whoever put a torch to that flume, I'll kill him," he vowed.

Casting his eyes heavenward, he looking up at the dark, forbidding clouds. "Come on, rain, God damn ya," he shouted. Then, he shook his head at his own foolishness and trudged over to join the bucket brigade.

It was the worst day of Meg's life. Hour after hour, she bent over the wounded firefighters, rubbing butter on minor burns and bandaging more serious ones. A few of the men were so badly burned that there was nothing she could do except put a cold cloth on their foreheads and pray that God would swiftly release them from their agony.

By mid-afternoon she was exhausted, but still she worked on, ignoring the knifelike pain in her lower back and the tears of fear and anguish that poured down her cheeks. The shifting wind had caused the fire to move away from the camp into the dense forest beyond but still, the thick smoke and searing heat made it almost impossible to draw a free breath.

There was little conversation among the women tending the injured, but as the afternoon waned, expressions grew

329

more grim and tempers more frayed as stamina and medical supplies rapidly dwindled. They were losing the battle, and they all knew it.

Around four o'clock, Meg suddenly heard a shout from the people on the bucket brigade. Looking up apprehensively, she was aghast to see them staring at the sky, grinning and slapping each other on the back like drunken revelers at a party. Then she felt the first heavy drops of rain and the same grin spread across her face.

Far above them, there boomed an ominous clap of thunder, and suddenly the heavens opened up. Never had Meg seen it rain so hard, the big drops pelting down furiously, feeling like needles against her skin. But despite the icy, drenching rain, people were dancing, clapping and whooping with joy and triumph. The ground beneath her quickly turned into a quagmire of mud, and wearily she pulled herself to her feet, staggering over to an unburned Douglas fir and leaning against it.

All around her she could hear the heavenly sound of sizzling as the heavy downpour doused the flames. Blinking rain off her eyelashes, she inhaled deeply of the freshening air and uttered a quick prayer of thanks. Then she closed her eyes, allowing herself the luxury of a moment's rest. Her respite was short-lived, however, as suddenly she felt a hand clamp down on her shoulder. With a startled little scream, her eyes flew open and she turned to stare into the enraged countenance of her soot-covered husband.

"What in the holy hell are you doing here?" he demanded.

Ignoring his obvious anger, Meg hurtled herself against the rocklike wall of his chest. "Oh, Geoff," she cried, clinging to him as if she'd never let go, "I've been so worried about you. No one had seen you for hours!"

330

"I'm fine," he said curtly. "Now, what in the hell are you doing here?"

Meg released his shoulders, her lips thinning. "I'm here helping, of course," she said defensively.

"God damn it, Megan!" he exploded, "are you nuts? You're pregnant!"

Despite the noise of the rain and the fire and the joyful cheers of the firefighters, at least fifty heads turned in their direction.

Meg had had enough. "I know I'm pregnant," she hissed, keeping her voice low enough that she was sure no one could hear her. "And I am sick and tired of being reminded of that fact. There is nothing wrong with me, Geoffrey, I am simply going to have a baby. Millions of women have done it before me, and millions will after. And whether you want to believe it or not, this is not just *your* baby I'm carrying, it's mine, too. If I thought for a minute I was doing anything to endanger it, I wouldn't be here. Now, move out of my way. There are still people who need my attention."

"Megan," Geoff said, his low voice more frightening than his shouting, "you're not going anywhere but home."

"Don't tell me what I'm going to do, Geoff. I will go home when I'm ready."

"You'll go home *now!*"

Meg closed her eyes, trying hard to block out the sight of the quickly gathering crowd. "All right," she said quietly. "I refuse to argue with you in front of the entire town, so I'll go. But when you get home, we're going to have this out once and for all."

"You're damn right we are," Geoff growled. Taking her firmly by the hand, he led her over to a nearby wagon.

"Matt," he yelled, motioning to the burly lumberjack who had stood guard at their door the night Geoff's hand

331

had been crushed, "Mrs. Wellesley needs to go home now. Will you drive her for me?"

"Sure, boss," Matt replied, lumbering over to the wagon.

With a quick twist of her wrist, Meg wrenched her hand out of Geoff's grasp and stepped up on to the wheel. She didn't protest when she felt his hands grasp her waist, thinking he meant to help her into the wagon, but she looked at him in bewilderment when instead he lifted her down and turned her back toward him. "Kiss me before you go," he said softly.

"In front of the whole town?"

"Exactly."

She reached up to place a chaste kiss on his dirty cheek, but he turned his head and for a brief moment their lips melded. When he pulled away, Meg looked at him beseechingly, wondering if his quick caress meant that he wanted to put aside the hard words they'd exchanged earlier that morning.

"Now, go home and take a nap. I'll be there later."

Meg searched his face for something—anything—that would tell her what she so desperately wanted to know. But his expression was impassive, and all she could truly discern in the amber depths of his eyes was a great weariness.

"Be careful," she said quietly.

Geoff nodded, lifting her up on to the wagon's high seat. "I will, but I think the worst is over."

"Thank God," she murmured.

Geoff opened his mouth as if to say something further, but then closed it, settling for a quick squeeze of her hand. "Get her home safe, Matt." The big man nodded and turned the wagon toward town.

A strange sense of foreboding niggled at Meg, and she

looked back over her shoulder. Her last vision of Geoff was the heartbreaking sight of him standing in the middle of the clearing, his hand wearily kneading the back of his neck as he stared dismally at his charred forest.

Chapter 29

As much as Meg had resisted leaving the site of the fire, she was grateful when she finally reached home. Matt Davidson saw her to the door, and after assuring him that he didn't need to stay with her, she closed it behind him and slid to the floor in an exhausted heap.

Lord, what a terrible day, she thought dismally. Tears sprang to her eyes as she thought of the eight men who had died fighting the fire and the forty or fifty others who had been injured.

At least the blaze hadn't reached town. That was something to be thankful for. But the personal loss for Geoff was enormous. By Meg's calculations, one-third of his timber was destroyed. The cost of removing the burned trees and replanting new ones would be astronomical, and she wondered if even Geoff's pockets would be deep enough to sustain the staggering loss. "It doesn't matter," she said aloud. "The only thing that matters is that he wasn't hurt."

Vaguely, she thought about the rumors she'd heard up at the camp that the fire had been intentionally set, and a brief vision of Peter Farnsworth swam before her eyes. Could his hatred toward her have become so acute that he would actually set fire to Geoff's flume, risking the lives of everyone in town? Meg shuddered, unwilling to even consider the possibility. She'd never be able to live with herself if she thought she was in any way responsible for the horrific events that had taken place that day. But how could the flume have caught fire unless someone deliberately put a torch to it? She shook her head, visualizing again the ugly black scar running down the mountain to the river—all that remained of Geoff's hard work.

How must he be feeling, now that his flume was nothing more than a charred ruin? He had told her once that he'd worked on it for two years, designing, constructing, testing. There was always such excitement in his voice when he talked about it—eagerly describing how this type of timber transport would revolutionize the lumber industry, saving money and man hours and lives by replacing the slow and dangerous skid roads with the safer, faster, and more economical wooden chutes.

He'll just have to build another one, Meg thought stoutly. The original plans for the flume had, thank God, been spared, since Geoff kept them here at the house, instead of in his shack at the camp. Tomorrow morning, first thing, she'd suggest that he ride out to the mill and talk to Hank about cutting the necessary lumber to begin rebuilding.

Tomorrow. Meg was determined that tomorrow, she and Geoff would settle this terrible misunderstanding about the loan money and then begin working together to rebuild what they'd lost today. With that bracing thought, she smiled and hauled herself to her feet.

Lord, but she was tired. Never in her entire life could she remember feeling such body-numbing exhaustion. Trudging over to the staircase, she paused and looked up. The steep flight seemed to yawn endlessly before her, and for a moment, she considered how much easier it would be just

335

to walk into the parlor and collapse on the settee. But the promise of a pitcher full of clean water and the big, soft bed in the master bedroom was enticing enough to make her gather her muddy skirts and lift her foot to the first step.

"It's only one flight," she told herself firmly, "and once you get to the top, it will be worth it." With all that had happened today, she wanted nothing so much as to wake up in Geoff's arms, and that wouldn't be possible if she slept on the settee.

Geoff . . .

Meg smiled just thinking about her handsome, passionate, mercurial husband. How she hoped he would come home tonight. She wanted so badly to see him, touch him, tell him she loved him.

The fire today had been a revelation, proving to her once and for all how little material things mattered when compared to human lives. The lost timber wasn't important. What was important was that she and Geoff settle things between them and admit their love for each other.

Meg's expression became dreamy. Despite today's tragedy, or maybe because of it, she was sure for the first time that Geoff truly loved her. She'd seen it in his eyes when he'd helped her into the wagon and squeezed her hand. And knowing that, the problems and misunderstandings between them seemed insignificant. They loved each other; that was all that mattered.

Just the thought of how wonderful it would be when they finally put things to rights between them brought a light to Meg's eyes, and with an energy that only a minute before she wouldn't have thought possible, she skipped lightly up the stairs.

* * *

She thought she'd been asleep only a few seconds when she felt Geoff's side of the bed dip beneath his weight. "You're home sooner than I expected," she murmured, reaching out to run her hand down his arm.

A noncommittal grunt was his only response.

"Is everything under control up at the camp?"

Another grunt.

"You poor darling, you're too tired to even talk, aren't you?"

No response.

Meg smiled sympathetically and lowered her voice to a whisper. "Are you awake enough to at least give me a good night kiss?"

She felt him lean toward her and drew a quick breath in anticipation of his lips touching hers. It was then that she noticed an unfamiliar sweet scent that she'd never smelled on him before.

"When did you start wearing bay rum?"

"A long time ago."

Meg let out a sharp scream of terror. The voice that had answered wasn't Geoff's.

Her fingers instinctively curled into talons and she struck out, blindly trying to scratch at the intruder's face. *"Who are you?"* she shrieked. *"What do you want?"*

She gasped as a heavy body covered hers and a pain shot all the way up her arm to her shoulder as strong hands grasped her wrists, forcing her arms down and behind her. "I'm the man you're going to marry," came a snarl from close to her ear. "And what I want is to give you that kiss you just asked for."

Meg's scream of fear and rage was immediately muffled by Peter Farnsworth's smothering mouth. Desperately she tried to wrench away from him as he ground his teeth against her lips, but he was too strong for her. She opened her mouth to scream again and instantly his tongue invaded, choking her as it thrust obscenely in and out.

She felt his excitement mount and his breathing become ragged, and with a strength born of pure terror, she dug her heels into the mattress and bucked him off. For a split second, Peter released his hold on her arms, freeing her enough that she was able to rake her nails the length of his cheek.

With a startled cry, he reared back and Meg seized the brief reprieve to make a lunge for the other side of the bed. Desperately she scrambled to stand up, but he caught her by the back of her nightrail, throwing her back down on the mattress and dealing her a mighty blow to the temple.

Meg's head exploded with pain, then a blessed darkness descended.

When she came to, she was still lying on the bed. She raised a hand, rubbing her pounding temple, then slowly opened her eyes. The room swam before her for a moment, then her vision cleared and she looked up to see Peter sitting next to her.

"Why did you make me do that?" he asked calmly.

Meg turned her head away, unable to bear the sight of him. "Geoff will kill you for this," she said quietly.

"Oh, I don't think so," he chuckled. "In fact, I don't think the great Mr. Wellesley is going to be doing much of anything, anytime soon."

Meg's head snapped around. "What are you talking about?"

Peter smiled, a smug, self-satisfied grimace that made her blood run cold. "He's a hard man to dispose of, that husband of yours. The runaway log didn't do it, the fire

338

didn't do it, but an ax handle across the back of the head never fails."

For a moment, Meg feared she was going to pass out again. She pressed her fingers hard against her temples and drew several deep breaths, struggling to stay conscious. "Are you saying that you've killed him?" she choked.

"No, not at all," Peter answered conversationally. "I've just . . . waylaid him. As a matter of fact, whether Mr. Wellesley lives or dies is no longer my decision. It's yours."

"Oh, my God," Meg moaned, "what are you planning?"

"It's very simple, really. You get up, get dressed, pack a bag and leave with me tonight, and your husband lives. You refuse, and he dies. As I said, his fate is in your hands."

"You're insane!" Meg shrieked, lunging at him with clenched fists.

Peter easily deflected her assault, again pinning her arms behind her and pushing his face close to hers. "Don't ever say that, Megan," he hissed, a maniacal gleam glazing his eyes. "Do you understand me? I don't want to hurt you since I love you so much, but if you say that again, I'm afraid I'll lose my temper, and then I can't be responsible for what might happen."

Meg swallowed hard, realizing that it was crazy to provoke him. The man was capable of anything. Solemnly, she nodded her understanding. She had to remain calm and try to keep him calm also. She had no doubt he might seriously hurt her if she angered him.

"Why are you doing this, Peter?" she asked quietly. "The agreement has been satisfied. Geoffrey told me that he paid your father all that was owed."

Peter snorted derisively. "I told you before, the agreement means nothing. That was my money-grubbing father's idea, not mine. All I wanted was you, and since I never expected you to be able to raise forty thousand dollars, I went along with the agreement, knowing it was the easiest way to get you."

Meg shook her head, gazing at him in genuine bewilderment. "When did you form this . . . attachment for me? You never showed the slightest interest in me until last year."

"Oh, but you're wrong!" he protested, grinning lecherously. "I've been fantasizing about having you since I was thirteen. And in the end, I always get what I want."

"But, I thought you and Jenny . . ."

"Jenny was nothing but a convenience," Peter scoffed. "A man has needs, and Jenny served a purpose. I just closed my eyes and pretended she was you."

Meg felt a surge of nausea sweep over her and closed her eyes, praying she wouldn't vomit. When she finally spoke again, her voice was so soft that Peter had to lean closer to hear her. "If I agree to leave with you tonight, will you release Geoffrey?"

"Of course," he shrugged. "Why wouldn't I? He'll never find us."

Meg nodded slowly, knowing she had no choice but to go along with Peter's insane plan. As she'd long suspected, he was truly mad, and refusing to accompany him would be tantamount to signing Geoff's death warrant . . . and probably her own as well. "All right," she agreed. "I'll go with you, as long as you give me your word of honor that Geoff won't be harmed."

Peter's face lit up with the easy, boyish smile that so belied his true character. He couldn't believe how simple it had been to gain Meg's acquiescence. Why hadn't he thought to tell her he had Wellesley in his clutches before this? If he'd only known how easily she would believe his lies, he could have saved himself a lot of time and trouble.

340

"Quit worrying about Wellesley and get packed," he ordered. "We have a long trip ahead of us, and I want to be out of here before daybreak." Rising, he stepped away from the bed, allowing Meg to get up.

Quickly, she walked to the opposite side of the room, then turned and shot him a hopeful smile. "Would you leave me for a moment and allow me some privacy to get dressed?"

"Not a chance," he smirked, lying back down on the bed and propping himself up on an elbow. "I've waited ten years to see you naked . . ."

Again Meg felt her gorge rise, but she swallowed it back, determined not to let him see her fear and revulsion. "All right," she said. "Tell me what I need to pack."

"Just some riding clothes. We'll buy whatever else you need when we get to Sa . . ." He broke off. "Before we leave the country."

Meg nodded and turned away, hoping her face hadn't betrayed the fact that she'd noticed his slip. *Sa . . . Sacramento? San Francisco? San Francisco! That must be it. He had said they were leaving the country. They must be sailing from San Francisco.*

As desperately as she wanted to believe him, Meg had grave doubts that Peter was really planning to release Geoff. But still, on the slim chance that he would keep his word, she had to find some way to try to leave Geoff a message as to where they were heading. But how, when Peter wouldn't leave her alone for even a moment? Surreptitiously her eyes swept the bedroom, looking for anything she could leave as a clue. Her gaze drifted over to the far wall, lighting on her dressing table. Suddenly, she had an idea, but in order to put it into action, she first had to find some way to distract Peter.

Turning her back to him, she took a deep, girding breath

and lifted her nightgown over her head, unveiling every lush curve of her body to his lusting gaze.

"My God . . ." he groaned, his eyes raking her rapaciously. He darted a quick glance toward the window, assessing how much time was left till daybreak. Not enough. "Soon," he told himself, reaching down and stroking his erect manhood. "As soon as we're over the pass."

With a deliberate swing of her hips, Meg sashayed over to her armoire, angling her body to give him a tantalizing view of the side of her breast, then squatting down to pull out her valise. Straightening, she sauntered across the room to the dressing table, fishing idly through the articles lying atop it as if trying to choose what to take along. She bent over, knowing she was probably risking rape, but determined to distract Peter enough that he wouldn't notice what she was actually doing. With a quick, furtive movement, she tipped her box of powder, spilling its contents across the dressing table. Then, with the tip of one long nail, she hastily scratched *"P.F."* and *"S.F."* into the scented dust.

"Get dressed, Megan," Peter gasped from the bed, massaging himself lewdly. "We've got to leave."

Mentally begging Geoff's forgiveness, Meg turned full front toward Peter, blinking innocently. "I'm sorry. I didn't know we were in that much of a hurry."

Peter's jaw dropped as he gaped at Meg's naked body, and for a moment she was sure he was going to rape her right there. But he forced his eyes away, again glancing out the window. "Unfortunately, we are. Now get dressed."

Meg nodded, emitting a shuddering sigh of relief, and hastened back to the armoire, pulling out a riding habit and quickly donning it. Stuffing a warm nightgown, a clean blouse, and some underwear into the valise, she snapped it shut and declared herself ready.

Peter got up off the bed, picking up his jacket where he'd thrown it on a chair and walking toward her. "Come on," he leered, suggestively squeezing her bottom, "let's get out of here and go somewhere where we can be alone." Grabbing her hand, he cupped it around his huge erection. "I'm gonna have a present for you tonight that's going to make you forget Geoffrey Wellesley ever existed."

Despite her vow not to anger him, Meg wrenched her hand away from his hot body and turned toward the door, glancing hopefully at the dressing table as she passed by.

Chapter 30

It was nearly seven in the morning before Geoff finally arrived home. He pulled his house key out of his pocket, then noticed that the door was unlocked. Ordinarily, his keen senses would have alerted him that something was wrong, but he was so tired that he merely shrugged and pushed the door open. He trudged through the foyer and paused wearily at the bottom of the stairs. Like Meg the night before, he looked up the steep staircase, but unlike his wife, he couldn't find the necessary energy to make the climb. Instead, he dragged himself into the parlor and fell on the settee. He'd sleep for a few hours. Then, tomorrow morning he'd go to the sheriff. As much as he longed to simply kill Peter Farnsworth and be done with it, he knew it was far better for everyone involved to let the authorities handle him. But one way or another, Geoff vowed, the man's vengeful spree of violence was over.

With an exhausted sigh, he closed his eyes. He didn't wake again for fourteen hours.

"Meg," Geoff called, sitting up on the settee and looking around groggily. "Meg, what time is it?"

He waited a moment; then, hearing no response, he stood up, stretching his tortured muscles. "God, I'm dying," he groaned, raking his fingers through his tousled hair and walking into the kitchen. "I must have used muscles yesterday that haven't been stretched in years." He looked around at the empty room in surprise, then frowned.

"Meg!" he called again, retracing his steps and entering the foyer. "Are you upstairs?" Still he received no response. "Now, where the hell is she this time?" he growled, irritated that his wife never seemed to be where he thought she was. He squinted at the grandfather clock in the dimly lit foyer. Nine-fifteen. She couldn't be at the mill, and she wouldn't be at Virginia's this late at night. She must already be in bed, he decided. Swinging around the newel post, he climbed the stairs.

As soon as he walked into the master bedroom, he knew something was wrong. The room was dark, but he could tell Meg wasn't in bed. Quickly, he lit a lamp, his apprehension growing by the moment. Holding the lamp up, he looked around.

"Jesus Christ, what's going on here?" he muttered, as he took in the rumpled bed, the clothes strewn haphazardly over the back of the chair, and the nightrail lying abandoned in the center of the floor. He shifted his gaze over to the open armoire and his breath caught in his throat. Meg's valise was gone. Throwing his head back, he emitted a loud wail of despair. She had left him.

Heavily, he sank down on the side of the bed. "Well, you should have expected it, you stupid ass," he accused. "You pushed her and bullied her and antagonized her till she finally had enough." His words trailed off as he felt the tight, barely remembered sensation of impending tears clog

345

his throat. Shit, he hadn't cried since he was a kid, but he felt like he was going to cry now.

Pressing his lips tightly together, he lay back on the bed, throwing an arm across his forehead and swallowing hard over the choking knot in his throat. Reaching out, he picked up a pillow, hugging it to him and burying his face in its softness.

Suddenly, his head jerked up and his eyebrows drew together. Again, he lifted the pillow to his face, inhaling deeply. "What the hell?" He took another sniff.

Bay rum . . . *the pillow smelled like bay rum!*

There was only one man in Wellesley foppish enough to wear that scent . . .

With a bellow of rage that could be heard all the way out to the street, Geoff hurled the pillow at the wall. "You're a dead man, Farnsworth!" he shouted, his voice reverberating off every wall of the house. Jumping up, he grabbed on to the bedpost and squeezed until his knuckles turned white. Farnsworth's throat. This was what he was going to do to Farnsworth's throat. Forget the sheriff, the lawyers, the juries . . . the man was as good as in his grave.

His eyes blazing and his breathing labored, Geoff looked wildly around the room, trying to find anything that might give him a clue as to where Farnsworth had taken Meg.

"Get a hold of yourself," he ordered. "You've got to think!" With a tremendous effort of will, he fought back his rage, then hurried out into the hall and picked up another lamp from a table, carrying it back into the room and lighting it. The brightness of the room increased considerably and he nodded in satisfaction.

He walked over to the bureau and stared down into an open drawer. A pile of handkerchiefs, a pair of white cotton gloves, and a letter lay neatly stacked inside. Absently, he picked up the envelope and carried it over to the light, peering at the neatly printed name in the upper right hand corner. "Willamette Jewelers, Portland, Oregon."

"Oh, no . . ." he groaned, a terrible premonition seizing him. Ignoring the guilt that stabbed him over reading someone else's mail, he pulled the single sheet of paper out of the envelope and quickly scanned the brief missive.

Dear Mrs. Wellesley:

Thank you for sending the list of items you wish to have appraised for sale. Although it is impossible to estimate the collection's worth merely by description, it sounds lovely and we would most definitely be interested in having the opportunity to examine the pieces further.

Please let me know when you are planning to be in Portland and we will set up a time, at your convenience, to meet.

We are hopeful that we will be able to come to a satisfactory agreement regarding the acquisition of your jewels.

Sincerely,

Henry Lovette, Prop.
Willamette Jewelers

Geoff dropped the letter and pressed the heels of his hands hard against his eyes. Meg hadn't lied to him. She *had* tried to sell her mother's jewels, just as she'd said.

His eyes clouded with remorse, Geoff gazed reluctantly down at the date of the letter. Three weeks ago . . . that was before Lawrence had even told him about the debt. And he, in his arrogance and anger, hadn't believed her. He'd stood right here in this room and accused her of lying. God, what a fool he was! How was he ever going to convince her of how sorry he was for not trusting her word?

"Now isn't the time to worry about it," he told himself firmly. "You can't do a damn thing to rectify this until you find her." Resolutely he shoved the bureau drawer closed and again started searching the room for any clues that might point to Meg's whereabouts.

He walked over to the armoire, trying to remember all the clothes in her wardrobe so he could figure out what she'd taken. The only thing he could tell was missing was an old riding habit. "They must be traveling," he whispered to himself. "Riding." He checked her shoes and nodded in affirmation. Her boots were gone.

"Okay," he said aloud. "So they're riding. But where?" Carefully, he perused the room again, his eyes lighting on the dressing table. He immediately noticed Meg's powder jar lying on its side and hurried over to investigate. Strange. Her combs, brushes, and mirror hadn't been disturbed. They were all there, lying neatly arranged as she always kept them. But what had happened to the powder? If Meg had spilled it, why hadn't she cleaned it up? It wasn't like her to be so careless.

Reaching out, Geoff set the jar back on its base, then leaned closer, noticing a pattern of some sort in the dust. His eyes widened as he realized that the pattern was actually letters. She *had* tried to leave him a message! *"P.F.— S.F."* he said aloud. *"P.F.—Peter Farnsworth!"*

A great jolt of fear ripped through him as his suspicions were confirmed. Taking a deep breath, he again bent over the dressing table. "Okay, sweetheart, so the *P.F.* is Peter Farnsworth. Now, what's *S.F.?*"

He straightened, planting his fists on his hips and staring out the window. *S.F. Something Farnsworth? Somebody Farns-*

worth? Who else was there besides Peter? George? Again Geoff peered closely at the letters scratched into the talc to make sure he hadn't misread them. He shook his head. The mark was definitely an "S," not a "G."

Frustrated that he couldn't think of what *S.F.* would signify, he paced the length of the room. *"S.F. S.F.,"* he muttered. "It has to be somebody . . . or something . . . or someplace. *Someplace . . ."*

His eyes narrowed as a possibility dawned. *S.F.—San Francisco! The son of a bitch is taking Meg to San Francisco! Dear God, he must be intending to take her out of the country!*

"Over my dead body," Geoff snarled. He took one last quick look around to see if there was any other clue he might have missed. Satisfied that there wasn't, he rushed out of the room and down the staircase, nearly tearing the front door off its hinges as he ran for his horse.

He had to catch them and catch them quick. In Meg's condition, there was no way she could ride all the way to San Francisco. Christ, the trek over the mountains alone would kill her!

Throwing himself into the saddle, Geoff kicked his horse into a gallop, heading straight for the Farnsworth home four blocks away. George might know where Peter was, and Geoff intended to use whatever means necessary to pry the information out of the old man if he did.

He arrived at the Farnsworth house and was off his horse before the animal even came to a full stop. Leaping up on to the front porch, he ignored the ornate knocker and began beating on the door. "Open up, Farnsworth," he bellowed, his voice so menacing that several people strolling by paused to stare at him incredulously. "Farnsworth? I know you're in there. *Open this goddamn door or I'll kick it in!"*

"Good God, I'm coming!" came an indignant response from inside the house. "Just hold your horses."

349

A second later the door opened to reveal George Farnsworth standing in his nightshirt, his expression livid. "What the hell do you want, Wellesley? My son isn't here."

"I know your goddamned son isn't here," Geoff shouted, pushing his way into the foyer. "What I want to know is, where is he?"

George glowered at Geoff angrily. "Just who the hell do you think you are, busting into my house at this time of night and demanding . . ."

"Your bastard of a son has kidnapped my wife!" Geoff roared, grabbing the smaller man by the front of his nightshirt and nearly lifting him off his feet.

"No . . ." George shrieked, shaking his head vehemently. "You're crazy."

"I'm *not* crazy," Geoff retorted, giving him a hard shake. "When was the last time you saw him?"

"Yesterday afternoon."

"When? What time?"

"About five, I think."

Geoff slowly released the old man, giving him a disgusted little push as he set him away. "Then he must have taken her last night. Christ, that means they've got more than twenty-four hours on me."

George yanked his nightshirt back into place indignantly. "Why do you think Peter took your wife?" he demanded. "There's no reason for him to have anything more to do with you people. The debt is paid."

"I know the debt is paid," Geoff gritted, "I paid it!"

"Then why?"

"Because your son is insane, Farnsworth! You know it, I know it, the whole town knows it. He hates me, and he's obsessed with Megan. What more reason do you need?"

"Peter is *not* insane," George bristled. "And I need a

350

whole lot more than your wild accusations to make me believe—"

"Shut up and listen!" Geoff ordered. "I don't have time to stand here and argue with you. Peter broke into my house last night, went to my wife's bedroom, and kidnapped her. But sometime before they left, she managed to spill her powder box and scratch a message into the dust."

George gaped at him in disbelieving horror. "What did the message say?"

"It said, 'P.F.—S.F.' That good enough for you?"

To Geoff's astonishment, tears of anguish welled in the old man's eyes and spilled over on to his cheeks. "My poor boy," he moaned, shaking his head. "What happened to my poor boy to make him do things like this?"

"I don't have any idea," Geoff snapped, hardening himself against the ripple of compassion he felt. "And I don't care. All I want to know is, where you think he might have taken Meg. Has he said anything recently about going to San Francisco?"

"San Francisco?" George asked blankly. "No. He *has* been in touch with someone in Mexico. Someone he says he met when he was in Texas. I don't know who, though. He never said much about why they were corresponding."

Geoff's eyebrows drew together in confusion. "If he's heading for Mexico, why would he go by way of San Francisco? It doesn't make any sense."

"What makes you think he's gone to San Francisco?"

"The message," Geoff muttered absently, his mind elsewhere as he frantically tried to determine why Peter would go to San Francisco.

"You mean you think the 'S.F.' in the message means San Francisco?"

"Can you think of anything else those initials would mean?"

"No," George admitted.

"That must be it," Geoff said, trying hard to convince himself that his hunch was right, even though it didn't make much sense. If *"S.F."* didn't mean San Francisco, then he was completely at a loss as to where to begin his search, and he couldn't bear to face that possibility.

"Are you going to San Francisco, then?" George asked.

"Of course I'm going to San Francisco! What else can I do?"

"Peter does have a lot of friends there."

Geoff's eyes lightened with renewed hope. "He does? Do you know any names?"

For a long moment, George stood and looked at the distraught man, fighting a terrible battle with himself. "What are you going to do to my son if you find him?"

Geoff's mouth thinned into an ominous line. "What would you do to a man who has tried to kill you, stripped you of your livelihood, and kidnapped your wife?"

George gasped. "Stripped you of your livelihood! Are you insinuating that Peter was responsible for the fire you had the other day?"

"Somebody torched my flume, Farnsworth. Who do you suppose did it?"

"Peter wouldn't do such a thing!" George exploded. "I know he wouldn't."

"Well, he did," Geoff snarled, stepping forward aggressively. "Then he absconded with my wife. And you, old man, are going to help me figure out where. Do you understand me?"

George shook his head despairingly. "The boy needs help. He's sick, Wellesley."

"He's also dangerous," Geoff hissed. "Now, come on, we're wasting time."

George let out a long, defeated sigh. "Come into the

office and we'll see if there's anything on his desk that might help you."

Together, they walked into a small room off the hall. George lit a lamp and began shuffling through the mountain of papers on the desk. Geoff joined him, picking up and discarding sheet after sheet. Ten minutes later, they'd found nothing.

"That's all of it," George said, shrugging. "You see, Wellesley, you're wrong."

Geoff threw the man a furious glare, then lifted a corner of the blotter. A small slip of paper fluttered to the floor. Bending down, he picked it up, drawing in a sharp breath when he read the few words scrawled across it. *"Pier 42, The Hispañola."* Shoving the paper into George's face, he hissed, "Still think I'm wrong, Farnsworth?"

"Lord have mercy," George moaned, his head dropping to his chest. "Why, Peter? Why? I gave you everything!"

Ignoring the old man's plaintive cry, Geoff turned away and headed for the front door.

"You're not going to kill him, are you?" George shouted, racing after Geoff and grabbing his arm.

"I'm going to get my wife back," Geoff growled, shaking off the man's clutching fingers and stepping out on to the porch. "Whatever it takes, I'm getting my wife back."

With a sob of misery, George watched Geoff mount his horse. Then, with an exhaustion borne of years of despair, he slowly closed the front door.

Chapter 31

"Peter, please, I have to stop for a while. *Please!*"

Peter's lips thinned with irritation as he shot a look back at Meg. She had pulled her horse to a halt and now sat slumped wearily over the animal's neck.

"We just stopped two hours ago," he growled, wheeling his horse around and riding back to where she waited. "Don't think I don't know what you're trying to do, Meg."

"I'm not trying to do anything," she protested wearily. "I'm just so tired . . ."

"You're not that tired. You're just trying to stall around enough to let Wellesley catch up with us before we reach San Francisco."

Meg's heart sank as she realized that Peter was obviously on to her game. Stalling was exactly what she was trying to do, and for most of the day her ruse had worked very well. Obviously, though, she'd pushed her luck too far. "I'm not stalling," she whined. "If Geoff were following us, he'd have caught up by now. It's just that, well, you know, in my condition . . ."

"Your condition is something we're going to take care of the second we get to South America," Peter vowed through gritted teeth. He had been enraged when Meg had first mentioned her pregnancy and further incensed that he hadn't already known about it. From what she'd said, it sounded like he was the only person in Wellesley who didn't. He supposed that really wasn't all that unusual, since he wouldn't lower himself to associate with the residents of the two-bit town where he'd had the misfortune to be born, but still, he was surprised his father hadn't mentioned it to him. Unless, of course, he hadn't known either.

"What are you talking about?" Meg gasped, jerking her head up and staring at him apprehensively.

"You heard me. There's lots of native women where we're going that will know how to put an end to your . . . indisposition."

"Don't try it, Peter," Meg warned, her voice deadly. "You try to force me to take anything that will jeopardize my baby and I'll kill you."

"Oh, sure you will," he sneered. "You're so sick all the time, you can hardly hold your head up. Just how do you think you're going to kill me?"

"I'm warning you, Peter. Don't even think about it."

Peter intended to do much more than "think about it." He was determined that Wellesley's baby would never take his first breath of life, but that was in the future . . . after they reached Bolivia. Right now, it was far more important to let Meg know that he wasn't about to allow her to threaten him.

"Don't you ever talk to me like that again, girl," he snarled. "You'd be wise to remember just who is in charge here."

Meg instantly regretted her rash words, knowing that Peter would never let down his guard enough for her to escape unless she lulled him into thinking she was too weak and too sick to attempt it. "I'm sorry," she said contritely. "You know I didn't mean it. I could never kill anyone for any reason. But Peter, surely you can understand what my baby means to me."

Peter laughed cruelly. "Too bad for you that it obviously doesn't mean as much to its father."

"What?"

"As you said, it doesn't look like Wellesley is coming after you. Guess he doesn't much care about you *or* his kid."

To her despair, Meg was beginning to think the same thing. When they'd first left town two nights before, she'd been certain that Geoff would come after them. Even if he no longer cared what happened to her, she knew he cared about his unborn child. But as the next two days had passed and there had been so sign of him, she was beginning to have doubts about even that. Maybe he was just so fed up with her obstinacy and stubbornness and the many ways he thought she'd deceived him that he didn't deem her to be worth rescuing. If only she'd had time to tell him how she really felt about him . . . if only they'd had time to work out their problems . . . if only . . .

"Don't think about those things," she told herself fiercely. "He'll come. You're carrying his baby—his heir. He'll come."

Determinedly, she turned her thoughts back to her present situation. "Please, Peter, I just have to get down for a minute and rest." Without waiting for his consent, she dismounted and made a great show of staggering over to a large tree and collapsing beneath it. "I need to sleep. Please? Just for an hour or so?"

"No!" Peter bellowed, grabbing her horse's reins and throwing them at her. "Now, get up and let's get moving."

Meg didn't have to work very hard to force the tears that sprang to her eyes. "I can't go on," she mewled pitifully. "You're trying to kill me, aren't you?"

356

As far as Peter was concerned, that suggestion was beginning to sound more and more enticing. Nothing was going as he'd planned. Megan—the woman he'd fantasized about for so many years—was in reality a whining, sickly, demanding ninny who could neither skin a hare, saddle a horse, nor even cook a pot of beans without fainting, hurting herself, or burning something.

And as far as the passion he'd been anticipating so hotly, well, that had gone right out the window when she'd told him she was pregnant. Even if he was willing to ignore the fact that she was carrying Geoffrey Wellesley's baby, her constant bouts of nausea, coupled with her incessant complaining, had very effectively killed his desire for her.

"Things will be different once we get to Bolivia," he told himself for the hundredth time. "I'll get rid of the damn kid and hire servants to do the heavy work so she won't have to do a thing . . . except please me." He smiled lasciviously, just thinking about what he planned to have Meg do to please him.

But first, they had to get to San Francisco, and if they didn't get moving, they were going to miss their ship.

"Get up, Megan," he commanded, his voice menacing, "you're not going to sleep, and you're not going to make us miss the sailing. Now, get off your rump and on that horse."

Meg let out a dispirited sigh, but did as Peter bade, too wary of his volatility not to. Wearily, she hauled herself up into the saddle and again began to meekly follow him down the rutted trail. They came to the crest of a hill and she chanced a quick look behind them, praying that she might see Geoffrey galloping after them across the emerald valley below. She didn't.

"He's not coming," Peter sneered, noticing where her gaze was roaming, "so quit your damn dawdling and ride."

They inched along a high ridge for another several hours until Meg really did think she might fall off her horse from exhaustion. The constant jostling was making her sick to her stomach, and her head pounded so fiercely that she could hardly focus her eyes. Finally, she could take no more and pulled her horse to a halt. "I'm stopping here," she announced to Peter's back.

"No, you're not," he retorted, turning around to glare at her as she dismounted.

"Yes, I am. We've been riding for at least eight hours, and I can't go on."

"Get on the horse, Megan," Peter warned.

"No."

"Megan . . ."

"There's nothing you can say that's going to make me get back on this horse today, Peter! You can yell at me, you can hit me, you can even kill me, if you want to, but I'm not riding any farther." Throwing him a look that dared him to do any of the things she'd just suggested, she tossed her horse's reins at him and walked over to a shady spot where she sat down.

"Don't you tell me what we're going to do!" he shouted, leaping down from his horse and striding over to where she sat. "Get up!"

"I said no," she answered calmly.

"Don't make me punish you, Megan."

Meg was too tired to be frightened by his threat. "Go ahead and punish me," she challenged. "There's nothing you can do that would be worse than what you've already done."

"Want to make a bet?" Peter exploded, his hands clenching into fists. "I haven't done anything to you . . . yet."

"Oh, yes, you have," she shouted back, so angry she

358

didn't even consider the danger she was putting herself in by defying him. "You've taken me away from my home and my husband, you've told me you're going to destroy my baby, and you've threatened to abuse me if I don't do your bidding. So why don't you do it, Peter? Why don't you just pull out your gun and shoot me? At this point, I don't much care."

Like the bully he was, Peter backed down. Turning away, he walked over to the edge of the ridge and let out a hoarse scream of frustration, then threw himself on the ground.

Meg ignored him. Oddly enough, his infantile behavior was somehow comforting. He didn't have the courage to carry out his dire threats and she knew it. Oh, he might get mad enough to hit her, and God knew, she didn't want that, but he wasn't going to truly hurt her. He wanted her too much sexually to do that. Hopefully, as long as she continued to fake being ill, she could stave off his lust a while longer. Long enough, at least, to try to escape. Now that she was convinced that Geoff wasn't going to come after her, she had to do some serious planning. The one thing she did fear was that if Peter actually got her as far as South America, he would find some way to destroy her baby, so she had to get away before they boarded the ship in San Francisco.

But until she could come up with a viable plan, she would continue to employ the tactics that had worked for her today. She'd found that alternating between whining at him and standing up to him served her very well, and she intended to keep right on doing it. Maybe she could even be unpleasant enough that he'd decide he didn't want her after all and abandon her in San Francisco. She doubted it, but just thinking that it might be a possibility gave her the courage to go on.

She closed her eyes and let her mind drift. As always at these moments, her mind filled with thoughts of Geoffrey. What was he doing right now? Working at his camp, rebuilding his flume, sitting in Portland with his attorney, filling out a divorce petition?

For two days, she'd harbored the fear that Geoff might think she'd left with Peter of her own accord. What if he hadn't found her crude message scratched into the powder on her dressing table? What if he had, but hadn't understood it? Most distressing of all, what if he had, but just didn't care?

"He'll come," she whispered, knowing that she no longer really believed her own words. "He has to come . . ."

Geoff *was* coming and Meg would have been ecstatic if she had known how close he actually was.

The first day, he'd ridden like the devil himself, making up most of the distance Peter had put between them with the long head start. Finally, after sixteen hours in the saddle, Geoff had stopped and rested, only to continue his grueling pace the next morning. By nightfall of the second day, he found traces of a fresh campfire and knew that they were only a few hours ahead of him. He'd catch up tomorrow.

But it wasn't until late the next afternoon when he heard Peter's raging temper tantrum that he realized how close he really was.

"They're right over on that ridge," he muttered with grim satisfaction. Quickly, he led his horse into a dense copse of trees so he couldn't be seen from the higher elevation. His first thought was to close in immediately, especially since it was obvious that Farnsworth was in a rage. But when he didn't hear any answering cries from Meg, good sense prevailed and he sat down to wait until full dark. There was no sense putting her in any more danger than necessary, and the quickly gathering clouds portended a black night, which would give him the distinct advantage of surprise. He would wait.

It seemed like an eternity before it was dark enough that Geoff felt ready to make his move. Tethering his horse, he sneaked forward on foot until he was within a hundred feet of Peter and Meg's small camp. He squatted silently behind a bush, straining his ears to hear.

"I've got to go water the horses before we turn in," he heard Peter announce.

Meg didn't answer.

"Get over here so I can tie you up."

This time Meg did respond, and when Geoff heard the resigned exhaustion in her voice, his eyebrows shot up with alarm.

"You don't need to tie me up, Peter. I'm not going anywhere. I just want to sleep."

"I said, get over here. Now, move it."

Geoff's fists clenched and it took all the control he could muster not to burst into camp that very moment. But he waited, hoping to use the time Peter was gone to rescue Meg and get her out of harm's way before he went back to deal with him. There was silence as Peter trussed Meg up, then Geoff heard the distinct sound of horses being led away. He waited another ten seconds, then sneaked around the perimeter of the camp, approaching Meg from the back and clapping his hand over her mouth to keep her from crying out.

She immediately started to fight him, her legs flailing

desperately in the dust as she tried to ward off this new, unknown tormenter. "Shh, baby, it's me."

Meg was just opening her mouth to bite down into the fleshy part of his palm when Geoff's words registered. Whipping her head around, she stared at him, tears of relief filling her eyes.

"Hello, Mrs. Wellesley," he smiled, his voice thick with emotion as he removed his hand. "Don't make a sound. I'm going to get you out of here."

"My hands are tied behind me," she whispered.

He nodded, then pulled a knife out of his belt and neatly severed her bonds.

"Oh, Geoff!" Luckily her unthinking cry of welcome was muffled against his shoulder as she launched herself into his arms. "I thought you weren't going to come."

"Not going to come?" His subdued whisper held a distinct note of disbelief. "You thought I wouldn't come for you?"

"Well, I . . . oh, I don't know!" Again she buried her face in his shoulder, clinging to him fiercely.

"Shh, Megan, sweetheart," he crooned, running his hand over her tangled hair. "Don't cry. We've got to get you out of here before Farnsworth gets back."

"Are we just going to leave?" she whispered incredulously. "Geoff, he'll follow us. I know he will. If he comes back and finds me gone, he's going to know you've found me and he'll come after us."

"Don't worry. I'm just going to get you out of here, then I'll come back and take care of him."

"Geoff, you have to be careful! The man is insane, and he hates you. I know he'll kill you if he gets the chance."

"He won't get the chance," Geoff assured her, his face dark and forbidding. "Now, come on. I'll show you where I have my horse."

Geoff took her hand and the two of them inched quietly out of the clearing, staying under the cover of trees and shrubs until they reached the place where Geoff had left the horse.

"Thank you," Meg choked, when they finally reached the sanctuary of the copse of trees.

Geoff tipped her chin up with his forefinger, wishing that there was enough light that he could see her face clearly. "For what?"

"For . . . for everything!" she sobbed, again catapulting herself into his embrace. "For not abandoning me, for risking your life to come after me, for forgiving me . . ."

Geoff smiled and gave her a gentle kiss. "We'll have plenty of time to talk about how wonderful I am later," he chuckled. "Right now, though, I want you to climb up in this tree while I go take care of Farnsworth."

"Climb up in a tree?"

"Yes," he nodded, grasping her by her waist and lifting her to a branch eight feet above the ground.

Meg sat down on the branch and grabbed the tree's massive trunk, teetering precariously for a moment. "Why do I have to stay up here?" she gasped.

"Because this way, if something happens to me and Farnsworth comes looking for you, you'll have the advantage of seeing him before he sees you."

"Oh, Geoff . . ." Meg moaned, not even wanting to consider the possibility that something could happen to him. "Please, I don't want you—"

"Don't argue," Geoff interrupted hastily. "Just once in your life, let me say something that you don't argue with."

Despite his curt words, Meg could tell by his tone that he wasn't angry with her. "I'll do whatever you say," she said quietly.

"Good. Now, take this gun." From out of the darkness,

a six-shooter suddenly appeared in front of her. "If you see Farnsworth coming for you, shoot the son of a bitch."

Meg nodded.

"And don't, for any reason, get out of this tree until I come back and tell you to. Understand?"

Meg remained silent, not wanting to make that promise when she knew that if there was trouble and she thought she could help, she wouldn't stay put for a minute.

"Megan?" Geoff repeated, his voice insistent. "Do you understand me?"

"Yes."

"And you promise you'll stay up there, regardless of what you might hear?"

Again, he was met with silence.

"Meg . . ."

Mumbling a quick plea of forgiveness for the lie she was about to tell, she answered, "All right. I promise I'll stay here."

"Good," Geoff nodded, seeming to be satisfied. "Now, I'm going back to the clearing and wait for Farnsworth. I'll be back as soon as I can."

"Please be careful," she pleaded, her voice breaking.

"I will." With a last reassuring pat to her dangling foot, he slipped away. Meg's eyes followed his shadowy form for a minute. Then he disappeared into the darkness.

Geoff paused when he reached the clearing, crouching down and scanning the area to see if Peter had returned. He hadn't.

Geoff waited silently, gun drawn, senses alert. But so intense was his scrutiny of the area leading down to the stream that he didn't hear Peter's stealthy approach from behind him.

"Wellesley . . ." Peter hissed, his voice as sibilant as a snake.

Geoff whirled around to find the barrel of a Colt .45 six inches from his face. With catlike speed, he threw out an arm just as Peter fired, deflecting the shot harmlessly into the air. The gun flew out of Peter's hand, clattering as it skidded along the rocks. With a bellow of frustration, Peter leaned down and grabbed a large stone, swinging his arm in an arc and smashing it against Geoff's temple.

Silently, Geoff crumpled to the ground.

High up in the tree, Meg heard the shot. She let out a startled little scream, then quickly clapped her hand over her mouth. She waited, her nerves so taut that the entire branch shook. Somewhere, off to her right, a twig broke. "Geoff?" she whispered into the darkness. "Geoff?"

There was no answer, and a terrible fear gripped her. What if it wasn't Peter who'd been shot? What if it was Geoff? She had to find out. She *had* to!

Sticking the gun into her waistband, Meg climbed down from her perch and ran in the direction of the gunshot. She burst into the clearing, then came to a skidding halt and let out a sharp scream of terror when she saw Peter looming over Geoff's prostrate form.

"You maniac!" she shrieked, charging at him like an enraged mother bear. "I'm going to kill you!" Wrenching the gun out of her riding skirt, she brandished it wildly in his direction.

Peter turned and gaped in astonishment at the wild-eyed virago waving the big gun and running toward him. "Don't do it!" he screamed, backing away. "He's not dead!"

"You're lying," Meg screamed, stopping directly in front of him and digging the barrel of her gun into his stomach.

Peter's eyes filled with fear. "Megan, please, don't do this. I'll let you go. I'll . . ."

"It's too late," Meg hissed. "You killed him. You killed

my husband . . . the man I love . . . the father of my child. And now, I'm going to kill you."

They were standing near where Geoff lay, and just as Meg pulled back the gun's hammer, there was a movement from the ground. Suddenly, Peter disappeared from her line of sight. There was a loud thump as he hit the ground, then a scream of pain as two meaty fists began cruelly pummeling his face. Meg looked down in confusion, not fully understanding how her quarry had suddenly ended up on the ground.

"Run, Meg!" Geoff yelled, dealing blow after punishing blow into Peter's bleeding face. For the briefest second, he looked up to see if she was doing as he ordered.

It was the second Peter needed. Pulling up his knees, he kicked Geoff in the stomach, bucking him off and then rolling over and over with him as the men continued to grapple.

Meg screamed as the combatants approached the steep edge of the ridge. Running after them, she shrieked mindlessly at them to stop.

Just as they reached the edge of the cliff, Peter broke Geoff's hold, leaping on top of him and wrapping his hands around his throat.

Meg reached the two men and watched with terror as Peter inched Geoff closer to the cliff's edge. Realizing that he intended to push Geoff over the side, she plunged headlong into the midst of the battle, kicking Peter as hard as she could with the pointed toe of her riding boot.

The unexpected attack caused him to loosen his grip around Geoff's neck for just an instant, but it was enough to give Geoff the upper hand. With a herculean effort, he forced his arms between their bodies, breaking Peter's hold. Peter's arms flew outward, swinging crazily in large, arcing circles as he tried to regain his balance. Geoff seized

366

his momentary advantage and grabbed Peter by the shoulders, hurling him off his body. Peter rolled away, grabbing desperately at the air as his legs slipped over the side of the cliff.

Then he disappeared.

Chapter 32

Meg opened her eyes and looked up into the worried face of her husband.

"Welcome back," he said softly.

"What happened?" she asked, running her fingertips across her forehead in bewilderment.

"What happened is that you saved my life," he smiled, so relieved she had finally regained consciousness that he could hardly speak.

As memory came rushing back, Meg squeezed her eyes shut and shook her head. "Peter . . ."

"Shh," Geoff crooned, gathering her in his arms and rocking her like a baby. "He's gone, sweetheart. Don't think about it anymore."

"Oh, Geoff, when I saw you rolling toward the edge of that cliff . . ."

Geoff halted her words with a gentle kiss. "It's over, baby. All over."

Meg opened her eyes, noticing for the first time that a trickle of blood was running down the side of his face. "You're hurt!" she gasped, pulling out of his embrace and sitting up. "Bleeding!"

Geoff lifted his hand, wincing slightly as he ran his fingers over the gash near his temple. "It's nothing. He hit me with a rock, but it's just a flesh wound."

"Oh, Geoff," Meg moaned, her voice still sounding vague and disoriented, "I'm so sorry . . ."

"Hush, baby. There's nothing for you to be sorry about. It was bound to happen, but it's behind us now."

Meg lowered her eyes, trying hard to come to terms with the horror she'd just witnessed. "He would have killed you if you hadn't killed him first, wouldn't he?"

"Yes," Geoff said quietly.

"Then it had to be done."

Geoff frowned, not liking the wan resignation in her voice. Somehow, he had to pull her out of the lethargy she was slipping into. "Why didn't you stay in that tree?" he asked suddenly.

Meg's focus sharpened as her eyes flared with indignation. "I'd think that would be obvious."

Geoff was enormously relieved by her response. He'd been right to annoy her. If there was anything that would get Megan back to normal, it was questioning a decision she'd made.

"You told me you'd stay there," he reminded her.

"Well, I lied. And you should be grateful."

"I am," he admitted, pulling her back into his arms. "You saved my life."

Meg pulled away and looked at him in bewilderment. "Why do you keep saying that? What did I do?"

"If you hadn't kicked Farnsworth, I don't think I could have broken that stranglehold he had on me. You're an incredible woman, Megan Wellesley."

"Thank you," she whispered with a small smile.

"The sun's going to be up in a couple of hours. Do you think you'll feel strong enough to ride once it's light?"

"Of course. I'm strong as an ox and I want to go home."

369

"But I heard you telling Farnsworth how exhausted you were."

Meg threw him a smug smile. "I faked all that. It was a good way to slow him down and give you a better chance to catch up to us, although I was beginning to think you weren't coming."

Geoff's brows drew together. "Megan, did you really doubt that I'd come after you?"

"Well, I hoped you would," she hedged, "but with everything that has gone wrong between us, I . . ."

"Oh, sweetheart," Geoff groaned, wrapping his arms around her and pulling her down in the tall mountain grass, "none of that matters. You're my wife, and I love you. That's all that counts."

"Do you really love me?" Meg asked, a sheen of unshed tears brightening her eyes.

"Oh, God, baby, if you only knew how much. You can't imagine how I felt when I found you gone. At first, I thought maybe you'd just up and left me."

"Me, leave you?" Meg gasped. "Why would I do that?"

"Because I'm a stubborn, bullheaded fool."

"You're not!" Meg protested. "You're—"

"I know, I know," Geoff chuckled. "I'm wonderful and romantic and heroic. You said that before, and I'm happy you feel that way. But the truth is, Megan, I've acted like a stupid ass most of the time we've been married, and I'm sorry."

"Oh, Geoff," Meg sighed, "I'm the one who should be sorry. I blackmailed you into marrying me, then I didn't tell you about the debt . . ."

"I know you weren't after my money," he said softly. "I found the letter from the jeweler in Portland."

"You did?"

"I wasn't prying," he added hastily. "I was just going

through the things in our bedroom, trying to find something that would give me a clue as to where you'd gone. It was when I thought you'd left me and I was desperate . . ."

"Geoff," Meg said seriously, "will you tell me something . . . truthfully?"

"Yes."

"If you had found that I'd left you of my own accord, would you still have come after me?"

There was a long pause, then Geoff slowly nodded. "Yeah. I would have. Even if I'd thought you didn't want me, I'd have tried to find you."

"Because of the baby?" Meg whispered.

"No. Because I love you."

"I love you, too," Meg choked.

"Are you gonna cry again?"

"Why?"

"Because this shirt is soaked already and I don't have another one. Really, Megan, you've got to quit bawling or I'm going to catch my death of cold!"

Meg started to laugh and her tears receded. "Maybe I cry so much because I'm pregnant."

"Maybe," Geoff acknowledged, running his hand lovingly over her stomach. "Is everything okay down there?"

"Yes. She's in there good and secure."

"You mean, *he's* good and secure."

"Oh, all right, have it your way."

They chuckled, then lay quietly together for a few minutes. Finally, Geoff propped himself up on an elbow and looked down at her earnestly. "Meg, you know what I said a minute ago about the baby not being the reason I came after you?"

"Yes?"

"Well, I don't want you to get the idea that I don't care about the baby. I do . . . very much."

"Oh, Geoff . . ."

"No, let me finish. I want children, sweetheart. Lots and lots of them. I hope we have so many damn kids that we have to build another wing on the new house to hold them all. But thirty years from now, when they're grown and gone, there will still be the two of us. You're the most important thing in the world to me, and I want you to know that baby or no baby, I would have come for you."

"Oh, Geoff," Meg sighed, "I love you so much." She leaned forward and kissed him. "In fact," she added, her eyes taking on a devilish glint, "I couldn't have chosen a better man to blackmail into marriage if I'd had my pick of anyone in the whole world."

For a moment Geoff stared at her in disbelief, then he started to laugh. For a long time afterward, they lay snuggled together, kissing, fondling, and watching the sun come up. It was truly the dawn of a new day.

Their arrival in Eugene the next afternoon caused quite a stir.

Geoffrey was a well-known figure in the bustling city. He often traveled there on business and was well acquainted with many of the city's most influential citizens.

Normally, his appearance in town caused an immediate flurry of excitement among two select groups—business mavens eager to align themselves with the famous timber baron, and society dames who would spring into action planning soirées in his honor. These parties were always eagerly anticipated, since they afforded Eugene's socially ambitious mothers the rare opportunity of parading their unmarried daughters before the handsome and wealthy Mr. Wellesley.

But his arrival in Eugene on this day was far different from any the town had known before. First, he did not come in his private railroad car, as was his usual habit. Rather, he arrived on horseback—and in the company of an unknown lady. Second, the couple appeared on Main Street looking as ragged and unkempt as an itinerant lumberjack and his woman.

The first to see them was Florenzia Mirada, one of the town's most influential dowagers. Florenzia took great pride in her Italian heritage and in the fact that her grandfather had immigrated from New York to Oregon many years before and had made a fortune manufacturing the crude ties used in skid roads.

Florenzia was strolling down the boardwalk, idling away the afternoon with a bit of window shopping, when she first spotted the bedraggled couple. Normally, she wouldn't have given them more than a cursory glance, but something about the man seemed familiar. She squinted against the bright sun, examining the horseman more closely.

"My stars in heaven," she gasped, poking her friend, Rebecca Hargreave, solidly in the stomach with her elbow. "Look at that couple riding toward us. Do you know who that man is?"

Rebecca was so myopic that she could barely discern that there *were* people riding down the street, much less make out anyone's features. "No, I'm sure I don't," she answered, a bit testily. "You know I don't wear my spectacles in public."

"Well, I'll tell you," Florenzia gushed, delighted that Rebecca's bad eyesight gave her the chance to break the news. "It's Geoffrey Wellesley!"

By this time, Geoff and Meg were close enough that

Rebecca could make out a few details of their appearance—at least enough to tell that they were dirty and shabbily dressed. "Oh, don't be silly, Flo," she scoffed. "That's not Geoffrey Wellesley! It's some filthy lumberjack heading north to look for work."

"I thought that, too, at first," Florenzia agreed, "but I'm telling you, Rebecca, that's Geoffrey Wellesley. After all, I should recognize him. He casts his eye at my Constanza every time he's in town, and nothing concerning my daughter escapes me."

Rebecca threw her friend a dubious look. Constanza Mirada was a dear young woman, but unfortunately, God had not seen fit to extend her beauty to her face. It was highly unlikely that Geoffrey Wellesley would cast his eye at Constanza with anything but pity.

"I'm sorry, my dear," Rebecca said stoutly, "but you're mistaken."

"I am not," Florenzia insisted. "It's him!"

"Flo," Rebecca reasoned, "why would Geoffrey Wellesley come riding into town dressed like a tramp, and in the company of that slovenly woman?"

"I don't know," Florenzia admitted. "It doesn't make much sense, but I know it's him. Here, I'll prove it to you!"

Stepping out into the street, she waved her arm over her head in an attempt to gain Geoff's attention. "Oh, Mr. Wellesley, yoo hoo!"

"Oh, Christ," Geoff growled, looking over at the madly waving woman. "Just what we need."

"Who's that?" Meg asked curiously.

"You don't want to know."

By this time, Florenzia had caught up to them, and after throwing a dismissive glance at Meg, she turned her full attention on Geoff. "I told Mrs. Hargreave it was you. But, whatever happened to you, my dear? You look a bit . . ."

"The worse for wear?" Geoff finished for her.

"Well, let's just say, you don't look quite like your usual impeccable self."

"We met with a bit of trouble on the road," Geoff said simply. Then, gesturing to Meg, he said, "Mrs. Mirada, allow me to present my wife, Megan. Megan, Mrs. Florenzia Mirada."

"Your wife!" Florenzia gasped rudely.

"Yes," Geoff confirmed, his voice hardening. "My wife."

Florenzia shot Meg a look that told her that she had been judged and found clearly wanting. "Well, what a surprise! When did this happen?"

"Happen? You mean, when did we get married?"

"Yes, of course. When did you get married?"

"About three months ago."

"Well, I never!"

"Pardon me?"

"I mean, I'm just surprised we didn't hear about it."

Geoff smiled thinly. "I'm surprised you didn't, either. Now, if you'll excuse us, we need to go freshen up a little."

"Yes," Florenzia muttered, her eyes again raking over Meg, "I can well understand how you might want to do that. But, tell me before you go, Mr. Wellesley, how long are you and . . . your wife going to be in town?"

"Just overnight. We're on our way home and we just stopped to get a little rest."

"Oh," she answered, sounding deflated. "I was hoping there might be time for a small gathering . . ."

"Not this time, I'm afraid, Mrs. Mirada. You see, we're really still on our honeymoon."

And, tipping his hat, he nudged his horse away, leaving Florenzia Mirada standing open-mouthed in the middle of Main Street.

* * *

"That was terrible of you," Meg admonished, as they walked through the front door of the Hotel Eugene.

"I know," Geoff admitted, "but that old bat has the ugliest daughter in three counties, and every time I'm in town, she tries to make a match between us. I just couldn't resist."

Meg shot him an arch glance out of the corner of her eye.

"Quit looking at me like that," he grinned. "I didn't mean to sound heartless. Constanza is a pleasant enough girl, but a man would have to pull the sheet over her head before he could find the courage to get in bed with her."

Meg burst out laughing, causing many heads to turn their way as they proceeded through the opulent lobby. Several people glared disapprovingly at them, bristling that such obvious riffraff would dare enter the lobby of the Eugene.

They approached the registration desk and a small, pinch-mouthed man frowned across the counter at them. "May I help you with something?" he asked coldly.

It was Geoff's turn to bristle. Pulling himself up to his full, imposing height, he riveted the little man with a quelling stare. "Indeed, Mr. Pennyman. I'd like my regular suite, if it's available."

The astonished Mr. Pennyman peered closely at Geoff's bearded, dirty face. Showing no sign of recognition, he croaked, "Your regular suite?"

"Yes," Geoff nodded. "Number six-forty-one."

"Six-forty-one!" Pennyman blustered. "But that's our best suite. I'm sure that's not the room you mean, sir. It's . . . very expensive."

"I'm aware of how much the suite costs," Geoff said icily. "I rent it every time I'm in town."

Pennyman blew out a long, defeated breath. "My apologies sir, but I'm afraid I'm not familiar with . . ."

"Wellesley," Geoffrey barked, losing all patience with the snobby little clerk. "Geoffrey Wellesley."

Pennyman's eyes turned into huge round circles behind his spectacles. "Mr. Wellesley?" he gasped. "Oh, I'm so sorry! Of course, your suite is available!" Whirling around, he grabbed a large key from out of a cubbyhole behind the counter. "If you'll just tell me where your luggage is, I'll have a boy . . ."

"We don't have any luggage."

"No luggage?" Mr. Pennyman blurted, before he could catch himself.

"No luggage. Now, there are several things I'd appreciate you doing for me."

"Oh, yes, certainly, sir. Anything."

"First of all, I want two baths sent up. Then, I want someone to go pick up some clothes for both myself and my wife . . ."

"Your wife?" Pennyman exploded, his face becoming positively apoplectic.

"Yes, my wife. Now, as I was saying, I want a suitable traveling dress for Mrs. Wellesley and a pair of pants and a good flannel shirt for myself."

"Yes, yes," Pennyman muttered, writing furiously on a small scrap of paper. "Underclothing?"

"I beg your pardon?"

"Will you be needing underclothing?"

Geoff turned to Meg, raising his eyebrows questioningly. She shook her head.

"No, that won't be necessary."

"Sleeping apparel?"

This time Geoff didn't even look at Meg for an answer. "No. That won't be necessary either."

Pennyman gulped, embarrassed by the trace of laughter in Geoff's voice. "Consider it done, Mr. Wellesley," he said, laying down his pencil and focusing on a point somewhere around the middle of Geoff's chest. "Anything else?"

"Yes. After the baths and clothes are delivered, I want two suppers brought up. Roast beef if you have it, or steak. Green beans, bread, pie, and potatoes—lots of them—with no pepper."

"Pepper, sir?" Pennyman questioned, peering up at him curiously.

"No pepper," Geoff repeated, throwing Meg a wink.

Pennyman wrote some more, then again laid his pencil aside.

"How about your horses? Or did you travel by wagon or carriage, perhaps?"

"We came by horseback," Geoff nodded. "They're tied up right outside. Have someone take them over to the livery, feed them, and rub them down. I'd like them delivered to the train station by tomorrow morning at eight. We'll be leaving on the eight-thirty northbound. That reminds me, we'll need train tickets. Just book us as far as Portland. I'll pick up my private car there."

"Yes, sir, I'll see to it."

Geoff started to turn away, then looked back over his shoulder at the flustered man. "Oh, and one more thing."

"Yes, sir?"

"Please see that no one disturbs us after our supper is delivered."

"Oh, no, sir. Absolutely not."

Geoff nodded and took Meg's arm, steering her toward the lavish, sweeping staircase at the rear of the lobby.

Glancing down at her, he was surprised to see her staring back at him, a look of wonderment on her face.

"What's wrong?"

"Nothing," she murmured, shaking her head. "It's just that I've never seen you act like that before."

"Act like what?"

"Like . . . like *Geoffrey Wellesley*."

Geoff shrugged. "The pompous little ass deserved it."

"You were pretty hard on him, Geoff."

Geoff threw her a baleful look, but turned back and called, "Mr. Pennyman?"

"Yes, Mr. Wellesley?"

"Thank you for your help."

"You're most welcome, Mr. Wellesley."

Horace Pennyman watched as Geoff and Meg disappeared up the staircase. His nerves taut as violin strings, he leaned back against the solid security of his registration desk and raised a shaking hand to his forehead.

"What's the matter, Horace?" asked a bellman standing nearby.

"Well, I'll tell you, Willie, I learned something today."

"What's that?"

"You know how they always say that the rich are eccentric?"

"Yeah? What about it?"

"Well," Horace sighed, a little smile playing around his tight little mouth. "They are."

Chapter 33

Meg leaned back in her chair, rubbing her stomach and groaning with contentment. "It's amazing how much better a hot bath and a hot meal can make you feel."

Geoff nodded and lit a cigarette, looking at his wife speculatively for a moment, She'd been quiet during dinner, and he wasn't sure whether it was from exhaustion or whether she was still plagued by memories of the tragedy up on the ridge.

"This really is a beautiful room," Meg ventured, looking around the sumptuously appointed suite.

"Yeah, it's a decent hotel for a town this size."

Meg looked over at the large tester bed longingly. "After four nights of sleeping on the ground, I'd say it's far more than decent."

"Meg," Geoff said suddenly, "is everything okay?"

She looked at him, surprised by his unexpected question. "What do you mean?"

Geoff stubbed out his cigarette and leaned across the small table, taking her hand. "I mean," he said gently, "are you really all right?"

"Yes," she nodded, summoning a smile. "I'm really all right. But I do have something I want to tell you."

Geoff looked at her questioningly, wondering what secret she could be harboring that would make her so anxious. "What is it, sweetheart?"

Meg stared at her lap for a moment, then said quietly, "I want you to know that Peter didn't . . . touch me. He wanted to at first. He even told me he did." She shuddered delicately at the memory of Peter's crude words. "But I pretended I was sick, and he was so disgusted by my constant complaining that I think it made him change his mind."

"Oh, Megan," Geoff breathed, getting up from his chair and coming around the table to pull her into his arms, "my poor baby. Is that what you've been worried about tonight? That I would feel differently about you because of the time you spent alone with Farnsworth?"

"Well, yes," she stammered, leaning her forehead against his chest. "I have been worried that you might not . . . feel the same toward me anymore."

Geoff's voice was very soft when he next spoke. "Megan, look at me."

Slowly she raised her eyes.

"Now I want you to listen to me very carefully, and then we're not going to talk about this anymore. All right?"

"Yes."

"I am very, *very* glad that Farnsworth didn't hurt you. But, even if something *had* happened, it wouldn't have changed my feelings toward you. I love you, sweetheart, and nothing will ever change that."

Meg let out a long, shaky sigh. "Thank you," she whispered, her voice thick with tears, "thank you for telling me that."

Geoff hugged her tightly for a moment, then suddenly pushed her away. "Oh, no, you don't! You're not going to start crying all over my new shirt!"

Meg smiled tremulously, dashing her tears away with the back of her hand. "Geoff?" she asked softly. "Will you do something for me?"

"Of course," he answered, brushing away a tear that still clung to her cheek. "What would you like me to do?"

To his complete surprise, a rosy blush bloomed on her cheeks. "Would you take me over to that big, soft bed and make love to me?"

Geoff's breath caught in his throat, and with a smile that told her he would be more than happy to grant her request, he swept her up in his arms and carried her over to the bed.

He laid her down and slowly, tenderly began undressing her, his shaking hands the only sign of his rapidly mounting excitement.

Their lovemaking that night was different than it had ever been before—slower, richer, more profound. It was as if the near loss of each other had added a new dimension to their relationship, lending their love a depth of emotion that neither of them had ever known before. Forever after, Geoff would say that it was that night at the Hotel Eugene that they truly became man and wife—bound together not only by the physical fulfillment they found in each other's arms, but by a spiritual bond that interwove their very souls.

Despite their fatigue, they made love for hours, kissing till there was no breath left in their lungs, caressing each other in hidden little places they'd never known existed, and whispering words of love and commitment that heretofore had never been voiced.

And when, finally, Geoff acquiesced to Meg's fevered pleas for release, it was as if the physical union of their bodies set up an inferno within them that destroyed forever the last great barriers of mistrust and misunderstanding.

When the storm had at last passed, they lay together

quietly, their emotions too strong for words. The night aged, their kisses waned, and for the first time, they drifted into the sublime slumber enjoyed only by those who truly know love.

Meg woke to the sound of Geoff's laughter. Groggily, she turned to look at him, not sure whether she was amused or annoyed by his early morning exuberance.

"You're happy this morning," she murmured.

"I'm in love," he announced, flashing her the signature Wellesley smile that had broken hearts on two continents.

"Really? With whom?"

"Come here, you little witch," he growled, pulling her over on top of him. "Kiss your husband and tell him you love him."

All vestiges of drowsiness fled and eagerly she complied, kissing him lustily and saying, "I love you. Now, answer my question."

"What question?" Geoff asked, his voice becoming husky as she ran her tongue across his lips.

"Who are you in love with, Mr. Wellesley?"

Slowly, he began rotating his hips against her, insinuating his stiffening shaft intimately between her thighs. "Who do you think?"

"I've heard lots of rumors," she teased, reaching down and beginning to caress him.

"Rumors about who?"

"Well, how about Constanza Mirada?"

Geoff's moan of pleasure trailed off into a disgruntled snort. "Not likely."

"Oh, that's right," Meg crooned, her fingers playing havoc with him. "It couldn't be her, since you'd have to pull the sheet over her head before you dared get in bed."

"Right," he mumbled, his jaw clenching as Meg ran her palm across the hot, wet tip of his erection. "Guess again."

"Hmm . . . Margaret Collins?"

Geoff's eyes flew open in astonishment. "The Sunday school teacher?"

Meg shrugged elaborately. "It was just a guess."

His eyes closed. "Wrong again. She's way too prim for my taste."

"Should I guess again?"

"Yeah, but you better make it good, because you only get one more."

"Oh," Meg sighed, feigning distress, "then, I guess I better think on it for a minute." Slowly, sensuously, she slipped down the length of Geoff's body, pausing to stare hungrily at his manhood. "I know who it is," she said breathlessly.

"Who?" Geoff rasped.

"It's that Megan Taylor."

He smiled beatifically. "You're a smart girl. How did you guess?"

"Because," Meg drawled, running her tongue sensuously around his pulsing length. "I've heard that she's not prim at all."

"You heard right," Geoff gasped. Suddenly, all conversation ceased as Meg took him into her mouth.

She stayed as she was for several long moments, touching him, tasting him, caressing him with her hands and mouth until both of them were breathless with desire.

When, finally, neither of them could bear delaying their ecstasy any longer, Meg slithered her lithe body up his, and swinging one leg across his hips, eased herself down on his rigid staff.

Unlike the previous night, this morning's coupling was swift and frenzied, an erotic glut of the senses that climaxed almost immediately, leaving them both panting and sated.

Meg collapsed on Geoff's chest, her breathing labored, her heart pounding. "Tell me," she whispered, "is *that* why you love me?"

"Yeah," he admitted, "that, and about ten million other things."

Meg smiled. It was the answer she'd wanted to hear.

They finally arrived in Wellesley two days later, and Meg knew she'd never been more glad to see anyplace in her life.

"Home," she murmured, gazing out the window of Geoff's private railroad car. "Three days ago, I didn't think I'd ever see it again."

Geoff crossed the gently swaying car and gave her a quick hug. "You're home and safe, sweetheart, and no one is ever going to force you to leave again."

She nodded, returning his hug and giving him a soft, loving kiss. "You're my hero," she whispered. "My knight in shining armor."

Geoff chuckled, secretly delighted with her effusive flattery. "Unfortunately, your knight is going to have to abandon his lady fair."

"What? You're abandoning me? And in my condition?"

Geoff smiled at her melodramatic tone. "Yeah, but only briefly." Sobering, he added, "I'm going over to the sheriff's right away. I have to report Peter's death and give a statement about what happened."

"Oh, Geoff, do you have to do that right now?"

"I want to get it over with."

Meg nodded resignedly. "I understand, and don't worry. I can walk home alone. It's only four blocks."

"You're not going to walk home alone," Geoff admonished. "I'll go with you."

"You don't have to," she protested. "I'll be fine, really."

"Megan, I have to walk the horses home, anyway. Now, quit arguing. The train is coming to a stop, and I don't want people to think we're bickering. There's going to be enough talk as it is."

Geoff was more right than he knew. They hadn't even completed the short walk home before word began to spread that the Wellesleys were back. No one knew for sure where the couple had been, but there was much speculation that something wasn't right. After all, they'd arrived by train, but they had two horses with them. Why?

By six o'clock that evening, everyone in town had heard some version of the shocking events of the last few days—most of them incorrect. Wild rumors abounded. Some said that Meg had run off with Peter Farnsworth and that Geoff had come after the lovers, killing Peter in a jealous rage. Others, perhaps remembering the tragic Jenny Thomas, insisted that Peter had kidnapped Meg at knifepoint and that by the time Geoff found his wife, she was more dead than alive. Still others maintained that it wasn't Geoff who had killed Peter at all. Rather, it was Meg, who, having somehow gotten free while being held hostage for ransom, had stuck a knife between Peter's ribs.

For their part, Meg and Geoff remained secluded at home for the next two days, unaware of the outrageous and disturbing speculation raging about town.

When the truth was finally told, it came from a most unlikely source. George Farnsworth climbed up in the church pulpit shortly before the end of the Sunday morning services and, in a griefstricken but commanding voice, explained to his neighbors what had really happened. He made no excuses for his son's behavior, but merely asked the town to forgive Peter and to treat Mr. and Mrs. Wellesley with the respect and concern they deserved.

When Geoff heard about George's public atonement, he rode over to the Farnsworth home and spent a private half-hour with the old man. No one, including Meg, ever knew exactly what transpired during that conversation but, from that point on, there was no more trouble between the Wellesleys and George Farnsworth.

For Meg, the weeks following the kidnapping were halcyon. She and Geoff were enjoying the heady excitement of a passionate and loving marriage, her new house was progressing according to plan, or so Geoff told her, and now that she had reached her fourth month of pregnancy, she was no longer sick and pale, but rather, had an aura of happiness and contentment about her that even the most jealous of Wellesley's spinsters couldn't deny. She was completely and utterly happy, secure in her husband's affections, and confident that nothing could ever come between them again.

Therefore, when she opened her front door one bright morning in September and found Reverend Caldwell's young son shyly holding out a message for her, she never dreamed that the few words contained therein were going to cause her entire life to turn upside down. The message seemed so innocuous:

Mrs. Wellesley,

May I please call on you tomorrow morning at ten o'clock? There is a matter I must discuss with you.

John Caldwell

Meg told the reverend's son that she would be happy to receive his father the following morning and sent him on his way. After the boy left, she wondered briefly what the minister might want to discuss with her, but confident that it would be a matter of minor importance, she soon put it out of her mind.

Chapter 34

"The fact is, Mrs. Wellesley, you're not legally married."

For a long moment, Meg just stared at the stiff-backed gentleman sitting next to her on the settee, then she broke into a rippling cascade of laughter. "But that's absurd, Reverend Caldwell. Of course Mr. Wellesley and I are married. Reverend Martin performed the ceremony and Mrs. Martin even gave us a reception on the church lawn!"

"I know that," Reverend Caldwell said patiently, "but the fact still remains, your marriage isn't legal."

"Now, wait a minute," Meg said, holding up a hand. "Let's start from the beginning. You're saying that because the marriage certificate was never signed, the wedding wasn't valid? That Mr. Wellesley and I have been living in si . . . in an unconsecrated state all these months?"

The reverend cleared his throat uncomfortably. "I'm afraid so. And due to your, ah, delicate condition, I feel the situation must be rectified with all due haste."

"I couldn't agree more," Meg nodded, her face ashen with shock. "The one thing I don't understand is why Reverend Martin never mentioned this either to my husband or myself."

"But he did!" Reverend Caldwell blurted. "Shortly

before his transfer to Astoria, Mr. Martin wrote out long and detailed notes for me regarding issues at the church that still needed to be resolved. Your marriage was number one on that list."

"That's very well and good," Meg retorted, "but why didn't he ever mention it to us?"

Caldwell shifted uncomfortably on the settee, wishing he could think of a tactful way to let Mrs. Wellesley know that Mr. Wellesley refused to sign their marriage certificate.

"Perhaps if I show you Reverend Martin's journal," Caldwell suggested hopefully.

Meg shrugged. "Certainly." Sidling a little closer to the minister, she peered down at the large, flat book he held in his lap.

"As I understand it, you were married in May."

"Yes. May twenty-ninth."

Caldwell nodded, thumbing through several pages of the journal until he found the one he was looking for. "You see? The entries start here." He pointed to a neatly scribed note under the heading of June 18.

"Spoke to G. Wellesley about signing marriage certificate."

He flipped several pages, then again paused on the page headed June 27.

"Reminded G. Wellesley about marriage certificate."

July 3.

"Saw G. Wellesley at cafe—marriage certificate."

July 14.

"Wrote note to G. Wellesley regarding marriage certificate."

To Meg's mortification, the entries went on and on and on—well into the month of August. Then they abruptly stopped.

"Why are there no more notations after August twenty-first?" she asked. "Did Mr. Wellesley sign the certificate at that time?"

"No," Reverend Caldwell said slowly. "That was the week Reverend Martin left."

"Oh. But since you've taken over his pulpit, you've never mentioned it to my husband?"

Caldwell swallowed hard. "Well, actually, I did, once."

"And?"

"And he said he'd come in the next day and sign the documents."

"But he didn't?"

"Unfortunately, no."

A long moment passed before Meg trusted herself to speak again. When she finally did, her voice had a strained, brittle quality to it. "I certainly appreciate your taking the time to come over here this morning." Regally, she stood up, her stiff posture and tightly set mouth the only indications of her discomfiture.

"No trouble at all, Mrs., ah, Miss . . . *Mrs.* Wellesley," he answered, scrambling to his feet also. "I'm sure this is all just an oversight that can be easily corrected. I know how busy your husband is."

"Yes," she smiled thinly. "He is very busy. Especially since the fire. As you can imagine, the task of clearing the dead timber and replanting has taken up an enormous amount of time."

"Yes, of course it has," Caldwell commiserated. "Such a tragedy." To the minister's credit, he didn't mention that the fire had taken place well after the last entry in Reverend Martin's journal. "But you will talk to your husband . . ."

"Of course," Meg nodded. "We will attend to this situation immediately."

"Very good," the reverend smiled. "I know how embarrassing it would be for you if word of this, ah, oversight became public knowledge, so the sooner, the better."

"Absolutely," Meg agreed, opening the front door and handing the man his hat. "Hopefully, if Mr. Wellesley's schedule permits, we'll be in to see you by the end of the week."

"Excellent. I'll be available any time."

"Thank you, Reverend. Good day."

Meg barely got the door closed before she burst into tears.

"Why, that's the craziest thing I've ever heard!" Virginia gasped, setting a cup of chamomile tea down in front of her weeping sister. "Of course you have to tell him."

"Ginny, you don't understand! Reverend Martin reminded Geoff at least ten times about the certificate and he still didn't go in to sign it. There has to be a reason!"

"There could be a million reasons," Virginia said. "He was busy. He forgot. He—"

"Didn't want to!" Meg finished, breaking down in another torrent of gusty sobs.

"Don't be ridiculous! Why wouldn't he want to? The man is madly in love with you."

"The man is keeping me as his mistress!" Meg wailed. "My child is going to be a . . . a bastard!"

"Meg!" Virginia gasped. "How can you even think such a thing?"

"How can I not?" she retorted, looking up at her sister miserably. "What would you think if you were me?"

Slowly, Virginia sank into a chair. "Drink your tea," she said absently.

Meg shook her head. "Do you still have that sherry?"

"Spirits! It's not even afternoon yet! Have you totally lost your reason?"

"Maybe I have. With everything I've been through in the last six months, I would certainly have cause."

With a long sigh, Virginia reached over and patted her sister's hand. "Meggie, listen to me. You *have* to talk to Geoff about this. When he comes home tonight, just sit him down and *calmly* tell him what Reverend Caldwell told you."

"And what if he tells me he doesn't want to sign the certificate?"

"He won't."

"What if he does?"

"He *won't!*"

"I wish I were as sure as you are."

In truth, Virginia wished she were as sure as she sounded. "Come on, now," she encouraged, "dry your eyes and drink your tea. Everything is going to be fine. Why, I bet when you remind Geoff of this, he'll insist that you two go down and sign the documents tonight!"

"Do you really think so?" Meg asked hopefully.

"There's not the slightest doubt in my mind." Virginia held her breath for a moment, waiting for a lightning bolt to strike her dead for that one.

"Well, okay," Meg sniffed, rising from her chair and pulling on her gloves. "I guess you're right. I should remind him about it."

"Absolutely," Virginia beamed. "Just go home and do it."

"I will."

"Promise?"

"I promise."

* * *

She didn't.

She meant to, she really did. She spent the rest of the afternoon preparing Geoff's favorite supper and mentally rehearsing how she would bring the subject up. But when Geoff got home that evening, he was so excited and full of news that she couldn't get a word in edgewise. He spent a whole hour before dinner eagerly extolling the benefits of the improved design he'd just completed for his new flume. And when he finally wound down on that subject, he started right up on another—telling her about the building crew's progress on their new house and assuring her that they'd be able to move in before the first snow.

And after supper, he said something so startling that once his words were out, there was no possible way for Meg to broach the touchy subject of their marriage certificate.

They were sitting in the parlor, quietly sipping their after-dinner coffee, when suddenly Geoff took one of her hands, lifting it to his mouth and gently kissing it. "I want to tell you something," he murmured. "These last couple of weeks have been the happiest of my life, and if it were in my power, I would stop time right now."

"You would?" Meg croaked. "What do you mean?"

"I mean," he whispered, pulling her head down to his shoulder and burying his lips in the dark cloud of her hair, "that right now, this very second, I feel like my life is perfect. I don't want anything to ever change between us, Megan. I just hope that fifty years from now, we feel exactly the same way about each other that we do today."

Meg sighed. Tonight was definitely not the night.

The next morning, Geoff banged through the kitchen door, grabbed a piece of toast off a baking tray on the stove, and said, "Come give me a kiss, woman. I'm late."

Meg turned from where she was stirring a pan of scrambled eggs and looked at him in surprise. "You mean you're not going to eat breakfast?"

"Naw," he said, wiggling his eyebrows at her meaningfully. "I had enough upstairs to keep me going till dinner."

"Geoff!" she gasped, scandalized as always by his earthy innuendos. His high spirits of the evening before had translated into a long night of lovemaking. They had made love twice before finally going to sleep, only to wake up shortly before dawn and do it again.

At first, Meg's mood had been subdued, almost bittersweet, but Geoff had been like a randy boy, and she soon found herself being swept away by his lusty playfulness. The night had been wild, exciting, exhausting—and Meg had wished it would never end.

"Oh, by the way," he said, his mouth full of toast, "we're invited to a party Saturday night, so don't plan anything."

"A party? Where?"

"Greg and Vickie Stevens are giving it."

"We have to go way out there? Why, they live almost out to our new house. That's such a long trip."

"You'd better get used to it," he laughed. "You're going to be making that trip a lot, once we get moved. Anyway, it's just a few people getting together, but Greg asked us to join them, and I figured it would be okay, so I accepted."

Meg turned back to her eggs, nodding slowly. "Yes, it's . . . fine."

"Don't you want to go?" he asked, walking up behind her and wrapping his arms around her thickening waist.

"Sure, I do," she said quickly. "I don't mean to sound so unenthusiastic. You know how much I like Greg and Vickie—and he's doing a wonderful job at the mill. I guess I'm just a little . . . tired."

With a knowing chuckle, Geoff nipped her ear, running

his hands up her stomach and cupping her full breasts. "I'm not surprised. I don't think we slept more than twenty minutes the whole night."

Meg giggled and threw him a shaming look. "Don't you have to go to work?"

"Yeah," he sighed, reluctantly releasing her after one last squeeze to her round bottom. "I do."

Turning toward the door, he grabbed another piece of toast. "Take a nap today," he advised, grinning. "You deserve it."

At Meg's shocked little gasp, he grinned wider. "By the way, will that new dress you're making be ready by Saturday night?"

"Why do you ask?"

He shrugged and threw her a devilish grin. "Because your others are getting a little tight."

He barely made it through the door before the egg-covered spatula hit it.

Chapter 35

"Megan, come on! We're going to be late!"

Meg put the stopper back in her perfume bottle and hurriedly grabbed her reticule. "I'm coming," she called, dashing over to the mirror for one last check of her appearance. "Don't know what difference it makes," she grumbled. "By the time we get all the way out to the Stevenses, I'll be so windblown that everyone will think I haven't combed my hair all day."

"*Megan!*"

"Yes, yes! I'm on my way!"

She sped down the stairs, but paused when she got to the bottom, turning in a graceful little pirouette to show off her new dress.

"How do I look?"

"Gorgeous," Geoff said absently. "You always look gorgeous. Now, *come on.*" He turned toward the front door.

"Geoffrey Wellesley! You haven't even looked at me, and you're the one who demanded I finish this new dress by tonight. The least you could do is tell me if you like it."

Turning back toward her, Geoff's eyes slid appreciatively up and down Meg's pale blue dress. It was beautiful. The high neck topped an intricately smocked yoke, exquisitely embroidered with tiny flowers. The material was then gathered under her breasts by a row of tiny, tucked pleats and hung to the floor in a series of loose folds which would modestly accommodate her increasing waistline as her pregnancy advanced.

"It's lovely," Geoff said sincerely, reaching out and tracing the delicate embroidery with a fingertip. "I had no idea you did such beautiful handwork."

"There are lots of things I do beautifully that you don't appreciate," Meg said tartly, still not ready to forgive him for ignoring her efforts.

Geoff grinned and ran his hand down the front of the dress, pausing to gently stroke her round stomach. Leaning close, he whispered, "There's one thing you do beautifully that I appreciate a lot."

"Oh, you're terrible," she huffed, slapping his hand away and picking her shawl up off the table. "I swear, that's all you ever think about."

"Not *all*," he protested, taking a step closer and pulling her against him.

"Well, practically all," she amended. A tiny smile curved the corners of her mouth and she lifted her lips for a kiss.

The old grandfather clock in the corner ticked off a full thirty seconds while they stood and kissed. Finally, Meg pulled her lips away and took a determined step backward. "Didn't you say we're in a hurry?"

"Yeah," Geoff mumbled, pulling her back into his arms. "We are, so we'd better do this quick." Dipping his head, he sucked her lower lip into his mouth, his palms sensuously massaging her excited little nipples, his fingers frantically fumbling for her buttons.

"Where are the buttons on this damn thing?"

"In the back," Meg answered smugly, gripping his wrists and firmly pushing his hands away from her breasts. "And we're not 'doing this' at all! I spent two hours getting ready tonight, and I'm not going to arrive at this party looking like I just crawled out of bed."

"You won't," he promised, a familiar huskiness creeping in his voice. Meg's eyebrows rose in alarm.

"Geoff! This is insane. Now, stop it." But even as she uttered the words, her hand dropped down and cupped him intimately. "Now, look what you've done," she giggled.

"No, look what *you've* done," he shot back, his words trailing off into a pleasured groan.

"We're not going to get out of here until we do this, are we?"

Geoff smiled triumphantly and shook his head. "Not a chance."

"You're insatiable," Meg muttered, even as her nimble fingers deftly unbuttoned the front of his trousers. Reaching inside, she released his throbbing erection, then stared down at it appreciatively.

Geoff saw the path her eyes were taking and with one sweeping movement, lifted her full skirt up to her waist and shimmied her pantalettes down her legs. "Quit looking at me like that," he ordered thickly, "you're making me nuts."

Grasping her by her waist, he lifted her off the floor. "Put your legs around me, like you did that day in your office."

Meg did as he bade.

He walked into the dining room and set her on the edge of the table, again hiking up her skirts till the many yards of loose, flowing material pooled around her. Leaning toward her, he whispered, "We're definitely going to be late." Then, thrusting his hips forward, he entered her with one smooth lunge.

"I know," she gasped, her words ending in a sharp little scream of pleasure.

"And, you—know—what?"

"What?" she panted, clamping her legs tighter around him.

"I—ahhh—don't—give, oh God—a—*damn!*"

They gave a simultaneous groan of ecstasy. Geoff's grip loosened and Meg fell back on the table, breathing hard.

"You know what?" she giggled.

"What?"

"I don't give a damn either."

"It's a nice evening, isn't it?"

"Hmm?"

"I said, it's a nice evening."

"Oh, yes, lovely. Perfect."

Geoff shot Meg a puzzled look as they traveled along under the starlit sky. She had been very quiet since they'd left the house, and he hoped he hadn't worn her out so much with their quick encounter on the table that she would be too tired to enjoy the party.

But fatigue was not what was plaguing Meg. Now that the blaze of excitement that always accompanied their spontaneous bouts of lovemaking had faded, she was again brooding about the marriage certificate.

All week she had tried to find an appropriate time to broach the subject of the unsigned document, but the right moment had never seemed to present itself. Every night before Geoff came home from the timber camp, she told herself that tonight she would ask him about it . . . tonight she'd find out why he was reluctant to sign it. But something always seemed to prevent it. One night he had come home so late, she'd already been asleep. On another, *he* was so exhausted that he dozed off during dinner and retired immediately afterward. And the other nights, he had been so passionate—so playful or carnal or sensuous—that she hadn't been able to bring herself to risk spoiling the moment with a possible confrontation.

But tonight, after the party, they had to talk. Tomorrow was Sunday, and she knew she wouldn't be able to face Reverend Caldwell if she and Geoff hadn't settled the issue of the certificate.

"You're awfully quiet," Geoff noted. "Are you tired?"

"No," she answered, shaking her head. "Just enjoying the ride."

Geoff nodded, seeming to be satisfied with her hastily formulated excuse. "It's beautiful out here at night, isn't it?"

"Yes. I'll be glad when we move into our new house." She didn't notice the secret little smile that curved his lips.

A half-hour later, they reached a fork in the trail that led either to the Stevens' house, or to their own. To Meg's surprise, Geoff steered the team to the right, heading up the path toward their new house.

"What are you going this way for?"

"There's something I want to check at the new house."

"But Geoff, we're so late now . . ."

He shrugged. "A few more minutes won't matter."

Meg frowned at him, but he pointedly ignored her.

They pulled up in front of their new house and Geoff set the brake and jumped down. Walking around the back of the wagon, he stepped up to Meg's side and held his hands up. "Come on."

"I don't want to go in, Geoff. Just do what you need to do and I'll wait here."

"No," he said, gesturing impatiently for her to jump down. "I want to show you something inside."

"Oh, for heaven's sake! It's going to be pitch dark in there. What do you expect me to be able to see?"

"Quit arguing and come on! We're wasting time."

With a snort of frustration, Meg leaned forward and allowed him to lift her down. Arm in arm, they walked up to the house, but when they reached the door, Geoff paused, bending down and lifting her into his arms.

"What are you doing?"

"Carrying my bride across the threshold," he answered, nuzzling his nose into the curve of her neck.

"Geoffrey William Wellesley, put me down. Do you understand me? Right now!"

"Lord, talk about a reluctant bride!" he laughed, then lifted a booted foot and gave the front door a push.

The door swung open and suddenly the room inside blazed with light.

"Surprise!"

Forty people surged forward, all of them holding lamps and candles, and calling out greetings and congratulations.

Meg looked around in astonishment at the huge gathering, then turned toward her husband, her eyes huge with wonder. "You knew about this?"

"Sure," he laughed, setting her on her feet. "So did everybody else in town. I never thought we'd get away with it without you finding out."

"Well, you certainly did," Meg assured him, then turned to hug Virginia, whom she suddenly found standing next to her.

"If you'll follow me, Mrs. Wellesley," came a voice from the back of the crowd, "there are a few things I'd like to show you."

Meg craned her neck in the direction of the voice until her gaze lit upon the shiny, bald pate of Benjamin Spoffard. "Oh, Mr. Spoffard," she giggled delightedly, "are you here, too?"

"Of course," answered the beaming little man. "Who else could I trust to hang these beautiful draperies?" Turning, he gestured expansively to the full-length green velvet drapes at the parlor windows. "Come see how nicely your furniture selections have worked out."

Like a child in a candy store, Meg eagerly followed the little man from room to room, alternately clapping her hands with excitement or sighing with appreciation over the beautiful furnishings placed so artfully in the big, airy rooms.

When Mr. Spoffard finally finished his tour, Meg hurried down the stairs, scanning the sea of heads for Geoff. She spotted him over by the massive stone fireplace, talking to two tall blond men, neither of whom Meg recognized, but who looked so much alike in their classic, Nordic handsomeness that she thought they must be twins. The men were both accompanied by women; one, a delicate brunette with features and coloring not unlike her own, and the other, a petite blonde with sea-blue eyes and hair the color of fresh honey. Hesitantly, Meg approached the chattering group.

"Ah, here she is now," Geoff grinned, hooking his arm around her waist and pulling her close. "Megan, I'd like you to meet some very special guests."

Meg smiled expectantly.

Geoff paused a moment, letting her curiosity build, then, with unmistakable pride in his voice, announced, "These are my brothers, Seth and Nathan, and their wives, Rachel and Elyse."

Meg's mouth dropped open. "Your brothers?" she gasped.

"Well, a couple of them, anyway. Two of the six, to be exact."

"The two most important ones," Nathan interjected, giving Geoff a good-natured punch on the shoulder.

"I'm absolutely delighted to meet you," Meg enthused, instantly charming the handsome men. "Are you gentlemen twins?"

"No," Seth's wife, Rachel, answered wryly, "and most of the time, they aren't gentlemen either."

The group broke into a peal of laughter, causing many of the guests in the room to look their way.

"Have you ever seen a more handsome family?" Beatrice Lennox gushed, turning toward Trudy Phillips.

"No," Trudy sighed, "I can't say as I have. Why, I believe those brothers of Geoffrey's are even more handsome than he is!"

Beatrice's gaze swung over to Howard Phillips, Trudy's husband of thirty-five years. "You always were partial to blond men," she teased.

Trudy looked over at her balding, potbellied husband and smiled lovingly. "Yes, I was."

By this time, Rachel and Elyse had separated Meg from the men and were pelting her with questions.

"How long have you been married? Geoff was so vague in his letter."

"Did you *really* not know about the party?"

"Is it true you blackmailed Geoff into marrying you?" This last blunt question came from Elyse, who was instantly riveted with a withering glare from Rachel.

Meg held up her hands, laughing. "Just a minute. I can only answer one question at a time. Geoff and I have been married for five months, I didn't know a thing about the party—or that the house was anywhere near ready, for that matter—and yes, I did blackmail him into marrying me."

404

She leaned forward conspiratorially. "And I don't regret it for one minute, because if I hadn't, I'm sure he never would have realized I was even alive."

Rachel nodded approvingly at Meg's frank response, her respect for her new sister-in-law growing by the minute.

"Who wouldn't have realized who was alive?" asked a beautiful blond woman who had suddenly appeared at Elyse's side.

Meg's eyebrows shot up haughtily at the young woman's presumption in joining their private conversation, but Elyse started to laugh. "Better get used to her, Megan. You're related to her, too."

"I am?"

"You sure are. This is Paula, Geoffrey's baby sister."

"Oh, for heaven's sake, Elyse," the vivacious woman huffed. "I'm twenty-three years old, I'm married, and I have a house full of kids. When are you going to stop calling me 'baby sister'?"

At Paula's comment about a houseful of kids, Rachel mouthed the word "two" to Meg, and held up two fingers. Meg chuckled and gazed happily at the three charming women, feeling like she'd just been accepted as a member of a very exclusive club.

"Is your husband with you, Paula?"

"No," she sighed. "Luke had to stay home with the kids. He's a blacksmith in Colorado, and the only way he'd marry me was if I promised we'd live on his money, not mine, so we can rarely afford to go anywhere together."

Meg looked at Paula sympathetically, but Rachel laughed and waved away her concern. "When you meet Luke O'Neill, Meg, you'll understand that no hardship would be too great to bear if the reward was having him for a husband. I'm madly in love with him and I've only met him once."

Paula grinned. "Watch it, Rachel, or Seth is going to hear you and get jealous."

"Oh, I don't think so," Rachel smiled, gazing over at her tall, handsome husband adoringly. "Seth knows he doesn't have a thing to worry about."

"Do you all have children?" Meg asked a bit shyly.

This time it was Elyse who answered. "In this family, Meg, you'll find that everyone has children. Seth and Rachel have a baby son, Ethan, and a five-year-old daughter from Seth's first marriage."

"Her name is Amelia," Rachel interjected, "and if I'm not mistaken, she's around here somewhere."

"She's hiding over there on the staircase," Paula advised her.

"That little devil," Rachel grumbled affectionately. "I knew she wouldn't go to bed."

"And how about you?" Meg asked, directing her question at Elyse.

"Nathan and I have a little boy who's five, a baby girl who's almost three, and another one on the way."

This statement was met by squeals of delight from Rachel and Paula. "You didn't tell me!" Rachel cried, hugging Elyse.

"I just found out myself," Elyse smiled. "I'm not due till spring, so I haven't told anyone but Nathan."

"This is wonderful!" Paula bubbled. "We have so much to celebrate tonight."

"And I could celebrate a lot more happily if I could get that child to bed," Rachel frowned, catching sight of Amelia hanging over the banister. "If you'll excuse me for a moment, I think I'll give it another try."

Paula also excused herself and walked over to join her three brothers by the fireplace.

"Let's see if we can find a quiet corner and sit down for

a moment," Elyse suggested. "With both of us in the family way, I'm sure we'll be forgiven."

Meg followed her sister-in-law over to a small alcove off the main hall. With a sigh, Elyse sank down on a tapestried settee. "I don't know why I'm always so tired the first three months."

"I know," Meg agreed. "Tired, sick, out of sorts, confused . . . I find the whole experience rather trying."

Elyse looked at her in surprise. "Are you saying you're not intending to follow the great Wellesley tradition of having as many children as possible in as short a time as possible?"

"I hope not," Meg sighed. "I know Geoff wants a big family, but I'm not sure I'm cut out for a brood of children. Actually, I'd be very happy with one or two."

"It'll never happen," Elyse warned, wagging her finger sagely in Meg's face. "There's not a single one of those seven brothers who would be content with 'one or two.' I've never seen any group of men as crazy about children as they are."

"I know," Meg nodded. "Geoff is very excited about this baby."

"And he will be about the next one and the next one and the next one," Elyse predicted.

"Oh, Lord, don't say that." Meg laughed. "I don't even want to think about that many 'next ones.' "

The women sat quietly for a moment, then, suddenly, Elyse said, "You know, Meg, the next baby is bound to be easier than this one."

"I've heard that, too. The first one always seems to be the hardest. At least that's what my sister, Virginia, says and she has five, so I guess she should know."

"I didn't exactly mean that."

Meg turned toward Elyse curiously. "You didn't?"

"No. What I meant is . . . well, I know about some of the problems you and Geoff have had, and believe me, I can understand how difficult it is to be pregnant when your marriage isn't secure. So can Rachel, for that matter. She left Seth for several months when she was carrying Ethan and . . ." She paused ". . . and Nathan and I weren't even married when Colin was born."

Meg's eyes widened. "You weren't?"

Elyse shook her head, her eyes taking on a faraway look. "No. In fact, Colin was six months old before Nathan even knew he existed."

Meg couldn't contain her gasp of astonishment. "How did that happen?"

Elyse smiled. "It's much too long a story to tell you now but, someday, when we have several uninterrupted, private hours . . ."

"I want to hear it," Meg nodded, feeling a kinship toward this new sister-in-law that she hoped would grow into a lifelong bond.

"And you shall," Elyse promised, squeezing her hand. "Now, come on. We better go back and mingle. After all, you're the guest of honor, and I shouldn't monopolize all your time."

As they stood up, Meg caught Elyse by the wrist and whispered, "Thank you for sharing your secret with me. It means a lot to know I'm not the only one who has had some . . . difficulties."

"Oh, my dear," Elyse chuckled. "You don't know the half of it. There's not a woman in the world who can marry one of the Wellesley brothers and not have a few 'difficulties'! That's one of the things that makes them so exciting."

Chapter 36

The party was wonderful. The many guests chatted, ate, drank, and spent a good deal of time smiling at Meg and Geoff. By nine o'clock, Meg was exhausted just from returning smiles and acknowledging good wishes. When she saw Geoff approaching her, she was sure he intended to suggest she retire upstairs to their sumptuous new bedroom to take a little rest, and she couldn't wait to accept. She was wrong.

"Will you come with me, please?" he whispered. "I need to say a few words to everyone."

"Come with you?" she asked, puzzled. "Where?"

"Just over to the fireplace. I figured we could stand on the hearth step. It's the closest thing we've got to a dais."

"Oh, Geoff," she sighed, "I'm so tired, I feel like I'm going to collapse. You're not going to talk for long, are you?"

A flicker of concern crossed his eyes and, quickly, he shook his head. "Only for a minute. I promise."

"All right."

Geoff guided her through the crowd and stepped up on to the hearth, giving her a hand up next to him. He signaled for quiet and immediately the crowd hushed as forty pairs of eyes turned toward him expectantly.

"Dear friends and family," he began, making a special effort to nod at his brothers and sister. "Thank you all for joining us for our celebration tonight. I know how hard it was for many of you to keep this party a secret . . ." Here he paused and gazed pointedly at Trudy Phillips, causing several women in the audience to titter. ". . . And I appreciate your discretion. My thanks especially to Greg and Vickie Stevens for organizing this splendid evening, and to my brothers, Seth and Nathan, and their wives, Rachel and Elyse, for traveling so far to be with us on this special night. And, of course, a special word of thanks to my irrepressible sister, Paula O'Neill, without whom no party is truly complete."

These last accolades were met by enthusiastic applause.

"Now, I have something I want to say. As most of you know, my marriage to Megan has been a very large topic of conversation around town for the last several months. We realize that there have been some . . . unusual circumstances surrounding our marriage, but none of them, no matter how bizarre or how tragic, has seemed to capture everyone's imagination quite as much as the rumor that has circulated this past week. I am speaking, of course, about our marriage certificate."

Meg's smile froze on her face.

"The rumor is that our marriage is not valid, at least in the eyes of the law, since the marriage certificate was never signed and witnessed. I can easily put an end to that rumor, since it's not a rumor at all. It's a fact."

He paused, allowing the throng of old biddies at the back of the room to have their moment of triumph. Then, with a wry crook to his mouth, he continued.

"As I said, it was recently brought to my attention, and

410

apparently, to everyone else's as well, that Meg and I never signed our marriage certificate. As you know, we had a very small, private wedding and in the hustle and bustle of that day, we forgot. Plain and simple. We forgot."

Briefly, his eyes raked the crowd as if daring anyone to dispute that statement.

"It's true that both Reverend Martin and Reverend Caldwell reminded me on several occasions that the document still needed signing—and I still forgot. But despite my poor memory, I do want to make it perfectly clear that never, at any time, did Meg and I consider ourselves anything but married. We were duly joined in Holy Matrimony on May 29 of this year by Reverend Martin at the First Presbyterian Church, in the sight of God and in front of two witnesses. *We are married.* It is only the legal registration of that marriage that was overlooked."

Several ladies in the crowd sighed.

"My first thought in planning this party tonight was to try to make amends to all of you who were unable to attend our wedding. I decided the next best thing would be to invite you here to witness the signing of our marriage certificate."

Another round of sighs.

"But then, I got to thinking that that was rather anti-climactic. You would probably much rather attend a wedding than a simple legal procedure. So I spoke with Reverend Caldwell and he and I determined that there was no reason why Meg and I couldn't just get married again."

The ladies were now nearly swooning.

"But before that second wedding can take place, I have to ask someone in this room a very important, very private question."

Turning away from the crowd, he looked down at Meg

who gazed back at him rapturously. "Will you marry me?" he whispered.

Meg's heart was so full of love and joy that she couldn't answer. Instead, she looked up at her beloved husband, her eyes brimming with tears, and nodded. Slowly, Geoff lifted her hand and placed a gentle kiss on her knuckles.

Turning back to the crowd, he grinned devilishly. "She said yes."

A lusty cheer arose from the assemblage, and suddenly, Meg found Reverend Caldwell standing at her side, his prayerbook in his hand.

"Did you tell him?" she whispered, leaning close to the smiling cleric.

"Me?" he asked, shrugging innocently. "I thought you did."

Meg shot him a dubious look, but before she could quiz him further, she spied Virginia hurrying toward her, carrying a huge bouquet of flowers. With a smug smile, Ginny handed the flowers to Meg and gave her a quick kiss.

"Will everyone take their places, please?" Reverend Caldwell requested.

To Meg's surprise, Seth, Nathan, and Greg Stevens lined up next to Geoff, while Virginia, Paula, Rachel, and Elyse flanked her. It was almost as if they'd practiced.

"Dearly beloved . . ."

This time, as the ancient words were intoned, Meg felt none of the quailing apprehension she'd suffered at her first wedding. There was no fear that Geoff would refuse to repeat the vows, no worry that he'd change his mind and abandon her right in the middle of the service.

And this time, when the minister said, "You may kiss the bride," there was no curt "No thanks." Instead, Geoff wrapped his arms lovingly around his wife and kissed her far longer than propriety dictated, causing at least three of the overly excited ladies in the crowd to burst into noisy tears.

"Now, you're finally, really, truly mine," he whispered, as he lifted his lips from hers.

"Forever and ever," she answered softly.

As they turned to accept the crowd's felicitations, Virginia stepped forward, handing Meg's flowers back to her. "Better than the first time, isn't it?" she whispered.

"Oh, yes," Meg smiled, her face a vision of happiness. "Better than I ever could have dreamed."

Epilogue

"Now, who the hell is at the door at this time of morning?" Geoff growled, turning over and staring bleary-eyed at the clock.

"What time is it?" Meg groaned.

"Seven o'clock."

"I feel like I've only been asleep about fifteen minutes."

Geoff chuckled and gave her a lusty pat on her bare bottom. "You have."

"Don't do that," she complained irritably. "Just go down and see who's at the door."

"Okay," he yawned.

Groggily, he sat up, pulling on his wrapper and shoving his feet into his slippers.

"All right, all right, I'm coming," he yelled, stomping clumsily down the stairs.

Yanking the door open, he stared in disbelief at Reverend Caldwell.

"I'm sorry to bother you so early," the minister apologized, his face flushing with embarrassment at Geoff's state of undress, "but I have my first service at eight o'clock and I felt that I just had to take care of this little matter before I did anything else."

"What little matter?" Geoff asked, squinting at the papers the reverend held clenched in his hands.

"Your marriage certificate, Mr. Wellesley. You and Mrs. Wellesley forgot to sign it last night."

Bursting into laughter, Geoff turned toward the staircase. "Megan!" he roared. "Get down here *right now!*"